QUEEN OF BLADES

StarCraft®

Queen of Blades

Aaron Rosenberg

POCKET STAR BOOKS
New York London Toronto Sydney

An *Original* Publication of POCKET BOOKS

A Pocket Star Book published by
POCKET BOOKS, a division of Simon & Schuster, Inc.
1230 Avenue of the Americas, New York, NY 10020

This book is a work of fiction. Names, characters, places and incidents are products of the author's imagination or are used fictitiously. Any resemblance to actual events or locales or persons, living or dead, is entirely coincidental.

ISBN-13: 978-0-7434-7133-6
ISBN-10: 0-7434-7133-4

10 9 8 7 6 5 4 3 2 1

This Pocket Star Books paperback edition June 2006

POCKET STAR BOOKS and colophon are registered trademarks of Simon & Schuster, Inc.

Cover art by Glenn Rane

Manufactured in the United States of America

For information regarding special discounts for bulk purchases, please contact Simon & Schuster Special Sales at 1-800-456-6798 or business@simonandschuster.com

To Jenifer, my Queen,
and to Adara and Arthur,
our own wonderful brood.

ACKNOWLEDGMENTS

Thanks to Luke for the introductions, Chris for his input and enthusiasm, and Marco for running the show. I'd also like to thank the people at Blizzard, who built this great setting and these cool characters, and the StarCraft fans, who help bring it all to life.

HISTORICAL NOTE

The events of this book take place roughly six weeks after the events described in the *StarCraft* novel *Liberty's Crusade*.

QUEEN OF BLADES

PROLOGUE

THE WORLD WENT DARK.

Not just a darkened sky—no mere nightfall could produce such utter darkness. No, this was the dark of captivity, confinement, blindness. Nothing visible, no light, no shadow, only a smothering visual shroud. A stark contrast to the blinding lights and sudden bursts of color from just before.

I struggle to make sense of my surroundings. Where am I?

Nothing but blankness answers, and an instant later a far larger question looms up, erasing the first. Who am I?

A wave of panic rises deep within, bile carried along its edge, threatening to drown me as I realize I cannot remember. I do not know who I am!

Calm, I tell myself. Calm. I force the panic down, pushing it back by sheer will, refusing to let it envelop me. What do you remember, then?

Nothing. No, brief flashes. A battle. A war. Horrid,

horrible foes, great monstrous beings surrounding me, dwarfing me. Betrayal—though I cannot recall the act itself I can still taste the bitter realization of it. Abandonment. Desperation, a last frenzied struggle. The feel of sinewy flesh pinning me, choking me, killing me. The light fading around me as the numbness creeps in.

And now this.

Where am I? I stretch my senses to their limit, probing my surroundings. The results, though hazy and disjointed, form a single conclusion.

I am being carried.

I can feel the movement, the gentle rocking motion. Not directly—something cushions me, envelops me, holds me all around. But that cushioning is moving, and me with it.

I try lashing out, but my limbs will not cooperate. I feel sluggish, drained—drugged. Senses dulled, body leaden, but nerves oddly on fire. I am burning from within! My flesh crawls, creeps, melts, morphs—I have no control over my own form anymore. I am changing.

Around me I can feel others shifting. They are not confined as I am—they are free to move, though their minds are oddly blunted. They are my captors, conveying me in my confinement.

I can hear their thoughts, slithering across me, through me. A part of me recoils but another part—a newer part—welcomes their intrusion. Vibrates in tune with their gibbering, allowing the patterns to resonate through me. Changing me further, bringing me closer to those waiting just beyond.

The part that is still me, the old me, recoils in horror. I cannot, I will not become one of these! I must escape! I must be free! My body is captive but my mind soars, reaching out for help, any help. I scream, desperate for anyone to hear.

And, far away, I know that my pleas have been heard.

Help me!

Rubble lay everywhere, evidence of a city in flames, a world in demise. Buildings had fallen, vehicles were crashed and crushed, bodies littered the ground. A sign still stood near the edge of the destruction, its scorched surface reading "Welcome to"—the name New Gettysburg only a jagged hole with blackened edges. All manner of bodies, from the pale flesh of the Terrans to the smooth hides of the protoss to the sinewy blades of the zerg. People, those not yet dead and unable to evacuate, ran screaming, wailing for help. Some brandished weapons, crazed beyond rational thought, desperate to defend themselves and their families. Others cowered, weeping, unable to face the end of their world. A few hid or ran, hoping to escape their fate.

The Swarm ignored them. It had a higher agenda.

The battle had not gone as expected. The Terrans had put up a strong fight but with fewer soldiers than anticipated. The protoss, the hated protoss, had appeared as always, gleaming in their battle suits and glowing in their arrogance, but had rapidly lost focus, dividing their attentions as if facing not one but two opponents.

In some places the Swarm had sighted Terrans battling protoss, a strange but welcome sight. Yes, it had been a strange battlefield, the sides constantly shifting. But that was for the Overmind to consider and digest. For now, the conflict was over, the battle won. The remaining Terrans posed little threat and the protoss had vanished once the outcome was clear. For some reason they had not razed the planet, a fact which had allowed the Swarm to discover and claim a previously unexpected prize.

Now, their linked minds already turned from this conflict to those stretching out before them, the zerg marshaled their forces and prepared for their victorious departure.

One brood cleared a path, removing any obstructions, whether flesh or stone or metal. A second brood followed close behind, its ranks protectively closed around its prize. Near the center several ultralisks moved in close formation, their back-spikes almost touching. Between them were four hydralisks, thick arms linked to support the large oblong they held. Through its rough, sticky shell the cocoon pulsed with light, though its faint glow was lost amid the fires and flares and explosions that had once been this city.

"Carefully," warned the brood's cerebrate, observing their progress through the overlord floating just above the sphere. Because the celebrant itself could not move, the airborne overlords served as its eyes, ears, and mouth. "The Chrysalis must not be harmed!"

Obedient to its will, the ultralisks shifted slightly

closer and slowed their pace, allowing more time for the brood before them to open the way. Their heavy feet crushed bone and metal and wood without thought or pause as they lumbered on, shielding the Chrysalis from attack.

"We have it, Master," the cerebrate announced in the depths of its own mind. "We have your prize."

"Good." The reply echoed from within, rising from the deep well of the zerg hive-mind. "You must watch over the Chrysalis, and ensure that no harm comes to the creature within it. Go now and keep safe my prize."

Accepting the Overmind's orders as always, the cerebrate redoubled its efforts, making sure its brood's defenses were secure. The Chrysalis would be protected at all costs.

On the zerg marched, the city burning around them. At last the Swarm had gathered itself within a vast crater where once the city's vaunted lake had stretched. Now the surface was glass-smooth, seared by the force of the protoss's landing ships and unmarred by the heavy feet that had trekked across toward the city under siege.

"We are ready, Master," the cerebrate declared, arraying its brood around the Chrysalis.

"I am well pleased, young Cerebrate," the Overmind answered, the warm glow of its benediction washing over the cerebrate and through it all the members of its Swarm. "And so long as my prize remains intact, I shall remain pleased. Thus, its life and yours shall be made as one. As it prospers, so shall you. For you are part of the Swarm. If ever your flesh should fail, that flesh shall be made anew. That is my covenant with all cerebrates."

As the cerebrate swelled with pride, a great darkness descended upon the crater, a shadow of the mass that drifted into view high above them. Beyond the upper reaches of the planet's dying atmosphere hung a massive storm, a swirl of orange and violet gases that spun around strange flickering lights. They moved faster and faster, the colors merging in their fury, until the center of the storm collapsed in upon itself, light and color giving way to a shadowy circle far darker than even the space hovering beyond.

"Now you have grown strong enough to bear the rigors of warp travel with the Swarm," the Overmind stated, its words sending a thrum of power through the Swarm. "Thus we shall make our exit from this blasted world and secure the Chrysalis within the Hive Cluster upon the planet Char."

As one the first brood rose, soaring high above the ruined city. They broke free of the planet's weak, fading grasp and approached the storm above, pulled into that yawning, beckoning darkness at its center, and vanished. The cerebrate felt their transit through the hive-mind link all zerg shared and allowed a spark of contentment to linger within its own mind. Then the Overmind summoned it as well, and the cerebrate called its brood together, linking them tightly for travel through the warp. They rose from the crater, letting the power of the Swarm fill them as they ascended, and soon the darkness had drowned out all thought, all sense, as it carried them across the vastness of space to their destination.

And within the Chrysalis, faintly visible through its thick skin and viscous contents, a body writhed in pain. Though not conscious the figure within shifted, stirred, unable to lie still as the zerg virus penetrated every cell, changing DNA to match their own. Soon the Chrysalis would open and the new zerg would emerge. All the Swarm exulted with the Overmind.

And, as they departed and Tarsonis died behind them, the mind trapped within the Chrysalis screamed.

CHAPTER 1

Jimmy!

"Aaahh!"

". . . but of course Mengsk—pardon me, Emperor Arcturus the First—claims this was all necessary. According to his spokesperson, the new Terran Dominion is doing everything necessary to remove the alien threat and make the colonies safe once more. It has been almost two months, however. In this reporter's opinion . . ."

Jim Raynor lay back down, eyes staring up at the steel-gray ceiling. He ran one hand over the sweat-drenched stubble atop his head and felt himself smile despite the adrenaline still coursing through him. A quick glance showed a hologram playing on his console, the tall, slender man captured within conveying his report with style despite or perhaps because of the battered leather trench coat and slouch hat he wore.

Mike Liberty. One of the few people left Jim called friend. Still reporting on Mengsk, even now.

Still trying to get the truth to people who didn't want to hear it.

". . . still reeling from the loss of the Dylarian shipyards," Mike was saying now, and Raynor cocked his head to listen.

"Arrest warrants have been issued for James Raynor," his friend was reporting, "though it is still unclear what happened. Why would the hero of Antiga Prime suddenly turn rogue? And why, after so many months saving lives, would he unleash such destruction on the Dylarian shipyards? According to the Dominion Raynor's attack could have crippled the fleet, putting everyone at risk in the case of another alien attack." He could hear Mike's voice dropping and knew what he would see if he glanced up—his friend was leaning forward slightly, a faint smile on his face, suddenly a friend confiding instead of a journalist reporting. "Perhaps Emperor Arcturus is simply enraged at the thought that anyone could walk away from his new rule, particularly one of his most prized associates. And perhaps these charges have been manufactured as an excuse to pursue Raynor, rather than letting the public realize that perhaps the Emperor's mandate is not as universal as he might claim."

"Heh!" He couldn't help laughing at that one. Go get 'em, Mike! But the hero of Antiga Prime? Where did he come up with this stuff? The accolade was as phony as most of Mengsk's charges against him.

Of course, the charges were true this time. He had struck the shipyards. He'd had to. When he'd belted

Duke, Mengsk's favorite lackey, and stormed off the ship after Tarsonis, Raynor had expected to be on his own again or perhaps down to a handful of his troopers. He'd been unprepared for the wave of support he'd received from his men. All but a handful had walked with him, and he'd found himself the head of a small army. But they were an army without transport, and he knew that Mengsk would never let them leave so easily. So they'd needed ships, and quickly. It had seemed safer to go after the shipyards and the vessels housed there than to try stealing active ships from those still loyal to Mengsk.

It hadn't been that simple, of course. Mengsk had guessed his move—whatever else he could say about the man, the self-styled emperor was an excellent strategist—and had dispatched Duke in his own flagship, the *Hyperion,* to head them off. That had been a mistake.

Knowing he wouldn't get any more sleep now, Raynor sat up and rubbed at his jaw under his short beard, grinning at the memory. Duke was a capable ship commander, perhaps, and a good general for all his faults. But he was used to fighting on level ground, going up against fleets and scoutships. He hadn't been prepared to wage a battle through the shipyards, where his own men couldn't shoot for fear of hitting each other or a ship. Raynor had had no such compunctions. If a ship was holed they moved on to stealing the next one. He'd lured Duke in close, then used the shipyard's own machines to grapple the *Hyperion* and lock her in place. Then he and his boys had overrun it.

Still laughing, Raynor stood up and crossed the room, heading for the handsomely appointed bathroom. Duke's short fuse had cost him the *Hyperion*, and Mengsk had received the first public defeat of his new Terran Dominion before he'd even declared its formation. Raynor had left with the *Hyperion* and a dozen other ships, his own private fleet, leaving Duke bound and gagged behind him.

Of course, it had gone downhill from there.

His smile dropping away, Raynor wrenched open the polished wooden door and glared at the room beyond. Marble sinktops, porcelain tiles, handsome faucets and fixtures—this place looked more like a fancy hotel than a ship captain's quarters. But they had been Mengsk's, and the big man did like his comforts. Raynor had been tempted to rip them all out, but it would have taken too long. He'd considered taking a simpler room for himself, but his crew had insisted. He was the captain now and these were his quarters. So he put up with the luxury and did his best to concentrate on other things.

Unfortunately, there wasn't much else to concentrate on. Since taking the ships Raynor had become Public Enemy Number One. Every soldier in the Dominion was hunting for him, and his face was plastered on every colony. Not that it bothered him—he knew better than most what Mengsk was capable of and what he did to those loyal to him, and had no desire to go back. Being the law didn't change anything. You stood by your people or you weren't worth standing by. Raynor honestly believed that, and Mengsk's betrayal had made his own desertion easy.

The question, however, was what to do after he deserted. He hadn't thought much about it at the time, since he'd planned to go off alone. But having others with him changed that. They looked up to him, depended upon him, sat patiently waiting for his orders. And he didn't have any. Oh, they'd stolen the ships, of course. And they'd hit a few outposts, singed a few patrols. But he didn't know what to do next. He didn't know where he was going. It had been six weeks and he still had no idea.

All those years as a marshal, Raynor had told himself he was independent, self-sufficient. It had been true, at least in part. He'd survived on his own resources, acted on his own judgment. His mandate had been loose enough and broad enough to give him a lot of freedom. But there had been a mandate: to protect the people of Mar Sara. After he'd joined Mengsk he'd gotten a new mandate: to protect the people from the Confederacy and from the aliens. What was his mandate now?

He'd quit out of rage, he knew. Rage at Mengsk for what he'd done. For whom he'd betrayed.

Rage over Kerrigan.

He could still taste the fury he'd unleashed at Mengsk for deserting her like that, leaving her to the zerg and whatever else was crawling across the planet's remains.

Hell, he could still feel the tender new skin across his knuckles where he'd punched Duke after the iron-haired general had ordered him to stand down. He was still angry.

But being angry wasn't getting him anywhere. And after that initial fury had faded he found he didn't know how to lead the way his people expected. They'd become rebels, but what were they really rebelling against? And how?

Mike was a more effective rebel, in his own way, sending out these rogue broadcasts from hidden stations. Reporting on what Mengsk was really doing to consolidate his power and telling people what had really happened with the zerg and the protoss and the Psi-Emitters.

The zerg and the protoss. Hell, half the time Raynor thought he sounded raving mad talking about this stuff, or even thinking it. Alien races battling over humanity, acting out some ancient feud, with the colonies caught in the middle? It was insane.

But it was too real. He'd seen too much of it to ever think otherwise.

Still, perhaps he was cracking up. That would at least explain the dreams.

They'd been ambushing him since Tarsonis, lying in wait for the instant he closed his eyes each night. As soon as he laid his head down and drifted off, the dreams began.

Nightmares, really. Each was the same. He was trapped, confined, bound somehow without rope or shackles, unable to move or resist. Shadowy figures hovered over him, pressing in on every side as he lay helpless, wanting to scream but unable to open his mouth. That was the dream.

Until last night.

This time it had been different. He had not been bound at all, and had retained control of his limbs, though they felt heavy and slow and oddly numb. He was standing on a pale ground, soft grayish-white like old teeth or bleached bone, and every movement kicked up small puffs of it, which drifted across his feet and brushed against his ankles. The material was oddly dry, neither cool nor warm, and disintegrated upon contact.

Ash. He was standing on a field of ash. It stretched as far as the eye could see, coating every surface, even the rocky black hills that rose off to the sides. Clouds of it swirled through the air, obscuring his view of two small purplish moons and a ringed red planet that hung overhead. He could taste the ash when he breathed, feel it coating his lungs. The entire planet was ash, as if it had been razed once and never recovered.

But he had more pressing matters than studying the landscape. As he stood, getting his bearings and trying to shake his limbs back to some semblance of activity, dark figures appeared in the distance, closing the gap between them and him with frightening speed. Soon they towered over him, their sulfurous breath hot on his skin. He tried to keep them all in sight and not look at them at the same time, knowing somehow that staring at them would drive him beyond the brink. The quick glimpses he caught in his peripheral vision reminded him of zerg—tough skin and stretched frames exuding tentacles and spikes and spines. But these were larger than any zerg he had faced, darker, distorted. They terrified him, and he could feel his heart racing in his chest, his breath coming short, his skin breaking out in a clammy sweat. A small whimper escaped him and he clenched his jaw, trying to prevent similar sounds from emerging.

Though they were all but brushing against him he found he could somehow slip past these shadowy figures, and in a moment he was shambling across the ash-buried ground, trying not to stumble as he forced his legs to their maximum speed. The hills stood beyond, the distance to them uncertain because the ash hid telltale shadows, but he knew if he could only reach them he could find cover. Plumes of fire and smoke rose behind them—volcanoes, judging from the ash—and he knew the soot and smoke would help hide him from view. If he could make it over the ridge he could vanish into the haze. He could escape. He urged his limbs to cooperate, to move, and ran as fast as he could.

It was not enough.

The figures were closing in, spines wriggling in anticipation, tentacles lashing the air, and he could hear them hissing their excitement. He could hear their flesh dragging across the ground, sending clouds of ash everywhere. He could even hear the drool dripping from their lips. Soon they would have him surrounded, cut off. Their long limbs would wrap around him, binding him, and the chase would be over. Then the real torment would begin.

Desperate, he wheeled about, searching for a way out, a weapon, anything. He needed help!

But nothing was there. Only the ash and the monsters and him.

One of the creatures oozed forward, its hard, slick flesh protruding long spines like a crop of hair, and reached for him with spike-studded limbs. His flesh burned where it touched him, acid shooting through his veins as the spikes broke his skin, and he thrashed uncontrollably. His head jerked about, red hair tangling and temporarily obscuring the sight of what was waiting. Then the tentacles tightened and, as his lungs were squeezed dry, a single cry escaped him.

"Jimmy!"

That was when he woke up.

"It can't be," Raynor mused as shucked his pants and stepped into the shower. A twist of the silver-inlaid handle activated the needle-sharp spray—real water; nothing but the best for Mengsk!—and the shock of ice-cold water removed any last vestige of sleep along with the dirt and sweat and dried blood. He stubbornly shut the shower off after the regulation thirty seconds and waited patiently for the hot air that followed, leaving him dry and awake and slightly flushed as he exited and grabbed a cleaner shirt and pants from his closet. All the time his mind was still spinning, trying to make sense of the dream, trying to ignore the clues it had received.

"It just can't be," he told himself again, tugging on his boots and then sliding into his jacket. The gun belt went around his waist automatically, his blaster settled comfortably at his thigh, and he was heading for the door, snatching up his hat on the way out.

The *Hyperion* was a big ship, a full-sized battle cruiser, and it had ample space for weapons, supplies, and small scoutships. But it had also been Mengsk's flagship, and the former terrorist wasn't about to creep down narrow gangways or shuffle up cramped steel-railed ladders. Raynor shook his head yet again as he walked along a broad, carpeted hallway, soft lighting rising from the tasteful wall sconces spaced evenly down both sides. Between the doors, paintings hung. It all resembled a stately mansion rather than a spaceship, let alone a warship. He wondered if Mengsk was more upset about losing the ship's weapons or about losing the scotch, cigars, and other treats he'd kept onboard.

Skipping up the wide curving staircase, Raynor finally reached the command level and, tugging open the heavy door, entered the control room. His control room. It was as ostentatious as ever, a grand ballroom festooned with monitors and consoles, a dining room filled with operating stations, a helm fashioned from wood and tile and blanketed in velvet and silk.

"Sir!" Matt Horner saluted from the command chair and made to vacate it, but Raynor waved him back down. Horner was a good man, if a bit young and idealistic—he had actually joined the Sons of Korhal to make a difference and still believed in such things as patriotism and justice. He'd learn someday, though Raynor regretted the fact. For now he was a good second-in-command and an excellent ship captain.

"All's quiet, sir," Horner told him, and Raynor nodded, leaning against a console midway between the command chair and the navigation controls.

"What are your orders, sir?" Horner asked, and Raynor shrugged.

"As you were, son." He saw the disappointment etched across the younger man's face and felt the guilt wash over him again. He'd seen that same look many times, on Horner and others, in the past few weeks. They had all been so eager to follow him, so convinced he would lead them to do the right thing. And instead he'd led them here. Here where they sat waiting, doing nothing but fending off the occasional stray ship, biding their time until Mengsk learned their whereabouts and sent the fleet after them.

Why weren't they doing more? Raynor knew they wondered that. Every morning Horner asked for orders, and every morning he had none to give. He had lost his sense of direction. Breaking from Mengsk had been the right thing, Raynor was sure of that, but he wasn't ready to attack the Dominion outright and he just couldn't seem to find a good middle ground between inactivity and all-out war.

As Horner sank back into the command chair,

Raynor let his mind drift again, and once again it returned to the dreams. Particularly to this most recent one. It refused to leave him. It had been different from all the others, and not just because of the details and his freedom of movement. It had been more intense—the edges sharper, the colors brighter, the air charged with something that had crackled about him, raising his hair on end. Excitement? Fear?

Anticipation. Something was going to happen. And soon.

"I need a planet, Matt," he said finally, causing the younger man to look up.

"Sir?" For an instant Matt's face was blank, his eyes puzzled, and then he lit up. "Yessir! A new base of operations! A launching point for the revolution! A rallying ground for the—"

"No, just a planet," Raynor interrupted, knowing he had to shut his subordinate down quickly. "One that matches a particular description."

Stepping up beside Horner, he began inputting details into the navigational system. "Warm," he muttered to himself as he typed, "though not unbearably so. Air a bit sticky and filled with ash. One visible sun. Two small moons. Red ringed planet nearby. Covered in ash, pale gray, at least an inch thick. Some hills and small mountains, black rock rather than dirt. Fire and smoke all around. Probably volcanoes everywhere. No vegetation or animal life." The terms came back to him easily, a holdover from his days as a marshal on Chau Sara describing plots for potential colony use. He finished typing in the description and stepped back as he let the computer search its files for a match, staring off into space through the wide portholes that lined the front of the room.

It couldn't be her.

She was dead. He knew it. He hadn't seen her die, admittedly, and if anyone could survive such odds it would be her, but still . . .

Tarsonis has been overrun. The zerg had taken the entire planet. It had been six weeks.

And if she had survived she would have contacted him. Hell, she would have shown up in his room at night, without anyone seeing her slip onboard.

Then again, maybe she had. Just not in the way he would have expected.

She was a telepath, after all.

Sarah Kerrigan. She of the flaming red hair, the emerald-green eyes, and the wide smile. The girl with the knowing look and the deadly grace. Former Ghost, former assassin, formerly Mengsk's most trusted lieutenant.

Kerrigan. His friend. Almost his lover. Certainly the attraction had been there on both sides—they had both felt it. And had almost acted on it more than once. But the timing had never been right. That was the way with wars—they got in the way of other things.

She had called him a pig the first time they'd met. She'd been right—he couldn't help the thoughts that rose when he first saw her, glorious and dangerous and crowned with that mane of firelit hair. But they'd gotten past that. They'd become friends. She and Mike were the only two he'd really trusted out of Mengsk's inner circle, and the three of them had been tighter than brothers, tighter than spouses, experiencing the close bond that only forms when death is the price of failure.

Kerrigan. Mengsk had left her to die on Tarsonis, amid the zerg Swarm. And she was calling to him now. In his dreams. It had to be her. No one else called him Jimmy, not since he'd learned to talk.

"Sir?" Horner was gesturing toward the console, and Raynor set aside his reverie to study the readout.

NO MATCHES FOUND IN SYSTEM

"Damn." He'd hoped Mengsk's maps would have it. At least then he'd know that the place itself was real, if not the dreams about it.

"Sir?" Horner was watching him.

"Yeah?"

"Sir, we could still find it."

Raynor thought about it for a second, then shook his head. "Nah. Probably doesn't exist."

This time Horner frowned. "Sir, may I?" He gestured at the console, and Raynor nodded. Swiveling it over to the command chair, Horner began typing, his fingers flying across the keys. "Size of moons?" he asked without looking up, and Raynor searched his memory of the dream.

"Small," he replied. "Half those of Mar Sara. Purplish in color."

The younger man nodded and typed in something else. "Size of ringed planet?"

Raynor shut his eyes, trying to recall the brief glimpse he'd had of it. "Say the size of Tarsonis," he said finally.

"Gravity?"

He recalled the feel of his feet on the ground, of the ash swirling about him. "Normal. Full Terran gravity." Then he remembered something else. "High sulfur content in the air. High oxygen count, too." He had felt almost light-headed when breathing, despite the ash's almost choking him.

"Yes, sir." Horner finished typing and entered the search. A moment later three locations sprang up on the map that dominated the central screen. "Three potential matches, sir."

Raynor just stared at him. "How'd you do that?"

This time Horner grinned, flushing slightly. "Used an algorithm, sir. Input the details for the system and cross-referenced them with star maps." He indicated the three glowing dots on the screen. "None of them explored, sir. That's why they weren't in the nav system. But based on their suns and planets and moons, these three could fit."

"Hunh." Raynor shook his head, impressed. Horner was so eager to please, so quick to obey any order, he sometimes forgot the kid had been helming a starship before joining up.

He studied the three locations on the map. The first one was the closest by far. But as he stared at it he felt . . . wrong, somehow. Not bad, not good, just cold, disconnected.

He glanced at the second dot. Same feeling.

Then he looked at the third dot—and almost fell over from the wave of fear and tension that hit him. He broke out in a sweat just staring at it, and somehow it seemed to flare brighter, though he knew it hadn't.

"That's it," he whispered, gesturing toward the third dot, and Horner realigned the screen, centering on the dot and focusing in upon it.

"Got it, sir," he said as a string of numbers appeared beside it. "Set course?"

For a moment Raynor hesitated. That was the world he'd seen in his dreams. He was sure of it. That was where Kerrigan was.

His first impulse was to grab a scoutship and head out alone, at maximum burn. But that wouldn't have been smart. Tarsonis had fallen to the Swarm, and Kerrigan with it. She couldn't have escaped them. That meant they had her. It would explain the nightmarish figures in his dreams—zerg, but more so, somehow more powerful and more terrifying than the creatures he had already faced.

Subtlety wasn't the issue here. Speed was. Speed and firepower.

Something else, as well. For the first time since they'd hit the shipyards, Raynor felt energized, alive. He had a purpose again. It might not last, but for now it was enough. And his people needed that same purpose. They wanted him to lead them? All right, now he had someplace to lead toward.

Stepping over to the command chair, he claimed the mike and switched it to open broadcast through his ships. "Attention, all units," he announced. "This is James Raynor. We are about to mount a rescue mission. I believe some of our people from Tarsonis were taken captive by the zerg. I have coordinates for a planet where I think they were taken." His hands tightened on the mike as he remembered the feel of those creatures closing in. "We're not gonna stand by and let those filthy critters run off with our friends. We're going out there, guns blazing, and we're gonna take them back. And we'll blast every zerg that gets in our way." He took a deep breath, then continued. "We depart in two hours. Anyone who doesn't want to go can leave now. I won't hold you to anything. This could be a fool's errand we're off on. It could be our deaths. So don't go if you're not ready for that." He glanced at the screen again, and at the dot that seemed to wink at him. "If any of our people are there, I'll tear the place apart to find them. And we won't leave without them."

He switched the mike back off and tossed it to Horner. "Matt, set a course, maximum burn."

"Yes, sir!" Horner began typing in commands enthusiastically, but paused to look back up at him. "Sir, do you really think so? That some of our people are there? Being held by the zerg?"

"I hope so, Matt," Raynor answered, turning away to study the dot again. "I certainly hope so."

• • •

Two hours later the *Hyperion* prepared to jump, the rest of Raynor's rebellious little fleet trailing behind it. Ten people had left before the ships could depart, out of over four hundred. The rest had signed on for the mission and whatever came out of it. Most had been excited, jittery, and he knew only part of that was the thought of rescuing fallen comrades. They were all just pleased he had taken decisive action. He was leading, and they were ready to follow. He just hoped they weren't following to their dooms.

Sitting in the captain's chair on the *Hyperion,* Raynor watched as space folded around them, letting the massive ship glide from normal reality and accelerate rapidly toward the ash-covered world of his dreams.

We're coming, Kerrigan, he called in his head. I hope you're still there, because we're coming to get you.

CHAPTER 2

TWO WEEKS LATER RAYNOR STOOD ON THE BRIDGE and looked down upon the world he had dubbed Char. Even before Horner jockeyed the *Hyperion* into orbit he could see the smoke rising from several spots around the dull gray world, and the flares of orange and gold that often preceded them. Judging from their preliminary scans the entire planet was caught in the throes of constant volcanic activity and in places it looked as if the ground itself might be unstable, still fluid from the repeated superheating beneath it. They had maneuvered past a larger red planet on their way in, dodging its wide golden rings, and spied two small moons as they braked just beyond Char's atmosphere.

This was definitely it. The world in his dreams. The dreams that still haunted him every night, and sometimes during the day.

Yes, they had gotten worse. He was having them more frequently now. Warp travel was exhausting—something about the body not being designed for moving at that speed and the mind not being able to process the information around it. Because of that he, like the rest of his people, had found himself dozing off several times a day, anywhere for a few minutes to an hour. And each time the dreams had returned when he closed his eyes.

Nor had they remained the same. The dream of those horrific zerglike monstrosities looming over him had continued, but with each dream he had less space to run, less room to move, less chance of escape. Less and less hope, as the monsters loomed larger and larger until they blotted out the sky.

His body had been altered as well within the dreams. It had stretched and contorted, shifting out of control, twisting and turning as if given a mind of its own and an urgent need to escape his consciousness. At first he had thought it was merely bad luck of the kind that filled bad dreams—tripping over a loose rock, twisting an ankle on uneven ground, fingers slipping from the haft of a gun. But slowly Raynor had realized that these were not accidents. In the dreams his own body was turning against him. It was siding with the monsters, working toward his capture and destruction.

His cries had become weaker as well. The calls of "Jimmy!" had faded to whispers, then to gurgles, then to mere gasps, as his throat tightened against him. Even his voice was no longer his. During the last dream Raynor had stood stock-still as the monsters descended, waiting until they had surrounded him. Then he had dropped to his knees and flung his arms wide, head back, waiting to receive them. He had woken from that dream with a laugh bubbling up his throat, a laugh of joy and victory and exaltation. And something else. A phrase that had wafted through him just as the dream ended, something that reverberated through every cell of his body and set his hairs on end.

"Behold the power of that which is yet unborn!"

It chilled him to the bone, those words. Because even though he could not identify the speaker, he knew they were talking about him. About her. About Kerrigan. What were they doing to her? Hold on, Raynor had thought desperately that morning as he'd staggered into his bathroom and ducked his head under the faucet to chase the last vestiges away. Hold on, Kerrigan. We're almost there.

And now he was. Here he stood on the *Hyperion*'s bridge, looking down upon Char itself. Knowing that Kerrigan was down there somewhere.

If the dreams were right, the zerg were there too. Raynor didn't see any sign of them but he knew that meant nothing. The deadly Swarm was capable of hiding all traces from even the strongest scans. Hell, he'd walked, slept, and rode right above them on Mar Sara, maybe for months, without ever realizing it. Sometimes he still wondered what would have happened if he hadn't put down near that first outpost, or run into Mike and that bodyguard of his. Would he have been another one of the casualties, his corpse obliterated by the protoss like everything else on the planet? Or had he been destined to get off that world before it died, to leave his home behind and take to the stars on some larger mission?

"Sir!" Horner's shout brought Raynor back to the present, and he jerked around. But something caught his eye as he turned, and he stopped, focusing on the speck floating off to one side of Char. The speck that quickly resolved itself into the shape of a Terran Dominion warship.

"I see it," Raynor assured his second, shifting to get a better look. "Can we identify it from here?"

"Yes, sir." Horner's fingers danced on the keyboard again, and after a second he had an answer. The audible gulp beforehand gave it away. "It's the *Norad III*, sir."

The *Norad III*. General Duke's ship. "Great." Keeping his eyes on the ship, Raynor backed across the room until he was next to the control chair. "Any signs of support?"

"Two carrier ships and a science vessel, plus one cargo hauler," Horner confirmed. Now Raynor could see the smaller smudges beside the first one.

"No other battleships?"

Horner frowned at his screen and tapped it again, as if he couldn't believe what he was seeing. "No sir," he finally replied. "The *Norad III*'s by herself."

"Hunh." Raynor rubbed his chin, thinking. The *Norad III* wasn't really by itself, of course—it had four other ships with it, making up a small fleet. But Matt was thinking in terms of a space battle, where the only important ships were the battleships and their fighter complements. If this were war Duke would be here with a half-dozen warships behind him. That meant this wasn't an all-out attack, on either Char or his little rebellion. Not that Duke could have predicted his arrival here—even if Mengsk had a spy onboard, as Raynor knew was possible, he hadn't given anyone but Horner the coordinates for this place. And he knew Horner was too idealistic to betray him. So if Duke wasn't here for him, why was he here? And without backup? Though then again, the *Norad III* was a heavy warship, one of the Behemoth class, and could carry more than a thousand soldiers and two dozen star fighters, so he wasn't exactly defenseless. Plus he had those carriers, which meant he had ample ground forces on hand. But you only used ground forces when you didn't want to damage the area. What was there on Char to damage?

"Only one way to find out," Raynor decided, and nodded to Horner. Taking the hint, the younger man stood and stepped aside, letting Raynor take the chair. "Matt," he said as he sank into the plush seat, "give the *Norad III* a holler. No reason not to be neighborly."

The younger man stared at him as if he'd gone mad, but did as instructed. A moment later the front screen's expanded view of Char vanished, replaced by a familiar face with a square jaw, a heavy brow, and a head of neatly chopped steel-gray hair.

"Raynor!" General Edmund Duke spat at him before the connection had even stabilized. "You've got a lot of nerve showing your face, you mangy dog! I oughta put you down right now!"

"Give it your best shot," Raynor replied, feeling his temper rise despite himself. Damn, but Duke always managed to rile him! He steepled his fingers, a gesture he'd seen Mengsk use more than once, to keep from clenching his hands into fists. "You don't have the firepower to take us," he pointed out brusquely. "The *Norad III* might take out the *Hyperion* but we've got ten more ships and you've got only four, and none of them any good in a firefight." He saw the muscle twitch in Duke's jaw and knew he was only saying what the older man already knew. They stared at each other for a minute without speaking.

Duke broke the silence. "What do you want here, anyway? Looking to set up your own little kingdom now that you've cut loose?"

"I could ask you the same thing," Raynor replied, leaning forward. "Why so far from home? Doesn't the Dominion need you anymore?"

"I'm here on a special mission," the general replied pompously. "The Emperor asked me to handle it personally."

"Really? Must be important," Raynor said. He tried to keep his face blank, failed, and wound up grinning. "You bringing him a drink? Maybe shining his shoes?" He saw the older man's eyes narrow and knew he'd scored a hit. Duke was such an easy target.

His adversary didn't break down, though. Duke was made of stronger stuff than that, and despite his other faults he wasn't stupid. "Wouldn't you like to know?" he replied with a laugh. "Oh, I bet you would. In fact, I bet you're here for the same reason."

Had Duke had the dreams too? No, that was impossible—Kerrigan had despised him as much as Raynor did. But why else would he be here? Maybe Mengsk had dreamed, though. Despite the betrayal that had led to Kerrigan's death the two had been close, and Kerrigan had been one of the former terrorist's most trusted lieutenants. Had she reached out to him, prompting him to send Duke on his behalf? Raynor didn't let any of that show on his face or in his voice when he replied, "Oh? What reason?"

"Don't play coy with me, boy," Duke snapped. "I know what's going on here. A lot more than you do, in fact." He looked smug, far too smug for a man who was only bluffing.

"You don't know anything," Raynor countered, though he wasn't so sure. He wasn't used to bantering like this, and wished Mike were here. Liberty had a definite gift for talk and probably would have had Duke spouting secrets about his mother by now.

"Oh, don't I?" This time it was Duke who grinned. "How're you sleeping, boy?"

He knows! Raynor sat back in shock. *Why else would he have asked that? Mengsk must have had the same dreams!*

"Yeah, gotcha," Duke chortled, and Raynor realized he'd let his surprise show. "Like I said, I know what's going on here. Just stay out of my way, boy. If you want to live, that is."

"Keep talking, old man," Raynor snapped back.

"Keep talking and stay in that shiny ship of yours and don't cross me. I'm not in the mood."

The older man's face had paled and his eyes were almost hidden under his brow now. His voice was little more than a rasp as he growled, "Listen, punk! I sure as hell don't take orders from no jumped-up beat cop who thinks he's a rebel!" The muscle in his jaw was practically dancing now, and Raynor thought he could hear the scrape of teeth grinding together. "Only reason I'm not taking you apart right now is I've got other fish to fry! But you give me any more of your lip and I'll storm over there and drown you like the dog you are! I'll personally tear a hole in that fancy ship of yours and plant my boot so far up your—"

Raynor cut the signal mid-rant and sat back in his chair. Something wasn't right here; he could feel it. Perhaps because of the time he'd spent with Kerrigan, he had learned to trust his instincts.

Something about that whole exchange had been off. Oh, Duke hated him, he knew that; the feeling was certainly mutual. And the older man's antagonism hadn't been faked, especially that last outburst. Nor had the taunts been a lie—Duke did think he knew something Raynor didn't. He was almost certain Mengsk had also had dreams from Kerrigan and had sent Duke to check them out. So what was wrong?

It was Duke's hesitance to fight, he finally decided. The man was practically a rabid dog, and Mengsk had been forced to leash him several times during the war to keep the general from overstepping his bounds and destroying Mengsk's plans with a mindless charge. Even if the *Norad III* was alone, Duke still would have come after them, at least enough to fire a warning shot or two. Plus he could always send his soldiers and attempt to board—if those carriers were even half-full he'd have enough men to swamp them easily. Why hadn't he?

"Matt," Raynor called, and Horner was standing at his elbow an instant later. He almost laughed but knew it would offend the younger man. "You sure the *Norad III*'s the only warship nearby?"

"Absolutely, sir." Horner's head bobbed up and down. "I did a full sweep, then another two to be sure. She's got nobody."

"Hm." That could just mean Mengsk couldn't spare any other ships. And the *Norad III* was a capable vessel. "How's she look?"

Horner understood him. It was one of the reasons he liked his second—the young man was able to make sense of his verbal shorthand. "Weapons ports open, sir, and shields up. She's definitely in combat mode." He frowned. "I did get two strange things, sir." Raynor waited for him to continue. "Those carriers are reading as more than half-empty. And I got a signal off Char's surface. From the *Norad III*."

"A second reading?" Raynor glanced at the screen, which had reverted to its view of Char. *Norad III* hovered off to one side, still little more than a smudgy outline. But she was clearly there.

Ah, but perhaps not all of her.

"Get me Duke again," he ordered, and Horner hopped to obey. A moment later Duke's face was once again on the screen. Raynor was amused to see that the older man's jaw was still just as clenched.

"You went down there, didn't you?" he asked immediately, not giving the general a chance to start shouting at him again. "You've already been to the surface. Your carriers are mostly empty. Plus we're getting a reading from your ship down there—one of your shuttles. And it's still there." He watched Duke's face as he spoke, and was pleased to see the other man's eyes narrow farther and his jaw become so rigid it was a wonder he could breathe. "You lost most of your men and at least one shuttle checking the place out." He leaned forward again. "What happened, Duke? Natives too much for you? Already get your butt handed to you?"

"Shut your mouth, punk!" Duke finally shouted, losing his temper completely. "You try it, you're so tough! Those zerg'll eat you alive!"

"So you did encounter them," Raynor mused aloud. "Too hot for you, eh?" He laughed. "Mengsk won't be happy. Sends you to do a simple task and you botch it royally."

"Shut up!" Duke roared. "I didn't fail! She's not here! Or if she is she's got the entire Swarm here with her! Nobody could get her out of that! Nobody!" Then his mouth clamped shut as he realized what he'd said.

"I can get her," Raynor assured him, and cut the connection again. He sank back into his seat, excited and chilled at the same time.

Kerrigan was here! Duke's ranting had confirmed it. Or at least Mengsk had been convinced she was, which meant Raynor wasn't crazy. Even if this was all some zerg trick, it was better than him just imagining things.

That was the excitement. Kerrigan had sent the dreams, and she had meant for him to come here. This was the place. And, despite everything, she might still be alive.

Then came the chills. Because this was the world from his dreams, the world of zerg more monstrous than any he'd seen before. And the zerg were definitely here. They'd already defeated Duke and driven him back off the surface. And one thing he had to admit was that Duke was a good man in a fight. The *Norad III* was a top-of-the-line battle cruiser, fully loaded. And he'd brought two carriers, each filled with ground troops, most likely the best Mengsk had to offer. But they hadn't been able to hold the surface, or even their drop point. Which meant the zerg were here in force.

He had to go down there. He knew that. He'd come this far; he'd never forgive himself if he didn't go. Neither would Kerrigan, for that matter. But what about his people? Could a bunch of ragtag rebels stand where Duke's army had fled?

Once again he was assailed with doubts. Did he have the right to risk all of them for one woman who might not even still be alive? Could he ask them to risk their own lives for hers? And what kind of leader would ask them to make that choice?

"Sir?" Horner stood nearby. "What are your orders?"

Raynor rubbed his palms into his eyes, hoping to drive some sense into his brain. He started to tell his second that he didn't know, that he was having questions, but quashed that impulse quickly. That wasn't what Horner wanted to hear. It wasn't what anyone wanted to hear. One thing he had learned from Mengsk was the importance of appearances. Even if you were tearing yourself up inside, you couldn't let it show. Not the leader, anyway. You had to present a calm face, a reassuring voice, and a clear purpose. Otherwise your people lost faith in you. And that was worse than making a mistake, even worse then costing some lives, because once they lost faith they'd be just as lost as you were.

"We're going down," he announced, sitting and tapping in the commands for open broadcast. "Make sure the *Norad III* doesn't pick this up," he instructed, and as Horner hopped back to his station Raynor grabbed the mike. "Attention, all ships," he announced. "This is Raynor. We are going down. I repeat, we are going down. All ships prepare landing parties, heavy gear, full combat mode. Expect opposition. It's gonna get hot down there."

He had already clicked off the mike and stood up when Horner stiffened at his console. "Sir!"

"What's wrong, Matt?" He was standing at the younger man's side in an instant.

"The *Norad III*'s opened her bay, sir!"

"What?" Raynor leaned in closer, studying the readout on Horner's screen. Had he finally pushed Duke far enough to force an attack?

"One shuttle and three star fighters," Horner announced a second later, deciphering the scrolling information. "Heading toward the surface, sir."

Raynor leaned back, nodding. He could hear the relief in Horner's voice. It wasn't an attack after all. At least, not one on them. He had pushed Duke into action, but not into coming after them—Duke was going planetside again to search for Kerrigan once more. Or to rescue survivors form his earlier attempt. Well, that was fine. Maybe they'd distract the zerg long enough for his people to get in and out safely.

"Matt, you've got the ship," he told the younger man, clapping him on the back. "Make sure she's still here when I get back, eh?" The younger man nodded, his face lit with pride, and Raynor knew Horner would give his life to keep the *Hyperion* safe. Hopefully it wouldn't come to that.

Well, we're here, he told himself as he exited the bridge and headed for the shuttle bay. *Time to get down there and take a look.*

CHAPTER 3

CHAR WAS EVERY BIT AS UGLY IN REALITY AS IT had been in his dreams, Raynor decided as he hopped down from the shuttle. His boots crunched into the surface, sending small puffs of ash swirling up around his ankles, and he was glad for the rebreather covering his nose and mouth and the attached goggles covering his eyes. He'd considered wearing his combat armor but had decided against it—though the suit would have given him strength and protected him against minor damage, it wasn't good in tight spaces and had only a limited power supply. Besides, he'd seen zerg cut right through armor. He was better off relying on agility, especially since he didn't have his bike handy.

Squinting against the setting sun, he studied the landscape. Bleak; that was the word for it. Ash and rock as far as the eye could see, topped by smoke and more ash and some flame. No plants, no animals, nothing moving but him and his people, who were all off the shuttles now and clustering around them, forming discrete units within the whole. That was exactly what he'd instructed before they touched down. He didn't want an army down here—too easy to attract attention. Better to split into small groups and scout around, figure out what was where. Hopefully one of them would spot the Swarm and find Kerrigan without getting noticed.

"All right," he called over the command channel. "All crews, stay frosty, and keep your eyes peeled for our target. Remember, not only are we up against the zerg here, but our old pal General Duke may be creepin' around too." He bit back a sigh, the harsh landscape already depressing him. "Let's hope this trip wasn't a big mistake," he muttered, then hoped they hadn't heard that part.

Shaking it off, Raynor shouldered his rifle and motioned his crew closer. If someone had tailored a planet to be inhospitable they couldn't have done a better job. He'd felt the futility of this place through Kerrigan's dreams, and it was worse now. But he had two things going for him that he hadn't had in those nightmares.

First off, he was awake and alert and armed.

Second, he wasn't alone.

He planned to use both advantages to their fullest.

"I want a sweep of the area to our northwest," he told Lisa Mannix, the sergeant he'd picked as his second here. "Quiet and careful. We don't know where they're hiding."

"Yessir." She snapped off a quick salute and began organizing the others into pairs, then assigning them sections on the grid. Calm and efficient, Mannix never seemed to get riled, which Raynor appreciated. He'd worked with her a few times under Mengsk and had been pleased when she'd joined his revolt, saying she couldn't stomach what had happened on Tarsonis. On the *Hyperion* she was easygoing, friendly, almost playful, but down here she was all business, and only minutes after they'd landed she had everyone moving out, canvassing the ground for any trace of their foes—or the woman they'd come to rescue.

"Sir, you need to see this!" It was one of his troopers, Chuck Ayers, a short older man who'd been a career soldier under Duke and had followed him to Mengsk and then walked away. He was one of Raynor's top choices for a mole, and he kept the man close to keep an eye on him, but so far Ayers had proven to be nothing but an asset. Now he was standing with his partner, Ari Patel, on either side of a small crevice, guns out and at the ready. Raynor stepped up beside them, Mannix right behind him.

"Check it out." Ayers gestured toward the crevice, and Raynor studied it. It was small, barely three feet across, and perfectly circular, with a raised lip around a deep hole. It wasn't so much a crevice as a sinkhole or a crater—or an entrance. The ash was thinner here, exposing the black rock beneath, and the inside was rough and lumpy. But the edge was razor-sharp.

"Small volcano," Mannix suggested, crouching to get a better look. "Planet's probably riddled with them. We'll have to watch our step."

"Hm." Raynor squatted as well, still staring at the hole. "Could lead to caverns, though," he suggested. They all knew what that meant. The zerg had shown a clear affinity for the underground. If this hole did lead to tunnels beneath the surface, it probably also led straight to the Swarm.

Mannix eyed the hole. "Too small for us," she decided finally. "Too easy to get stuck." She frowned. "Too small for most zerg, too."

Raynor nodded and stood up, absently brushing ash from his pants. She was right—only zerglings could fit through that. The hole might lead to the Swarm but it wasn't going to provide Raynor and his crew with access, or be a way for the zerg to sneak up behind them.

"Drop a sensor," he told Ayers, moving away from the crater. "We'll keep an ear on it. Good catch, though." The soldier saluted, already reaching for the pack at his side. Each of the troopers had at least one sensor, and they were all keyed into everyone's else's comm unit. If the zerg crept past this crater they'd all hear it.

They kept moving, Mannix making sure the pairs were spread out across the grid. Raynor stayed beside her, rifle at the ready, but most of his attention was taken up listening to the other squad reports.

"Got a hole!" one announced. "Too small," they called back a moment later. "Dropping a sensor." Others had the same results. This area had seen strong volcanic activity not too long ago and the ground was still pocked with the resulting craters. That pattern of discovery and dismissal lasted for a full ten minutes.

"I've got zerg!" someone shouted. Raynor immediately pinpointed the individual. It was Lance Messner, from the *Nemesis*. Raynor was running toward Messner's location even as he shouted for Mannix and the others to follow.

The *Nemesis* shuttle had been next to theirs, and their teams were not far apart. It took Raynor only ten more minutes, running full out, to reach Messner. He was afraid he'd be too late, but the young trooper was still standing when he skidded to a halt.

"Where?" Raynor demanded, searching all around, his rifle barrel following his eyes. Messner pointed down, and Raynor realized there was a crevice between them. This was not a crater like the others but a narrow split in the ground, and he could see deep into the earth below it. And, somewhere down there, something was moving.

"You're sure it's zerg?" he demanded, and Messner nodded fervently.

"Sir, yes sir!" the trooper replied. "I heard them, sir! That chittering sound they make, like giant beetles in a feeding frenzy!" It was an apt description, and not one likely to be confused with anything else on this world.

Mannix was beside him by now, with the rest of their squad falling in behind her. Raynor dropped to his haunches to peer into the crevice. Yes, he could hear what Messner had described. It was definitely zerg. Not close, and perhaps not even aware of them, but definitely there.

"All right, we've got zerg," he announced, standing

up again. "They're not coming up through here but we know they're below us. We've got to assume they know we're here, too. I want the squads to double up," he told Mannix, who nodded. "Defensive formation. Continue the scouting, though. We need to find a way in."

While Mannix organized the men, Raynor squeezed the bridge of his nose between thumb and forefinger, trying to will away the headache he felt forming. He shut his eyes—

—and found himself alone, the sky turned darker, the sun vanished but the moons high. His rifle was gone, as was his pistol and even his boots. He stood there, the ash drifting between his toes, and watched the horizon darken further, but not from the onset of night. This was a more organic darkness, a wave of creatures moving toward him, their dusky hides drowning the light as they came.

In what seemed an instant they were around him, and he spun, searching for a way out. He had none. They were everywhere, surrounding him and then pressing in upon him, his flesh taking numerous cuts from the spikes and blades and claws on every side. They towered over him, trapping him in their shadows, and he shuddered even as a wave of relief rippled through him. Not just relief, but pleasure, excitement—he was happy to see them! He was glad they had found him, glad they were so close, glad they were touching him. Their limbs tangled about him, making it difficult to tell where one ended and another began, and he was glad of that as well. Glad he was one with them. One of them.

"Sir?"

The touch on his arm startled him, and Raynor fought back the reflex to fire, shoving his rifle point away from a surprised Mannix. The men were arrayed behind her, waiting. Messner, who had been crouching beside him at the crevice edge, was still straightening up, as he had been when Raynor had shut his eyes. A second, maybe two, he realized; that's how long I was out. It seemed so much longer. Long enough for the dream to reach me. Was I asleep? Or is it just that much stronger planetside?

"Let's go," he told Mannix, and she nodded, whatever concerns she'd had vanishing before the task at hand. They set out again, their squad and the Nemesis team combined, men circling the center, never leaving a quadrant unwatched or uncovered. It was slower this way but much safer, especially now that they knew the zerg were below them. Raynor wasn't taking any chances.

"Sir, we've got a problem." It was Horner, calling on his private link, and Raynor responded, making sure the command circuit was off so the conversation wouldn't be broadcast.

"What's wrong, Matt?" he asked. It had been several hours now. They hadn't found a single entrance they could use, though they'd seen plenty of craters and several more crevices. The zerg were still down there, visible through some of the cracks, but if the Swarm had detected their presence they weren't attacking yet. Either they didn't know or they had something more important to do, Raynor thought.

"We've got readings, sir," Horner continued. "Incoming ships."

"Duke's reinforcements?"

"No sir," Horner replied, and the fact that he didn't sound pleased made Raynor uneasy. Whatever was coming, his second would have preferred Terran Dominion warships. This couldn't be good. "It's protoss, sir," Horner explained, and Raynor resisted the urge to shoot something, anything.

Protoss. Here. Now.

It made sense, in a way. Everywhere he'd seen zerg, the protoss had arrived as well. Often the tall, graceful aliens had appeared after the zerg had infested a world and had then wiped the planet clean—not just of zerg but of everything: all higher life-forms, all traces of civilization. That's what they'd done to Mar Sara, his homeworld. He already knew that zerg and protoss were bitter enemies and fought at every turn. The protoss seemed determined to eliminate all traces of zerg and followed them around like cosmic exterminators, cauterizing whole worlds to prevent the Swarm from spreading. If the zerg were here on Char, of course the protoss were as well. Or would be soon.

"Keep me posted," he told Horner, but he was already thinking through the possibilities. They'd teamed with the protoss several times before to eliminate zerg—the zerg wanted to corrupt and absorb Terran life while the protoss just wanted to stop the zerg, so it was an easy choice of allies. Could he strike a deal with the protoss again? The last time he'd seen them had been on Tarsonis, when Mengsk had ordered his men to engage the alien race despite their common enemy. Mengsk had wanted the Psi-Emitter's to do their job and summon the zerg in force so they would destroy the Confederacy's Capital World. He hadn't wanted the protoss to interfere and stop the process. It had been part of the reason Raynor had walked out—but would the protoss know that? Or care?

"How did they find this place?" he wondered aloud, ignoring Mannix's questioning glance. Every other time the protoss had followed the zerg to a Terran world, but in many cases they hadn't arrived fast enough to have been tailing the Swarm. On Chau Sara and Mar Sara, for example, the zerg had been there for weeks or even months before showing any signs, and the protoss had only arrived after the damage was done. So what were they doing here now? Had the zerg been here on Char that long? If so, they'd have the entire planet mined and mapped—and Raynor had brought his men into a killing ground.

But what if the protoss had come here for another reason? What if, this time, it wasn't the zerg they had tracked? The zerg were telepathic, Raynor knew—the entire Swarm was linked together and members could communicate instantly across entire planets. He suspected that the protoss were also telepathic, though their warriors seemed to have more autonomy than did the zerg. He didn't think the protoss were a hive-mind, but what if they were psionic? Kerrigan had to be incredibly powerful to reach across space to both him and Mengsk. What if she'd reached out to the protoss as well? Or what if they'd simply received the dreams unbidden, the signal so strong it had struck them on its way to him? The dreams definitely involved zerg, and that might have been enough to attract the protoss.

Of course, that didn't mean their presence was a good thing. Not given their tendency to annihilate any planet the zerg had tainted. And Char was definitely tainted.

"Listen up, people," Raynor announced on the command channel. "We've got protoss incoming as well. We don't know whose side they're on. Don't shoot first, but don't let down your guard."

If they were lucky, he thought as he beckoned to Mannix, the protoss would keep the zerg busy for him. Maybe they'd even blast open a way down to the zerg tunnels, and he could simply follow them in. It wasn't likely, though.

"I want to know where they land," he told Mannix. "They might lead us in. But be ready to fall back to the shuttles if I give the word. If they start lighting this place up we'll hightail it back to the *Hyperion* and wait for the smoke to clear."

"Yessir." She glanced around. "We haven't found a way down yet, sir. If the protoss don't show us one, how much longer you want to look?"

Raynor thought about his dreams, and the woman sending them. "As long as it takes, Sergeant. As long as it takes."

Part of him, however, knew it wouldn't be that long. The dreams were getting more frantic and more distorted. He could feel Kerrigan's urgency. Whatever was going to happen, it was going to be soon.

"We got a hole!" someone shouted, and Raynor shook off the foreboding to scramble toward the trooper. It was Deke Cavez, the youngest member of his team, tall and slight and fast enough to run down a hoverbike on foot. Cavez was standing by a crater with his partner, Melinda Squire, and Raynor could already see that this one was larger than the holes they'd found before. It was at least five feet across and its lip rose a full three feet from the ground, creating a short cone. The sides were rough and ash-covered, but the interior glittered a glossy black.

"It's big enough," Mannix confirmed, peering into the crater. "Looks like it runs all the way down, too. We should be able to—" The rest of her sentence was cut off as she stumbled back, barely avoiding a scythe blade that lashed out and up from inside the crater. Raynor caught her as she fell, shoving her farther back as he brought his rifle to bear, its barrel rising along with the snakelike creature that sprang up from the hole, flared head darting about to study them, scythe-arms already twitching for a second attack.

A hydralisk. Raynor had seen them before—hell, it had been a hydralisk and some zerglings that had caused his encounter with Mike Liberty, the same encounter that had led to his meeting Mengsk and Kerrigan. The same encounter that had ultimately led him here. He owed the hydralisk for making him who he was today.

He repaid the favor by opening up with his gauss rifle, firing a row of metal spikes deep into the snake-like zerg's head. It toppled to one side, the impact driving it to the ground, the glow already fading from its eyes. It hadn't seen Raynor yet and he hoped it had died before revealing their location to the rest of the Swarm.

"Right." He glanced over at Mannix, already back on her feet. She nodded. "All teams, converge. We got us a hole. We're going in, but be warned—the zerg're already down there, and they know about this entrance. Let's just hope they don't know we're coming."

But somebody does, he thought as he watched Cavez and Squire leap into the crater, followed by Ayers and Patel. *Kerrigan must know we're here. I'm coming, darlin'. I'm coming.* Then it was his and Mannix's turn, and, shouldering his rifle, Raynor jumped feetfirst into the darkness.

CHAPTER 4

THE CRATER TURNED OUT TO BE THE TOP OF A long, straight chute. The sides had cooled long ago, but the lava that had erupted through it had been hot enough to melt the rock to glass, and the walls were water-slick and perfectly smooth. Raynor plummeted like a stone, bruising arms and legs whenever he bumped against the sides, careful to keep his head tucked in and his limbs wrapped around his rifle. The fall felt endless but it was probably less than a minute before he spied a glow below him, and then he was curling into a ball and striking the floor hard enough to leave him dizzy and gasping.

"All right, sir?" Cavez offered him a hand, and after a minute he took it. The youngster looked unfazed, but then he'd jumped in first and so he'd had a minute to recover. Raynor did his best not to show just how wobbly he was—wouldn't do to let his men see him collapse like a little girl.

"Fine, thanks," he rasped, clambering to his feet and

leaning back against the wall while he waited for his vision to clear. Behind him he heard a thud and a groan that could only be Mannix, following him down. Ayers was there to help her up and move her out of the way and suddenly Raynor knew he didn't need to worry about looking weak. They'd all need a minute to recover. It was one hell of a drop.

He glanced around, squinting to see better. Two glowsticks lay on the ground nearby, producing the light he'd seen, and he realized they'd been lit to provide a clue to the sudden stop at the end. It was a smart move, and he wondered which of the four troopers had thought of it.

The glow wasn't much, but as his eyes adjusted he could make out more of the space where they'd landed. It was broad and high, at least four feet above his head and wide enough for four men abreast. He'd have preferred something narrower, since that would have kept the zerg from mobbing them, but it couldn't be helped. The rough corridor extended in both directions without branches, and he noticed it had a slight incline. The lower end pointed back the way they had come.

"Which way, sir?" Mannix asked, wincing slightly as she popped her neck and worked her right shoulder back into joint. Two more pairs had arrived, one-fourth their crew, with the others and the full Nemesis squad still topside.

"Not sure yet," he admitted, pushing off from the wall and walking a little ways down the corridor. If the zerg were in this tunnel they hadn't noticed them yet or were too far away to be detected. He had a feeling they weren't here—the chute had been long enough to get them down here but that didn't mean it ran all the way to whatever level the Swarm was using. He knew they liked it deep. But the lava had flowed up from here, which meant there had to be a way down from this point. He just had to find it.

"All right, Kerrigan," he muttered. "I'm here. Now where the hell are you?"

Closing his eyes, he was instantly thrust back into the nightmare version of this world. This time the monster-zerg already had him surrounded, and as he lifted his hands to shield himself he saw that his skin had darkened, but unevenly, his flesh now blotchy and gray, almost green, clearly unhealthy. Yet his body felt strong, capable, powerful. Energy thrummed through him, invigorating him, setting his hair on end—

Raynor forced his eyes open again, cutting the dream off abruptly. It had been waiting there for him behind his eyelids, ready to spring the instant he fell into darkness. He was almost afraid to blink, in case it came back into that space and pulled him away. But his gamble had worked. The dream was stronger here than it had been on the surface. Kerrigan was closer.

Walking past his curious troopers, he stalked a dozen paces in the opposite direction and closed his eyes again.

One of the zerg was touching him, its scythelike limbs poking into his mottled flesh, but it was not attacking. There was no force behind the thrust, no aggression—it was merely a way of making contact. And through that contact came a voice, deep and cold, a voice that resounded through his bones and sent chills up his spine. Yet for all that, it felt strangely comforting.

"Welcome," it said to him. "The Swarm embraces you."

The shock of that message popped his eyes back open and Raynor stood there a moment, gasping, before turning back to his crew. "This way," he told them, barely able to spit the words out. The dream had been stronger this time than before. Part of that was the urgency, he knew, some impending event that Kerrigan was desperate to avoid. Part of it was simply that the dreams were getting worse, their story playing out to an unpleasant end he desperately tried not to acknowledge. But part of it was proximity. He was sure he was right. Kerrigan felt closer this way. He was leading his men in the right direction.

The corridor dead-ended a hundred paces farther down, but just before that point Cavez spotted a branching. A narrow passage split off to one side, its sharply angled walls and irregular path evidence that it was a natural fissure. The rock here was slate gray rather than black and they could see a darker patch at the far end, either volcanic rock or an opening. Either way it was their best option, and they headed toward it, creeping along single file. Ayers took the lead, with Patel right behind him.

"It's another passage," Ayers called back, and sounded like he was about to elaborate when he let out a wheeze and then a short gasp. Patel's rifle sounded, the report deafening in that narrow space, and Raynor cursed from his spot four men back. It had to be zerg! And here they were, unable to retreat, unable to form ranks, emerging one by one like peas popped loose from a pod. This was likely to be a slaughter.

He had to do something fast to even the odds, and he did it. Grasping a heavy sphere from his belt, he primed it and lobbed it overhand. The grenade flew past him, over Mannix and Cavez and Squire, and disappeared into that darkness where Patel had ventured after Ayers.

"Grenade!" Raynor shouted, dropping to a crouch, and Messner behind him and Mannix before him did the same. He hoped Patel had heard.

Then the grenade went off, sending a shock wave back through the passage. The walls shook and slivers of rock fell, slicing flesh and canvas and leather, bouncing off metal. But the ceiling held, the floor didn't crack open, and an instant later Patel called out, "All clear!"

They hustled then, stealth forgotten, wading into the smoke and dust, and a minute later Raynor was out of that narrow fissure and into a much wider corridor, his back against the wall, rifle at the ready. Patel had a nasty cut along one arm and looked like he'd been worked over by a dozen large drunks, but he was still standing and still had a grip on his rifle. Ayers hadn't been so lucky. The veteran trooper lay on the ground just beyond the fissure's exit, blood pooling beneath him from the gaping hole in his chest and from the places where his arms had been. The hydralisk had stopped him from shooting by shearing both arms off at the elbow, then it had gutted him. They hadn't even heard the first blow. Fortunately the hydralisk hadn't been expecting a grenade. Judging from the body it had taken the impact full force in the chest and head, and had been squashed like a bug against the far wall. Raynor hoped it had been painful but knew it probably hadn't.

"Well, they know we're here," he said, shaking his head. "Nothin' for it, then. Leastways we don't have to be quiet anymore." He clicked his rifle over to full auto, and heard many of the troopers doing the same. "Get hold of the other crews," he told Mannix. "Relay it back if you can't get a signal to them from down here. Get everyone down here. We're gonna need 'em." Mannix nodded and called Messner to her, presumably to coordinate the process of reaching the other teams. Raynor knew he could trust her to take care of it. Soon they'd have everyone down here with them, roughly three hundred troopers. He hoped it would be enough.

He watched for another minute as the rest of the two teams made their way through the fissure. Squire and Cavez moved Ayers' remains off to one side. Gina Elani, one of Messner's team, bandaged Patel's arm. Everyone was ready. Then, because this tunnel ran in two directions and he could see several branches already, Raynor gritted his teeth and closed his eyes.

More of the monster-zerg were touching him now, their claws and spines jabbing but not penetrating his skin, and the voices had amplified, creating a ringing echo behind his eyes and between his ears. The words were the same, though.

"Welcome. The Swarm embraces you."

Shuddering, Raynor opened his eyes, reassuring himself that it was just a dream. Then he walked to the other side of the fissure and let the dream take him again. It took all his willpower to come out of it, to step away from that cold, clammy, smothering greeting, but he had his answer. He gestured in that direction.

"This way," he told his people.

As they followed him down the natural hallway, he hoped Kerrigan was worth it. And he hoped the scene in his dream was only an interpretation of her fear, not a peek at what was really going on inside her head. Because if it was accurate, they might all be doomed. And Raynor knew it would be his fault for bringing them here, to this world, to these caverns, to this mess.

The tunnels continued, one leading to another. Raynor used the dreams to find his way through each intersection, following the stronger path each time. And each time he had to force himself back to the present, back to his own flesh and blood, wrenching his mind from that stifling welcome that awaited him in the darkness. The urge to scream welled up within him and he fought it back, tightening his grip on his rifle until he was surprised the barrel and stock didn't have his fingerprints squeezed into the hardened plastic.

They encountered several more zerg. Each time it was only a small group of the aliens and each time Raynor's troopers made short work of them, though not without cost. Patel had survived that first attack with a wound to one arm and made it through a second unscathed, only to have his face bitten off by a zergling that leaped from a small hole in the ceiling and tore into him on the way down. Gina Elani, the petite trooper who had bandaged Patel's first wound, was sliced in half by a hydralisk when she stopped to give one of her fallen teammates a hand up. That teammate died as well, his chest ripped open even as Messner fired a full clip into the zerg's back. Others also fell, many Raynor knew only a little and some he didn't even recognize except as names on a list. He vowed to look up every last one of them if he made it out of this alive. They deserved that much.

The small zerg groupings were probably due to the narrow passages and crooked tunnels. Once or twice they found themselves in wide corridors like the first one below the chute, but those never lasted. These caverns were natural, never altered by zerg or any other, and they started and stopped, twisted and turned, dove and rose at random, going from avenue-wide to stairwell-narrow in a heartbeat and doubling around razor-edged corners or ribboning off out of sight. Cracks in the floor led to other levels, as did holes in the ceiling, but some of those gaps led to tiny pockets instead, and it was impossible to guess what lay beyond each opening. One trooper died because he dropped down through a crack and fell into a magma pool, burning to ash in an instant. Another thrust his head up through a hole above and cracked his skull against the rocky ceiling of the two-foot-high space. He might have survived if he hadn't broken his neck when he fell back to the tunnel below.

Raynor's dreams—they were more like waking visions now, always threatening to overlap reality and overwhelm his sense of self—were all that kept them going. He heard several troopers muttering behind him, wondering how he could possibly know where to go in this maze, but Mannix and the other sergeants shushed them quickly. No one really wanted to believe he didn't know the way, anyway. That would only make this worse.

Finally Raynor led them down a short, almost straight tunnel, high enough for him to carry another trooper upright on his shoulders and wide enough for him to fling his arms out without scraping the sides. At the other end was a wide arch, its surface stone but covered by a pulsing gray-black matter that looked less like the fungus it was than exposed brains. It was the zerg ooze, the creep that had showed their presence on several planets as it crept across the surface, matching their spread beneath. It meant that Raynor and his people had finally reached a place here on Char where the zerg had made themselves at home.

"Sir!" Cavez pointed, and Raynor followed his gesture, catching his breath as he saw the shape suspended near the center of the arch. It was an eye, a human eye, or at least it would have been if humans grew twenty feet tall. A cluster of thick tendrils trailed behind it and were wrapped around what looked like massive web strands crisscrossing the arch. The eye hung from them like a horribly altered spider, wriggling as they approached its web.

"Somebody blind that ugly sucker!" Raynor shouted, and Squire took aim and fired. A single spike plunged deep into the eye, dead-center on its massive pupil, and with a grating squawk the eye burst, showering them with bits of jellied goo. The tendrils still clung to the web, twitching slightly.

"Guess there's no sense knocking," Raynor muttered to Mannix beside him, and she mustered a weak smile in return. The eye had obviously been a sentry, and it had seen them approaching this whole time. The Swarm knew they were here.

"Get ready!" Raynor shouted over his shoulder, knowing Mannix would relay his message to the squads too far back to hear him. "We're about to have company!"

As if his words had been the trigger, a flutter of shapes appeared on the far side of the arch, casting shadows upon the web there. Then the strands burst and the Swarm was upon them.

Earlier, in that fissure, Raynor had wished for more room. Now he would have killed for less. The tunnel here was broad enough for three men to stand together, and the archway filled that width. That meant the zerg had enough space to charge in a cluster, spilling through the arch and threatening to engulf his troopers by numbers alone. A narrower space would have forced the zerg to trickle through instead of flood and they could have held them off more easily. Still, the goal wasn't to hold them but to get past them. Raynor didn't need to close his eyes to know that Kerrigan must be on the other side of that arch.

Getting through was going to be a problem, though. He shot a hydralisk through the head with his rifle and then drew his pistol and shot another that had been about to gut Mannix from behind. Steadying his pistol barrel atop and across his rifle, he fired one and then the other, blasting anything in his way. Zerglings were everywhere, leaping at men's heads or chewing through their arms or clamping those massive jaws around their ankles, tangling limbs and guns and leaving them vulnerable. The hydralisks were right behind them, as were the mutalisks, both using their spikes and blades to carve through the human forces. Raynor saw Squire go down, scythes from two different hydralisks meeting in her chest, her rifle shoved down by the blows and discharging at her feet, kicking up rock shards as the spikes struck the ground. Messner fell beneath a pack of zerglings and was literally ripped apart—Mannix saw it as well and was kind enough to put a bullet through the young trooper's head before he could register the pain. Raynor's troops were good, well-armed and well-trained and well-motivated, but they were drastically outnumbered. The tight quarters—wide enough for them to be surrounded but not wide enough for them to back away—didn't help. The zerg were all linked together, speaking to each other's minds, and that let them move as a single body. Raynor's people weren't so lucky. They stumbled against one another, blocked one another's shots, and sometimes even shot each other. That didn't help.

"We need to get inside!" he shouted to Mannix. They were back-to-back, firing at anything that came too close—more than once he'd had to jerk his gun away to avoid shooting a trooper. "We don't have time for this!"

"Let's go!" she shouted back. "Everyone, form up on me! Cover fire!" Not everyone heard her through the tumult, but enough did and some twenty men and women grouped around them, all facing outward. They began walking as a clump, locking step to avoid stumbling, firing in all directions at once. Every time someone emptied a clip the neighbor took over, covering that angle until they had reloaded. The zerg couldn't get to them, couldn't breach that wall of steel and plastic and powder. They made it under the arch, and then they were inside. The rest of the troopers were still in the tunnel, and they waited until Raynor and Mannix were past the arch before unleashing a rain of bullets. The zerg were forced to turn their attention to the larger threat again and swarmed down the tunnel, leaving the handful around Raynor with a moment to breathe and look around.

"What is this place?" one of them, a young man named Fedders, whispered. He was shaking slightly, and Raynor couldn't blame him. What they'd just been through, and what they were seeing now, was enough to shake anyone.

This chamber was far larger than the tunnel beyond it, wide enough for a shuttle to fit within and tall enough for one to stand upright without grazing the domed ceiling. The walls were covered in creep, which shed a faint light that pulsed all around them, leaving Raynor slightly nauseous. Zerg moved here and there in the room, smaller zerglings like giant maggots writhing through mounds of creep piled at intervals upon the floor while hydralisks and others stood guard.

"It's a breeding ground," Raynor told the others, remembering what Mike and Kerrigan had told him once about an encounter on Antiga Prime. "It's where the zerg are born." At the center of the room was a cluster of zerg, at least forty of them, including hydralisks, ultralisks, and even the airborne mutalisks. Off to the side he spotted two massive, sluglike creatures, their sides pulsating as if lit from within, perched on mounds of creep and festooned with streamers of similar organic material—Raynor remembered they were called cerebrates and were essentially zerg commanders. He could see several zerg eggs, pulsing green and red upon their mounds of creep. But between the zerg at the center he saw something far larger, something that glowed and gave off sparks like small lightning. He knew immediately that was his target.

"Everyone, on me!" he shouted, raising his rifle and slamming home a fresh clip. "We need to breach that thing!"

The zerg heard him coming, or sensed him, or simply anticipated his attack. "Cerebrate!" one of the cerebrates shouted, its voice an odd rasp that cut at Raynor's ears and produced a dull throb behind his eyes. "The Chrysalis is opening! Do not allow any Terrans near it!"

The second cerebrate lifted its front end toward the archway and, responding to its mental commands, the lesser zerg pulled away from the cocoon and charged toward the Terrans. The other cerebrate hunched closer to the strange pulsing oblong, like a protective mother warily circling her prize egg.

Raynor and his team braced themselves for the moment of contact. Just before the zerg reached them, however, Mannix pulled a grenade from her vest, primed it, and lobbed it at the approaching creatures. It struck just before a hydralisk and blew the creature apart as it detonated, the blast taking several others with it and battering a dozen more aside. Raynor quickly fired into those dazed zerg, killing them before they could recover. Then the rest were upon them and he was back to firing pistol over rifle and rifle under pistol, swiveling the barrels left and right to keep his front covered.

"Get going, sir!" Mannix shouted at him, nodding her chin toward the cocoon. "Take care of that thing! We've got this!"

Raynor hesitated only a second, then nodded. "Stay frosty!" he hollered, then fired both guns on full auto in a semicircle before him. The zerg there were blasted to bits, and before any others could fill the gap he had charged through and was past them. Behind him he heard another grenade go off, and the sound of gunfire increased. Mannix and the others were covering his charge. He knew, deep down, that it would probably mean their deaths. They knew it too. But this was the job. This was why they'd come.

The creep underfoot clung to his boots and Raynor's outright run turned into a stumbling jog, but he still covered the distance to the cocoon before any other zerg could come after him. He ejected the spent clips from each gun and reloaded as he slowed to avoid crashing into the thing. He targeted the approaching cerebrate, but it paused and swiveled away, inching back until it had vanished into the haze of creep strands that hung in tatters from the ceiling. Now it was just Raynor and the cocoon.

The thing was easily twice his size, he realized as he examined it more closely. Its surface was pocked and pitted, lumpy like thick porridge, and it writhed as he watched. The thing, that shell itself, was alive! It was still giving off sparks, and his hair stood on end as he approached it. But Raynor didn't back away.

"Kerrigan?" Reaching out, he set one hand upon

the thing, feeling the jolt as his fingers touched it through his gloves. He could just make out a shape within, twisting, limbs flailing against the cocoon's pulpy shell. But this couldn't be Kerrigan—even though he could see only a hazy outline, the figure within had too many limbs.

Perhaps it was the touch of his hand against it, or the sense of his proximity. Perhaps it was simply a matter of timing. But whatever the reason, as he watched Raynor saw first one limb lash out, then another, striking the cocoon near the top—and slicing through, a wicked spike drilling its way out. The cocoon stretched as the rest of the spike tried to tear free, its sticky surface pushed to the limit. Another hard thrust came from within, a second spike appearing, the cocoon's upper edge distended farther—and then it burst like a rotten melon, the skin peeling away and the interior spurting forth. Without the surface tension the rest of the skin fell away limp, pooling on the ground, and Raynor stepped back to avoid suffocating within its slick folds. Thick, oily liquid followed it down, washing across his boots and spreading a thin sheet across the chamber floor. The creep absorbed it and thickened, growing darker, and its pulse became stronger. But Raynor didn't notice that. He was too busy gaping at the figure that stood revealed as the cocoon—what he now remembered the zerg calling a Chrysalis—fell away.

Kerrigan was a tall, powerfully built woman with a fine, full figure that had sparked the thoughts that had led to her calling him a pig when they first met. She had pale skin turned almost tan by her travels, piercing green eyes, a lush mouth a little too wide for her heart-shaped face, and a glorious mane of fiery red hair she kept tied back when she worked. With her intelligence, her combat skills, and her telepathy, she was a fascinating, graceful, deadly woman. She was the most stunning and infuriating woman Raynor had ever met.

This was not Kerrigan. This was some winged horror from his worst nightmares. It was nothing like the woman he had loved.

Or, rather, it was. But it wasn't. Raynor still stared, his weapons forgotten, the battle behind him forgotten. Nothing mattered, nothing even entered his head but the woman—the creature—before him. It had Kerrigan's stature, her build, even her face. The skin was wrong, though, a mottled green that looked slick somehow, like the flesh of a dolphin or a seal. In many places it was hard and glossy, a protective shell, though he could see no pattern to the protection's placement. The armor extended to spikes over one shoulder, at the elbows, along the back of her hands, and along her legs. The eyes were still the same shape but yellow instead of green, a bright yellow with strangely shifting pupils. The hair, that wonderful red hair, was now stalks, somewhere between tentacles and spikes, sharp and cylindrical but limp around her face and segmented like an insect's legs—or a human's bones. The part that threw him the most, however, the part that had made him think it could not be her, was what had torn through the Chrysalis, what he had seen flailing within the cocoon just before that.

The wings.

This figure had wings, great majestic wings, the wings of a giant bird or a bat—if that creature were armored like an insect and had no fur or feathers or skin for covering. For the wings were nothing more than pairs of elongated, segmented spikes, great hooked claws protruding from her back and reaching down to her knees. Even as he watched they flexed, their tips dripping ichor like a spider's fangs, and he somehow knew they were seeking prey.

This figure was not human. Yet its face, its features—they were Kerrigan. Or at least they still bore traces of the woman she had been. It was Kerrigan if she had been twisted, remade as a parody of herself.

Kerrigan, transformed. Into zerg.

Now the dreams made sense. It had all been real, not just a cry but a warning and a message. She had shown him what was happening to her, bit by bit. He remembered the welcome again, and that sense of both loathing and acceptance that followed it. All of that had come from her.

As if to cement his understanding he heard a voice now, both in and out of his head. It was so deep it echoed and so cold it made his teeth ache. And it was a voice he had heard twice before. Once when it welcomed him in his dreams and once when it announced the "power of that which is yet unborn!" Now that voice spoke a third time, its words slithering up and down along his spine.

"Arise, my daughter," it cried, and there was no mistaking its exultation. "Arise . . . Kerrigan," it crowed, and all the zerg in the chamber bowed their heads. All except one.

"By your will, father," the figure in the Chrysalis remains said proudly, head raised high. Her voice was deeper, more resonant, and it echoed in his ears and in his head as if each word carried layers of meaning and emotion, too much for him to catch all at once. The words rolled across and through him, sending shivers down his spine. "I live to serve." She stepped down, gracefully exiting the bits of shell and fluid, standing tall in the chamber. Kerrigan had been an imposing woman, her head up to Raynor's shoulder. This new figure could have looked him in the eye, if she had deigned to notice him. She did not, and he couldn't decide if he was relieved or disappointed by that. Despite her radical transformation, he could still see Kerrigan's strength, the vibrancy and purpose that had attracted him in the first place. In some ways he was even more drawn to her now, mesmerized by her new form and the new power he sensed within her. He knew he should be repulsed, sickened, but he was fascinated instead. A part of him wondered if that was also part of her change, if this overwhelming attraction was a chemical or mental assault, but he couldn't believe that, especially since she had not even seen him yet.

What the figure did see, however, was the fight near the archway. Mannix and a few of the other troopers were still alive and still battling the zerg, and Raynor watched as the woman's brow furrowed and her eyes blazed with anger.

"Let all who oppose the Overmind feel the wrath of the Swarm," she announced, her wings flaring out behind her, and at her words the zerg increased their attack, biting and stabbing and slicing with renewed frenzy. Mannix fell to a vicious blow from a hydralisk, her head toppling several meters from her body, and the blow severed another trooper's arm as well. Others fell right behind her, and in a moment Raynor was the only one left alive.

The zerg had not survived unscathed, but they didn't seem to notice their losses as the remaining creatures regrouped and turned back toward the center of the chamber, their cerebrate still directing them from its corner of the chamber.

"Well done, Cerebrate!" that same strange cold voice boomed again. "What I have wrought this day shall be the undoing of my enemies!" Then every zerg turned toward Raynor, and he felt the wave of their hatred wash over him. "Let not a Terran survive. . . ." the voice commanded.

Raynor struggled to raise his rifle. Though he knew the odds were hopeless, he planned to go down fighting. But his rifle wouldn't move. Glancing down, he saw a hand on the barrel, a speckled green hand with bladelike nails effortlessly stopping him from bringing the weapon to bear. Looking back up, Raynor found himself meeting the gaze of the creature from the Chrysalis. It was a cold stare, the eyes bright but emotionless, and the pupils danced independently, leaving glittering trails in their wake. It was the look of an alien, with no trace of the woman he had known.

"Mother of God," Raynor gasped, unable to stop himself. "Kerrigan, what have they done to you?"

CHAPTER 5

THE OTHER ZERG SLOWED TO A STOP, SEVERAL only an arm's reach away. They froze then, unmoving, and Raynor listened dully to the conversation taking place around him, numb despite the fact that his fate hinged upon the outcome.

"Destroy the Terran," the cerebrate demanded. "The Overmind commands it."

"This Terran is mine," the former Kerrigan stated, her tone leaving no room for argument. "I will dispose of him in my own fashion. Leave us." The other zerg remained there, not approaching but not retreating, and she bristled, quite literally, as the spikes that had been her hair rose above her head and her wings arced upward, vibrating with her rage. "Leave us!" she repeated, and the other zerg bowed.

"As you command, o Queen," the cerebrate acknowledged. It did not move but somehow it seemed to dim, the pulsing along its sides fading slightly, and Raynor knew it had focused its attention elsewhere. The lesser zerg passed through the arch and vanished from view. Even the giant maggots had disappeared, Raynor realized as he glanced around. The chamber was completely empty save for the two of them and the inactive cerebrate—and the remains of his soldiers here and beyond, mingled with those zerg they had slain.

With the Swarm out of sight, Raynor stopped trying to raise his rifle, and she released her grip as well, letting the weapon fall back to his side. He stepped away to stare at her more easily and she met his gaze calmly, her hair settling back down around her face, though the tips angled toward him, looking uncomfortably like animate weapons. Her wings also dropped back down to drape around her, but rustled slightly, giving Raynor the uncomfortable sense that they could act without her conscious control.

"Sarah," he asked finally, reaching one hand toward her face but stopping it just short of touching her, fascinated and repulsed by her altered appearance. "Is that really you?"

"To an extent," she replied, the commanding echo fading from her voice and leaving her sounding more like the woman he remembered. She looked down at her hands, turning them this way and that, flexing the long fingers, extending the vicious claws. The tips of her wings echoed the movement. "I'm far *more* than I once was, Jim." At the sound of his name he started, and she glanced back up at him, her hands clenching into fists. "You shouldn't have come here," she warned him. He thought he heard sorrow, perhaps even pity, in her voice, and that shook him. Sorrow she'd known in plenty, but Kerrigan hadn't been one for pity.

Her words also confused him. He shouldn't have come? "But the dreams," he argued. "I dreamed you were still alive . . . that somehow . . . you were calling to me." Had he been wrong? Had this all been a mistake? A trick of his own mind? But how could he have known what was happening to her then? How could he have heard that voice inside his head if not through her? She must have been sending those dreams!

"I was," she admitted. She seemed to dwindle slightly, the patches on her skin fading, the wings folding in upon themselves, and her hair turning softer and more pliant, until she resembled the Kerrigan of old once more. She turned her face from him, but he could hear the pain in her voice and imagine the look upon her face. It was the same face he'd imagined when she had called to him for help back on Tarsonis, when Mengsk had left her to die. "While I was in the Chrysalis," she explained, "I instinctively reached out to you and Arcturus telepathically. Apparently, Arcturus sent *Duke* here to reclaim me. . . ." Raynor could hear the bitterness behind that last remark, and in the soft bark of laughter that followed.

"Yeah, he's a little busy building an empire," he said, "so he sent his lapdog to stand in." He laughed. "You shoulda seen his face when I showed up."

She smiled, a sad smile but a familiar one. "I can imagine."

"I'm here now, though," Raynor pointed out. "And

so are you. We can get you outta here, Kerrigan. We can get you someplace safe." *We can undo what they did to you,* he wanted to say, but couldn't. Not that he needed to—Kerrigan had been able to answer his thoughts even before, and now she seemed far more powerful. She was already shaking her head, and the mottling was resurfacing, as if reflecting the turmoil within.

"But that was *then,* Jim," she told him, turning to face him again. "I'm one of the *zerg* now. And I like what I am." She raised her arms high, the shell-like spots shifting across her limbs and torso as she moved, creating a moving layer of protection. Her hair rose and reached for the roof as well, yearning upward, and her wings rose to their full extension, flaring out behind her. Even in the dim light of the creep, he could see her eyes flashing. "You can't imagine how this *feels* . . . ," she told him finally, lowering her arms again, and somehow he knew she was talking about more than just the physical changes. The wings remained up, as if determined to remind him how much she had changed.

"I am one with the zerg now," she said, smiling. "It is wonderful, Jimmy. It envelops me. It makes me whole. I can never be alone again."

"They called you a queen," Raynor said, remembering the cerebrate's comment as he left, and her smile grew wider.

"Yes, I am. The Queen of Blades." She raised her right hand, fingers spread wide, and the blades sprouting from her fingertips rippled in response. So did the spikes on her head and the wings at her back.

"Guess you're not gonna give up bein' royalty," he said, shaking his head. She didn't bother to reply; she didn't need to. He could read her reply in her smile.

"So what?" Raynor asked, backing a step away and shifting the grip on his rifle in case he needed to raise it suddenly. "Are you goin' to *kill* me now, darlin'?"

"It is *certainly* within my power," she told him, and he knew she was right. Even before her transformation Kerrigan had been the deadliest fighter he'd ever seen. Her skill with a gun was amazing, but her prowess with knives was nothing short of phenomenal. He could only guess what she could do now with the blades part of her own body and her stature and speed enhanced by the change. Mike had told him once about Kerrigan's killing an entire roomful of soldiers single-handedly, in a matter of minutes, without ever being touched. She probably could have handled all the troopers by the archway on her own now. A part of him wanted to see her in action, to admire her new talents. The rest of him wanted to run screaming. Instead he stood very still and waited to see what she decided. The ball was definitely in her court.

Kerrigan flexed her finger-blades again, waving them menacingly in his direction, and for an instant Raynor thought he was dead. She was still smiling that sad smile from her past, however, and she did not move to close the distance between them. "But you're not a threat to me, Jim," she told him finally, stepping away and widening the gap. "Be smart," she warned him, that echo creeping back into her voice. "Leave here now, and never seek to confront the zerg again." That last statement was issued like a command, and he felt the force of her words and of her personality bearing down on him, compelling him to submit.

"Doesn't look like I have much choice," he muttered, hoping that would be enough to placate her. For a moment they stood there, both armed but neither attacking, the tension almost visible between them, like a flicker of light. Then the moment passed and Kerrigan turned, dismissing him utterly.

For a second he considered raising the rifle after all, shooting her from behind. At this range he couldn't miss, and for all her powers and organic armor and mottled skin and scary hair, a clipful of iron spikes would still finish her. He was sure of it. Well, almost sure.

But he never got the chance to test that theory. As Kerrigan turned away her skin paled, then became transparent. In an eyeblink she had vanished completely, fading from the edges in until finally nothing remained. Raynor was alone.

Kerrigan was still nearby, he knew. She had gone invisible, just as she had done when she'd been a Ghost. He'd thought the process required a specialized suit of combat armor. Apparently he'd been wrong. Or perhaps the Queen of Blades simply no longer required such props.

The Queen of Blades. The name sent a chill racing through him. By adopting that title, she had made it clear that the transformation had been a full success.

Sarah Kerrigan was gone. Only the Queen of Blades remained. And she was not inclined to be friendly.

Still, she had let him live, and Raynor certainly wasn't complaining about that.

Holstering his pistol but keeping the rifle ready, he staggered back to the archway and through it, forcing himself to examine the remains of his team as he passed them. They'd earned the right to hold his gaze, and it would be insulting for him to look away just because it made him uncomfortable. He made sure he knew each face, each name, before turning away and passing through the arch again. There were more troopers on the far side, most of them stretched out on the floor. But a few still stood, leaning against the tunnel walls, and these gave a ragged cheer when he appeared.

"Sir!" It was Cavez, bandaged and battered but still alive. The tall young man limped over to Raynor as he carefully stepped through the pile of bodies littering the ground. "Are you all right?"

"I'll live," Raynor admitted, embarrassed to realize that he had not been wounded beyond a few scrapes and cuts. Cavez was far worse off, but here was the trooper asking about his health instead of the other way around. Still, he knew it was more than just his wound status that Cavez was checking on. The trooper wanted to know whether Raynor was prepared to take charge again.

I'm not fit to lead, Raynor thought as he studied the handful of survivors. *It's my fault you're hurt, my fault* your friends are dead, my fault we're here. I dragged us across the galaxy and sacrificed a hundred or more men just to chase down a woman who doesn't even want me around. Put that way it sounded ridiculous, and he had to stop himself from laughing—he could feel the laughter bubbling up inside, fueled by near-hysteria, and he knew that if he started laughing he might not stop. Instead he forced himself to concentrate. Cavez was hurt, as were most of the others. He needed to get them to a medic, and that meant getting topside again.

"Right," he called out, "find a partner and form up! We've got to retrace our steps as best we can. There might be faster ways out, so keep your eyes peeled for those, too. Let's go."

He motioned Cavez to fall in with him and together they marched back down the corridor, checking the sides and up above for any sign of the zerg. But they saw only rock and bits of creep. Whatever zerg had survived the recent battle were gone. Raynor tried not to think about where they might be now.

It took hours for the battered band to reach the surface. They saw no zerg along the way but still had to contend with confounding directions, irregular passages, unstable tunnels, boiling magma pits, and other dangers. Most of the surviving troopers were wounded, no one not well enough to walk back but several not fit enough to be of much use after so much hiking, and they moved slowly even in the wide, straight tunnels.

Raynor had one of the men out front as a scout and another in back as a rear guard, the two soldiers instructed to stay as far away from the rest as was safe, as quiet as possible, and as observant as anything. Neither of them called in any problems, not that he'd expected any. Kerrigan—he still couldn't manage to call her "the Queen of Blades," even to himself—had been awakened now as part of some larger plan, judging from what that voice had said. The zerg they'd seen so far on Char were probably all scurrying to be part of whatever she intended. That would definitely keep them all busy while Raynor and his people escaped onto the surface once more. He'd figure out their next move once they were all back aboveground where they belonged. "If man was meant to live in caves," he muttered, "he'd have much thicker skin, much weaker eyes, a thick fur coat, and a serious slouch. That's why we invented lifts, lights, and lasers."

"What was that, sir?" the nearest trooper asked, tilting a bandaged head in his direction.

"Nothin', son," Raynor replied. "Nothin' at all."

They followed the same path back that they'd taken down, at least as far as they could. In several places they had to deviate—at one point a cave-in had apparently occurred after they'd left, perhaps triggered by the fighting down below, and a narrow path was sealed tight with rubble, the air around it thick with dust. A tunnel they'd used before was still there, but whereas it had been a steep slope down, now it was a steep climb up, with nothing but glass-slick walls on either side, and

Raynor didn't think any of them could make that trip in their current state, including him. Both times they scouted the area and eventually found an alternate route that took them away from their original entrance point but kept them heading upward. That was the most important thing, Raynor felt; to keep moving up, toward the surface and the sky and the ships. Popping up a mile away from their starting point wouldn't matter as long as they did eventually pop back up. The idea of staying down here forever was far too depressing to consider for very long, and he shoved the thought away every time it surfaced.

Finally Cavez, who had taken the role of lead scout, came running back down a corridor, a big grin plastered across his dirty, blood-smeared face. "I can see daylight, sir!" he announced happily, and the others cheered and laughed and shouted. A few even cried, and no one razzed them for it.

"Good man," Raynor said, blinking back tears himself. "Lead the way." He followed close behind the young trooper, and sure enough he soon stood at the base of a short, wide chute that showed sunlight at the top. The distance was too far to jump but they gave one of the troopers, a thick-bodied man named Non, a boost up into the chute. He pressed his back against one wall and thrust his legs straight out in front of him, his feet solidly against the wall opposite. Then, his arms spread wide for balance, he began walking his way slowly up the chute. It took half an hour, but eventually he was able to peek over the rim.

"All clear, sir," he called back down, and everyone breathed a sigh of relief. Raynor had been afraid of another Ayers tragedy and was glad this time was different.

"Over the edge, soldier," he called up. "This is no time for sightseeing." Non chuckled, saluted, and shoved hard with his back and legs, swinging his arms up and forward at the same time. His back left the wall just as his hands caught the opposing lip, and he levered himself over the edge and out of the chute altogether. A moment later his face reappeared, and he dropped a rope to the others waiting below. Raynor handed it to Cavez, who was fast and light, and the trooper walked up it quickly until Non was able to reach down and help him the rest of the way. Then the two of them began hauling everyone else up out of the tunnels.

When it was finally his turn Raynor tried his best to help them, bracing himself against the chute wall with his back and his feet, but he was exhausted and still a bit numb and finally he gave up and let them pull him up, doing little to aid their efforts. At last one of the troopers, Ling, reached down and clasped his hand, and Raynor used the added leverage to pull himself over the chute's lip and back onto solid ground. He collapsed, ignoring the ash that rose about him and turned him chalk-white from its debris, and simply lay there for a moment, staring up at the sky. Then the day's events caught up with him and, without intending it, he closed his eyes.

CHAPTER 6

THIS TIME THE DREAM WAS DIFFERENT, IF DREAM it was. He was standing in a thick, rough-walled tunnel, able to see the stone walls and floor clearly despite the lack of light. He could feel the rock beneath his bare feet, taste the hint of sulfur in the air, scent a tantalizing trace of blood and flesh in the still, stale air. His senses were alive, his body tingling with energy. He felt amazing.

The zerg were all around him, as they had been in so many of his dreams, but they weren't frightening anymore. They had shrunk, for one thing, or he had grown—either way, the creatures no longer towered above him but were at eye level or lower. They were not crowding him, either, merely standing nearby. And the air of unfamiliarity, of strangeness, of distance, had faded, only a hint remaining around the edges. Before these had been monsters, horrifying creatures whose very forms he could not comprehend, let alone their minds and motives. Now he understood them all too easily, and that lack of mystery stripped away his fear. How could he be afraid of these creatures when he knew their names and could speak to them as an equal or even a superior?

In fact, he was speaking to them now, he realized. But the words pouring from his mouth were not in fact his. They were Kerrigan's.

She was addressing the enormous sluglike creature, the one that resembled a flesh-cannon, the cerebrate. "Cerebrate," she told him, "you watched over me during my 'incubation,' and I am grateful to you." It fluttered slightly, and he was surprised to realize it was pleased and proud. It had never occurred to him that zerg might possess such emotions, and a part of his mind wondered if he was simply assigning human traits in an effort to understand them better. That felt right, and he suddenly realized he was not the only one having this thought. Kerrigan had thought much the same thing and reached the same conclusion. The mind sought to apply familiar patterns when facing unfamiliar events or beings, and despite her recent transformation a large portion of Kerrigan's mind was still human. "It is my wish that you continue your vigil," she was saying now, "so that I might strengthen my powers to better aid the Swarm."

No! Raynor wanted to shout. Don't play along with them! You're not one of them! Don't help them, they're the enemy! He struggled to beat his hands against his head, to tug at his hair, to do something, anything, to derail those thoughts of duty and involvement. But unlike in the other dreams, he was not in control here, not even of his own body. He was merely an observer, with no power to affect Kerrigan's actions or the events that flowed from them.

He had missed the last thing she said while he was mentally flailing, and now the second cerebrate, the one that had stayed near her Chrysalis during her emergence, was speaking. It horrified Raynor that he could tell the creatures apart so easily.

"Though you be the *favored* servant of the Overmind," this cerebrate snapped, and Raynor could hear the anger in its voice, "you would do well to remember that you are just a *servant.* You know of our grand mission, Kerrigan. Would you put your personal *whims* before the *will* of the Overmind?"

The other zerg backed away, feeling the tension stretched between their two commanders and anticipating a fight. Raynor expected it as well, knowing Kerrigan's temper better than most, and so he was surprised when she did not attack the cerebrate, which appeared to have no physical defenses. Instead she simply straightened and gave him a single hard, haughty glance. Her bone-wings stirred, however, and flexed toward the cerebrate, eager to carve the slug to shreds. Raynor could sense Kerrigan's response to that as well: part horror that a part of her new body could be so disobedient and willful, and part delight that her new form possessed such protective instincts of its own.

"Do not cross me, Zasz," she warned him, chin high, eyes narrowed. "I will do as I see fit." Then deliberately, insultingly, she turned her back on him. "And not you or any other cerebrate shall stand in my way."

Zasz bristled at her tone and her clear snub. The organic cannon body tensed and its inner light began pulsing more rapidly until the entire body was aglow with quick flashes of light. Several of the surrounding zerg edged closer, chittering their leader's rage, claws and spines and scythes raised to strike on the cerebrate's behalf. The fool was going to attack! Raynor could feel it, and a surge of excitement shot through him, a surge he knew immediately was not his own. Kerrigan had known what she was doing when she spoke. She had deliberately pushed the cerebrate beyond his breaking point. She wanted Zasz to order an attack so she could destroy him and claim his brood as her own. And she would destroy him, Raynor knew. The cerebrate was a leader, a strategist, not a fighter. Kerrigan was both, especially in this new incarnation. The cerebrate was immobile, vulnerable, and relied upon its brood to fight for it, while Kerrigan could outfight any of them. She would carve her way through the other zerg and then destroy Zasz himself.

But before the cerebrate's brood could attack a voice cut across them all, paralyzing them with its deep timbre and rolling pronunciation, a wave of sound that washed over them and left them stunned and speechless. It was a voice Raynor had heard before, though he had fervently hoped not to hear it again.

"Let her go, Zasz," the voice intoned. "The greatness of her spirit has been left to her that the Swarm might benefit from her fierce example. Fear not her designs, for she is bound to me as intimately as any cerebrate." The voice chuckled, the sound leaving Raynor feeling dirty somehow, as if it demonstrated a humor beyond his ability to understand and one that found amusement with concepts and actions he would find repugnant. "Truly," it explained, "no zerg can stray from my will, for all that you are lies wholly within me. Kerrigan is free to do as she desires." The voice faded, leaving Raynor weak in the knees and short of breath, and he knew he was not the only one reacting so strongly. Kerrigan had been overwhelmed by the voice as well, and so had Zasz and the others.

The cerebrate quickly untensed. Its brood members backed away as well, lowering their limbs to show they meant no more harm.

"By your will, Overmind," he acknowledged. Raynor knew the creature had hoped for a different decision, but he also knew that they would not have to worry about this cerebrate, unless and until the situation changed. No zerg would dare stand against the Overmind's orders, he realized. Until that voice spoke, Zasz had been determined to convince Kerrigan to do things his way, by force if necessary. Now the Overmind had instructed otherwise, and the cerebrate would carry out those directives to the best of its ability.

"Cerebrate," Zasz said, apparently to the second cerebrate. "You must see that she comes to no harm. My brood will remain behind to protect the incubation chamber from further desecration."

"My brood will die to protect her," the other cerebrate replied.

"As it should," Kerrigan stated simply.

Raynor felt her turn and walk away, taking it for granted that the second cerebrate's brood would follow. And they did. Raynor knew now, through Kerrigan's thoughts, that the cerebrates themselves did not travel—they were too large and bulky to move. Instead they led their troops mentally, particularly through their overlords. Thus both of these cerebrates could remain in the incubation chamber, but Zasz would be focused upon events here while the other cerebrate's mind would be following the activities of its brood, which would accompany Kerrigan.

Another cerebrate sat in one corner of the chamber. Raynor had not noticed it there before; it had somehow masked its presence before this. Now he saw it plainly, however, and somehow knew that this cerebrate was older and more powerful even than Zasz. Indeed, this third cerebrate, Daggoth, was the Overmind's right hand. Daggoth's brood was clustered about it, and now several hydralisks detached themselves from this cluster and approached Kerrigan. "Cerebrate, take these, the deadliest of my minions," said Daggoth. "They shall aid you in your search."

"They shall be put to good use," Kerrigan assured him, and the zerg fell in with the others behind her. Daggoth retreated mentally, intent upon his own tasks, and Zasz had gone silent, leaving only Kerrigan and her new followers.

"We must attack at once," she told the second cerebrate. It occurred to Raynor that this one had no name, and as soon as he thought it he knew why. Among the zerg, names were a matter of recognition, only given to those who had served the Overmind long and faithfully. Both Zasz and Daggoth had won that honor. This cerebrate was young and had not yet distinguished itself. Kerrigan, of course, was a special case, which might explain Zasz's resentment—she had retained her original name and had been given another upon her rebirth. But she was still speaking to the cerebrate, and Raynor struggled to focus on her words. "Once I have—"

"Sir?"

It took Raynor a moment to separate himself from the last vestiges of the dream, to realize that he was not stalking through an underground chamber with a zerg brood anymore but lying upon the planet's surface. Cavez was leaning over him.

"Sir, everyone is clear," the trooper reported. Raynor nodded and accepted the younger man's hand up, shaking his head both to disperse the ash that clung to his hair and rebreather and to clear the dream-traces from his mind. What had Kerrigan been about to say? he wondered. Where was she attacking? Much as he hated the dreams, hated this last one particularly because it showed him how comfortable Kerrigan was in her new role, he wished Cavez had waited an instant longer to wake him. That lost information might prove immensely important.

Too late to do anything about it now, however. Brushing the more stubborn bits of ash from his goggle lenses, he glanced around and took stock of their situation. Twenty-three soldiers. That was all he had left of the three hundred or so who had followed him down. And many of the survivors were wounded, some badly. They had weapons and plenty of ammo—several of the more experienced troopers had been alert enough to scavenge clips from the bodies of their fallen friends. No food to speak of, of course; they hadn't planned to be down here that long. Everyone carried a canteen of water and a few emergency rations, but most of that had been consumed on the trek down, or given to the injured to give them strength for the return march.

"Back to the shuttles," he announced finally, patting one soldier's shoulder where she sat, head between her raised knees, arms limp at her sides. "Let's go, trooper," he told her as gently as he could. "Plenty of time to rest when we're back off this rock." He gave her a hand up.

That was it then, he admitted to himself as they gathered their gear, helped the injured to their feet, and began walking toward the shuttle beacons indicated on their comm units. The mission was over. He had failed. He'd come here to find Kerrigan, which he had, and to save her, which he couldn't. She didn't want to be saved, and even if he'd had the means to undo whatever the zerg had done to her, he didn't have the manpower to take her from them. Hell, he wasn't sure Mengsk did, even with the Dominion at his beck and call. The only thing he could do now was get the hell out of Dodge, mourn Kerrigan, and move on. And hope to hell she didn't come after him.

They were a long way from the shuttles, both because they'd walked a good distance before finding the chute down and because they'd wound up taking a different route back to the surface. Fortunately this part of Char was easy going, only a few low hills and shallow valleys, and they plotted a direct line back to the shuttles from their current location. Raynor led the way, with Cavez and Non right behind him, and the troopers settled into their pace quickly, falling into the lockstep rhythm of a forced march. Raynor matched it as well, and the steady beat and monotonous scenery soon lulled him into a half-sleep, leaving him still awake enough to walk but not really conscious.

Apparently, that was enough to trigger the dreams again.

He was on a ship now, and for a second he thought this was just a normal dream, or even a memory of something. Then a shadow moved in the corner of his vision and he saw a limb, long and sinewy, brush the corridor wall. The limb ended in a massive scythe of jagged bone, and he knew at once that he was back in Kerrigan's head. There were zerg beside her, and now he realized he could hear more of them behind, rustling and scraping and hissing as they moved down the steel-gray hall.

The zerg were inside a ship somewhere.

How? was his first thought. Zerg couldn't operate vessels—they traveled through some sort of organic space tunnel; one of Mengsk's men had tried to explain it to him once, but all he'd gotten was that they could open warps between worlds without using any tech. And, judging from most of the zerg he'd seen, they wouldn't have the manual dexterity to operate a Terran ship anyway. Normally the zerg left ships alone, targeting the people, or they sent their massive mutalisks and tiny, explosive scourge up to attack the vessels from the outside. How could they be in one now? And it was definitely a Terran ship. He recognized the standard plastic wall panels, the utilitarian gray carpet, the recessed lighting along the juncture between walls and ceiling. He'd spent far too much time on ships like this in the past year.

And, it occurred to him, of course Kerrigan would be able to operate a ship. Which meant the zerg could now as well.

Why? was the second question that popped into his head. If they could travel in space unaided, why would the Swarm want a ship at all? What were they doing there? But then he remembered the last words he'd heard Kerrigan speak in his previous dream. "We must attack at once," she'd said. Did the attack have something to do with a Terran ship? And whose ship was it? His were in orbit, he knew, but so were Duke's. Despite a slight pang of guilt, he hoped it was one of Duke's ships she had invaded. Maybe, if he was really lucky, it was the *Norad III* herself. Let the old bastard deal with her face-to-face!

As Kerrigan moved farther along the hall, however, Raynor noticed more details, and his heart sank. The blank, brushed metal walls, the dull carpet covering the floor, the recessed lighting, everything functional but not quite bare-bones military—this wasn't a warship. It definitely wasn't the *Hyperion*, but it wasn't the *Norad III* either, or one of the carriers. It could be one of his smaller ships, or Duke's science ship or cargo ship. Then a handful of people emerged from a door up ahead and Raynor knew he'd been right. These were civilians, techies and researchers. Regardless of whom they worked for, they were defenseless against the zerg now racing down the corridor toward them.

One woman screamed as she looked up and spotted the aliens for the first time. She fell, her legs giving way from shock, and just lay there sobbing as they approached. A hydralisk made quick work of her, and the sobbing stopped abruptly. Another woman had backed away, clawing at the door she had just exited, so panicked she forgot how to use the door panel. A zerg speared her from behind, his claw passing through her chest and denting the door. Then it shook its arm and her body was tossed aside, blood spraying the halls and everyone present. Several drops struck Kerrigan and she brushed them away with one hand, then absently licked her fingers.

Two of the civilians, a man and a woman, had been near the back of the group and had not yet been attacked. The man saw Kerrigan's motion and gasped, his eyes traveling up and down her form and his skin paling as the sight registered fully.

"She's infested!" he gasped. He threw an arm up in front of the woman, a ludicrous gesture given the zerg rapidly surrounding them. "Stay away from her!" he shouted, though whether it was a plea to the approaching aliens or a warning to the woman Raynor couldn't tell.

"Call for help!" the woman cried, and hearing her shook the man from his daze. He punched a button on the door panel, the Emergency Call button, and blue lights began flashing all along the corridor. A siren sounded as well, and now more people appeared in the hall from other doors and intersections, screaming and cursing as they saw the zerg. The man's heroism cost him his life, a zerg tearing his head from his shoulders, and the woman followed, her chest split in half and her organs torn free before the scream had died on her lips.

Raynor was forced to watch, unable to wake up or turn away, as the zerg continued their march through the ship, slaughtering everyone in their path. A squad of armed soldiers appeared finally, still buckling on their armor, and Raynor was only a little cheered to notice the Terran Dominion insignia. Whatever Kerrigan was up to, she had invaded one of Duke's ships.

"You'll never make it out of here alive, bitch!" one of the troopers shouted, firing his gauss rifle on full auto into the approaching brood. Several zerg were hit, and two fell with steel spikes through their throat and eyes.

"See?" another trooper bellowed, laughing as he swung his weapon around to fire upon them. "They ain't so tough!" He let loose a barrage and more zerg died. "These critters bleed just like anybody else!" he shouted, and several of his comrades cheered.

Kerrigan had not been hit, however. A chill raced up his spine as he saw why. One of the troopers aimed at her and fired, a cluster of iron spikes racing toward her. She raised one hand and the spikes simply stopped in midair, slamming to a quivering halt as if they'd run into a wall. A second gesture and the spikes spun about and leaped toward the trooper, punching him into a wall from the impact. The spikes pierced not only the man but the wall behind him, and his body was left hanging there as the rifle slipped from his dead hands.

Kerrigan stalked forward, blocking and sometimes reversing the attacks aimed at her. Behind her zerg fell, but Raynor knew she didn't care. They were expendable. Only she mattered—her and her mission here.

One of the troopers spotted her through the zerg swarming around and past her. "We got company!" he shouted, then gasped as he saw her more clearly. He started to back away, and his eyes bulged as he stopped, frozen in place. Kerrigan held him there, paralyzed, as she stepped up behind him and rammed her finger-blades through his back, slicing his spine to ribbons. Before his body had toppled she was gone again, moving to the next man, her wings writhing with impatience, every barb angling toward her next target. A single glance fried that trooper's mind, and she was already looking for a third as he swayed and fell, blood leaking from his eyes and ears.

It took mere seconds for Kerrigan to move through the opposition, and even from behind her eyes Raynor had trouble following her movements. He had always known, from the moment he first saw her, that she was fast and deadly. His experiences with her in the field had verified that, and Mike had told him about the incident on Antiga Prime, when she had dispatched an entire room of armed men with nothing but a knife and a pistol. She was even faster now, however, and she no longer needed any weapons but the body the zerg had given her and the mind-powers she had always possessed but had been unwilling or unable to use. Men died quickly, too fast to scream, and then the corridor was clear of her foes again and the remaining brood members were climbing over the bodies.

"This way," Kerrigan commanded, turning toward a stairwell, and the zerg followed her obediently. Several more people died, both civilians and soldiers, as she descended the narrow metal stairs—many of the zerg had been forced to wait above, unable to navigate the tight space, and judging by the sounds they were killing anyone who ventured too close. Kerrigan did not pause or deviate but headed to the very bottom and then down a long, narrow, unremarkable gray hall. She obviously knew where she was going. It was definitely a science vessel she was on, not a cargo ship—it was too small for cargo. But why would she go after a ship like this? Why not take out the *Norad III* instead? That was definitely the bigger threat.

"Here," she said finally, stopping at the heavy blast-door at the far end. The keypad lock was much more complicated than any of the others on the ship, and Raynor realized that he had never seen this door before. Nor did he know what lay beyond it. But Kerrigan clearly did.

She didn't bother trying the lock. Instead she grasped the handle with one hand, plunged the fingers of her other into the thin seam between the door and the wall, braced herself with her feet wide apart, and twisted from the waist. The door groaned, shuddered, and tore loose, and she tossed it aside. The room beyond was dark and smelled of stale air, but small lights blinked somewhere within, and Kerrigan smiled.

"Good," she said. "What I seek is within. Soon—"

Beep.

"What the f—?"

The beep woke Raynor from his walking slumber, as did the curse that followed. The sound had come from his comm unit, though he realized hazily that he had heard it echoed behind him as well. The curse had been from Non.

Glancing at his wrist, he saw the screen still displaying the terrain grid he'd selected at the start of their march, their path traced along it and ending at—nothing.

The dot that should have been there was gone.

The dot that marked the location of the shuttle's beacon.

"Sir," Cavez started, "we just—"

"I know, I know!" Raynor snapped, still staring at his screen. What had happened? Where was the beacon? For that matter, where were the beacons for the other shuttles, which had been displayed as well, but dimmed, to distinguish them from the *Hyperion*'s?

Glancing behind him, he saw everyone looking at their wrists, shaking them, pushing buttons. Everyone's displays were the same, all equally blank. A quick check confirmed that the comm unit had just refreshed its information, as it did periodically. The beacons had shown clearly before, but when it scanned for them this time they were gone. Something had happened in between. Something to the shuttles.

The troopers had covered most of the distance back already, and Raynor charged up the hill before him, glancing at his screen to confirm what he had already seen. The shuttles were just over this rise. Panting from the exertion, using his hands to wave away the ash that rose about him, he reached the top of the hill and stared down into the valley below. The valley where they had left the shuttles.

The valley that was empty save several wide swathes where the ash had been scattered or burned away, dark rock and dull soil showing through. That, and the bodies he saw crumpled here and there near those swathes.

"No!" he shouted, barreling down the hill, rifle ready though he could already tell he wouldn't need it. Whatever had happened here was long over. The shuttles were gone.

CHAPTER 7

"DEAD, SIR," SAID ONE TROOPER, THE YOUNG woman he had helped up before, moving away from the body she had been examining. "Zerg, looks like."

"Same here," a second soldier confirmed, straightening up from another body. Raynor nodded. It was the same with the body he'd examined, a man named Sanchez who'd piloted the *Hyperion*'s shuttle. Sanchez had been torn to shreds, and the damage certainly matched what Raynor had seen from the zerg—hell, it matched what he'd witnessed just hours ago in the tunnels.

The zerg had clearly been here. And they had killed all his shuttle pilots and taken his shuttles. But why? The zerg had never needed shuttles before—their overlords could move through space unaided. Why would they want his shuttles?

His comm unit beeped again, registering an incoming signal, and Raynor accepted it and opened the channel, still glancing around, his mind still struggling with what had happened here. The voice that reached him quickly demanded his full attention, however.

"Mayday, Mayday!" It was a woman's voice and didn't sound familiar. "Can anyone hear this?"

He was about to reply when another voice cut in. "Roger that," it answered, and Raynor recognized Duke's gravelly snarl. "This is the *Norad III*. Go ahead." He was surprised to hear Duke answering a call personally, and decided to eavesdrop as long as he could. Perhaps he'd learn something useful. Like maybe what had happened to his shuttles.

"Sir!" Raynor could hear the relief in her voice. "Sandler, sir, from the *Amerigo*. We're under attack, sir!"

"Who's firing on you?" Duke demanded, and Raynor knew the general had assumed he was behind this. Which was fair—if their situations had been reversed he would have accused the vindictive little ass in a heartbeat.

"It's not an outside attack, sir," Sandler replied quickly. "It's an invasion. They're on the ship!" Raynor thought he could hear gunfire behind her, and screams.

"Who's on the ship, Captain?" Duke demanded. "Who are you fighting?"

"Zerg, sir," she said. "It's the zerg! They're here!" At first Raynor thought the last statement was meant just to reiterate the *Amerigo*'s plight, but then he heard more gunfire, followed by a loud scream, a short hiss, and then silence.

"Sandler? Sandler!" Duke shouted. There was no reply. Raynor checked his comm and saw that the line was still open, the channel active. But no one responded. "Damn!" He turned to Cavez, about to say something, when his comm beeped again. It was a different call, and this time it was one of his own ships.

"Sir, this is Warriton on the *Chandler.* We're being attacked by zerg, sir—-from inside the ship!"

Another call followed right behind it. "Sir, Lieutenant Physon reporting from the *Harper.* We've been breached! The captain is down, and we're taking heavy casualties!"

As a fourth caller, Ragay from Duke's carrier ship *Trillium,* called to report the same conditions, Raynor finally realized what had happened. The zerg had taken his shuttles, and probably any Duke had sent down as well, but not because they needed them for travel. Travel wasn't the point. The shuttles gave them access to ships, which meant the zerg could get inside easily and then kill everyone onboard. Unlike Terran boarding parties, the zerg weren't worried about their own safety, or about keeping the ship intact—they would survive even if the ships crashed. Not that the Swarm cared about losing a few soldiers. It was the perfect way to bypass all defenses, especially since Kerrigan could steal the access codes from the shuttle pilots' minds before killing them. She'd invaded Duke's ships the same way, using his shuttles or more of Raynor's, and had probably reached out mentally to get the codes from someone on each ship as the shuttles were about to dock. Which meant the zerg were infiltrating each of his and Duke's ships right now.

Including the *Hyperion*.

Quickly he punched in the codes for his command ship.

"Matt!" he shouted as soon as the channel opened. "Matt, can you read me?"

"Sir?" Horner sounded the same as ever, and Raynor breathed a sigh of relief. His second wouldn't sound so calm if there were fighting taking place onboard.

"Listen, Matt, there's not much time," he said quickly. "The zerg are about to attack. Get everyone ready. And get people to the lifeboats—you may need them. I want you to—"

"What do you mean, sir?" Horner interrupted. "We haven't seen anything on the scopes except the shuttles returning. No sign of zerg at all. But we can talk about this in person when you get up here."

"When I—?" Raynor closed his eyes. For once the dreams did not come. "Matt, where is my shuttle now?"

"About to dock, sir." He could hear Horner's confusion. "But you know that already."

"No, I don't," Raynor explained slowly. "I'm not on that shuttle. Listen to me, Matt. Lock down the shuttle. Seal the shuttle bay, lock it all down, don't let anyone in or out."

"But sir, I—all right." Though he obviously didn't understand, Horner obeyed as always. Raynor heard the sound of typing, then a small "Hunh." "That's odd," Horner said finally.

"What? What's wrong?"

"There's an override," Horner told him, still typing. "I can't lock it down. It's your code, sir. What's going on?"

Raynor cursed, wishing there were something he could do. But there wasn't. He was trapped here on Char while the zerg swarmed through his ships, and now they were about to take the *Hyperion* as well.

"Can you override the override?" he asked.

"No sir," came the reply. "That would defeat the purpose." Despite the situation Horner chuckled at the thought, and the sound tore at Raynor. He was just a kid!

"There's got to be some way to stop them!" he demanded. He pictured the *Hyperion*'s layout and cursed Mengsk's ego. Those wide, impressive stairways didn't have any doors on them, no way to seal off the levels. The zerg would have free rein once they exited the shuttle bay. "Whatever you do, don't let that shuttle dock!"

"Well," Horner started, then hesitated. Obviously he'd thought of something but didn't want to say what. He still sounded calm, a lot calmer than Raynor, though from the way his voice rose Raynor could tell the kid was scared. He had every right to be.

"What, Matt? There's no time!"

"I could perform an emergency warp-jump," Horner explained.

Raynor understood at once. Pilots and navigators planned warp-jumps very carefully, often for hours beforehand. That was because a single mistake could send a ship millions of light-years off course, turn it inside out, or worse. Plus the warp engines usually needed a few hours to warm up. Jumping without preparation or planning was sheer madness.

"Do it," he said, pleased to realize he wasn't even shouting. "That's an order, Matt."

"Yes sir." He could hear Matt typing furiously and knew he was entering the commands for the warp-jump. Raynor keyed in his own personal code to override the safety measures that would normally stop the *Hyperion* from jumping so abruptly. That was all he could do.

At last he heard a chime in the background, indicating the ship was ready to move. "Good luck, Matt," he whispered.

"Same to you," Horner replied. "Jim." And then he was gone.

Raynor felt a mild surge of relief. At least the *Hyperion* wouldn't be overrun. Even if they impacted a star, or warped through a black hole, it would be better than being killed by zerg aboard their own ship.

He just wished there were something he could do for his other ships. The *Hyperion* was the only one that had powerful enough engines to tear open a warp that quickly. None of the others could move that fast, and with an emergency jump his command ship hadn't been able to take any of the others with her. They were stuck up there, dealing with the zerg, and he was stuck down here with no way to reach them.

But there was one possibility.

Raynor quickly keyed his comm unit to a different frequency. Almost immediately he got another voice.

"Who is this?" someone, a young man, demanded.

"This is Jim Raynor," he replied. "Get me General Duke right now."

Duke's voice came through a second later. "What the hell are you playin' at now, punk?"

Raynor swallowed his irritation. There wasn't time. "Listen, Duke," he said desperately. "I know we don't like each other much but I need help." He ignored the general's laugh and plowed on. "My ships are overrun by zerg," he explained quickly. "And my shuttles were all stolen. I need you to send men to clean my ships out, or at least rescue my people. I know they're on your ships too, but you've got the firepower to deal with them. I don't."

There was a pause.

"Duke, do you hear me?" Raynor demanded. "They're killing everyone on my ships! Your soldiers are the only ones who can help them now. Please!"

Another brief pause, and then Duke finally replied. He laughed.

"You want me to save your people?" he said after his laughter subsided. "You thumb your nose at me, turn your back on Mengsk and the Dominion, steal our ships, make me look like a damn fool, and then you want me to help you? To rescue the same people who walked out on me at your say-so? Boy, you got some big brass ones, that's for sure, but not a lot for brains."

"Look, blame me if you want, that's fine," Raynor offered. "Come down here and arrest me, I'll go quietly. You can try me, execute me, whatever. But don't blame my people for this. Don't kill them for my mistakes. Please, Duke, I'm begging you."

"Well," Duke said slowly, "that you are. And that's a thought that'll keep me warm on many a cold winter night." He chuckled again before his voice turned to gravel. "But you dug this ditch, boy, and now you're lying in it. And all those deaths, they're on your head. Hope that helps you sleep at night." And with that he broke the connection. A moment later Raynor saw a dark shadow cross the sky, dwindling as it went, and he knew the *Norad III* had left Char and headed back to the Dominion, at least one of its ships trailing behind it. Duke had turned tail and fled. Raynor couldn't blame him for wanting to steer well clear of the zerg, especially after those same zerg had taken down at least one of his own ships from the inside, but he swore if he survived all this he'd hunt Duke down and make him pay for leaving his people to die up there.

"What do we do now, sir?" Cavez asked him. Raynor shook his head.

"I don't know," he admitted. He glanced skyward again, squinting to make out the shapes that were his ships hovering just beyond the atmosphere. He kept expecting to see them come crashing down, and told himself that at least there might be some survivors.

He had thought it couldn't get any worse.

Suddenly a blinding light lanced across the sky, forcing him to shield his eyes. The light struck one of his ships and enveloped it, creating a glow that was visible even amid the sun's rays. The ship was clearly lit, a nimbus playing about it, and then that aura collapsed inward and the ship crumpled like a paper ball. When the light faded the ship was gone, not even a trace left behind.

"What?" Raynor gaped at the empty space. One of his ships had just been destroyed, completely obliterated. What could do something like that?

But he knew the answer immediately: the protoss. Scanning the sky, he saw one of their lovely, delicate-looking ships hovering not far from his little fleet. Now he remembered Matt's telling him, just before he came planetside, that a protoss ship was about to exit warp in their immediate vicinity. Obviously this was that ship.

But why had it destroyed one of his vessels?

Again the answer came right away: because of the zerg. The protoss were fanatical about destroying all zerg and even all traces of their existence. And now the zerg were on his ships. So the protoss were going to destroy them there, and his people along with them.

The beam burst forth a second time, illuminating, enveloping, and then obliterating another of his ships. Then it struck once more. Raynor's comm unit pinged again just as the third ship ceased to exist, and he glanced down hurriedly. Then he stared. A new dot had appeared on his screen, which had shifted from the local grid to a wider planetary one. The new dot was right beside one of his ships but was heading toward Char. A lifepod! Or perhaps one of the other shuttles! That meant survivors!

His hopes were dashed, however, as the protoss fired again, this time on the escape vessel. All Raynor saw with his eyes was the beam itself—as the new dot vanished from his comm unit.

Other dots appeared, each originating from one of his ships and heading toward Char's surface. And each time the protoss shot it down. One of the shuttles must have evaded the beam, however, or at least avoided the full brunt of the weapon—it wobbled on his tiny screen, clearly damaged but still descending in a long, loose spiral. Raynor quickly marshaled his troops.

"We got survivors!" he shouted, waving his rifle over his head. "Let's go, let's go!" The soldiers fell in behind him and began running toward the projected crash site. Meanwhile Raynor monitored communications in case anyone made it out alive, or one of his remaining ships managed to cleanse itself of zerg, or the protoss contacted him directly about a temporary cease-fire.

Two other shuttles made it down to Char's atmosphere, taking damage from the protoss but not enough to disable them. But up above the protoss were destroying the rest of Raynor's ships.

"Sir?" It was Leanda Bluth, captain of the *Harrison*.

"Yes, Leanda?" She was short and rounded and had bobbed blond hair streaked with brown. She smoked cigars and drank some horrible homebrew of her own invention and cheated outrageously at poker. He liked her.

"The zerg have overrun the ship, sir. Everything except the bridge, and they're at the doors now. I'm sorry, sir."

"Don't be," Raynor told her gruffly. "You did a good job, Leanda. Thanks."

"Yes, sir," she replied. "Good luck, sir." Then she deliberately closed the channel.

A minute later, the protoss beam sliced into the *Harrison.* The ship was too large to be enveloped completely but the beam struck section after section, disintegrating whatever it touched. Raynor couldn't tell which areas had already been hit and which were being hit now. He did notice, however, when the *Harrison* went off-line. And he watched through the clouds of ash and smoke as, bit by bit, the ship was carved into nothingness. Finally the beam vanished, leaving nothing but a gap in the sky where his ship had been.

The *Harrison* had been the last one. All of his ships were gone now, and all his people save those with him, the handful on the *Hyperion if* Matt had kept the ship intact, and whoever had survived in those downed escape pods. All those people who had followed him, believed in him, trusted him. All dead. Dead because of him.

He shoved the thought from his mind, though he knew it would haunt him forever after. Time for that later. Right now he had survivors to find.

• • •

They reached the closest of the three signals forty minutes later. It was a shuttle rather than a lifepod, and they saw the smoke from its damaged engines and singed fuselage before they spotted the ship itself. The protoss beam had caught it a glancing blow, incinerating one wing and ruining most of the engines, but the pilot had managed to coast the damaged craft down in one piece. As Raynor and his men topped the rise they saw that the shuttle had its doors open and that several people were standing beside it. Despite their small numbers, the sight lifted his heart, and abandoning all caution, he ran toward them.

"Sir!" One of the figures stepped forward, left arm cradled protectively against her body, head bare to let her long hair drift in the mild breeze, ash giving her a faint streak across the blond. "Lieutenant Abernathy, sir, from the *Chandler.*" Other than the wounded arm, she looked unharmed.

"Lieutenant, it's damn good to see you," Raynor told her. He did a quick head count. She had twenty-three people with her, roughly half the shuttle's capacity. Four of them were civilians but the rest were soldiers, and fully armed. No one seemed to have suffered anything worse than cuts, scrapes, bruises, or broken limbs.

"Sir, the *Chandler*—," one of the soldiers started to ask. Raynor just shook his head.

"We've got two other escape pods," he told them. "I need to round up whoever's in them." He beckoned

Cavez over—he'd discovered during the return trek through the tunnels that the young trooper was smart, resourceful, and very reliable. "Cavez, Abernathy," he made the quick introductions. "Stay here, patch people up as necessary, and inventory anything we can use." He selected five troopers at random. "You, you, you, you, and you. Come with me." Then he was off and running again, heading for the second location. The five troopers kept up easily. Behind him he could hear Abernathy and Cavez organizing the shuttle and the remaining soldiers. It would be as good a place as any to set up camp for the night.

The second craft was also a shuttle, though more badly damaged—the protoss beam had sheared through its middle and the ship had broken in two upon entering the atmosphere. The beacon was in the front half and from a nearby hill they spotted the back half a valley away. Four soldiers, including the pilot, had survived in the front half. No one was alive in the rear section, though the pilot said he'd had almost the full forty packed inside it. Bodies were strewn between the two halves, and Raynor insisted that the soldiers with him gather the corpses and place all of them in the shuttle's front section, which they stripped of its supplies and other useful bits. One of the four survivors had a leg injury, and Raynor ordered her to stay with the others by the wreckage. Then he and the three healthier soldiers from that shuttle moved on to the third and final location. He would have liked to keep everyone together but knew that if anyone was alive but injured, time might be of the essence.

This one was a mere escape pod, barely large enough to house six people. It had apparently evaded the protoss beam entirely, or perhaps been too small to be noticed. Unfortunately whoever had piloted the pod was unskilled and had skimmed it off a nearby cliff, judging by the scrape across the rocks there and the matching furrow in the pod's underbelly. It lay on its side in a small crater, and Raynor suspected the crater's lip was all that had kept the pod from rolling farther.

For a second Raynor hesitated. None of his ships had carried escape pods. This had come from one of Duke's ships, either the cargo ship or the science vessel. Which meant that anyone within it worked for the Terran Dominion, and might shoot him on sight. He considered walking away, but couldn't bring himself to do it. Char wasn't that friendly a place, at least not what he'd seen of it so far. He couldn't leave any survivors to fend for themselves. Hell, he'd probably even have offered Duke a chance to join forces. Probably. Still, he loosened his pistol in its holster, just in case.

"Hello?" Raynor called as he approached the pod. Its hatch was partially open, though it looked less like a deliberate action than a result of the damage it had sustained. "Anyone in there?"

Listening closely, he thought he heard a faint reply.

"We're coming in," he warned in case they were armed. The hatch was badly crumpled and it took all four of them to pry it open enough for entrance. Finally it yielded to their efforts and peeled back enough for Raynor to slip through.

The pod's interior was a mess. Basic supplies were normally bolted to the walls or held in mesh pouches, but these had all come loose upon impact and were scattered everywhere. The pod had six harnesses, all spaced evenly around the walls, and two of them were empty. The other three held people, two men and a woman. One of the men was clearly dead, an emergency prybar embedded in his skull. The woman's head hung at a bad angle and as Raynor edged around he saw that her eyes were open and glazed. The other man had what looked like a shard from a structural support piercing his abdomen, but he groaned and shifted as Raynor's shadow fell across him.

"Help . . . me," the man gasped, and Raynor looked around desperately for the pod's med-kit. There! He scooped it up and moved to the injured man's side, then opened the kit and began rummaging through it.

"I'll do what I can," he said bluntly. He could already tell from the amount of blood pooled at the man's feet that the wound was fatal. But he wasn't about to say that. Finding the painkillers, he injected the man with enough to numb him. "Which ship are you from?" he asked. He didn't recognize any of the people, who were clearly civilians rather than soldiers.

"The *Amerigo,*" the man said softly, his eyes already

losing focus and his words slurring slightly as the painkillers did their work. "We got out when that . . . monster appeared. Had to . . . warn someone."

"Monster? What do you mean?" Raynor leaned against the wall beside the man, his pulse quickening. He suspected the answer but needed to be certain. The *Amerigo* had been Duke's science vessel, he remembered. He'd heard its Mayday.

"Not . . . zerg," the man explained, shaking his head and wincing from the motion. "Not one . . . I'd seen before . . . anyway. Like a woman . . . but one of them." Kerrigan! Raynor tried to keep his voice even, knowing he shouldn't excite the man too much but determined to find out as much as he could.

"She was on the *Amerigo,* this zerg woman?" The man nodded, the painkillers now apparently in full force, because the movement didn't seem to bother him. "What was she doing there?" His dream, or vision, of her had been real! And she'd been on the *Amerigo*. Which meant that strange door on the bottom level had been there as well.

"Searching . . . the files," the man replied. "Old . . . logs."

"Old logs?" Raynor frowned. "She was there for old travel data?"

Again the man shook his head. "No, not travel." He smiled grimly. "Doesn't . . . matter . . . now. No . . . secrets . . . left." He took a deep breath before continuing. Raynor tried to ignore the bubbling sound that made, or the froth that appeared at the man's lips. He knew this questioning wasn't helping the man any, but the guy was already dead. And he needed to know why Kerrigan had attacked.

"*Amerigo* . . . was a Terran science vessel," the man explained. "Every science vessel . . . had the same secure room on the bottom level. Files. Ghost Program."

Raynor felt the chill grip him. "*Amerigo* was part of the Ghost Program?"

The other man shook his head. "No. We just . . . carried . . . the files. Every science vessel did . . . in case Ghost . . . operatives needed help or . . . repair." By the way he said "repair," Raynor could tell he didn't mean first aid, and he remembered Kerrigan talking bitterly about the training she'd received as a Ghost, and the conditioning they'd forced upon her.

"She wanted the files," he muttered. "That's why she attacked."

"Won't . . . do her . . . any good," the man managed, the words creating pink bubbles around his mouth and his eyes dimming. "All . . . encrypted." He coughed up the last word, along with blood, and gasped, his eyes opening wide. Then a rattle emerged from his throat and the man went limp.

Raynor climbed back out of the pod, barely aware of his actions. He told the soldiers to gather anything they could use and then stood off to one side, waiting as they searched the tiny vessel. He was too busy thinking about what he'd just learned, and what it meant.

Kerrigan had been a Ghost, a telepathic assassin for

the Confederacy. She and the others had been heavily conditioned, with strong psychological and chemical blocks to keep them from misusing their abilities. She'd told him once that Mengsk had rescued her from all that and helped remove many of those blocks. That's why she'd been so loyal to him.

But some of those blocks had remained. Despite what he'd seen her do, Kerrigan had not had access to her full potential.

And those files contained the key to unlocking them. If a Ghost's conditioning weakened, the files would instruct the scientists on how to reinstate them. But that meant they could also be used to remove the blocks by working backward.

Now Kerrigan had those files. No wonder she'd targeted the *Amerigo* personally—as a former Ghost she knew what it would contain. And she'd used those memories, and her skills, to gain access to that room. He had no doubt she'd managed to decrypt the files, probably pulling the necessary codes from one of the scientists who hadn't made it out in time. Now she would be able to unlock her own mind, destroy any lingering conditioning, and rid herself of those restraints. Her full power would be unleashed.

Raynor shuddered. What had the zerg just unleashed upon them all?

CHAPTER 8

BY THE TIME RAYNOR LEFT THE LIFEPOD AND ITS dead trio behind, collected the other survivors from the second shuttle, and brought everyone he'd found alive back to the first, Cavez and Abernathy had put everything there in order and set up a base camp. They'd erected several large tents to house most of the men, flanked by smaller tents to handle the runoff. Operations and mess were set up within the shuttle itself, making use of its power cells.

"We total fifty-two, sir," Cavez reported as Raynor dropped onto the shuttle's surviving wing, using it as a makeshift seat. "We have enough rations to last us two weeks, more if we can find something to supplement them." He tactfully didn't mention that they'd seen nothing living on Char but zerg, and Raynor didn't think they'd get hungry enough to try eating the disgusting aliens. "Plenty of weapons," Cavez continued, "and a decent supply of ammo." He grinned. "We've even got powered armor, twenty-four suits in all—a few took damage from the shuttle crashes but we can probably cobble them back together, or use them for parts."

Abernathy took over. "We're okay where we are," she confirmed. "No extra-atmospheric communication, though. We've got the comm units patched through the shuttle, so we can maintain links among ourselves, but it doesn't have enough power to breach atmosphere." She shrugged. "The shuttle does have an emergency beacon, and I've activated it—it's self-contained and can run continuously for up to three years." None of them commented on the notion that they could be trapped here that long, though Raynor wasn't really worried about it. Hell, between starvation and the zerg he could probably arrange to die sooner and save himself the awkward waiting. Of course, someone might pick up the distress call and come rescue them. Even though they were on the far side of the galaxy, and the only people who knew they had come out this way were now dead as well, or hated their guts.

Still, stranger things had happened.

"Good work," Raynor told the two troopers. "Set some guys to stand watch and tell the rest to get some sleep. We'll sort out what to do in the morning." He lay back on the wing and was asleep within seconds.

Their situation didn't look any better the next morning. Everyone had needed the sleep—they had all gone through a rough time the previous day, whether they'd been underground or up in space—

and so in that regard they were better. But all those recent events, so catastrophic and so sudden, seemed surreal, and yesterday everyone had moved in a daze. Now, waking up to Char's cold little sun and the layer of ash that coated their tents (someone had erected a small tent over the wing while Raynor slept, for which he was grateful—it wouldn't have looked good if he'd suffocated in his sleep), it was difficult to deny the reality. They were really stranded here.

"We can repair the shuttle," one of the troopers, Deslan, suggested. They were all gathered around a fire Abernathy had built on the far side of the shuttle, using its bulk to shield the flames. Despite the constant volcanic activity it was cold, though Raynor knew it would warm up and become almost stifling later when the sun's rays and the constant flames and steam had mingled to cook the surface.

"With what?" Raynor asked, sipping from his cup and grimacing. Instant self-heating, self-rehydrating coffee did its job, forcing enough caffeine down your throat that you were awake and alert for hours even if you normally suffered from narcolepsy, but it tasted like moldy cardboard reduced to liquid and heated to somewhere between a boil and the center of the sun. He took another sip. "We don't have any spare parts," he pointed out. "Sure, we can scavenge a bit from the other shuttle and the lifepod, but what we need is an intact engine. Neither of them has one."

"Even if we did have the parts," Abernathy added, "we'd need the tools and facilities to effect repairs.

That means a full ship's cradle, a crane, a few arc-welders, and several other things we don't have."

"And what if we did get the shuttle working again?" Raynor asked them. "It's only good for short hops, you know that. The nearest inhabitable planet is—" He frowned, trying to remember what he'd seen on the charts coming in.

"—three days' travel," Non supplied. He shrugged, looking slightly embarrassed when several other troopers glanced at him. "I like to know where we are," he admitted.

"The protoss are still in orbit," a man named McMurty pointed out. "We could repair our communications system and contact them, ask them for help."

Raynor laughed. "And you think they'd say, 'Sure, want a lift home?' Not bloody likely. Protoss only care about one thing, and that's killing zerg. Either they'd ignore us or they'd kill us in case we'd been infected." He didn't bother to explain that the protoss had been the ones destroying their ships. The soldiers from the *Chandler* and the *Graceful Wing,* former home of that second shuttle, didn't know anything about that part of yesterday's disaster. Raynor had considered telling them but had decided it wouldn't do any good. They didn't need to know that humanity apparently had a second enemy to worry about, the very aliens who had seemed to be allies so recently. Perhaps it was all a misunderstanding, and if so that might come out later, in which case telling the others what had happened would only make it harder to overlook. But if it had been a deliberate act against them, it was one more complication, and telling these soldiers who had really destroyed their homes and their friends would only make matters worse.

"So what are we going to do?" Abernathy asked. Everyone else quieted to hear Raynor's answer.

"Well," he said slowly, "I reckon we're stuck on this rock for a while. Weeks, most likely. Could be longer than that, months or even years. We need to make preparations in case that's true." He glanced around. "We need to explore this planet thoroughly, make sure there aren't any dangers besides the ones we already know. Keep your eyes open for traces of animals, plants—anything at all. If we're lucky we'll find a new source of food so we can save the rations for emergencies. Clean water would be nice too." He drained his cup. "Watch out for zerg. We know a lot of them were here and belowground. They might still be there, and we could walk right past a tunnel entrance before realizing it was there." He didn't say anything about Kerrigan—again, his team didn't need to know about it yet. Bad enough the planet was infested with zerg; if they ever found out these zerg were led by a woman, a Ghost turned zerg assassin, it would almost certainly create a panic. Raynor needed everyone to stay sharp and keep hoping, and he wasn't going to tell them anything that might distract them from that.

"We'll start local," he announced, setting his cup on the ground, standing up, and stretching. "Grid out our surroundings, say a distance of ten miles. Cover it carefully, in teams, like we did yesterday. Look for tracks, tunnels, streams, anything at all. We're watching for two things, mainly—dangers and useful items." He gestured to Cavez and Abernathy. "You two are my lieutenants now." Both nodded, and Cavez puffed up his chest unconsciously, pleased at the field-promotion. "Each of you takes half this sorry lot," he said, hitching a thumb at the other soldiers, earning a few chuckles. "Assign sergeants if you want, that's up to you. Set a detail to keep this place while the rest of us search." He thought about it. "Might want to send a few back to the other shuttle, too—we cleaned out what we could but there might be some stuff we missed."

"Yessir!" Both of them saluted, and he nodded and moved away, leaning against the nose of the shuttle while they selected their teams—he knew from bitter experience that the worst thing you could do to subordinates was stand over their shoulders while they talked to their own subordinates. He needed these troopers to accept Cavez's and Abernathy's orders even when he wasn't around, and to realize that he trusted them to make their own decisions. That meant staying out of their way.

The two had been good choices, and in less than an hour people were assigned, equipped, and on the move. Cavez had put Non in powered armor and set him and five others to watch the camp—he'd deliberately chosen the five most wounded troopers, and Raynor admired the logic of giving them an important task that didn't require them to move around at all. He and Abernathy had then split the grid in half, Cavez taking one side and Abernathy the other. They'd given each squad a region to cover, and within those squads the sergeants set men to handle specific quadrants. It was all very organized. Raynor had slipped through the cracks, however—he wasn't in either unit so he hadn't been assigned a coordinate or a partner. Perhaps his lieutenants had assumed he would stay by the shuttle, but he was too restless to sit still. Instead he began walking aimlessly, not paying attention to his direction. Whenever he passed within sight of troopers he nodded, making it look like he was simply inspecting their progress, but in reality he was just moving to keep himself from thinking too much about their predicament.

As he walked, barely registering where he was going or his surroundings, Raynor let his mind wander as well. Not surprisingly, it went straight to Kerrigan. Instead of another dream, however, he flashed back to the first time they'd met.

It had been on Antiga Prime. He and his men had just landed there, with orders from Mengsk to take out the Alpha squadron guarding the colony's main road. Mike Liberty had gone with them to help rouse the people to rebellion, and they were conferring when she appeared.

She had seemed to appear out of nowhere—they had been dropped off on a low plateau and there was no cover anywhere, just flat rock and a strong wind. Yet one second they had been alone and the next a woman was standing beside them. And what a woman!

Kerrigan had been wearing her Ghost armor at the time, the gleaming, form-fitting suit accentuating her curves. Her long red hair had floated about her like an open flame. And Raynor had felt himself drawn to that flame like the proverbial moth.

Her features were not beautiful—they were too strong for that. Her eyes were too sharp and too vividly green, her mouth too wide and full, her nose too long. Her cheekbones and jaw were strong, proud, and unrelenting. Yet she was striking, all those features combining to create a face that fit her perfectly—proud and strong and utterly captivating. He had wondered what it would be like to kiss those lips, and what her body was like beneath that armor.

And she had heard him. She had just begun reporting on scouting when her eyes widened and she took a quick step back. "You pig!" she'd shouted at him.

"What?" he'd protested, though he knew the reason for her outburst and could feel his face turning red. He'd assumed she'd simply caught him staring. "I haven't even said anything to you yet!" he'd defended himself lamely.

She'd sneered at him then. "Yeah, but you were *thinking* it," she'd snapped, and his embarrassment had turned to anger. She was a telepath! He'd glared at Mike, who'd looked guiltily away, confirming his suspicions. The reporter had known! And hadn't told him! Not that telling him would have changed anything—he still would have reacted to Kerrigan the same way. But maybe he could have masked it somehow if he'd known she might read his mind.

That had been the start of their relationship, such as it was. He'd been attracted to her, definitely, but her being a telepath had cooled his lust considerably. He'd seen too many things, heard too many stories, and thinking about telepaths brought his own personal ghosts back to him all too clearly, Johnny and Liddy looming before him in mute testimony of the damage being gifted could do to ordinary people. He'd been short with Kerrigan for a while as a result, and had been surprised when Mike had stood up for her and told him to back off. He'd come to like the lanky reporter, and to trust his instincts, and Mike's obvious high opinion of her had probably been the start of his conversion. Plus, the more he saw of Kerrigan the more she impressed him, not just physically but mentally. She was a tough cookie, that was for sure, but she was also assertive and independent and brutally honest. Kind of like him. He'd been particularly amused when she'd flat-out told Mengsk he was crazy, after the terrorist leader had ordered them to rescue General Duke from the downed *Norad II*. And look what had come of that. Still, he—

Raynor's reverie was interrupted by a shadow. It fell across him, lengthening until it covered not just his own shadow but his immediate surroundings, and he heard a strange, almost musical hum in the air. Not wasting the time to look up, he dove to the side, rolling as he hit the ground, one hand going to his pistol. Finally he came to a stop, slamming up against a small spur that was probably a steam vent, and drew his gun, brushing away the ash he'd acquired in his roll and squinting toward the source of the shadow.

What he saw took his breath away.

He had seen protoss ships before, over Mar Sara and Tarsonis. But never in person. And never close enough to reach out and touch.

His first thought was that it was less a ship than a sculpture, and a beautiful one at that, all golden swirls and loops and stylized barbs. Next he thought of a moth or a butterfly, with long graceful wings hovering above a short, stubby body—but he quickly corrected that thought, because this was more like a hornet than a moth, its wings more angled, its body segmented and streamlined. Everything about it spoke of style and grace and speed. The hum he'd heard must have been its engines, he thought as the ship settled lightly to the ground mere feet from him, lightning playing about it and concentrated at the rear and along the base and the wings. Then the lightning dwindled, becoming infrequent flashes of light rather than a continuous arcing display, and the hum faded. The ship was powering down.

Raynor righted himself, wincing at the bruise his backside had taken from that spur, and clambered to his feet, pistol still in his hand. As he watched, a sweep of the ship unfurled, swinging out and down, revealing an oblong portal along one side and creating a gentle slope from that point to the ground. The portal irised open and a figure appeared, silhouetted against the glow from within the ship. Then the figure stalked slowly down the walkway, followed by another, and another.

The protoss had landed.

The first dozen to disembark were clearly warriors, wearing something that Raynor guessed was combat armor but which resembled his own armor the same way a classic painting resembled a crude sketch. The protoss were towering figures, easily seven feet tall, and in their armor they resembled great deadly insects, their bodies protected by shiny segmented shells whose pieces overlapped perfectly but slid about easily, allowing both flexibility and protection. Portions of the armor swept up from the chest, high over the flared shoulder-pieces and down to the back, resembling stylized wings. A gleaming light was embedded at the center of their chest, just below those arcs, and Raynor couldn't tell if the light was functional, decorative, or both. The protoss wore no helmets, their armor ending in a high collar that protected the neck alongside and in back but left the throat bare for full movement, and their long, peaked heads peered out from the welter of protective metal, glowing yellow orbs staring out from an almost featureless expanse of tough gray hide. They had no mouths and no noses, and Raynor wondered idly how they breathed—or talked. He didn't see any rifles or blasters, but each warrior's forearms were covered in unusually thick bracers, the armor flaring out over the wrist instead of sloping back from the hand. On the back of each bracer was a raised unit topped with a glowing dome, and he suspected they had integral blasters there.

The warriors spread out in a semicircle around the gangplank, and then a final figure appeared at the portal and began his descent. If the others were soldiers this was definitely their commander. His armor was at once more spare and more elaborate than theirs, the bracers smaller and more elegant and lacking the bulge Raynor took for weaponry, the shoulder-pieces wider, the breastplate replaced with a heavy collar, a pair of thick crisscrossed straps with a gleaming gem set where they intersected, and a wide segmented belt. The pieces gleamed platinum rather than bronze and were suffused with a faint golden glow. Over his shoulders and around his waist he wore long strips of fabric that created the sense of a loose open robe and a symbolic loincloth. They were made from some shimmering fabric, dark blue but with highlights that shifted from blue to gold to green as it caught the light. The commander's eyes glowed blue, a vivid blue like a strong flame, and Raynor found his own eyes turning again and again to that electric gaze.

As the leader reached the ground and his armored boots settled into the ash, barely raising a puff of white, Raynor recognized him. He had seen this protoss once before, on the screens of the *Hyperion*. They had been on Antiga Prime and the protoss had acknowledged their presence before descending to cleanse the planet. This was the Executor Tassadar, the High Templar, one of the protoss high commanders.

Knowing his name and knowing they had met before, even at a distance, made everything worse. This same alien, the very one who had destroyed his ships and killed his people mere days ago, had called those people allies only a few months before! Raynor's rage bubbled up within him and he had a sudden urge to charge forward and confront the protoss Executor. His legs refused to cooperate, however.

He had seen the protoss leader before, it was true. And he had spotted protoss—what they called Zealots, warriors—on Tarsonis as well. But only from a distance, and only in the heat of battle. He'd been busy then, distracted, unable to fully register their presence. He had no such blinders now, and staring at the tall, proud, graceful aliens arrayed before him, Raynor felt something he wasn't sure he'd really experienced before.

Awe.

The zerg were horrifying, terrible, enough to make even the bravest man quake with fear. But this was different. It was more than that, and less at the same time. He wasn't afraid of the protoss, or at least that wasn't all of it. He was afraid, but only because they were so much more than him. Raynor had learned confidence the hard way, by being forced to rely on himself and his own abilities to stay alive. He knew he was a capable fighter, a good tracker, a decent commander. He knew he could take most men in a fair fight. But facing these aliens he felt like a little boy again, clinging to his mother's skirts. For the first time he understood, really understood deep in his bones, that these were aliens, beings from another planet, another race, another culture. And that they were ancient compared to him. Humanity was a mere child beside the protoss, and not a particularly promising one at that.

As he stood there, fighting the desire to run away or duck and hide, Raynor saw the Executor's head swivel about, those glowing blue eyes searching for something. Then their gaze settled upon him, and he knew how a moth felt when it was pinned to a display by razor-sharp pins. Tassadar's gaze pierced him, rooting him to the ground, and baring his very soul.

"Come."

That was all the Executor said, but the word resounded through Raynor's head despite the distance between them. They don't talk, he realized abruptly. Not out loud. The protoss spoke mind-to-mind instead, and just now their commander had spoken to him. His voice was deep and soft and rolled over Raynor. If the zerg sounded like metal grating upon itself, or insects buzzing in rage, the protoss sounded like ocean waves or the rumble of thunder in the distance.

Raynor felt his right foot lift off the ground and his body shift forward to complete the step. The left followed. He had no control over his limbs, but obeyed the protoss's command like a sleepwalker, trapped within his own flesh. The protoss warriors stepped aside without a sound and he continued forward until he was inches from the Executor, staring up at him. Behind them the portal slid shut and the walkway coiled back upward, sealing the ship, but Raynor didn't care. His attention was locked on the towering, captivating figure standing before him.

Those blue eyes had never left him, maintaining their intense gaze, and now the Executor tipped his head to one side to better consider this strange guest. "James Raynor," the protoss acknowledged. "You were allied with Arcturus Mengsk during our prior encounters." Tassadar's eyes narrowed slightly. "You are no longer an associate of his?"

Raynor remembered, then, one of the other reasons he had walked out on Mengsk. On Tarsonis the protoss had landed ground forces, warriors much like these, and had fought the zerg hand-to-hand. And between them and the Terran forces they had been winning. The zerg were being driven back.

But that wasn't what Mengsk wanted. He wanted the Confederacy's Capital World to fall so that he could sweep in and create a new order, his Terran Dominion. The protoss were jeopardizing that plan, risking his revenge and his ambition. He couldn't allow that.

So he'd ordered his men to attack the protoss.

Raynor had refused. The protoss were their allies against the zerg! Raynor wasn't going to fight them, especially when the protoss had never attacked them directly. They had targeted Terran colonies only after the zerg had already corrupted them.

"No," he managed, dragging the word from deep within. The Executor's brow lifted slightly, and suddenly Raynor found he could move again. His words came more freely. "I don't work for him anymore," Raynor admitted. "I left after Tarsonis, after he turned on you. That wasn't right."

The Executor nodded, a mere dip of his long, tapered chin, but to Raynor it felt like a benediction, and a great weight lifted from his shoulders. He hadn't even realized how bad he had felt about that betrayal all these months, on the guilty thought that somehow he should have stopped it.

"You feel anger, and loss," the protoss leader commented then, and the sudden remark drove Raynor's mind back to the rage he had felt so recently. Rage directed at Tassadar himself. This time the protoss had turned on him, destroying his ships! He couldn't bring himself to voice the accusations, but apparently that wasn't necessary. The Executor heard them anyway, and looked away as if embarrassed.

"The Terran ships orbiting this world were yours?" Raynor nodded angrily, and Tassadar nodded in return, still not meeting his eyes. "Yes, they were destroyed by our hand," he confirmed.

Raynor couldn't hear a single trace of guilt in the alien's voice. "Those were my people up there!" he meant to shout, but the words come out in a whisper instead. "You killed them."

"Their deaths were caused by the zerg," Tassadar

countered, his gaze swiveling toward Raynor again. "Your ships had become infested by the Swarm. We were forced to take action." His mental voice was calm, patient, that of a parent soothing an upset child. Raynor resented being patronized, but couldn't shake the sense that, for once, perhaps it was deserved.

"The zerg invaded, yeah," he agreed. "But my people were fighting them! We could have rescued them! Instead you killed them all, and stranded us here!"

Tassadar stared down at him, those glowing blue orbs not angry but understanding, their light bathing Raynor in a sense of profound compassion. He knew that the Executor understood his frustration, his grief, and that he sympathized with him, and somehow that sympathy eased his pain. "Such was not our intent," the Executor told Raynor gently. "Yet your ships were lost to you. The zerg had overrun them. We detected little human life left on those vessels." His eyes narrowed, though not at Raynor. "Better it is to die a clean death, a warrior's death, than to become one with the zerg, as your people would have had they been allowed to continue."

Raynor shuddered, thinking of Kerrigan. Could they have done that to his remaining crew? Yes, that was the zerg way—they absorbed their fallen foes into the Swarm. So perhaps the protoss had saved his people from a fate worse than death.

"But you didn't have to destroy the ships," he managed, though much of his anger had faded in the face of the Executor's logic. "Now we're stuck on this rock."

Tassadar nodded. "Such was not our intent," he said again. Then, apparently judging the conversation over, he turned to his warriors, who had waited unmoving during the discussion. "Seek out the Queen of Blades," he instructed them.

"You know about Kerrigan?" Raynor was amazed.

"Her screams echoed across the void," the Executor replied, "the clarion of a new terror birthed upon the cosmos." Raynor thought he heard a hint of awe and perhaps even fear in the alien's voice. "Her mind is powerful, even now, and the danger she presents cannot be overestimated." He glanced at Raynor again. "I must ascertain her strength." His voice hardened somehow, the thunder behind it increasing. "She shall not threaten my people while I stand."

With that he turned back to his warriors. "Seek her out," he repeated, "and her forces. Do not oppose them directly, however. Merely find her and instruct me as to her location." Raynor was surprised that he could "hear," much less understand, Tassader's order, and realized a second later that the Executor had deliberately included him. In fact, the protoss leader had apparently done more than that, and Raynor found he could understand the protoss mental language as if he had been born to it. Right now, however, his mind was on something else.

"You're not gonna fight her?" he demanded, his surprise overwhelming his hesitance to speak so abruptly to the towering alien. "You just said she's a threat—a terror!" And, thinking back on what he'd seen her do since her transformation, and what he'd learned from that dying scientist, he had to agree.

"She poses a significant danger," Tassadar confirmed. "I must watch her carefully, that I might understand her capabilities."

"I can tell you her capabilities," Raynor muttered. "She's Hell unleashed."

CHAPTER 9

THE PROTOSS SCATTERED, EACH MOVING OFF IN a different direction. Tassadar, however, waited by his ship, standing as still as a statue. Though Raynor was right in front of the alien, he could tell the Executor no longer registered his presence.

One part of Raynor hoped the protoss got their butts kicked by Kerrigan and her brood. It would serve them right, the arrogant bastards. But that was only a small portion of his mind, the jealous, illogical part he tried to keep locked away. The rest of him knew it was in his own best interests for Tassadar to find and destroy Kerrigan once and for all.

Meanwhile, he had another concern. The protoss were wandering around Char, and so were his own people. He didn't want them mixing it up, especially when the protoss might still be their allies. Tassadar's explanation had made sense to him and he was no longer angry at the Executor for destroying his ships. Upset about the loss of them and his people, sure, and still mad, but now he was just mad at the zerg for forcing such a drastic response. In the protoss's place he would have done the same thing, and he knew it, especially since the Executor had told him there were few signs of human life left on the ships, and the alien had no reason to lie to him.

Walking away from the protoss ship and resisting the urge to glance back repeatedly to make sure the towering Templar wasn't sneaking up behind him, Raynor topped a small rise. He hadn't realized he'd walked quite so far, but from here he could see the second shuttle, and that gave him an idea of their camp's location. Quickly he raised his comm unit and set it to broadcast on the all-purpose frequency Cavez and Abernathy had selected.

"All units," he said into the comm, "all units, this is Raynor. The protoss have landed on Char. I repeat, we've got protoss here on Char. They're wandering on foot but they're after zerg, not us. Don't shoot at them. Repeat, don't shoot at them!"

Almost immediately his comm chimed with an incoming signal. "This is Ling," one of Cavez's sergeants reported. "We just spotted one of them, maybe half a mile away. Look like walking ants! He saw us but kept moving."

"Good," Raynor replied. "Leave 'em alone and they'll leave us alone."

Several other troopers called in to report protoss sightings, but the protoss did not attack them and the two forces slid past each other without incident.

McMurty, who had been over at the second shuttle, actually came out of the back half to find himself face-to-face with one of the protoss warriors, but said that after they stared at each other for a minute the warrior simply nodded and moved around him. "Nearly wet myself," the trooper added, laughing at his own fear, "but he couldn't've cared less!"

Raynor debated what to do next. His men were handling themselves fine and the scouting was continuing. Already one team reported a small stream and another had found a stagnant pond, which would be fine once they'd boiled the water or used detox pills from the shuttle's supply. Another team had discovered a cluster of large flat mushrooms around one crater and others were looking in similar places for more—there was no guarantee they were edible but it was the first plant life they'd found and it was certainly worth experimenting. Deslan claimed he'd seen something small and rodent-like darting into a vent as he approached—he hadn't been able to catch it, but if he hadn't been seeing things it meant there were at least small mammals here, and they could hunt them for meat.

No one had found any sign of the zerg, however. Had the monsters vanished somehow? Raynor doubted that—he knew they were capable of going off-planet without ships but assumed it would require massive energy. Something like that wouldn't be subtle and they'd have seen signs. So would the protoss, and Tassadar was still doing his impression of a boulder. No, the zerg were here somewhere. Most likely back underground. Then Raynor remembered he had a way to check. Taking one last quick look at the motionless Templar, he sat down and closed his eyes.

And nothing happened except that the world went dark.

Opening his eyes again, he frowned. Ever since they'd landed he'd had trouble keeping the visions away. But now that he wanted them they were gone? What gives? He tried again, squeezing his eyes tight and concentrating on Kerrigan.

And then he saw her.

But not Kerrigan as she was now, not the mesmerizing, terrifying Queen of Blades. No, the Sarah Kerrigan that appeared before him was the one he had known on Antiga Prime and several other planets since then, the same Kerrigan he'd talked to shortly before they'd all landed on Tarsonis during that last fateful mission. It was Kerrigan fully human.

She wasn't wearing armor, a rarity for her. Instead she was decked out in worn cotton pants, a soft work shirt, high leather boots, and a dusty leather jacket. Her hair was pulled back in a loose ponytail, strands of it escaping to frame her face, and other than the long knife strapped provocatively to one thigh she was unarmed.

And she was smiling.

Not her usual smile, either, which spoke of pain and towering self-control. No, this was a look he'd seen on her face only a few times, when he or Mike had managed to startle her into laughter. It was an unfeigned smile of genuine pleasure, causing crinkles around her eyes and a faint dimple in one cheek.

She was happy.

Raynor forced his eyes open again, dispelling the image. He leaned forward, arms across his legs, and took a deep breath, vaguely thankful for the rebreather that kept his lungs from filling with ash. He tried not to gulp air, knowing that would only make him feel worse, but he needed to slow his racing heart. What had that been? It wasn't a vision, a peek into Kerrigan's head as he'd been expecting. And it wasn't a memory—he'd never seen her wearing those clothes before. Was it simply a dream? It was certainly Kerrigan the way he'd always hoped to see her, without her constant defensiveness. But he hadn't really been asleep and it had been far too vivid to have been just a daydream.

Lifting his head, he glanced down the hill toward the protoss ship—and leaped to his feet, waving his hands to block the inevitable flurry of ash. Tassadar was gone! Looking around, Raynor spotted the Executor stalking to the top of another hill nearby, heading away from him. Without stopping to think about it, he ran after the alien.

Tassadar had long, quick strides, but he didn't seem to be in much of a hurry and Raynor closed the distance between them rapidly. He slowed when he was still about twenty feet away, then fell in behind the Executor. They must have spotted Kerrigan, he realized. Tassadar had told his warriors to inform him of her location. He must be going to confront her now.

Raynor knew he had to go along. Not to lend support—he suspected even the lesser protoss warriors were far more capable than he was at combat, and their race had years of experience against the zerg. No, he was going to watch. He wanted to see what happened when these two, Kerrigan and Tassadar, met face-to-face. It might tell him more about both of them, about their strengths and weaknesses. And it promised to be a matchup he didn't want to miss.

As they walked, Tassadar giving no indication that he had even noticed Raynor behind him, Raynor thought about the situation once more, and about his options. The protoss had landed and had been if not friendly, at least not hostile. That was a good sign and took one weight off his mind—he had only one enemy here on Char, not two. And the Executor had not intended to strand Raynor and his men on this world. Would the protoss actually consider helping them get off-planet, then? He'd thought the idea ridiculous when McMurty had suggested it, but now it didn't sound quite so preposterous. It would be worth asking, at least—he knew now that the protoss wouldn't kill him for daring to speak to them, so he really didn't have anything to lose.

He started to say something about it, then stopped. Better to wait until after the upcoming encounter, he decided. Besides, the protoss might not be in any position to aid them once they'd met Kerrigan. He wondered if he could figure out how to operate their ship.

Even if the protoss wouldn't give them a lift, their situation was looking up. They'd found some water and possibly some food, so survival here wouldn't be as awful as it might have been. And perhaps the protoss would at least carry a message for them, a distress call. Who would he send it to, though? They had left a handful of people behind before coming to Char—perhaps they would be willing and able to bring a ship and pick them up. Or perhaps one of the worlds nearby could mount a rescue mission. There were only fifty of them—a single small spaceship would be large enough to hold them all.

He considered the notion of contacting Mengsk directly. Yes, the emperor had named him a criminal. Would he send someone here to arrest him? Raynor had offered that solution to Duke and the sadist had laughed and left him here. But Mengsk would see the political value of capturing and trying Raynor. It would make him look strong and capable, and show what happened to those who opposed him. He might even order Duke back here, and the general couldn't refuse a direct order. The notion tickled Raynor. Sure, it would mean his death, but Mengsk might be willing to pardon the rest of his team if they swore not to oppose him again. That was worth something.

They had crossed several hills now, and walked through several small valleys. Raynor could feel an ache in his legs, and his feet were throbbing in his boots. He'd already drained what little water he'd had left in his canteen, and eaten the one ration he'd still had in his belt pouch, and his throat was dry, and his stomach was gnawing at him. But Tassadar showed no sign of weariness or discomfort and Raynor was forced to keep going as well.

Just how far were they going? Where was Kerrigan?

More than an hour, later Tassadar stopped abruptly. Raynor stumbled to a halt behind him and collapsed on the ground, not caring if the Executor moved on without him. He had to rest!

They were at the base of another hill, this one taller and steeper than most, and as Raynor studied it he realized the difference. The slope was not only steep but oddly textured, clearly rock but lumpy rather than smooth or faceted. The hill also curved around on both sides, and it was a more regular sweep than that of most mounds or protrusions. The final clue was a clump of mushrooms at the hill's base, not five feet from where Raynor had dropped. Each mushroom was easily a foot in diameter, with a wide flat head and a short stubby stalk, and they were brown and gray and speckled with white that matched the ever-present ash.

This was no hill. It was a crater. One of the largest he'd seen so far. And judging from the way Tassadar was looking toward the upper lip, Kerrigan was inside it.

It made sense, Raynor admitted as he leaned back. The zerg favored the underground, and a volcano would provide ready access from the surface world to the caverns beneath. He rested his head against the slope behind him and closed his eyes, just for a second—

—and he was inside the volcano, standing on the shallow bowl-shaped floor, admiring the dark glassy sides that rose around them. The rest of his brood clustered around him, and his wing-tips fluttered in anticipation.

He was inside Kerrigan's head again. And like her he was suddenly awash with excitement.

"Do you feel that, Cerebrate?" he heard Kerrigan asking the massive zerg through its overlord, which hovered slightly behind her. "The protoss are here, on Char. . . ." She paused, and Raynor had an odd swooping sensation, as if he had been flung across the room or been caught up by a strong wind. He knew Kerrigan had used her telepathy; he had felt it through their connection. "They have been here for some time," she announced, sampling the mental landscape as a dog would sample the air with its nose, tasting for scents and reading the information they carried. "Hiding," she finished gleefully.

"We must destroy them," the cerebrate suggested, though it did so diffidently. Clearly it had learned from watching her confrontation with Zasz. That had been Kerrigan against a named cerebrate, one of the Overmind's elect, whereas it was still nameless and unimportant. It had to be careful to avoid inciting her wrath. "The protoss are our ancient foe," it pointed out.

"Yes, yes," Kerrigan agreed impatiently, her wings clacking together. "We will destroy them, never fear. But first I want to know why they are here." She smiled. "And that is easy to discover, as they are waiting just over the rise." She took to the air, leaping up to the crater's lip, her wings spreading out behind her as if they could hold her aloft. From there she could see protoss ringing the crater, one of them possessing the golden glow that marked a full Templar. It was toward that figure that she jumped, landing lightly perhaps twenty feet from him and furling her wings around her like a barbed cloak. Behind the Executor and farther down the slope she saw a figure hunched on the ground, this one not wearing the protoss's glittering armor but ash-smeared fatigues and a worn leather jacket. A rebreather covered his face, but she recognized him nonetheless, and her smile grew at the thought of such an audience.

"Jim," she called softly, and Raynor heard her voice both in and out of his head. "Wake up."

And his eyes leaped open.

Kerrigan was standing before him, just as he'd seen in his vision. Her attention was fixed on the majestic protoss before her, but Raynor thought he saw her direct a quick glance his way—and wink. Then she was focused upon Tassadar again.

"Protoss commander," she called to him, her voice ringing across the landscape and causing Raynor's teeth to ache from the echo. "It was folly of you to come here." She stood proud and tall, not caring that her zerg were still climbing the crater's inner walls and had not yet topped the rise. Nor did she seem to care that the other protoss warriors were moving in from either side of the hill, massing behind Tassadar and behind her. Instead her wings unfurled, sweeping out behind her like a cloak, and she lifted her chin. "For I am Kerrigan," she announced, "and—"

"I know of you well, o Queen of the Zerg," Tassadar replied, cutting her off, "for we have met before." He executed a stately bow, bending at the waist until his torso was almost parallel to the ground, though his eyes never left hers. "I am Tassadar of the Templar," he informed her, humbly omitting his full title, his words rolling across them and enveloping Raynor in a tide of deep echoing warmth. Kerrigan smiled slightly, though whether she was acknowledging his introduction or showing that she had felt his vocal effects Raynor had no idea. "I remember your selfless exploits, defending humanity from the zerg," the Executor continued. "Unfortunate it is, to see that one who was once so honorable and full of life would succumb to the twisted wiles of the Overmind." To Raynor the alien sounded genuinely disappointed, as if Kerrigan had failed him personally and that failure was a great loss.

Kerrigan did not appreciate the sentiment. "Do not presume to judge me, Templar," she snapped, her wings rearing up and back, their tips jabbing toward him. "You'll find my powers to be more than a match for yours." She smiled again, though this was the humorless smile of a predator. "In fact," she said softly, her words driving ash before her as if they were carried on a strong wind, "I sense that your vaunted power has diminished since last we met. . . ."

Raynor wasn't sure what happened next. He saw Kerrigan leap forward, wings outstretched, claws extended, to swipe at Tassadar. But the Executor shifted to one side, sidestepping her attack. At the same time his forearms, now encased in a soft blue glow, rose and knocked her wings aside so that she slid past him without even grazing him.

That was what Raynor saw. Or thought he saw. Because both Templar and zerg were fuzzy around the edges, as if viewed through thick glass. Their bodies glowed faintly, his blue and hers a yellowish green, and they left strange afterimages as they moved.

Raynor blinked and looked again. Tassadar and Kerrigan were still standing as before, and a part of him knew they had not moved at all. But he was sure the attack he'd witnessed had just happened.

Now the Executor nodded slightly, as if acknowledging Kerrigan's statement. Or perhaps this was its response to her attack. "Mayhap, o Queen," he intoned. There was a trace of something in his voice, something that sounded suspiciously like humor. "Or," he continued, "is it only that I need not flaunt my power in such an infantile test of will?"

As the words left his lips Tassadar did the last thing Raynor would have expected—he ran. The Executor turned on his heel and did a graceful sideways leap, spinning down the hill in a smooth cartwheel motion and landing erect a good hundred feet from the base of the hill. The other protoss had apparently responded to some silent command because during the exchange they had crept silently down the hill as well, and now they were all grouped around their High Templar leader. Without another word Tassadar turned and led his Zealots at a full run around the hill and into the higher mountains that loomed beyond. The protoss moved so quickly that Raynor barely had time to register their departure before they had vanished from view.

Kerrigan watched them go, her wings twitching with rage. Her zerg had finally crested the lip and now surrounded her, though they kept a respectful distance from their enraged queen. Despite himself, Raynor couldn't help admiring her. She was magnificent.

"Foolish Templar," Kerrigan whispered, her words carrying easily to Raynor on the still air. "Prepare your defenses! I will come for you soon."

"Seek out the cowardly protoss," she instructed her brood. "Slaughter them all, but leave the High Templar, the so-called Executor, to me. Now go!" Her wings flared and the zerg fled, racing down the hillside and following the same path the protoss had taken. Only one overlord remained, fluttering slightly before her, and Raynor realized it was not one of hers.

"Kerrigan," the overlord said, and Raynor recognized the voice as that of Zasz the cerebrate, "I sense something strange about this Templar. Perhaps you should reconsider your attack."

She turned on the overlord, her wings snapping up to pierce its side and then slicing down and back to carve it open. "For the last time, Zasz," she hissed as the dying zerg fell to the ground at her feet, spraying ichor everywhere, "you question my motives and authority at your own peril."

"You dare threaten a cerebrate?" Zasz gasped, though his voice was fading as his emissary died. "You will be the doom of us all," he warned. Then the overlord shuddered and went still, the ichor that flowed from its wounds slowing to a trickle.

"My doom," Kerrigan told the unhearing zerg, "is a thing not of your making, and far beyond your power." Then she stalked past it, down the hill. As she came to Raynor she glanced at him, but this time she did not wink and her eyes, looking much like the vivid green he remembered, contained such sadness it took his breath away. The look vanished quickly, and she gave no other sign that she had seen him.

This time that was definitely a relief, he thought as he watched her go. He had seen Kerrigan angry before, of course, and it had always impressed him as the human equivalent of a tornado, violent and unpredictable and incredibly destructive. Now she was even worse, and he suspected her emotions were more unbalanced as well. Becoming zerg had reduced her self-control but increased her power, a dangerous combination. He was glad it was Tassadar and not him on the receiving end of her fury.

He understood the Executor's actions now as well. Tassadar was clearly a wise commander and had told Raynor he wanted to see Kerrigan's abilities for himself to determine whether she was a real threat. The

Executor knew that the best way to do that was to provoke her. But she had a lot more zerg than he had protoss, and in a fair fight they'd simply swarm him under. So he'd egged her on, ticked her off, and then run away. Making her chase him. Smart. This way Kerrigan was in hot pursuit and Tassadar could pick the battlefields. He'd probably stop a few times, let her get close, and see how she reacted, then take off again before her full brood could assemble and overwhelm him. It was a good tactic, the type of thing Mengsk might have done, though there wasn't anything underhanded about it, just a sensible approach to a new enemy of unknown capabilities.

"Well," Raynor muttered to himself as he stood up and dusted himself off, "I suppose I can't sit around here all day." Picking a few of the mushrooms to bring back, he headed off toward his base, though he glanced over his shoulder once in the direction both Tassadar and Kerrigan had taken. He wished he could follow them to see the outcome of this battle. No matter who won it was sure to be an impressive sight, and he hated to miss it.

CHAPTER 10

"WE'RE NOT IN BAD SHAPE, SIR," ABERNATHY reported the day after Raynor's first encounter with Tassadar. She and Cavez were meeting with Raynor inside the shuttle to discuss their situation. "We have several sources of water now—none of it particularly pure but all drinkable. The mushrooms are safe to eat and we've confirmed the presence of rodents and other small critters. We're rigging traps for them now. Hopefully we'll have fresh meat within a few days."

"That's good—too many of these rations and your stomach starts hankering for your boots," Raynor joked. "Did we manage to get anything else from the other shuttle or the lifepod?" He'd finally told his lieutenants about the lifepod, and they'd sent a team to examine it and to bury the bodies.

"Not much," Abernathy admitted. "A few more rations, an extra blanket, and one more pack of detox pills." She shrugged. "We pulled every part that looked intact, too, but the biggest thing we need to fix is the engines, and those weren't any better than these."

"Yeah. Well, we'll figure something out." He turned to Cavez. "That's the useful items—how about the dangers?"

The trooper shrugged. "Not much here, actually. Zerg, of course, though they haven't bothered us yet—we think the protoss are keeping them busy." That they were, and Raynor had already told his lieutenants a little about that. "No other large animals or even insects, and the small ones we've seen don't look poisonous. We do have to watch the terrain," he warned. "One of my men got scalded from stepping too close to one of those damn steam vents and Ling almost fell into a small crater—he caught himself just in time but his helmet came off." Cavez looked grim. "That crater was still hot. Cooked the helmet to slag in an instant. We've marked it so we don't step there by mistake, but any crater could still be live."

"Can't we just avoid the ones that're smoking and coughing up lava?" Raynor asked.

Cavez shook his head. "It's not that simple. Most of these things are dormant—they're not spitting anything up anymore. But they're still hot. The problem is, when the lava sits for a while it apparently develops a thin skin over it, just like soup does. And the ash settles on that skin, blending it with the rest of the landscape. So it looks just like the ground everywhere else, but it's actually lava right under the surface."

Raynor thought about it. "Don't we have infrared goggles? We can use those to check for hot spots."

His lieutenants looked a little embarrassed. "Yes, sir," Cavez replied. "We've already got men doing that. But it'll take a while to mark all the spots nearby, let alone all the ones within that ten-mile radius."

"Oh, right." Raynor felt stupid, and laughed at himself. "Guess that's what I get for thinking I'd turned clever," he admitted ruefully. "Okay, so we got zerg and we got steam and we got lava. Anything else trying to get us?"

Both lieutenants shook their heads. "There might be unstable rock formations in the mountains," Abernathy pointed out, "but we aren't going there at the moment so it's not an issue."

"Okay." Raynor scrubbed a hand over his face and then through his hair. "Well, looking around kept everyone busy for a day. What're we gonna do tomorrow?" He looked to his two lieutenants for suggestions.

"We can take apart the shuttle systems," Abernathy pointed out. "Put every man with electronics know-how on shuttle detail, try to figure out what's been broken and what we can do to replace it."

Raynor nodded. "That's good. But we can probably only get a few people working on this crate at a time. Say five at once?" The other two nodded. "Okay, put together three teams of five and get them on this. Rotate them around. What else?"

"We're setting traps," Cavez reminded him. "For food."

"Right, right." He shrugged. "How many know how to trap and hunt?"

"Only ten of us, sir." Cavez looked a little embarrassed. "I used to hunt with my uncle back home," he explained.

"Nothing to be ashamed of," Raynor assured him. "Did a little of that myself, and I can probably still set a decent snare." He thought about it. "Okay, get those nine on trapping detail. You're in charge of that. Maybe we can set up a rotating detail to collect mushrooms and water and look for anything else edible."

"We've got ten men checking the craters and marking the dangerous ones," Abernathy volunteered, guessing his next question. He gave her a smile in return.

"Okay, that's a start, but let's put another ten on that if we've got enough IR goggles to go around." She nodded. "So that's what? Forty-five out of forty-nine?" They confirmed his math. "Set the last four to guard the camp, a roving patrol, and we're good. That'll keep everyone from panicking for another week at least."

"What about the protoss, sir?" Abernathy asked. "Shouldn't we keep an eye on them, especially if they're fighting the zerg?"

Raynor grinned at her. "Just leave that to me."

It took him two days to track the protoss warriors. They had abandoned their ship where it had landed and had retreated into the mountains, hiding among the glittering spires and hollow cones. The mountains were more active than the flatlands in terms of volcanoes, and smoke and ash billowed from several peaks and leaked from smaller vents throughout the region. It made for excellent cover and the protoss were putting it to good use, especially since their glossy armor blended well with the obsidian that littered the area and their eyes apparently saw through smoke and soot without a problem.

Raynor had packed a week's worth of rations and ventured up among the peaks, determined to locate and spy on Tassadar and his troops. Cavez and Abernathy had the camp well in hand and everyone there had something to keep them busy for the rest of the week, if not longer. He wasn't really needed there. But someone had to keep track of the protoss, and of their battles with the zerg. It might as well be him. Besides, he knew both groups' leaders personally, which meant he might be able to predict their locations and activities.

Not that it had worked with Tassadar, at least at first. The protoss had proven adept at hiding their tracks, or perhaps simply left no impression in the loose ash of the mountaintops. He searched for two days, to no avail. Finally, however, he realized that he was going about things all wrong.

"Don't try to find where an animal's been," his grandpa had taught him when he was a youngster just learning to hunt and shoot. "Find where it needs to go and wait for it to show." That was what he should be doing here. The mountains were large enough that he could wander for weeks and never come across a single protoss. And the aliens had no mouths, which meant he had to assume they didn't eat or drink. So watering holes were out. But they were up here scouting and spying, and that meant finding good vantage points. The mountains had a lot of sharp spires of narrow cliffs, but how many provided cover as well as a good view of the landscape below? Especially in the direction of the zerg incubation chamber—he was assuming the Executor had some way of detecting zerg gathering spots, since protoss attacks had always concentrated on those locations, which meant they would know about the Swarm's hideout underground. So he searched until he found a gap facing the right way, a narrow cleft in the rock that led back to a space large enough for a small squad to hunker down. After refilling his canteen from a nearby pool, Raynor selected a good vantage point on a rock spur overhanging the nook, deliberately piled ash around and over himself for concealment, and settled down to wait.

He must have dozed off while lying there, because he dreamed of Kerrigan again. And once again it wasn't Kerrigan as she was or as she had been but Kerrigan as he'd wished her to be. She was wearing the same outfit as before, the shirt's top two buttons open to reveal a tantalizing hint of cleavage, and more of her hair had worked free of the ponytail, creating a loose cap around her face. The wind was blowing the hair about and she was laughing, brushing strands from her eyes and cheeks. Her hands were long and slender, strong, artistic hands, and the nails were painted a faint shade of green that complemented but couldn't compete with the green fire of her eyes. She was lovely.

Now he saw himself in the dream, a him to match her: Jim Raynor as he might have been in happier times. His hair was longer than the stubble he had now, still short enough to keep out of his eyes but just long enough to be tugged this way and that by the breeze, and long enough in back to brush his shirt collar. He was wearing familiar clothing, the same buckskin pants and denim shirt he'd worn as a marshal, but the combat vest was gone, replaced by a loose leather one. His gun belt still hung across his hips, but the holster was empty. He had no weapon. And he found he didn't care.

Approaching Kerrigan, he held out one hand, palm up. She smiled, blushing, and placed her hand atop his. Then he led her a few steps away and she turned to face him. He bowed, she curtsied, and they came together, their hands still clasped and extended to the side and their other arm around each other's waist. And they began to dance.

Then something stirred nearby, and Raynor woke up.

For a second he couldn't remember where he was or why he should care. All he wanted was to close his eyes again and return to the dance. But the sound came again, something hard and possibly metallic brushing against stone very close by, and he shifted, feeling rock beneath him and ash all around. Ah, right—he was waiting by a spyhole and hoping the protoss found it.

Apparently they had.

Peering over the edge of the overhang, he spotted a protoss warrior by the gap, looking out upon the valley below. The warrior had levered himself up and had his legs wedged into the gap to support his weight. His armor rubbing against the rock had been the noise Raynor had heard. A second protoss stood behind the first, arms raised across its chest but facing away, clearly standing guard.

Raynor waited patiently as the first protoss studied the scene below, then traded places with his companion. When both of them had looked their fill and then slipped away through the narrow passage leading back to the peaks, he rose, quietly, disturbing the ash around him as little as possible, and dropped into the gap. He didn't hear anyone running back so he waited a few seconds before following the same path the protoss had taken. He spotted the second warrior's head just as it disappeared around a boulder up ahead.

Now that he knew where they were Raynor was able to keep them in sight. He was careful not to get too close—Tassadar had apparently decided he wasn't a threat, at least when they'd met down below, but he didn't want to provoke the warriors and find out if that protection still held. Better to stay out of sight. Besides, right now he didn't need to speak to them, he just wanted to figure out where they were and what they were doing.

An hour later he located their camp. Their ship must have held more than he'd thought and the rest must have emerged later, because Tassadar had at least a hundred warriors crouching in a deep cleft between two peaks. The Executor himself sat cross-legged upon a short, wide boulder, and from where Raynor peeked around a rock the alien's eyes seemed to be closed. Was he sleeping? Or meditating? Or perhaps tracking Kerrigan through dreams, the way Raynor had a few times? There was no way to tell. But it didn't matter, really—he'd found them, and now he could watch them.

For the next day Raynor did exactly that. He located several good vantage points and alternated between them to keep from falling asleep or stiffening up. Each one gave him good cover and a decent view of the valley below. He'd also marked the three places where the protoss could exit the valley, and made sure to keep those in sight at all times. If they started moving he'd know about it.

Nothing happened for a while, however. The warriors below didn't mill about the way humans would, which Raynor found disconcerting. No walking in circles, no whittling stray sticks or carving small rocks, no chatting. No eating or drinking, either, which meant his first guess had been correct—they didn't need food the same way he did. They simply crouched and remained that way, not moving at all for hours on end. Then suddenly one would stand and stretch, performing a series of gymnastics before returning to his crouch in the exact same spot. It was eerie.

All of a sudden they were up and moving. Raynor had just raised his canteen to his lips to take a quick swallow when the protoss stood and began filing through the pass on the opposite side. Damn, he thought, quickly capping the canteen and getting to his feet. He sprinted around the valley and got to the pass before the last warrior had disappeared from view. Then he paused a second to catch his breath before creeping along behind them.

Tassadar led his warriors down and then through a second pass, emerging just above a small plateau. He ushered his troops out onto the clearing, and they marshaled there, clearly preparing for battle. But where were the zerg?

Raynor got his answer a moment later. First he heard faint clicks and hisses, and then suddenly the zerg came into view. They were marching—if he could describe their crawling and gliding and stalking that way—up the side of an old volcano not far below. The ground all around the cone had fallen away and this was the quickest way through the area.

Tassadar's warriors crouched and began creeping to the edge of the plateau. Then, in twos, they dropped over the edge, landing soundlessly on a small ledge below. From there they leaped across to the crater itself, using the flaring edges of their armor to cling to the rock. The plateau faced the side of the volcano, and the zerg were marching from front to back—they had not seen the protoss yet, and the Zealots were all safely hidden by the crater's lip.

After the last of the protoss had made the jump Raynor lowered himself onto the plateau and moved closer to the edge. He wasn't about to attempt that jump, though. Besides, he had a great view from right here.

He watched as the zerg continued their progress, climbing over the cone's lip and down into the crater itself. The surface looked solid, though Raynor remembered what Cavez had said. Certainly if it was just a skin the zerg would have crashed through, particularly the lumbering ultralisks, but they didn't have any trouble crossing. They probably had ways to detect the hot spots, he realized, much like IR goggles enabled his team to do.

After the zerg were all in the basin Tassadar gestured, and his warriors hauled themselves around the crater's edge, hand over hand, until they were evenly spaced about the lip. Then, at some signal Raynor couldn't see, they all heaved themselves up onto the lip in a single motion and dove down into the crater. As he watched, glowing spikes appeared from their forearms, extending over their fists, and he realized these energy blades were their primary weapons. The Executor himself perched on the crater's edge but did not participate in the conflict—instead he sat and watched, just as Raynor was doing.

The zerg were taken completely by surprise. The brood had been concentrating on getting across the crater and was unprepared for the sudden attack from above. Protoss were among them in an instant, carving through the zerg's tough skin with their energy blades, and a dozen or more zerg had fallen before the rest had time to react. Raynor saw four warriors close in on an ultralisk, each targeting a leg, and slice the massive zerg to pieces before it could bring its large scythe-tusks to bear.

One of the hydralisks reared up and hissed loudly as it turned and slashed at a protoss warrior, leaving a visible gash across his armored chest. The sound carried across the plains, and to Raynor it had a clear note of desperation. The zerg was calling for help! The protoss stabbed forward with one hand and swept the other in a wide outward arc, severing the hydralisk's limb and then impaling it through the head, and the hydralisk's cry faded, but Raynor could still hear the grating voice echoing and knew its warning had gone out.

Kerrigan must have been nearby because a moment later Raynor heard a strange rustling, scraping sound, like a bird's flight mixed with the sound of bones grinding together, and then she was there. She leaped down into the crater, her wings flared behind her and beating at the air, and landed atop a protoss warrior, her wing-tips cutting him in two even before her feet had touched the ground. Her zerg quickly rallied around her and began pushing the protoss back while Kerrigan herself glared about her, evidently seeking her adversary.

"Where are you, Tassadar?" she shouted, her voice making the nearby cliffs shake and causing rocks to tumble free. Raynor felt the vibrations through the plateau beneath him, and hoped it would hold. "Do your underlings always do your fighting for you?"

She glanced up and spotted the Executor, still sitting on the opposite lip, but before she could do more than sneer at him he leaned backward and fell from sight. Raynor, watching from above and behind, saw the High Templar fall in a graceful dive, arms spreading outward, then flip over and land on his feet in a small ravine far below. Somehow he had signaled to his warriors at the same time, and they turned and bolted from the crater, leaping over the edge and tumbling down after their leader. Most of them lacked his grace and precision, but they still managed to regroup in the ravine without major injury and marched quickly away, disappearing into the rocks.

Kerrigan had not hesitated either, and a powerful jump carried her to the lip a moment behind the protoss, her wings widespread to maintain her balance. But by the time she had reached that perch her enemies were gone, vanished into the warren of rock and lava that lay all about them.

"Run and hide, little protoss," she sneered after searching for a moment. "You cannot evade me forever. And when I find you"—her wings curled in like hands forming fists—"I will rend you into bits!"

Turning back to her brood, she assessed the damages. So did Raynor. Two protoss had been killed but their fellows had carried the bodies with them, leaving behind only a few drops of blood upon the ash and rock. Fully a third of the zerg brood had been killed or maimed, however.

"Eliminate the wounded," Kerrigan ordered, standing and walking around the crater, moving easily across the narrow lip as if it were a wide road. The unharmed zerg, obeying her command, quickly turned on their injured fellows, and the air was filled with blood and ichor until only the undamaged zerg remained standing. The wounded did not put up a fight.

Kerrigan had reached the far side of the volcano now, and leaped down, gesturing for her surviving zerg to follow her. They swarmed obediently up and over the lip and then down onto the narrow ledge below, and she led them in the same general direction Tassadar had taken, clearly intent upon finding him. Raynor doubted she'd succeed—despite her skills and whatever mental powers she now possessed, he had a feeling the Executor was ready for her. She wouldn't find the protoss until he wanted to be found.

The question, Raynor realized as he shifted his legs to sit on the plateau with his back against the cliff, was what to do now. Tassadar had disappeared. They might return to the same valley, and he would check it out, but the protoss would be foolish to use the same hiding place twice, and the Executor was clearly no fool. So he'd have to find them all over again. And right now, with them on the move and the fact that they had a head start and could run faster than he could, there was no way he could catch up. He'd have to wait until they went to ground and then find them all over again.

As he was levering himself back to his feet he heard a strange humming sound behind him. It was familiar, and after a second he recognized it. It was the sound of the protoss ship.

"Oh, now what?" Raynor asked as he twisted around and dropped onto his stomach. He peered over the edge of the plateau and stared down at the crater below.

The protoss ship was landing.

His first thought was that the zerg had attacked the ship and that was why it had relocated. It looked as if it had been in a fight—gone was the glittering gold and many of the majestic sweeps, and the hull was blackened instead. But then he looked again and realized that the configuration was different—this ship was smaller in general, stubbier, and lacked the elegance of Tassadar's. The hull was black, but not from damage—instead it had a black finish that was smooth without being glossy, reminding him of granite or black marble. Where it was not black the ship gleamed a dull bronze, weathered but still strong, and gave off a sense of immense age and endurance.

This was a different ship entirely. A second protoss vessel. What were two protoss ships doing here?

He watched, hunkered down, as the ship settled in, its base resting amid the ichor and blood of the slain zerg. The side irised open and the bottom lip elongated, creating a walkway. After a few seconds several protoss emerged and made their way down the gangplank and onto the crater floor.

At least Raynor thought they were protoss.

Just as the ship was slightly different, so these figures did not match the warriors he had seen before. They were of a similar height and moved with equal grace, but their armor was heavier, blockier, less streamlined and less elegant. It had the same matte finish as their ship, and seemed almost to absorb the light around it, so that the figures below were standing in shadow even though Char's small sun stood almost directly overhead. They had heavier brows, longer, sharper chins, and ridged plates at the temple and cheek that suggested horns, making them resemble armored lizards rather than insects. Their bracers, which had strange coils and wires running along their length, were thick enough to house the same energy blades, but they were darker than the rest of the armor, as if the shadows were coalescing around the figures' hands and wrists.

Then their leader emerged.

He was tall, as tall as Tassadar, but more hunched. Raynor had no idea how long protoss lived or how old any of the ones he'd seen were, but something about this new figure suggested great age. Despite that this leader moved gracefully, his feet making no sound as he stepped from the walkway to the ground. His face was longer than that of his warriors, his chin curling back up at its tip and flattening out, as if he had a majestic beard. His skin seemed almost purple, particularly just below the deep-set pale green eyes, but faded to white that shaded to ivory along his chin, and he had bone ridges atop his head and small barbs along his cheeks, like a great fanged lizard. Like Tassadar he wore long strips of cloth across his chest and shoulders and over his groin, but these were a soft black that glittered slightly like stars in the nighttime sky. Beneath those he had long robes with full, flaring sleeves, the fabric a rich red-brown like dried blood, cuffed in a softer brown like fur with strange sigils stretched all around. Massive epaulets covered his shoulders, overlapping plates of metal or perhaps bone scored with swirls and sweeps and pinned together by a gleaming crystal dome the deep purple of a twilight sky. A shadow traveled with this new protoss, shrouding him despite the sunlight, and Raynor shivered, feeling a chill emanating from the alien and his troops.

Who were these guys? he wondered. And what were they doing here on Char?

CHAPTER 11

RAYNOR WATCHED AS THESE NEW DARK PROTOSS gathered together and bowed their heads in either communion or prayer. Then they moved to the lip of the crater and effortlessly vaulted it to land lightly on the far side of the slope—the way the zerg had come, Raynor noticed. Intrigued, he abandoned his hiding place and cut down from the plateau, taking a narrow path that led him along the cliff and to the ground not far from the crater's base. He moved carefully, knowing the rocks there were not stable, but as quickly as he dared, and he still arrived in time to see the warriors descending into a wide cavern nearby.

"Underground again," he muttered to himself as he jogged to the entrance and peered inside. "Great." It was too dark to see much, but the cavern did extend backward and showed no sign of narrowing. At least he wouldn't be cramped. With a sigh he ducked beneath the low arch of the entrance and headed down, following the faint footsteps he heard somewhere ahead of him.

He didn't have to worry about getting lost, as it turned out. The cavern swept down, becoming a wide tunnel, and then opened into an even larger chamber. The curving roof here was easily a hundred feet above the rough stone floor and the walls were surprisingly smooth—where they weren't covered in creep. Because this chamber was infested by zerg and showed the signs of their presence. Not the least of which being the zerg themselves, who were massed down below. In their center was one of the massive sluglike creatures, the cerebrates. Raynor recognized this one as Zasz, the cerebrate who had defied Kerrigan. Apparently her response—killing his overlord—had not improved his attitude toward her.

"The Queen of Blades is not worthy of our support," Zasz was whispering as Raynor flattened himself behind a protrusion in the wall, hoping to escape notice. "She risks us all with her impatience and her temper. She is not zerg!"

If he was waiting for a reply from the Overmind he did not get one, and the cerebrate's muttering continued. "Her incompetence must be demonstrated! Her leadership is suspect. It must not continue!"

While Zasz ranted, Raynor risked a quick glance around. Where were those protoss? The tunnel had led straight here—no branches or nooks or anterooms—which meant they had come this way. But how could they have gotten past this many zerg without a fight? He looked around again, and almost jumped when he saw a section of the wall move a short ways below him. The patch of wall had looked normal until it shifted, and then he saw a tall, slender outline. Protoss! They could go invisible like Kerrigan, or at least partially—now that he looked carefully he could see the warrior standing there, and slowly he distinguished several others beside the first. Why hadn't he noticed them before?

The answer became obvious as he saw the first warrior turn sideways—and vanish. In a second Raynor was able to spot the protoss again, but the alien's armor had taken on the color and patterning of the wall behind him. Protective camouflage.

Now that he knew what to look for Raynor spotted several more protoss, all up against the same wall and taking on the wall's coloring and texture. But where was their leader?

As if his thought had been a cue, the leader appeared—near the center of the zerg brood, opposite Zasz and perhaps a hundred feet from the cerebrate. When he became visible his warriors went into motion as well, abandoning their posts along the wall and gliding down to the chamber floor, their footsteps almost inaudible and their forms still little more than shifting shadows.

The Swarm's response was instantaneous. The ultralisks stepped forward, locking their scythe-tusks together to form a protective barrier around their leader. The overlords and mutalisks took to the air, as did the tiny scourge, while hydralisks and zerglings ringed the ultralisks, facing outward. Every zerg writhed with anticipation, flexing claws and tails and baring teeth. They instinctively moved closer together as the protoss leader stepped forward, a pace ahead of his warriors—

—and held both massive, clawed hands up, palm outward, in the universal sign for peace.

"I am Zeratul, Praetor of the Dark Templar," he announced, speaking to the cerebrate. His voice was cold and dry, like old leaves, but a thrum behind the shaky surface suggested depths best left untapped. "I would speak with you, o Zasz of the cerebrate."

The cerebrate wriggled slightly. "Why would I speak with one such as you?" Zasz asked, though it seemed he did not expect a reply. "You are an enemy of the Swarm, and must be destroyed."

"Without a doubt you can destroy us," Zeratul agreed. "For we are few and you are many. But what then? Still you must contend with the Executor and his warriors. Still you must block the Queen from consolidating her power—by destroying you and claiming your duties and your brood for her own."

"What know you of our queen?" Zasz demanded.

"Only her greatest weakness." Though the Praetor's reply was spoken softly, every zerg stopped whatever it had been doing to listen to this conversation, sensing its potential to destroy a hated enemy and perhaps exact revenge for the drops that had been spilled. "Would you know it?" His words lacked Kerrigan's power but had another quality to them, a depth that spoke of great age and perhaps even wisdom.

Zasz was evidently swayed as well. "I would hear more of this weakness," he admitted.

"We shall speak together as equals," Zeratul offered. "I enter your brood unarmed to show my faith in the process." His arms had remained up this entire time, but now he gestured with them to make it even more obvious that he was unarmed. "Come meet with me and we shall discuss such matters."

For a moment no one moved. Raynor, watching from his safe perch along the tunnel, was sure the zerg would simply fall upon this Zeratul and tear him to shreds. Even with his warriors nearby, and with the power Raynor sensed around him, the strange protoss would be no match for a full zerg brood. Yet they didn't attack. Zasz simply swayed, as if debating, and his brood waited, twitching eagerly but not advancing.

"We will speak," Zasz finally confirmed. At its words the zerg around it pulled back, though reluctantly. The overlords, mutalisks, and scourge parted, to hover off in the chamber's corners, while the ultralisks backpedaled and the hydralisks and zerglings moved aside. Now there was an empty ring around the cerebrate. Zeratul stepped forward and walked slowly to the center of the room. The other protoss—the other Dark Templar, Raynor assumed—stepped back a few paces as well, until they were arrayed before the end of the tunnel. It looked almost like an elaborate dance.

"Speak, then," Zasz urged when he and Zeratul

were mere feet apart. Raynor could see strange shapes and flashes of color shifting beneath the cerebrate's skin and knew Zasz was eager, and growing impatient. "Tell us of this weakness."

"And so I shall," the protoss confirmed, leaning in slightly. His head tilted down, his body crouching a little to put him closer to the cerebrate's level. Raynor wondered how the protoss could stand being so close to the foul zerg, but Zeratul showed no hint of discomfort or even dislike. He looked as if he were relaying secrets to a close friend.

"Your queen," he informed the cerebrate, his voice little more than a dry whisper, "has one great weakness, as I said. A flaw that could easily prove fatal."

"Tell us!" Zasz demanded, the spots on his front flashing more brightly.

"Very well." Zeratul nodded, and with one arm gestured behind him. "The flaw is this: the same as the rest of your kind. The same that shall be your death!" With these last words a blade appeared above the outstretched hand, jutting from his wrist. It was much like the weapons Raynor had seen on Tassadar's warriors, an energy spike that glittered and glowed, but those had been a smooth, gleaming blue-white. This was a sparking hissing yellowish green, the same shade as his eyes, wisps of vapor rising from its edges. Beneath the hiss Raynor could feel a deep thrum through his bones and his teeth, and the room grew noticeably colder.

Then Zeratul pivoted, his cocked arm jabbing forward, and the blade struck deep into the cerebrate.

Zasz screamed, a horrible rending sound that tore Raynor's throat in sympathy. Despite his hatred for the zerg he felt pity for the creature. More than anything he wanted that horrible sound to stop. The Dark Templar remained where he was, his blade embedded in the cerebrate's flesh as Zasz convulsed in agony. The lights within him were spasming as well, colors and shapes appearing suddenly and without pattern, and the rest of the zerg writhed in shared pain. None of them attacked, however—evidently they were too shocked to move without a direct order, and Zasz was in no shape to give one.

After what seemed like minutes Zeratul leaned in, forcing his blade even deeper, and twisted his arm, causing the blade to widen the hole it had made. The screaming stopped abruptly and Zasz collapsed, his massive body limp.

Then Raynor saw a strange thing. A glow gathered from deep within the cerebrate's body, coalescing as it moved forward, until it passed through the gaping hole in its head and floated just above, a ball of yellowish light that wriggled and extruded small glowing tentacles in every direction. Somehow Raynor knew that this, and not that awkward shell, was the true Zasz. The ball rose, hovering there as if waiting for instructions or direction.

Then the Dark Templar struck. His blade lashed out, a great sweeping gesture, and the ball was sliced in two. The brilliant energy spike left trails of light and shadow behind it as it moved, and the ball's glow was smothered by the shadows, its own light absorbed even as it fell, its form collapsing until it was just a scattering of faint light and then nothing at all.

And the brood went wild.

They had not moved while Zeratul attacked Zasz, but when his blade carved open that glowing sphere a thrum went through the chamber, somewhere between a snap and a sigh, like a taut wire breaking. The zerg evidently heard it as well, and the sound drove them mad. Suddenly they were moving, but not as they had before. This was a true "swarm," with no coordination or purpose, and as Raynor watched an ultralisk stomped on a zergling, squashing it flat. Two hydralisks turned on each other, each of their scythes lashing out to slice deep into the other's flesh. Mutalisks dove into the crowd, spewing their acid on their fellow zerg, and scourge exploded against overlords and ultralisks alike, their suicidal detonations destroying the larger zerg and spreading ichor and blood and flesh everywhere.

In the midst of all this, Zeratul stood unmoving. The blade at his wrist had vanished, and now he merely watched as the brood turned upon itself. After a moment he nodded, then stalked back toward the tunnel. His warriors moved to flank him as he passed, and together they walked back up the tunnel and out of the cavern. Raynor hugged the wall as they passed, but if they saw him they did not acknowledge his presence. A moment later their footsteps had faded and he was alone with the zerg.

Not that they noticed him either. They were too busy killing each other. It wasn't murderous rage, though, he realized. He'd seen the zerg fight often enough to know how efficient they could be at killing. This was too careless, too sloppy. An ultralisk stormed across the chamber, its head swiveling this way and that as it moved, its scythe-tusks impaling smaller zerg. But it missed as many as it hit and it didn't finish off the zerg it wounded—instead it ran on, ignoring the damage it caused, until it reached the far wall. Then, as Raynor watched amazed, the ultralisk charged full force into the cavern, its tusks shattering with a sickening crunch. It reared back, clearly dazed, and repeated the attack, again and again, each time injuring itself more, until finally its head collided with a rocky spur, producing a loud crack, and the ultralisk fell to the ground, its skull caved in.

This was insane, Raynor thought as he watched the chaos below him. They weren't angry—they had gone mad!

He thought about that. Maybe they had gone mad. Or mindless, at least. This was Zasz's brood. The cerebrate had controlled them utterly. Raynor had noticed before that individual zerg had little autonomy—even the cerebrates were bound to the Overmind's will. Kerrigan was apparently an exception. She'd been allowed to retain her free will, and was loyal to the Swarm but could act independently. The other zerg were more tightly controlled. So, if Zasz had done all the thinking for his brood, and Zeratul had just killed him, where did that leave these zerg? Without a controlling thought. No wonder they were going berserk—they were mindless killers and all their restraints had just fallen away, but without a direction they simply lashed out around themselves.

A chill crept through Raynor as he retreated hastily toward the surface, keeping an eye on the carnage behind him. Fortunately the zerg were too distracted to notice him. The zerg's greatest strengths were their sheer numbers and their ability to act as one, he thought as he exited the cavern and took a deep breath, relieved to be back in the sunlight and open air again. Zeratul had found a way to sever the connection between individual zerg—he had killed one zerg, the cerebrate, and had effectively dispatched an entire brood. If he and his people could learn to do that, to target the cerebrates, they could end this war! They could destroy the zerg for good!

"It can't be that easy," he admitted as he walked away, heading back toward his camp. The Dark Templar had vanished, as had the other protoss, and he was too weary and too shaken by what he'd seen to go after them again. Besides, he had a lot to think about.

If all it took to destroy a brood was killing the cerebrate, why hadn't Tassadar done the same? Sure, the Executor had said he was here to study Kerrigan, but he'd fought the zerg before. Why not just target their cerebrates, render the broods helpless, and then mop them up? In that way the protoss would never lose a war against the Swarm, and the Swarm probably wouldn't have ever made it to Mar Sara and the other human worlds.

There was more to it than that. There had to be. Tassadar hadn't used that tactic because he didn't know it. But the protoss must have known about the cerebrates. And if they had, why hadn't they targeted them? It couldn't be that simple. Zeratul knew something he didn't, something even Tassadar didn't.

His mind flashed back to Zasz's death, and to the strange light show that had followed. It was the second time he'd seen a protoss battle a zerg commander, and the second time he'd seen something that didn't look quite real. What was he really seeing when Kerrigan and Tassadar fought, and when Zeratul destroyed that glowing sphere that came from Zasz? He didn't know, but whatever it was, that was the key to all this. Zeratul's killing the cerebrate hadn't been enough—the brood had been frozen during the attack, but they hadn't gone berserk until later.

Not until Zeratul had destroyed that ball of light.

Somehow that light was the key. And Raynor was pretty sure he couldn't hit something like that with a gauss rifle. Hell, he wasn't even sure he'd have seen it if not for Zeratul. So maybe it was only the Dark Templar who could do something like that. He wondered if they'd consider allying with him to wipe out the rest of the Swarm. Certainly Zeratul seemed less interested in testing Kerrigan than Tassadar had—the Praetor hadn't even asked about her, but had instead sought out and attacked Zasz.

Raynor shook his head. "Too much too fast," he muttered as he clambered over a small crater, careful not to step in its center until he'd tossed a rock there to see if the surface was solid enough to hold. He'd come here to rescue Kerrigan, plain and simple. Instead he was climbing around on the rocks, spying on not one but two groups of protoss, watching them alternately fight and taunt the zerg. It was all a little too strange for him, and way too complicated. Not for the first time, he wished Mike were here. The newshound was sharper than he was. He'd understand all this, and then he could explain it. But Mike was nowhere near, was off running his rebel broadcasts, which left Raynor to figure this out on his own.

CHAPTER 12

BY THE TIME HE STUMBLED BACK INTO CAMP, Raynor was exhausted. It was already late enough that most of his people were asleep, leaving only the night watch and a handful of others to notice as he staggered to his tent, crawled into it, shucked off his boots, and collapsed.

And, of course, he dreamed.

He and Kerrigan were still dancing, twirling and dipping to music he recognized as the old folk tunes he'd heard while growing up. It was music he'd heard when visiting his grandfather, and carried happy memories—dancing to it with Kerrigan only added to them, leaving him warm and content. Then the music shifted, slowing, and she stepped in close, her arms rising to wrap loosely around his neck. His own shifted to settle at her waist, his hands clasped at the small of her back. They were doing little more than swaying to the rhythm, occasionally shuffling a step forward or back. Their eyes were locked together, and hers twinkled with happiness, arousal, and something else—mischief. Her hip brushed against him as they took a step. Her chest rubbed against his as he stepped forward, and this time she didn't step back as quickly. Somehow she contrived for their bodies to connect repeatedly, though always in innocent, seemingly accidental ways. And all the time her face bore a look of calm enjoyment, but her eyes told the real story. She was toying with him.

Finally he couldn't stand it any longer. He tightened his arms around her, preventing her from moving away, and leaned in close. Her eyes widened slightly, though he knew she wasn't at all surprised. Her lips parted and her chin tilted slightly, so that her mouth met his. Their lips brushed, gently at first, then pressed together more firmly as they both gave in to the passion they felt. It was their first kiss. It was worth waiting for. It was gentle and sweet and demanding and a powerful hint of what might follow, and for a second after they pulled apart Raynor could not think, could not blink, could barely breathe for wanting her.

Then he woke up.

"So we've got two kinds of protoss out there?" Abernathy asked as the three of them gathered inside the shuttle for their customary morning meeting. Raynor nodded and gratefully accepted the mug of coffee she handed him.

"That's right." He took a sip, ignoring the way it scalded his tongue, and sighed in relief as he felt the caffeine kick in, jolting his system fully awake. "This second group calls itself the Dark Templar." In his memory he saw Zeratul again, with that sliver of darkness protruding from his hand and that cloak of cold and shadow wrapped around him, and shivered. "They're definitely dark, I'll give them that," he admitted. "Their tech, their mind-powers, whatever, seem drawn from cold and the dark. Like space."

"But we don't need to worry about them attacking us?" Cavez asked a little nervously.

"No," Raynor reassured him, "I don't think they'll attack us. We're not their targets here—either group's. The regular protoss are after Kerrigan. Near as I can figure, the Dark Templar just want to destroy the zerg."

"Sounds good to me," Abernathy said, and Raynor chuckled.

"Yeah, me too," he said. He'd already told them what he'd seen, including how the zerg brood had reacted. He didn't mention the sphere of light, however. He knew how it'd sound if he did, like he was losing his mind, seeing things. So he left that part out. "I'm hoping we can strike a deal with them," he admitted, "scratch each other's backs. We offer some extra firepower, they use their whatever-it-was to mess up the zerg, then give us a ride off this rock."

"How do we find them?" Cavez asked.

"I can find them," Raynor told him. "I did it once, I can do it again." He didn't mention that encountering the Dark Templar had been luck the first time. But why not let them hope a little? "I'll track down the other protoss too," he decided. "I want to keep an eye on both of them, and on the zerg, just in case anyone starts wandering through this area or decides they need to knock us off too."

"Do you want to take some of the men with you, just in case?" Abernathy asked.

Raynor shook his head. "No, I can move faster alone, and I'm used to it. Besides, everybody's got their assignments. No sense switching 'em now." He didn't point out the obvious—that even if every trooper went with him they'd be no match for the first protoss group or a zerg brood, and possibly not for the Dark Templar either. Safety in numbers only worked when you had the numbers on your side.

"We've got everything covered here," Cavez assured him, and Raynor clapped the young trooper on the shoulder.

"I know you do," he told the younger man. "You two don't need me hanging around all day." He grinned and took another slug of his coffee. "Better if I keep myself busy and out of your way."

The next day Raynor headed back out, looking for signs of any of the three leaders he sought. Immediately, however, he was faced with a dilemma: should he return to the mountains or head down into the lowlands, where cracked earth was broken up by small steam vents and pocked with fissures? He figured the protoss would head back up into the mountains, where they could find more cover and also have a better vantage from which to spot Kerrigan. But she wouldn't go up there. She'd stay down low, scouring the landscape for any sign of her foes, daring them to come to her. He knew that both from the Kerrigan of old and from what he'd seen of the new, awe-inspiring Kerrigan.

Plus something about his dreams told him she was south rather than north, low rather than high.

He had dreamed again last night, and again they had been dancing. They kissed, just as they had before, and then she pulled back, smirking, and twisted free of his arms. A quick, sly look at him and she was off and running, forcing him to chase her. He did so happily, laughing at the sheer joy of it all, loving the feel of the wind in his hair and the sight of her before him, her long red hair streaming about her.

She was quick, but he was taller and his longer strides ate up the distance, closing the gap until finally he could reach out and snag her wrist. The sudden shift in her balance caused her to stumble, and he bumped into her, the two of them toppling to the ground together. They landed on soft grass, amused and unhurt, and Kerrigan struggled to free herself, twisting her hand this way and that but to no avail. She was laughing the whole time, and so was he.

At last she gave up trying to escape and, suddenly changing tacks, shouldered him aside, causing him to topple onto his back again. Then she rolled over onto him, forcing the air from his lungs. He lay there, trying to catch his breath, and she pulled her wrist loose.

"Aha!" she shouted triumphantly, raising both arms to keep them free of his grasp.

Then she turned so she was lying atop him, face-to-face. And, grinning, she lowered her lips to his.

He woke still tasting her kiss.

Now, as he wandered through Char's strange, sulfurous desert, Raynor thought about his dreams again. He had dreamed of Kerrigan before, of course, starting back when he'd first met her—dreams of how that encounter could have gone differently, dreams of the two of them talking, dreams of them getting along, even dreams Kerrigan would have wanted to shoot him for if she had seen them in his head. But since landing on Char he'd been dreaming about her more and more, almost every time he closed his eyes. Was that just because he'd thought she was dead and now knew she was alive, if altered? Was it because he felt drawn to her, even more now than before? Because something about her, in her new form, was utterly captivating?

As he stalked across the plains, stepping carefully to avoid cracks and crevices and steam, he kept his eyes peeled. The Kerrigan of old would have disappeared, going Ghost on him, but somehow he didn't think this new Kerrigan would use that trick. She was bolder now, more confident. Maybe that was part of what he liked about her. He'd always felt Kerrigan's brashness was a mask for a lonely, self-conscious young woman. Now she was completely sure of herself and had no need for such tricks.

He came to the edge of a massive crevice that could easily have been defined as a valley. Looking out over it, shading his eyes against the glare of the hard-baked dirt and rock, he spotted movement. The ground seemed darker in one area, and at first he couldn't tell if it was actually moving or if the steam was causing ripples in the air, playing tricks on his eyes. He squinted, trying to get a better view, then finally gave up and pulled the binoculars from their case on his belt. With them raised he could see the disturbance clearly.

It was zerg, definitely. He could make out several overlords hovering above the ground, smaller shapes that were probably mutalisks darting between them. Below those were the massive ultralisks, easily distinguished now, and around them smaller shapes that had to be hydralisks and zerglings. One shape walked out in front, from this distance little more than a dark butterfly with legs, even through the binoculars. But he recognized the outline and the walk instantly. It was Kerrigan.

"Gotcha," Raynor muttered as he returned the binoculars to their case and studied the edge of the crevice before him. Off to one side a little ways he spotted a crack that angled down. It was wide enough for him to fit through, and if it ran all the way to the bottom he'd have an easy path. The crack was also narrow enough that levering himself back up it wouldn't be too hard, either, though he hoped he didn't have to do that with a full zerg brood in hot pursuit.

The crack petered out halfway to the valley floor but ended in a short ledge. Raynor found a second ledge about ten feet below the first one and jumped down, catching himself before he stumbled forward and fell. That ledge was only a few feet wide but another five feet over was a longer one that angled down into a trail, and after jumping onto it Raynor was able to continue his descent. By the time he had reached the valley floor, an hour or two later, he was sweaty and exhausted. And the zerg were closer.

Taking a few quick swallows of water and munching on some rations, he eased his way into the valley proper, hugging the wall behind him for cover. The zerg were still a good distance away, and he inched his way forward, being careful to stay as concealed and quiet as possible. He wanted to spy on them, not get killed by them.

Finally he found a small crack in the wall behind him, creating a nook barely as wide as his shoulders, and he tucked himself into the cramped space and waited. The zerg were close enough for him to hear them, and he strained to listen.

"Insufferable protoss coward!" Kerrigan was raging. Peeking around the edge of the nook, he saw her storming across the valley floor, her wings jabbing at the air with each step. "Tassadar cannot evade my wrath forever," she promised herself, her hands clenching into fists and beating against her sides. "I shall find him and—"

Her raving was interrupted by a faint rushing sound

overhead, and Raynor ducked back, glancing up as he did. It was an overlord, and he wondered where it had come from, since Kerrigan's own were still behind her with the rest of her brood.

"Kerrigan," the overlord called out, and he recognized the voice. It was the other cerebrate, Daggoth, the one that in his dreams had given Kerrigan the use of his warriors for her assault on the *Amerigo*. "Zasz is dead!" he informed her, his overlord floating nervously just beyond her reach. For a second Raynor wondered if Daggoth had heard how Kerrigan had treated Zasz's overlord back in the crater. Was he afraid she would attack his messenger as well?

This was not unwelcome news, however, and so she merely smiled up at it, a sharp-toothed, nasty smile. "Oh?" she purred, her wings curling about her contentedly. "Dead, you say?" Then her smile dimmed. "It is a pity that cerebrates cannot truly be killed," she said, which made Raynor sit up and take notice. What did she mean by that? "I expect," she continued, "that the Overmind will reincarnate him soon. . . ."

Raynor rested his head against the cool rock of his hiding place, trying to process what she had just let slip so casually. Cerebrates reincarnated! His first thought was to discount that as hocus-pocus—he'd heard people talk about reincarnation before, usually either old folks or young kids with starry eyes and crazy ideas. But then, this was Kerrigan talking. Even before her transformation she'd been as hardheaded and practical as . . . well, as him. And her becoming zerg had, if anything, stripped away any lingering frivolities. If she was talking about reincarnation, especially to a cerebrate, she was serious. Which meant the zerg commanders couldn't be killed, at least not permanently. His heart sank. The zerg had a ridiculous number of warriors and could always breed more. And now their commanders couldn't die. They were impossible to defeat.

Apparently the zerg had thought so as well, which explained the panic he heard in Daggoth's voice as the cerebrate replied, "No, he will not!" The overlord's agitation increased and Kerrigan looked up at it curiously. So did Raynor. "The protoss have devised some new attack," Daggoth explained hurriedly, "an attack powerful enough to nullify our reincarnation and give pause to the Overmind itself!"

Raynor wanted to shout when he heard that, and he had to bite down on his gloved hand to keep himself quiet. Zeratul! Whatever the Dark Templar had done to Zasz, it had been permanent. And it was throwing the zerg into complete panic!

"I had wondered," Kerrigan admitted, almost to herself, "why the Overmind felt so . . . distant from me."

"As had I," Daggoth replied, and Raynor could hear both surprise and sorrow in the cerebrate's tone. "You are a mere youngling, recently brought to the Swarm. I have served countless lifetimes, and ever have my mind and the Overmind's been one. Now there is an emptiness within me, and my cries to him fall without reply."

"Is it so hard," Kerrigan asked him then, her words condescending but strangely bitter, "to manage without the Overmind's guidance? To pilot your own course?"

"Such is not our way" was Daggoth's only answer, and Raynor saw Kerrigan's face twist in what might have been disgust. She was clearly not pleased, though Raynor knew she was perfectly happy to see Zasz gone for good. Still, she snarled as she digested the new information and considered it in light of other recent events, her wings twitching impatiently. "So," she said finally, the word little more than a growl. "Tassadar's plan was merely a diversion. I should not have underestimated him so." If anything she looked even angrier than before, and Raynor pitied the Executor when Kerrigan found him. If there was one thing she had always hated it was to be treated as if she didn't matter, and Tassadar's taunting her had merely been a ploy to keep her distracted. In truth, it didn't mean she wasn't important—if anything it matched the protoss's statement that she was of critical importance and of the utmost danger—but she saw it differently.

"Without its master," Daggoth was saying, "Zasz's brood has run amok, and even now threatens the Hive Cluster." His overlord turned, spotting one of the other overlords that still hovered over the rest of Kerrigan's brood. "Cerebrate," it called, addressing the nameless cerebrates whose brood Kerrigan now commanded, "you must eradicate the rampaging brood and stem any further damage it might cause." Daggoth's overlord twitched in what might have been fear. "I shall deal with the protoss myself."

"No," Kerrigan corrected, and the overlord froze in the act of turning away. "The High Templar is mine."

"We each must play our role, o Queen of Blades," Daggoth told her, and his words sounded suspiciously like a reprimand. Apparently Kerrigan thought so as well, and her wings swept up, grazing the overlord's sides and drawing a twitch of pain from it. "We must do as the Overmind might bid, were it to speak again."

"The High Templar is mine," she repeated softly, her words rolling with power. "You will handle Zasz's brood. I will find the protoss and teach them the error of their ways." Then she grinned. "The Overmind would approve this plan, were it still linked to us." To Raynor the last statement had the shape of a barb, reminding the cerebrate that he had no one to back him.

For a moment no one spoke, and Raynor could almost taste the tension. Would Daggoth prove to be another Zasz, he wondered, and defy Kerrigan's commands?

But Daggoth was an older cerebrate, and much wiser. "It shall be as you say," he declared finally. "My brood is in proximity to Zasz's own and will dispatch his raving subjects."

"Good." Kerrigan nodded. "When that is done, locate the protoss's craft and destroy it. I will not give him the option of escape." She turned away, wings furling, and Daggoth recognized the dismissal. His overlord flew off, presumably returning to the rest of its brood, leaving Kerrigan alone with her loyal zerg.

"Where have you gone, little Templar?" she whispered, her eyes narrowing. Raynor felt a strange pressure behind his eyes, and he thought he saw Kerrigan glance in his direction. Then the feeling moved on. "Ah," she sighed after a moment. "There you are." And she was off at a run, her wings flapping behind her and causing her feet to glide across the ground. Her brood moved with her, and in a moment Raynor was alone. He waited until he was sure they had all swept past before abandoning his hiding place and all pretenses of stealth and running after them.

The zerg ran for hours, seemingly tireless, leaping across small chasms and circling around larger crevices, before finally reaching a wide plateau that resembled the one on Antiga Prime where Raynor had first met Kerrigan. Tailing behind the zerg, drenched in sweat and gasping for breath, he skidded to a stop just in time to keep from falling onto the plateau as the last of the zerg jumped down.

The protoss were waiting for them.

This was the first group of protoss, one hundred strong, and they were arranged around the far edge of the plateau. Tassadar stood tall and proud before them, close to the center of the wide flat rock. His eyes were already locked upon Kerrigan, who had leaped down to the plateau first and was already stalking toward him, her wings spreading in anticipation.

"Trapped at last, little Templar," she hissed to him as she closed the distance. Her hands flexed, eager to carve into flesh, and her wings mimicked the gesture.

"This shall be our battleground, o Queen," Tassadar replied. "Face me here, and I will defeat you myself!" He did not step back or move at all as she closed the distance, and his large electric-blue eyes regarded her calmly as she paused perhaps five feet away.

"I face you now, little Templar," Kerrigan replied, baring her teeth at him, "and you face your doom!" She leaped forward, spinning as she did, and her wings spun around her, their blades whistling toward the Executor—

—and finding nothing but empty air. Tassadar was no longer there.

"Where?" Kerrigan wheeled about and spotted the High Templar the same time Raynor did. The protoss leader was now standing behind her, ten paces back, still looking unfazed. Raynor wasn't sure how he had moved so quickly, and Kerrigan didn't seem to care. She practically skipped across the distance, bounding up and spinning, then landing on one foot and leaping to spin again. It was beautiful, a ballet of death, her body transformed into a single whirling blade, and in the time it took to blink she had closed the gap and her blades had found flesh.

The flesh of a hydralisk, which collapsed in pieces, its body still twitching as the image of Tassadar faded from it.

"An illusion?" Kerrigan howled, turning back toward

the far end of the plateau, her eyes flicking across the assembled protoss warriors as she tried to locate her foe. Her lips pulled back in a sneer. "Are you afraid to face me, Templar?"

"So long as you continue to be so predictable, o Queen," Tassadar replied, "I need not face you at all. You are your own worst enemy." His voice echoed all around them but had no clear source, nor had his warriors moved when he spoke.

"You cannot hide from me, little protoss," Kerrigan warned him, her eyes narrowing. Raynor felt that same strange pressure and realized she was reaching out with her mind. After a few seconds she straightened from her crouch, focusing on one of the Zealots. "I know you are here," she called out, walking toward the warrior she had selected. "It does not matter that I cannot find you. You are a leader, little Templar, and you will not allow your men to come to harm." As she moved her wings stretched out behind her, and the sun's light caught upon them. Raynor thought he saw an iridescence stretch between her wing-blades, a sheen like a soap bubble linking the barbs and creating a faint skin across them. When he blinked it vanished, but after a second he saw it again.

Kerrigan had reached the warrior now, and she smiled at him. It was not a friendly smile. The protoss remained motionless, looking through her, arms crossed over his chest. She turned away as if to speak to her zerg, who waited impatiently where she had left them, and her left wing swept around as she turned, that sheen touching the warrior's neck. He did not make a sound as his eyes suddenly dimmed and his head toppled to the ground, rolling off the edge of the plateau. The body crumpled a second later, fountaining blood from its severed neck.

"Shall I kill another?" Kerrigan called out, smiling as she turned toward the next warrior in line. Her wings wriggled excitedly.

"Hold!" One of the warriors near the end of the line stepped forward, his armor and clothing changed as he moved, until Tassadar faced her. "Very well, o Queen. I am here. Now face me in battle."

"With pleasure," Kerrigan snarled, and launched herself at him.

Once again Raynor saw a strange layered image. He saw Kerrigan leap toward Tassadar, her wings lashing out at him, and saw the Executor dodge the blow. The protoss leader had no weapons and made no counterattack but Kerrigan pivoted away as if he had.

She spun again, the tip of one wing scraping across the Executor's chest and causing him to stumble. He allowed himself to fall, catching himself with one hand, and then kicked off the ground, pivoting up until he was upside down and supported on that hand before flipping back over and landing on his feet again.

Tassadar stepped forward, or tried to—suddenly he was hurled back into his warriors, who staggered but caught him and themselves before they fell off the plateau. This time Raynor thought he saw the Executor's eyes widen in surprise or perhaps pain. Or both.

Tassadar was suddenly tugged forward again, limbs flailing against air, until his face was inches from Kerrigan's. He swept his arms around, fists aimed for her head, but her wings blocked the blow and pinned him in midair like an enormous bug trapped in a spider's web.

That was what Raynor saw. But not *all* he saw. Because superimposed on that was another sequence of events, similar but grander, more electrifying, and more unnerving.

Kerrigan leaped toward Tassadar, her wings out, that rainbow sheen between them. Tassadar's body was suddenly enveloped by a blue glow similar to the one Raynor had seen around the protoss ship.

The Executor spun, raising one arm to block, and sparks flew as iridescence and blue lightning collided. His other arm lashed out and across in a solid backhand, blue flickers arcing behind it, and Kerrigan stepped back, her wings floating up to avoid that glow.

She moved in again, pivoting so one wing raked across him, and though he threw up both arms to block the blow the impact still hurled him backward, his glow dimming slightly.

Tassadar fell and flipped over, using Kerrigan's blow as momentum and one hand for support. As he moved, his right foot lashed out toward her head, the glow around that limb intensifying and extending outward like a blade. She jerked to one side, however, and the blow missed her.

Then her wings flexed and snapped forward, as if tossing something, and the iridescence shot forward like strands of a web, catching the Executor in the chest.

Kerrigan leaned back, her wings sweeping behind her, and the strands remained, yanking Tassadar forward. His glow grew weaker, particularly at the point of contact. He tried to lash out with both hands, focusing the glow there until his fists shone like twin beacons, but Kerrigan's wings blocked the attack. More sparks flew, and iridescence from the wings wrapped around the Executor's wrists, binding him tightly.

Then Kerrigan raised her wings and Tassadar rose with them like a puppet on taut strings. His glow had faded further and was almost gone except for a faint halo around the head.

"Now I have you, little Templar," Kerrigan purred, gazing up at her captive. "What shall I do with you?" she pondered theatrically, one finger resting on her chin, her other hand on her hip. After a moment she nodded. "Death, I think, but not too quickly." Then, as if for the first time, Kerrigan noticed the other protoss, who were still standing motionless around the plateau's edge. "Oh yes, I'd forgotten them," she commented. She glanced over her shoulder to her brood. "Kill them," she commanded. "Kill them all."

The zerg had been pacing and shifting and fluttering, clearly under orders and impatient to attack but unwilling to disobey. Now, with their queen's permission, they charged, their bloodlust no longer held in check. Raynor saw a mutalisk dive toward a protoss, its mouth open as it flew, and then it was past the warrior and circling back around. The acid it had spit at him as it went past ate through the warrior's armor, though his flesh, and apparently even through his bones, causing the body to collapse in pieces like a loose jigsaw puzzle. A pair of hydralisks had descended upon another and zerglings were everywhere, snapping and biting at limbs and preventing the warriors from blocking any attacks.

I've got to help them, Raynor decided, still watching from his safe location just above the plateau's near end. *Otherwise Kerrigan's brood will slaughter them all.* But what could he do? He had his pistol but no rifle, no armor, and no backup. He cursed himself for not taking the combat armor—it would have eliminated any chance at stealth but he could have kept up more easily and he'd have some firepower now, when he needed it.

Raynor glanced around desperately, looking for anything that could help, and his eyes passed along several of Kerrigan's brood floating a short distance above the others. Mutalisks, overlords, and scourge waited in the air for their queen to call them to battle. The small, fast-moving scourge had barely enough energy to go a few hours without sustenance, so they were perched in rows along the backs of the three overlords that floated in a rough line on the other side of the square, eagerly awaiting the command to launch themselves at the enemy.

Something about that arrangement struck Raynor oddly, and he glanced back again, but couldn't figure out what was bugging him. Instead he shifted his gaze to stare at the zerg ground forces, who were making short work of the protoss. The protoss warriors were taller, stronger, and much faster than the average Terran, let alone the zerg, and their armor was proof against at least glancing blows from zerg claws while their energy blades could cut through the tough zerg hide with ease. In a fair fight, the protoss would win easily. But right now they were severely outnumbered, the zerg using that advantage to swamp the protoss, three or four zerg attacking each warrior. Almost half the protoss were down already, and it would not be long before the rest followed.

Raynor wished there were something he could do. He liked the protoss—well, at least he admired and respected them. And he needed all the allies he could get these days. There had to be some way to even the odds. But that would require heavy equipment, which was back at the camp, or high explosives, which they used sparingly, and—

At the thought of explosives Raynor whipped his head back around to stare at the zerg fighters, particularly those overlords. That was it, he realized. The cerebrate who answered to Kerrigan, the new, namless one, lacked Daggoth's or even Zasz's experience. This new cerebrate hadn't known to keep his forces well apart, particularly the airborne ones.

Raynor drew his pistol and steadied it on a rock before him. He took careful aim, letting his breath in slowly and letting it out again just as slowly, lined up the sights—

—and fired.

He let loose with three rapid bursts, not sure that would be enough. But it was.

The first shot struck the farthest overlord, causing it to writhe in pain. His second burst missed because of the creature's motion but the third hit right near the first, widening its already gaping wound. Stunned by the sudden attack from nowhere, the overlord reeled back, unable to control its flight—

—and slammed into the overlord beside it.

Crushing the resting scourge between them.

The explosion threw Raynor back, his pistol slamming into his cheek and leaving him with a ringing head and a throbbing face. But the devastation on the plateau was far worse. The scourge were the zerg's suicide bombers, bred to explode upon impact. They detonated with enough force to destroy a shuttle or a fighter craft, and a handful of them could breach a starship hull. This had been a row of them, the explosion from the first adding to the impact on the others, and there was nothing here but flesh and bone. And the hard rock of the plateau reflected the blast back up, causing even more damage to those stuck upon it.

The zerg caught the worst of it. There were more of them, and they had less outward protection than the armored protoss. Zerglings were shredded by the explosion, as were the other two overlords. The mutalisks and hydralisks and ultralisks had thicker hides, but still those closest to the blast were torn apart, while those farther away were battered and bruised and broken.

Not that the protoss escaped unscathed. The explosion caught them by surprise as well, and several of them were hurled from the plateau, smashing into the rocks below. Those closest to the blast center were shredded, armor and flesh both, and all of them were tossed about like leaves on a strong wind.

Not even Kerrigan escaped.

Her back had been to her brood, all her attention focused on her captive, and the blast had caught her full force, knocking her to her knees, her wings lancing forward like a spider's legs to keep her from being smashed into the rock.

The movement had released Tassadar, who had also been tossed back but had caught himself with one hand on the plateau's lip. He hung there a moment, then swung the other arm up and, with an impressive heave, flipped forward, uncoiling as he did so he landed standing and facing the chaos.

For an instant the Executor studied the scene, his eyes flicking up once to where Raynor had crawled back to the ledge to watch what happened. He thought he saw Tassadar nod at him. Then the High Templar must have signaled his troops, because those warriors still alive and mobile grabbed up their fallen comrades and sprinted to the edge. For another second they paused there, silhouetted against the rocks beyond. Then as one the protoss dove forward, disappearing into the gorge below.

"No!" Kerrigan howled, wings flexing and thrusting her back to her feet. She was staring at the spot where Tassadar had stood before he jumped. "You cannot escape me so easily, little Templar!" And she ran to the edge, wings flapping behind her, and leaped off, half-gliding and half-falling as she pursued her quarry.

Her brood, those who had survived, gathered themselves and followed her, climbing or jumping or flying down as necessary. In a moment they were gone, and Raynor was left alone again, looking out on the devastation he had caused.

"Not bad for a day's work," he admitted, grinning as he rubbed gingerly at the bruise along his cheek. He'd saved the Executor's life, at least for the moment, and several of his warriors as well. If that didn't buy him some points with them nothing would. He wanted to collapse for a while—he was still exhausted from running after Kerrigan, and now he was battered from the explosion as well. But he knew he had to keep the brood in his sights.

"Okay, okay," he muttered to himself, holstering his pistol and climbing to his feet. Then, with a sigh, he began picking his way as fast as he could down to the plateau and to the gorge below, straining eyes and ears for any hint of the aliens he was determined to follow.

CHAPTER 13

FORTUNATELY FOR RAYNOR, KERRIGAN WAS NOT interested in concealing her whereabouts. Quite the opposite, in fact—she wanted Tassadar to know she was coming for him. Somehow she had summoned reinforcements, most likely claiming zerg from other broods, and her overlords and mutalisks and scourge flew overhead like vultures circling a kill, making it very easy to locate her.

Unfortunately, she was also moving very quickly. Far more quickly than an unarmored Terran could manage. Raynor again cursed himself for not wearing powered armor, and assured himself that he wouldn't make that mistake twice.

As it was, he found himself chasing the brood that was chasing the protoss, knowing he wouldn't be able to catch up until they stopped. Which meant he would probably reach them after the fight was over. He wasn't sure what point there was to arriving so late on the scene, but felt compelled to follow anyway. Maybe

Tassadar could hold his own long enough for Raynor to arrive, though he wasn't sure what a single pistol could do if a unit of protoss warriors were in trouble. He doubted Kerrigan or her cerebrate subordinate would fall for the same trick twice. But he knew he had to watch what happened. Maybe it was just that, despite everything, he still felt a need to be close to Kerrigan and to keep an eye on her. Or maybe he felt someone should at least witness her atrocities.

Kerrigan was fast but so were the protoss, and Tassadar had apparently decided that he needed time to regroup and to study what he'd learned so far. The Executor and his troops had vanished, leaving Kerrigan to howl with rage and scrape her claws and wings against the surrounding rocks, leaving deep gouges in their surface. Raynor could hear her shrieks two valleys away, and slowed his pace. This wouldn't be a good time to burst in on her and her brood, not when they were so clearly out for blood. In the absence of their real quarry they would probably take him as an acceptable substitute.

As he picked his way over the rocks, however, the howls and curses suddenly stopped. Had he been spotted somehow? He thought he was too far away for the overlords and other airborne zerg to notice, but he wasn't exactly sure how good their vision was. He flattened himself against a rock anyway, and then froze, listening hard.

"What have we here?" It was Kerrigan, and she was all but purring now. Damn! That had to mean she'd spotted prey, and he didn't think it was Tassadar. Raynor's hand edged toward his pistol. If the brood did come after him he'd take down as many as he could. Not that it would make much difference, but at least he wouldn't die feeling useless.

"Not the Templar, no," Kerrigan was saying to herself, and the scrape of bone on rock indicated that she was moving. Were the sounds getting louder, or was that just his imagination? "But equally as good," she decided. Raynor could hear her delight.

"Come out, little one," she purred now. "Come out and play. My brood is hungry for blood, and yours calls to us. Come out, little protoss. Show me why you smell different from your kin."

Protoss? Raynor let out a sigh. It wasn't him after all. But wait—smelled different? That had to be the other protoss he'd seen, the strange one that had killed Zasz.

Zeratul.

The scraping continued but was no longer getting louder, and Raynor risked stepping away from the boulder and glancing around. The zerg were still one valley over. He crawled up the hill, cursing softly as he put his hand too close to a steam vent, and paused near the top, using a small boulder for cover.

Kerrigan was standing down below, in the narrow rock basin of the valley. Her zerg were all around her, chittering angrily about the delay and excitedly about the prospect of new prey. He could see them clearly from here and could easily make out Kerrigan's wings, which were curling and uncurling with barely contained glee. She was facing a cavern at the valley's edge, and it seemed her words were directed toward that dark space.

Raynor saw nothing, but after a moment Kerrigan nodded. "Do not bother to cloak yourself, little protoss," she warned the empty air. "For I can sense you though I cannot see you. Show yourself to me."

Zeratul appeared before her, not forty paces away, his Dark Templar behind him. They must have used the same trick Raynor had seen them do before, when they went after Zasz, blending into their surroundings. It hadn't fooled Kerrigan, but the Dark Templar didn't look too concerned. In fact, Zeratul nodded at her as he stepped forward, a gesture that spoke of respect for an equal.

"Greetings, o Queen of the Zerg," the protoss intoned, his words echoing in Raynor's head. Just as before there was something dry and brittle about them, but at the same time they hummed with restrained power. "I am Zeratul, Praetor of the Dark Templar." He actually bowed to her, a deep, graceful bow from the waist, which seemed to amuse Kerrigan. "Your coming has been foretold."

"Has it?" she asked, and even from here Raynor could see the smile on her lips just as easily as he heard it in her voice. "And what do they say of me, Praetor?"

"You are a part of the culmination," the protoss replied. "But not the end of it." His eyes glowed brightly, and Kerrigan seemed almost transfixed by them. Her entire brood was motionless, held in thrall by the Praetor's gaze and words. "You shall show the way, the path that must be taken, the realigning of old truths no longer valid," he intoned, and to Raynor it sounded as if the protoss was reading from a text somewhere, or reciting holy scripture. "Yours is not the hand, but your very existence provides necessary instruction."

"The culmination," Kerrigan repeated. She raised her hands and stared at them, fingers fully extended, claws glistening in the fading sunset light. "And these are not the hands." Then she glanced up at Zeratul and her smile returned, widening into a predatory grin. "But even if these are not the hands, Praetor, at least they will be the culmination of your life." Then she was moving, bounding forward and swiping outward with both hands as if tearing apart a curtain—or a body.

Any human would have been ripped to shreds by the oncoming attack, Raynor knew, and he shuddered. For that matter, he suspected most protoss would have been carved open just as easily, Kerrigan's claws piercing their thick hide and glittering armor like tissue paper. Zeratul's flesh seemed no different, and no more protected.

But he was not there when her blows arrived.

Instead he had twisted away, dancing back in a strange shadowy blur, and from his wrists projected those glittering green blades he had used to end Zasz.

"So be it," he announced, his words ringing across

the rocks and making several zerg crumple to the ground, writhing. "We shall battle."

And then the battle began.

As with Kerrigan and Tassadar, Raynor saw two separate fights overlaid, the combatants matched in location and position but not in their actions. He was dimly aware that the zerg had been freed from their paralysis when Kerrigan attacked and that they were battling the other Dark Templar, but his eyes stayed locked on the two leaders and their private duel. Even the other zerg stayed clear of that conflict, respecting their mistress's wish for an undisturbed fight.

Zeratul sprang toward her, flipping over her as he approached, his blades stabbing downward. Her wings blocked the strike, however, fanning over her head so their spikes caught his blades and shoved them away. Then her wings snapped up, the tips poised to pierce him on both sides. But Zeratul twisted, and they could not find purchase as he sailed past. He landed behind her, pivoting to face her, arms raised and ready.

The sun slipped just below the horizon now, and the shadows lengthened, one of them enveloping the Praetor. The darkness thickened around him, wrapping over him protectively until only his glowing eyes could be seen clearly. Raynor strained to pierce that shroud and could just make out the Praetor's blades as patches of dim light, a marginally weaker shadow against the whole.

If the shadows bothered Kerrigan, she gave no sign of it. Instead she spun toward her foe, her wings lashing out again, carving open the darkness as they struck. An unwholesome yellowish glow had sprung up around her, enveloping every spur and spike and talon, and that glow chased away the darkness, leaving streaks of normal twilight amid the shadow.

Zeratul was not idle, however. He skirted his opponent, edging through the darkness, but the shadows did seem to confuse Kerrigan, who did not react to his changed position. When he was parallel to her he struck again, one arm sweeping down and the other up to trap her uppermost wing-blade between them.

Kerrigan screamed with rage and pain as the blow connected. Her wings reacted of their own accord, flexing, and Zeratul was knocked aside. He stumbled back, almost losing his footing, but recovered. The wings stabbed toward him, their tips aiming for his glowing eyes, and he barely blocked them, both blades rising and crossing each other. He caught the lowest wing-blade in that intersection and forced it up, sweeping the others along with it. Then, when his arms were fully extended and the wing high above his head, Zeratul whipped both arms up and around, driving his blades toward Kerrigan's unprotected torso.

He had not reckoned with her other wing, however. Kerrigan turned to face him, her second wing curling protectively around her, and Zeratul's blades glanced harmlessly off them. Then they flared outward, the tips angling down to pierce his extended arms. Raynor felt the Praetor shudder with pain and knew the protoss had bitten back a telepathic scream.

Now Kerrigan's other wing descended as well, piercing the Praetor's shoulder, and he was pinned between her wings, unable to free his arms enough to raise his blades. Blood dripped from the puncture points as Kerrigan lifted him up, held securely between her wings and stretched sideways before her.

"You fight well, little protoss," she admitted, idly running one finger along the wing he had struck before and licking off the blood or ichor that coated it. "Better than your Executor counterpart. But I am the Queen of Blades!" She leaned in so their faces were inches apart. "You cannot best me!"

"Battles are not fought by strength alone," the protoss told her, no longer struggling against her wings. "You are powerful, yes, but not invincible."

"I have beaten you," she pointed out, and Zeratul chuckled in reply, his body shaking slightly from the laughter. If moving like that with her wing-tips embedded in his flesh hurt, the Praetor gave no indication.

"You have won this battle, yes," he agreed. "But this was merely our first encounter. The next may go differently."

"Next?" Kerrigan regarded him curiously, and Raynor could read her puzzlement. She had the protoss pinned and helpless, primed for the kill. "What 'next'? Your life is over, little protoss," she said, dragging one claw across his cheek and carving a thin furrow in the thick skin there. "I have but to move and you will be no more." She glanced behind her, and Raynor looked around as well, seeing the rest of the valley for the first time since the battle had started. The floor was littered with zerg bodies, but here and there a protoss lay among them as well. Zeratul had started with perhaps a hundred Dark Templar. Now he had maybe half that number, and they were badly outnumbered.

"Your forces are overmatched," Kerrigan pointed out, turning to glance at Zeratul again. "My brood will destroy the last of them, just as I will slay you. Char will be rid of your Dark Templar, and you with them. Tell me, then, where and how will this next encounter take place? The protoss equivalent of Heaven?"

Zeratul seemed unfazed by his situation, or that of his troops. "You are overconfident," he warned his captor. "Such a fault is common in the young and powerful. It leads to dangerous assumptions, however, and in those assumptions you expose yourself."

Now Kerrigan's smile turned to a frown, and she bared her teeth. "Do not lecture me!" she shouted, spittle flying from her mouth—Raynor noticed that several drops struck her protoss captive and burned into his skin. "I am no weakling, no youth untrained in the arts of war! I am the Queen of Blades! And I am your death!"

Her wings plunged toward one another, intent upon skewering Zeratul between them.

But just as she moved, the darkness, held at bay by her glow and by the last glimmer of the setting sun, descended upon them like a heavy blanket. Zeratul vanished within its embrace, utterly consumed by the night.

And Kerrigan's wing-blades clattered against one

another as they collided, unimpeded by the body they had held not an instant before.

"No!" Kerrigan's scream was loud enough to echo across the landscape and shrill enough to shatter stone. Raynor clutched at his ears, sure blood was dripping from them, but unable to look away from the scene below. How had Zeratul done that? One second he had been pinned like a fly by a spider; the next he was gone.

Or was he? Raynor thought he saw a faint flicker within the shadows next to Kerrigan, tiny specks that might have been the Praetor's eyes. Just below those he thought he saw a second, longer flicker, like Zeratul's energy blades, though perhaps that was just his eyes playing tricks on him. What he did see, however, was the rest of the Dark Templar fading back into the shadows after their leader, leaving the zerg alone on the battlefield, stabbing at shadows and coming up empty. The protoss had vanished into the night. Even their fallen warriors were gone, spirited away by the others. It was as if the fight had never occurred, save for the evidence of the zerg bodies piled here and there upon the ground.

"You protoss are cowards!" Kerrigan shouted, wings flaring up behind her. Their tips still glistened with Zeratul's blood. "I have bested both of you, and both of you have fled like frightened dogs! Stand and fight me! Face your defeat and your death like true warriors!" But her words received no reply. Enraged, she turned and attacked a nearby rock, her wings slicing into it and then wrenching free, shattering the boulder in a cloud of dust and rock chips. Even that did not slake her rage, however, and as she turned toward her brood several of them shrank back, cowed by their mistress's bloodlust. Raynor ducked back as well, glad he was safe up on the hilltop. Even if she spotted him he could run and probably disappear into the next valley before her brood could reach him. At least he hoped so.

Kerrigan continued to curse her protoss opponents, insulting their honor and courage, but if she hoped to incite them to attack it did not work. After railing for several minutes and scoring the valley walls with her claws, she gave up. As she stood there, chest heaving from her exertions, hands clenched into fists, wings raised behind her, Raynor thought she had never been more beautiful. Or more deadly.

"What shall we do now, mistress?" one of the overlords asked, drifting closer but wisely staying beyond the range of her wings, and Raynor knew it was the cerebrate asking through his minion.

"We hunt," she snarled back. "Char is ours. These protoss cannot hide forever. We will find them and we will kill them all. Then we will display their bodies from the highest peak, that all might know what happens to anyone who crosses me!"

"Which shall we target first?" the overlord asked. "The ones who just escaped or the ones we fought earlier?"

"We hunt them both," Kerrigan replied, a small smile touching her lips. "Summon the rest of the brood," she instructed, her wings curling around her again like a cloak. "Summon them all. We will sweep across this world and annihilate any who stand against us." She glanced upward, directly at Raynor, and he knew she was talking to him. She knew he was there! And she was telling him that he and his people were just as much a target as the protoss.

I've got to get out of here, Raynor realized, shifting back behind the boulder. *I've got to get back to base and warn the others. We need to get ready. Kerrigan's just declared war on us all.*

But before he could move, he heard an unwelcome sound. Chittering and clacking and hissing, the sound of spikes and claws rubbing against rock and taloned feet scrabbling on stone. The zerg were coming. And they were coming from the next valley over, directly toward him.

Kerrigan and her zerg were in front of him, and reinforcements were coming at him from behind. He was trapped!

CHAPTER 14

RAYNOR LOOKED AROUND FOR ANY SORT OF cover. But the hill had little to offer beyond the rock he was already using. As on most of Char, the ground here had been subjected to countless lava flows from the volcanoes that dotted the landscape, and the hill was still covered by thick layers that resembled hardened syrup. The material was not particularly strong—more than once he'd put his boot through it while trying to climb—and out of desperation he drew his pistol and began using the butt to break a hole through the lava right by the boulder. In a few minutes he had carved out a small gap, exposing a slightly larger pocket below it, and wedged himself inside. Curled into a ball, he just fit, his head an inch below the rest of the hill. The boulder cast its shadow down upon him, which he hoped would help. Then there was nothing he could do but wait, and pray to anyone he thought might listen.

The sounds of the zerg grew louder as they approached, and he tried to push himself farther into the ground, sure that at any moment one of the brood would spot him and alert the rest. Then they'd dig him out of the ground like a carrot in his mother's garden and—he cut the thought off before it could explore the gruesome possibilities.

Now the zerg were on the hill itself, and he was sure he felt the lava around him trembling from their weight and motion. He didn't dare move his head and tried to ignore the prickling at the back of his neck that warned him he'd already been spotted.

"Cerebrate," he heard one of the zerg hiss, and the voice was uncomfortably close, "what is that, over there? By the—"

"Daggoth!" The shout cut off the zerg's question, and Raynor recognized the voice instantly. Kerrigan. She was still in the valley, from the way the sound echoed. "Greetings, Cerebrate! Come and speak with me, you and all your brood. I have strange tidings."

"As do I, Queen of Blades," the cerebrate replied. There was a strange reverberation to his voice, and Raynor realized that Daggoth was talking through an overlord somewhere on the hill. Of course the massive creature could not travel across Char's surface itself. "I and mine shall attend you."

The chittering and hissing and clattering increased, ringing in Raynor's ears, and then dulled as the brood climbed over the hill and down into the valley below. He couldn't believe his luck. That zerg had spotted him, he was sure of it, and it had been about to reveal his location to the others. Kerrigan had saved him. He felt a strange tug at his heart as he slowly unfolded from his hole and crept back onto the lava's surface, still sheltered by the boulder. Had she known he was there? Was her timing simply a happy accident, or had it been intentional?

He peered into the valley again. It was filled to bursting with zerg now as Kerrigan's and Daggoth's broods mingled. Kerrigan herself still stood near the center, and Daggoth's overlord hovered not far from her.

"Tassadar is not the only Templar on Char," Kerrigan informed Daggoth, her wings twitching as if impatient to resume the hunt. "There is another, Zeratul." She paused. "He is different," she admitted after a moment, her brows furrowing in thought. "Different from Tassadar and from any protoss I have heard of, indeed from any the zerg have encountered before. More powerful, but darker, much darker." Then she grinned. "Still, he was no match for me. Only guile saved him, and it will not again. We need—"

"Hold, o Queen," Daggoth interrupted, and even from here Raynor saw Kerrigan's eyes narrow. She'd never liked having people cut her off and obviously that hadn't changed. "There are more important matters at hand than your pursuit of these protoss."

Her wings curled slightly but Kerrigan showed no other sign of her anger. "What matters, Daggoth?" Her tone was barely polite, but there was more civility in it than she had bothered to offer Zasz. It was clear she respected this cerebrate far more than the other zerg she had dealt with thus far.

"There is the matter of Zasz's death," Daggoth pointed out. "None before have accomplished such a feat, severing a cerebrate's ties to the Overmind. We must assay how this was done that we may guard against it in future."

Kerrigan nodded. "Yes, this matter is one of great concern. What have we learned of the event?"

"The Overmind itself it studying the matter," Daggoth replied. "Hence its recent silence. Soon it will speak to us once again and unravel this mystery for us." His voice shifted, becoming more serene, even satisfied. "As for Zasz's brood, they are no longer a threat."

"Good." But Kerrigan was still focused on the protoss she had been pursuing. "And what of the protoss ship?"

"We have eliminated them," Daggoth assured her, earning a sharp look. Was that surprise on Kerrigan's face?

"'Them'?" she asked, but then she nodded. "Ah yes, of course. These new protoss did not arrive with Tassadar, thus they had their own ship."

"Both craft have been destroyed," Daggoth repeated, and Raynor fought back a stab of panic. He'd been counting on convincing Tassadar to give them a lift off this ashball. Now the protoss were stuck here too! And even Zeratul was stranded—the only people who could leave now were the zerg!

As he was pondering his drastically reduced options,

Raynor heard a strange thrum fill the air. Every zerg in the valley went utterly silent in an instant, all but the overlords going still as well. In the calm Raynor thought he could hear steam venting from somewhere nearby, and the distant roar of a volcanic eruption.

Then the silence was shattered by a voice, that horrible, oily voice that slid through his head and sent shivers through his bones, the one that caused his eyes to roll back and his throat to seize up. It was the zerg ruler, the Overmind.

"Behold," it called out, its words making the rocks tremble, "my long silence is now broken, and I am made whole once more!" Its exultation was almost unbearable, and Raynor sank to his knees, head clasped in his hands. "The cunning protoss have dared strike down that which was immortal," the Overmind stated, each word a clear pronouncement of doom for such audacity. "For the protoss who murdered Zasz are unlike anything we have faced before. These Dark Templar radiate energies that are much like my own. And it is by these energies that they have caused me harm." Now Raynor understood, through his own pain, why the Overmind sounded so outraged. The loss of a zerg, any zerg, was inconsequential. But the attack on Zasz had hurt the Overmind as well, and for that it was furious.

The zerg below shared its fury, and despite their continued stillness Raynor could feel the tension welling up from the valley. When the Overmind released them they would burst into a killing frenzy.

He knew he'd have to be far away by that point or risk being their first victim.

"Yet," the Overmind continued, and suddenly its tone changed from rage back to joy, "yet shall their overweening pride be their downfall!" Even Raynor listened intently, curious but dreading to learn what could have made the zerg leader so excited. "For when the assassin, Zeratul, murdered Zasz," the Overmind announced, "his mind touched with mine, and all his secrets were made known to me." Now the Overmind's voice soared, its sheer power driving a spike through Raynor's head and causing blood to run out his ears and nose. "I have taken from his mind the secret location of Aiur—the protoss homeworld!"

Even the zerg below seemed confused by this, though Raynor could feel their excitement as well. Whatever made the Overmind happy made them happy, and right now the Overmind was ecstatic.

Fortunately the Overmind was quick to explain the cause of its glee. "At long last, my children," it told the assembled zerg, "our searching is done. Soon we shall assault Aiur directly!"

And now Raynor understood. He had known from the first encounter on Mar Sara that the protoss hated the zerg with a consuming passion. It had never occurred to him that the feeling might be mutual, but apparently it was. The zerg hated the protoss right back, or at least the Overmind did—and all this time he'd been hunting for the protoss homeworld so he could attack it and destroy them once and for all. And now, thanks to Zeratul's attack, the Overmind knew its location.

Raynor wasn't quite sure how to feel about that. On the one hand, anything that turned the zerg away from humanity was a good thing. And the protoss had shown themselves capable of fighting off the zerg—what could an entire world of Tassadars and Zeratuls accomplish, especially when fighting on their home ground? On the other hand, the protoss would not be expecting an attack at home, and the zerg would appear without warning. He was sure the Overmind would send all his broods there at once, and he couldn't imagine that the protoss had the numbers to match the full Swarm. If the zerg wiped out the protoss, who would stand against them then? Who would protect humanity from their continued invasion?

Not that there was anything he could do about it. And not like he didn't have his own problems.

"Prepare yourself, my Swarm," the Overmind instructed. "We shall depart for Aiur at once."

"I wish to remain behind, father." It was Kerrigan who spoke, not surprisingly, though even her own zerg seemed startled at her insolence. "I have unfinished business with the High Templar Tassadar, and with this Zeratul."

"I would have you at the forefront of this invasion, my daughter," the Overmind told her, and though its words were gentle, the command behind them was unmistakable. Still Kerrigan was not cowed.

"I am honored, father," she replied, "and would

gladly participate in any capacity you deem appropriate. But surely someone must punish these protoss for daring to set foot upon our world, and for striking down our brother." She looked almost sorry about Zasz's death, and Raynor couldn't help but admire her skill. She was playing the role perfectly. "I would be that avenging hand, father. Give me leave to finish this matter and then join the Swarm on Aiur."

For an instant the silence stretched across the valley, and everyone, Raynor included, waited with bated breath to hear the Overmind's reply.

"Very well," it said finally, and the tension faded at once. "You may remain here, my daughter, to handle this matter. Upon its conclusion, however, I will expect you on Aiur to take over the leadership of our campaign there."

Kerrigan bowed, her wings sweeping down to brush the ground. "It shall be as you command, father," she replied, her voice that of the obedient servant, though the smile on her face showed that she had gotten exactly what she wanted.

The thrum vanished, leaving Raynor gasping with relief as the pressure in his head faded, and the zerg below began moving once more.

"Will you require assistance in your quest?" Daggoth asked Kerrigan through his overlord. Something in the tone suggested that he already knew her answer.

"My thanks, noble Daggoth," she replied, "but I am more than capable of destroying these meddlesome protoss myself." She nodded toward his overlord. "You may rejoin the rest of the Swarm and prepare for the departure to Aiur." It was an obvious dismissal.

The cerebrate did not take offense, or if he did he concealed his emotions well. "Very well" was all he said as his brood gathered itself behind his overlord. Raynor crouched, ready to duck back into his hole if necessary, but Daggoth's zerg turned toward the opposite side of the valley instead and he relaxed. "May your hunt prove fruitful," the cerebrate called back as his brood disappeared into the valleys beyond. "And may you join us quickly in our attack on the hated protoss homeworld."

"I do not join," Kerrigan muttered, watching the other brood's departure. "I lead." Her words were soft, but loud enough for Raynor to hear.

"Now," Kerrigan called out after the last of Daggoth's zerg were gone from sight, "the hunt continues." She turned, scanning the hill, and for an instant her eyes pierced Raynor where he watched. "My prey will never know what hit them." Raynor had the sinking feeling she wasn't referring to the protoss.

Enough of this, he thought. Moving quickly, he crawled backward down the hill until he was sure he couldn't be seen by the zerg in the valley. Then he turned and half-ran, half-skidded the rest of the way, hitting the ground at the hill's base hard enough to go tumbling. He righted himself quickly and broke out into a dead run, heading straightaway from the zerg as fast as he could manage. He'd seen plenty, and had learned even more today. It was time to get the hell out of here, before his luck ran out and they came for him as well. All this information wouldn't do him and his crew much good if he got killed before he could tell them about it.

As he ran Raynor considered everything that had happened today. He'd seen both Tassadar and Zeratul go up against Kerrigan—and seen both protoss lose. He'd seen things he wasn't sure were real but didn't think were hallucinations, either, things that made no sense but felt right. He'd learned more about the zerg, their leaders' immortality, and their newfound weakness. And he'd found out what the zerg wanted most: the location and destruction of the protoss homeworld.

He'd also found out, unfortunately, that both protoss ships had been destroyed. Maybe they could be repaired. Maybe, he mused, the parts from one could be used on the other! The zerg weren't tech-minded—they probably hadn't paid much attention to parts as they attacked the ships. They might have done only superficial damage, or missed the vital components, like the engines. It was worth checking out.

Of course, that meant talking to the protoss. Both groups. And while Raynor thought Tassadar would at least hear him out, he wasn't sure about Zeratul. Something about the Dark Templar scared him a bit, like the ghost stories he'd heard as a child. But then, the zerg were worse than any horror tale, and they were plenty real. He'd gladly work with another, lesser nightmare to get himself and his people safely away from the Swarm.

But first, he had to find them.

CHAPTER 15

"SO ALL THE ZERG ARE GONE?"

That was the first thing Cavez asked after Raynor told him and Abernathy what he'd seen. Which he had not been able to do until the following evening, because by the time he'd dragged himself back to base it was morning, and he'd collapsed in his tent. He was just glad he'd made it inside first—the last mile or so it was all he could do to keep placing one foot in front of the other. Hell, it was all he could do to keep breathing. He'd slept like the dead for the rest of the day, waking up only once when someone set a canteen of water and a tray of food just outside the tent flap. By the time the sun had gone down he'd felt almost human again, and he'd taken only enough time to splash water on his face before finding his two lieutenants. He hadn't even dreamed, he'd been so tired, and he was surprised to realize that he was disappointed. The images of him and Kerrigan, so happy together in a life that could never exist, were deeply frustrating, yes, but at the same time so comforting that he hated missing an opportunity to experience them again, however fleetingly.

"Almost all," he corrected Cavez now. They were inside the shuttle again and he was leaning against one wall, a cup of steaming coffee cradled in his hands. The smell and the warmth were as welcome as the quick energy boost. He didn't sit down, because he couldn't trust himself to get back up again. "We've still got one brood to worry about," he reminded them. "And they're only interested in one thing—killing every non-zerg on this rock."

"But they're after the protoss, right?" Abernathy asked from where she was perched on a seat. "That's what you said—they want the protoss dead."

"They're gunning for the protoss, sure," Raynor agreed. "But that doesn't mean they'll leave us alone. Figure if they see both us and the protoss they'll go for the protoss, but if we're all they see they'll happily settle for us."

"We've got the combat armor," Cavez pointed out. "We can hold our own in a fight. And if it's only one brood we won't have to worry about reinforcements. We can whittle them down, wipe them out."

"That we could," Raynor agreed. "But what would it cost? How many would we lose?" He shook his head. "I'd rather get us off this ashball without a fight, if I can." He took a quick sip of his scalding coffee, then grinned. "Of course, if we have to fight we're gonna kick some butt."

"What do we do now, sir?" Abernathy looked worried, and Raynor didn't blame her. She was a good soldier and a competent leader, but going up against uncertainties was always tough. Raynor had seen plenty of this before. Give a soldier a weapon and a target and he was good to go. But tell him something vague like "Prove your worth" or "Protect this land" and he ran into trouble. Soldiers needed specifics, who and what and where and when. And unfortunately Raynor didn't have that to offer. But he hadn't been a soldier—he'd been a marshal. He'd had to think on his feet and work with loose definitions and create his own specifics. He could do that again.

"Go over all our gear, all our supplies, all our weapons and armor," he told them now. "Start stockpiling food and water, but nothing we can't carry. Break down what we've got into small parcels and assign each one to a trooper. I want us ready and able to ditch this camp at a moment's notice." It might come to that, he knew. If the zerg spotted the shuttle they'd converge on it, and even with the armor he and his men couldn't handle an entire brood. They'd be better off leaving this place behind and disappearing into the mountains or the hills or the valleys, just as the protoss had.

The protoss. That was the second priority, right after keeping his crew safe. "We need to find those protoss," he said, thinking out loud. "Doesn't matter which of them we find, though I'd rather it was Tassadar. I've met him already, and maybe he's not the friendliest guy in the world but he didn't shoot me, either. That counts for something." He grinned at Cavez and Abermathy. "Can't just steal their ships, especially not when they outnumber us. We'll ask for a ride instead."

"Both of their ships were destroyed," Cavez reminded him.

"Maybe, maybe not," Raynor replied. "We'll need to check each one out, see just how badly it's been beat. We might be able to salvage some parts."

"Even if those ships are crippled," Abernathy said, "we might be able to jury-rig their engines to work on our shuttle."

They all glanced around them, considering the small craft. It had survived the descent surprisingly well, the hull still intact. One engine and one wing were gone, the other engine was badly damaged, but if they could rig a protoss engine to her she could fly. Maybe.

"It's worth a try," Raynor agreed. "First things first. We look for the protoss and offer to team up." He noticed Cavez's shudder. "Something wrong, son?"

"I just don't like the thought of teaming with aliens, sir," the young lieutenant replied.

"Me either," Raynor admitted. "But right now we need help to get off this planet, and I'd sleep with a rabid dog if I thought it would help."

"Do you think they'll help us?" Abernathy asked him as they stood up and made their way back out of the shuttle.

"Don't know," he admitted to her, downing the rest of his coffee in a single long gulp. "But I plan to put on my best manners and ask."

• • •

It took Raynor almost a week to locate the protoss again. They had gone to ground, both groups, evading Kerrigan and her zerg. Several times Raynor caught a glimpse of a protoss warrior gliding past along a mountain ledge, or stalking silently past a small volcano, or racing across the ash deserts. But each time it was only a glimpse, and when he looked again the protoss was gone. The zerg were apparently having as little success, and more than once he heard Kerrigan howling with rage, or saw score marks where she'd vented her displeasure on the rocks. He kept his men on full alert, four men in combat armor on guard at all times. Raynor had commandeered a suit for himself as well, and found it much easier now to race around the planet hunting the elusive aliens.

Finally, as he was perched atop one of the taller mountains scanning the horizon, a small splash of color caught Raynor's eye. Focusing on that area, he used the armor's targeting system to isolate and enhance the image. As he watched, the tiny splash magnified, details appearing until he could see it clearly. It was a protoss warrior, and the color he had noticed was the blue-white gleam of the armored shoulders. Now, though, he could see the blue color below that, and the blue cloth covering the groin. It was Tassadar.

"Gotcha," Raynor whispered. He leaped down from his peak, the armor's servos absorbing the shock easily, and bounded toward the Executor, who was now locked into his targeting system. The armor allowed

Raynor to race through the mountains as if he were merely jogging easily along a beach, and within minutes he had closed most of the distance. Every time he crossed a peak or ridge he glanced toward Tassadar again, making sure the protoss leader had not moved, and as he drew closer Raynor saw more and more of the protoss gathered in the small valley there. He had apparently found the current Templar camp.

He slowed his pace when he was only one ridge away, not wanting to startle the protoss. They were being hunted by the zerg, after all, and would probably react to any intrusion as a threat. His armor made him considerably more dangerous, but he wasn't sure he was a match for a protoss warrior, even so—certainly not for all of them at once. Besides, he wasn't here to fight. He paused to give himself a minute to think about what he was doing here. He wanted to talk. Tassadar had reacted to his emotions before, he was sure of that now, and would probably do the same here. He still felt a little anger at the protoss for destroying his ships but most of that had faded. He understood their reasons, and agreed with them. He'd have done the same thing. Now he was just determined to get his people—those who remained—to safety. And he needed the aliens' help to do that.

Convinced that he was now calm and as friendly as he was going to get, Raynor hauled himself up the last ridge and looked down into the small valley—just in time to see the last protoss vaulting the peak on the opposite side. They were gone.

"Aw, not again!" he muttered. leaping quickly down into the valley and charging across it. He jumped to the top of the far peak and saw the Zealots a short ways ahead of him, clearly on the move. Their energy blades were not extended and their armor looked the same as always, but something about their posture, the way they were moving, convinced Raynor—they were heading for battle.

"My timing sucks," he told himself, hurrying along behind them. He'd wanted to talk, and obviously that wasn't going to happen now, not when they were in a combat mind-set. They'd probably kill him out of reflex before he could manage a word. He couldn't afford to lose sight of them, though—it might take another week to find them again, and the zerg could stumble upon his camp at any time. He couldn't risk that. So he played the shadowing game, staying just close enough to watch and tail the protoss but keeping far enough back that he hoped they wouldn't notice him.

Maybe, Raynor thought as he stalked behind them, he could lend them a hand against the zerg. That might convince them he was an ally and make them more inclined to help him. Yeah. The more he thought about that, the more he liked the idea. He'd been itching to go up against the zerg now that he had armor again, anyway, to pay them back for all the men he'd lost down in the caverns, not to mention the ships. This would be a good opportunity for that. He could vent some of his frustrations, show the zerg humans weren't as helpless as they thought, and get in good with the protoss at the same time. It was a good plan.

And, like most good plans, it didn't survive contact with the enemy.

In this case, it was the enemy that was the problem. Because as Raynor clambered out of one crevice and saw the protoss warriors slowing as they crossed a wide plateau before and slightly above him, he also saw their opponents for the first time.

And it wasn't the zerg.

"Hail, Tassadar, High Templar and Executor of the Protoss," Zeratul called out as his Dark Templar arrayed themselves around him—he was standing near the back end of the plateau, facing the way the Templar had come. The strange protoss's mental voice was as dry as ever, but this time it lacked much of the power it had held when Zeratul had confronted Kerrigan. At least it didn't make Raynor's head ring as he found himself a good vantage point along the ridge bordering the plateau and settled back to watch.

"Dark Templar," Tassadar replied, coming to a halt several body lengths from his counterpart. His voice carried a strange hint of—was that disgust? It was different from the tone Raynor heard when Tassadar spoke to Kerrigan or mentioned the zerg. That had been more recognizable as hatred. This sounded less angry but more . . . bitter? "I felt your presence," Tassadar continued as his own Zealots settled in behind him, and Raynor noticed that their positions matched those of the Dark Templar. He wondered if it was deliberate.

"I am Zeratul, Praetor of the Dark Templar," Zeratul announced. They were the same words he had used to introduce himself to Zasz, Raynor remembered, but how different they sounded now! Then it had been a declaration of opposition, the bold proclamation of a warrior facing sworn enemies and daring to toss his name and rank in their faces. Now it sounded gentler, almost apologetic. If the protoss were human Raynor might have thought Zeratul was embarrassed but at the same time proud of his affiliation.

"I know of your kind," Tassadar replied, and his disgust was almost palpable. "You are heretics, cast out from our race. You are considered anathema." His warriors tensed behind him, preparing to spring, and glows sprang up around several of their wrists as they prepped their energy blades.

But Zeratul held out his hands, palms up and fingers spread, in a clear gesture of peace. Again it mirrored his encounter with Zasz, but its meaning seemed entirely different. Raynor, watching the Praetor speak to Zasz, had seen the move as a delaying tactic, a chance to find the right moment to strike. Now it seemed genuine.

"I have no desire to fight you, my brother," Zeratul called across the plateau, and Tassadar flinched as if he had been struck. "Though you despise me, we have no quarrel. We are allied here, on this world, in this battle. Our goals are one and the same. Surely you must see that?"

"I see only another foe," the Executor growled back, his hands clenching at his sides. "Another who would tarnish the legacy of the Templar and sully our honor." He raised one fist and his eyes blazed blue, dazzling even in the sunlight. "Defend yourself!"

And with that the Templar attacked.

It was a strange battle. Raynor had seen the protoss fight several times now, and from a similar distance. He had watched Tassadar and his Zealots fight Kerrigan and her brood and had seen Zeratul do the same. Both times he had been impressed by the protoss's speed, strength, and skill. They were either warriors born or heavily trained. Either way, he had been awed by them. Watching the protoss battle the zerg had been like watching a trained swordsman moving through a raging mob—the swordsman moved smoothly, gracefully, and wielded his blade with precision, while all around him the mob rampaged mindlessly, using nothing more than brute force and vast numbers to overwhelm.

But this time the swordsman faced another swordsman. Or rather, two bands of swordsmen faced each other.

It was an amazing display. Raynor was sure he missed much of it, because the protoss simply moved too quickly for him to follow. A Zealot would pivot forward, dancing as much as attacking, and his arm would lash out, blade crackling in the thin air, sparks appearing as the energy ignited stray bits of ash and soot. A Dark Templar would float forward to meet the attack, spinning around, one arm swinging up smoothly, glittering blade extended, and the two energies would cross, blue and green colliding, shedding flickers of shadow and brightness in all directions, dazzling the eye. Then the two combatants would pull apart and step away, only to circle and close and strike again. Not once, that Raynor saw, did a blade connect with flesh. Each blow was matched by a countermove, each blade blocked by another blade. This wasn't slaughter, or even bloodshed. It was a dance, a display, a show of skill and talent and art.

It was beautiful. And for someone like Raynor, who had grown up with harsher realities and rougher tools, it was a brief glimpse into another world. What would it be like to be from a race whose combat had become so stylized, so perfect, that it was poetry to watch? A race that could fight without wounding, win without killing, defeat with hurting? He couldn't even imagine it.

As their warriors battled, the two leaders had watched, unmoving. "Your warriors are well-trained," Tassadar commented after several minutes, his words halting, as if they had been dragged from him against his will. Raynor could hear the grudging respect in them.

"As are yours," Zeratul replied, returning the compliment more easily. He nodded at his counterpart. "Surely you see that they move the same, fight the same, think the same? Our ways are one." He took a step closer and his voice dropped, though Raynor could still hear him clearly. It was as if the Praetor was whispering, sharing a friendly secret. "We are but sides of the coin," he confided to Tassadar, "our paths different but our goals, our very foundation one and the same. Do you not recognize this truth?"

"Do not attempt to sway me with your lies," the Executor countered, taking a step back to maintain the distance between them. "I have been taught of your kind, of how you betrayed our race, how your broke with our people and severed every connection from us. You turned your back on us, on yourself, on everything that is protoss! You are not one of us!"

"Think past the old tales," Zeratul urged, taking another step toward him. "They are but stories created by your forefathers to explain our departure. Kernels of truth exist within them, yes, but buried within a field of deceptions."

"No!" Tassadar stepped back again, then straightened. "I will not listen to this! You shall not corrupt me!" And he struck at Zeratul.

The blow was so fast Raynor couldn't see it fully—he saw the protoss leader's arm slam forward in a blur, fist leveled at the Dark Templar's chest, but even his armor's targeting system couldn't clarify the image properly. It was simply too quick, too sudden. He thought he felt a rush of air from the punch, even here on his ridge, and knew that the impact would crush the Praetor's chest like an eggshell.

But by the time the punch landed, the Praetor was no longer there.

If Tassadar's move had been lightning-fast, Zeratul's

response was as quick as thought. There was no blur, no sense of motion—the Praetor was simply two feet to the left of his former position. It had happened in less than a blink, and Raynor's eyes twitched trying to adjust even as his brain registered the Dark Templar's change in position. It hadn't been an illusion, either, like the one Tassadar himself had used against Kerrigan. Raynor was sure of that, though he couldn't say why. He just knew that the Praetor had been facing Tassadar an instant ago, and now he was off to one side.

"You strike with force but no focus," Zeratul warned Tassadar, and something in his voice told Raynor that if the protoss had lips and a mouth they would be curved into a smile right now. "Do not waste yourself on such useless expenditures. Do not throw away your energy on uncertainties. Wait until the moment is truly right, then marshal your strength for the attack."

"Do not lecture me!" Tassadar roared, his words an uncanny echo of Kerrigan's retort to Zeratul during their battle, shaking his head to clear it. He attacked again, his moves even faster this time, his strikes more furious. Not once but three times his fists moved, so fast they seemed to punch all at once, in a neat row to the left, to the right, and dead center on the Praetor's chest. Raynor understood the logic behind it. The Executor was hoping to box his opponent in, hitting to either side to keep him from ducking out of the way again. He was counting on at least one punch landing.

But none of them did.

Zeratul moved again, sliding to the left before Tassadar's first blow landed—a move that somehow did not involve his legs or feet, simply his body's suddenly appearing two feet from its previous location. Then he was back in his former position, as the Executor's other two strikes passed harmlessly alongside him.

"Still you attack without concentration," Zeratul said, shaking his head slightly. "You use your body with full force, but not your mind. Why, when it is your mightiest weapon? Do not lash out with fists first," he cautioned, his own hand snaking out and latching onto Tassadar's wrist before the Executor could draw his hand back from his failed attack. "Target your foe with your mind first," the Dark Templar instructed, shadows welling up beneath his fingertips and wrapping dark bands around Tassadar's forearm. "When your mind is locked upon your opponent your fists may follow, and then they cannot fail to strike."

The darkness was rising now, sheathing Tassadar's arm up to the elbow, and Raynor could almost feel the Executor's attempt to jerk away. A spurt of swirling emotion burst forth from Tassadar, half pain and half fear, perhaps the first fear the mighty protoss had ever felt. And then that fear gave way to another emotion—rage.

"Enough of your confusions!" he roared, the thunder crackling beneath his words propelling Zeratul away from him with an almost palpable force. Tassadar flexed, blue arcs of energy flaring from his wrists, and the shadows fell away, shredded by the brilliant light.

"You speak in riddles to distract me," he accused the Praetor, taking a step back and raising both arms, high over his head, the lightning arcing between them. "But I will not be swayed!" As Tassadar lowered his arms, the lightning settled around his wrists, sweeping forward to form blades like those his warriors wielded, but longer, brighter, and filled with a crackling hum that made Raynor's hairs stand on end. These blades were not contained—or created—by bracers, he knew. They were a part of Tassadar himself, an expression of his own power. "Now we will see an end to your lies," Tassadar warned, taking one slow step toward his counterpart. "Once and for all."

The other protoss had left off their own duels, watching their leaders battle, and Raynor's eyes were locked on the conflict as well. He knew somehow that this was a match of epic proportions, one that would become part of protoss history. Assuming any of the witnesses survived to tell of it.

As he shifted to get a better view, Raynor caught a speck of movement from the corner of his eye. He twisted slightly to get a better look, and froze.

"Aw, hell," he whispered as he registered what he was seeing. His helmet automatically tracked and magnified the image, making it impossible to ignore.

It was the zerg. Lots of them, probably the entire brood.

And they were heading this way.

Raynor glanced back at the plateau, where Tassadar was still stalking toward Zeratul, energy blades extended. The protoss were all fixated upon them, too much so to notice the approaching Swarm. They'd be slaughtered.

"Well, this ain't gonna be good," Raynor muttered to himself. He levered himself up from his crouch and leaped forward, the suit's servos causing him to sail across the gap between the ridge and the plateau. He unslung the canister rifle on his back as he moved, swinging it around and into his hands as he landed, bending his knees to absorb the impact and taking a single step forward to keep his balance.

He found himself facing several dozen energy blades, wielded by several dozen angry protoss.

"Hold on!" Raynor shouted, raising the rifle over his head with both hands. "I ain't your enemy! They are!" He pointed, and many of the protoss turned to gaze past the plateau—

—just as the first of the mutalisks, guardians, and devourers swept down upon them.

"To arms!" Tassadar shouted, his feud with Zeratul instantly shunted to the background. "Regroup, my Zealots, and we will teach these zerg what it means to confront the protoss!" His right arm swept up almost lazily, the energy blade extending even farther as it arced above his head and sliced the leading devourer in two, its halves falling to the rock on either side of him.

In an instant the protoss were locked in battle, and Raynor with them. But right from the start, he could see how this was going to end.

"There're too many of them!" he hollered at Tassadar, shooting down a trio of mutalisks that had been poised to shred one of the protoss warriors. "We can't hold 'em!"

The High Templar either didn't hear him or didn't care, so Raynor turned to Zeratul instead. "We've got to get out of here!" he urged, firing a barrage to take down a cluster of approaching scourge that exploded just shy of the plateau, the shock waves almost tossing all of them off their feet. "When the rest of the brood gets here we're gonna be swamped!"

The Dark Templar had not moved since stepping away from Tassadar, and now he seemed to retreat into himself as he considered. Finally he nodded.

"The human is correct," he declared calmly. "This is not the time for our battle to conclude. We must abandon this battlefield and seek a more opportune time to end this conflict."

Tassadar heard that one, at least, and turned to stare at the Praetor, even as his hand caught another mutalisk and throttled it. "You would flee battle?" he asked, his eyes wide.

"You would stay and see your people needlessly slain?" Zeratul countered, and that struck home. Tassadar's eyes narrowed and he seemed about to attack the Dark Templar again. Before he could move, however, the Praetor leaped at him instead.

Raynor was shocked, and so, apparently, was Tassadar—the High Templar froze as Zeratul flew toward him, both arms extended, a band of writhing, searing cold darkness forming between them. Raynor started to bring his rifle up, but paused. He wasn't sure why, but some instinct told him not to interfere.

Before he could blink the Praetor had closed the distance, his shoulder colliding with Tassadar's chest and driving the Executor to the ground—

—as a mutalisk lashed out, its long snakelike tail scraping acid across Zeratul's shoulder and chest where the Executor's head had been an instant before. Blood from the resulting wound spattered Praetor and Executor both, and Zeratul twitched in obvious agony but refused to topple. He reared up instead, sending more blood fountaining from the whole in his side, and pivoted to face his attacker, which had wheeled about in midair for a second attack. Then the darkness between the Dark Templar's hands connected with the mutalisk's arcing tail and sliced clean through it as the mutalisk jerked back, wailing in pain. The effort must have exhausted the Praetor, however, and he dropped to his knees in a pool of his own blood. Tassadar was already up again, having rolled free of Zeratul and vaulted back to his feet, and he sliced the mutalisk apart with his blades before helping the wounded Dark Templar to stand.

For a second the two simply eyed one another, Templar and Dark Templar, blazing blue eyes and wise green ones. Then Tassadar's hand jerked, tearing a long strip from his uniform, and with it he bound the older protoss's wound. A surge of light welled up from his hands as he worked, and when he removed them the Praetor's wound was still severe but no longer spurting blood everywhere. Once that was done Tassadar nodded, surprising Raynor.

"You are correct," the High Templar said. "They have the advantage of us here, and remaining will merely lead to our own demise. We lose no honor in regrouping." He gestured, and his protoss gathered around him, leaving a cluster of zerg bodies in their wake. Zeratul's Dark Templar grouped behind him as well, making Raynor think of a circle divided in two halves. And he was right at the center of it.

He had been about to wish the protoss leaders good luck when he heard another voice, more familiar than theirs but less welcome, drifting across the landscape.

"I am coming for you, little protoss," came the words, echoing toward them and simultaneously ringing in his head. "Both of you, High Templar and Dark Templar, Executor and Praetor. Linger a moment longer and I will deliver you quickly unto death. Flee and I will prolong your torment for hours, days, an eternity." He couldn't pinpoint the location or even the direction, with the sound bouncing against all the rock nearby, but he knew she was close.

Tassadar still seemed tempted to remain and fight, particularly now that Kerrigan had called him out again. "We shall meet in battle soon, o Queen of Blades," Raynor heard his tight, angry thought, "and I shall slay you for the honor and safety of my people."

Kerrigan apparently heard him as well. "Your people?" She laughed. "Look around you, little protoss. These are all the people you have left!"

"What riddle is this?" Tassadar demanded of the empty air, his eyes blazing. "Though I may be outcast for recent actions still I am protoss, and still my race rules the stars!"

"Not for long," Kerrigan crowed back, her voice growing slightly louder. "The Swarm has gone to your world," she taunted, "to precious Aiur! By the time another day has passed your planet will be in cinders, and your race destroyed!"

Tassadar reeled as if he had been struck, and he wasn't the only one. Raynor saw the other protoss reacting with shock as well, staggering and scowling and shaking their heads. Zeratul and his Dark Templar seemed equally affected.

"Impossible!" Zeratul shot back toward the hills. "Aiur is concealed from your ilk, and its location remains secret!"

"Not from you, little protoss," Kerrigan answered, and now her voice seemed to be coming from right over the hill. "You know its location, don't you? And now, thanks to you, we do as well."

This time it was the Praetor who staggered backward, a wave of disbelief rising off him like steam, even as Tassadar turned toward him, the High Templar's eyes narrowing in rage.

"You!" His mental cry was the equivalent of a bellow, and Raynor winced as the telepathic shout struck him between the eyes. "What have you done?" But even as the tall protoss moved toward his Dark Templar counterpart, Raynor heard a distinctive whistling noise he recognized all too well. It was the sound of Kerrigan's wing-spikes slicing the air. She was close. Too close.

"Argue later!" he shouted at the protoss, stepping between the two leaders and making a shooing gesture with his rifle. "Let's get out of here! Now!"

Tassadar glared down at him, then at Zeratul, then slowly nodded, the motion clearly hard for him. "Yes, we will settle this later," he agreed finally, and turned away, leading his warriors toward safety. Zeratul matched him without a sound, and his Dark Templar fell in behind him.

"Is this your choice then, Jimmy?" Kerrigan called, and this time he knew the words were only inside his head, but no less real for that. "So be it. You and yours will suffer the same fate as your new friends."

"Damn." Raynor sighed, and then turned and bounded after the protoss, who were already running toward the far end of the plateau. "Looks like you're stuck with me," he told Tassadar as he caught up to the Executor. Then he glanced over at Zeratul, who was keeping pace beside them. "Hell, looks like we're all stuck together." The two protoss leaders looked at him, then at each other.

"You have much to answer for, Praetor," Tassadar informed Zeratul, and the tone of his statement made it clear he would personally make sure the Dark Templar paid whatever debt he owed.

Zeratul did not argue the point.

"Perhaps," he allowed. "If such as she said is true,

the blame is mine to shoulder, and bear it I will. For truly, guiding the Swarm to Aiur is the last thing I would wish."

They stared at each other for another instant, green eyes locked with blue. Then, at the same time, they nodded.

"You accept your responsibility," Tassadar stated. "This is a beginning, at least." He gave the Praetor one last glare. "Until I know the truth of this matter, you shall not leave my sight."

"Bound together," Zeratul agreed, his words thrumming with that strange power he had revealed before. "Thus the hands of fate entwine us, different strands woven together to create a stronger fabric for the whole."

Tassadar was less cryptic. "Your warning was timely," he told Raynor as they ran, "and we are grateful. You and yours may accompany us as allies."

As he opened a comm channel to call base and tell them to evacuate, Raynor thought about that. He'd set out looking for the protoss, either group, in the hope of forming an alliance. And he'd gotten one. He just hadn't expected to get it in quite this manner.

CHAPTER 16

"JIM."

Kerrigan was smiling, laughing, as she twisted just out of reach. He chased after her, but she managed to stay just beyond his grasp, her blazing mane streaming behind her as she ran.

"Wait," he called out, hands clutching air as he tried again and again to catch her. "Come back!"

"No," she said, turning to face him and skipping nimbly backward as he dove for her again. "You made your choice." Her words were light and her lips still wore that mocking smile, but her eyes were sad, so sad. She stepped up beside him and traced a finger along his face. "Now you're stuck with it," she murmured, her lips drifting up toward his, her mouth parting so close to his her could almost feel her skin against him. Then a searing pain sliced across his cheek and he reeled backward, hand lifting reflexively to cup the wound. Her fingernail had somehow transformed into a long, barbed claw, and she had cut him with it. He stared as she backed away, licking the blood from her fingertip, and shuddered at the look on her face and the hunger he saw in her eyes.

"Time to wake up, Jimmy," she told him breathily. "Time to face the consequences."

And he sat up, his cheek tender where he touched it.

It had been two weeks since they had joined the protoss. The first few days had been the worst.

"Get everybody out of there," he told Cavez and Abernathy over the comm. "No waiting, just do it."

"Yes, sir," they both replied, and he could hear Abernathy shouting orders a second later. Cavez remained on the link, however. "Where are we going, sir?" he asked.

"That's a damn good question," Raynor admitted. "Hell if I know right now." He shook his head. "Get everybody moving toward the mountains and let me know when you're en route. I'll have a better idea then."

He assumed that the mountains were where they were all going. Since fleeing Kerrigan none of the protoss had said a word. It was a bit eerie running across Char's twisted landscape in complete silence. A few times he'd heard odd murmurs behind him, what sounded almost like wind through trees, and he suspected it was protoss conversation he was overhearing—conversations among the Zealots or the Dark Templar, things he wasn't included in and so couldn't really make out. The two groups hadn't mixed at all, the Zealots staying on his left and the Dark Templar on his right, each following their respective leader, and he kept expecting them to split off from each other at some point. Which would leave him with a dilemma—which group would he follow? He knew more about Tassadar, had spoken to him directly, and felt the Executor was the more direct of the two, but Zeratul knew how to kill zerg, even cerebrates, and that was a power Raynor wanted on his side. Fortunately it hadn't come to a decision yet—the two leaders seemed content to move together for now, though they didn't speak to or even look at one another. Raynor resisted the urge to whistle to cut the tension.

Then things took a turn for the worse, as they usually did.

"Sir, we've got zerg!" It was Cavez, shouting into the comm as soon as Raynor responded to the ping.

"Where are you?" Raynor shouted back. He could hear the retort of gauss rifles and hisses and clacks mixed with screams in the background. He came to a dead stop, his suit compensating for the sudden halt, and the protoss instantly paused as well.

"We're still at the shuttle," Cavez admitted, sounding a little embarrassed. "Took longer to gather everything than we'd thought. Then the zerg showed up out of nowhere!"

"Dig in," Raynor ordered, using his suit's tracking systems to locate the camp from here. "Don't try to run—they'll cut you down. Center on the shuttle, put the armored troopers in front, and hold the fort. I'm on my way."

As soon as he closed the link he turned to the two protoss commanders, who were watching him silently. "They're hitting my men," he explained hurriedly. "We need to get them out of there."

He'd been half-expecting an argument. He didn't get one. "A commander's first duty is to his troops," Tassadar agreed. "You must go at once." Then, perhaps reading the surprise on Raynor's face, or the question that popped into his head, the Executor tilted his head and his brow quirked in what Raynor felt sure was humor. "We have allied with you," the High Templar assured him, "and we will accompany you in this rescue mission."

"Great." Raynor let out the breath he'd been holding. He glanced over at Zeratul, who hadn't spoken. "What about you?"

The Praetor shrugged. "Our fates are intertwined," he said, as if that explained everything. And maybe it did, because when Raynor turned and began running full speed back toward his base, both protoss groups ran beside him.

Even with his suit's servos and the protoss's natural speed, it took almost an hour to reach the shuttle. He could hear the fighting before he topped the last rise, and took some comfort in the fact that at least some of his crew were still alive and fit enough to fight. Then he saw the shuttle. At first glance it looked as if it had been decorated with strange bits of leather and bone, odd spikes and horns and barbs jutting out from every angle. Then his suit clarified the image. He was seeing the zerg swarming over his ship, and the men stationed around it.

"We're comin' in!" he bellowed into his comm unit as he barreled down the hill and across the small valley toward the shuttle. "Careful what you're shooting!" He unlimbered his canister rifle as he ran.

Then he was down there, and put a volley of spikes through an ultralisk that had raised its scythes to carve through the shuttle's side. The massive zerg fell, crushing several zerglings beneath it, and the rest of the brood turned toward Raynor, giving his troopers a momentary respite. Of course, that didn't help *him* much.

But a second later they forgot about him entirely, because that was when both groups of protoss descended upon them.

It was a short fight. This was only a small portion of Kerrigan's brood, actually, a handful of ultralisks and guardians with a few dozen mutalisks, hydralisks, and devourers and perhaps thirty zerglings. Those were the ones still standing when he'd arrived, anyway—his men had dispatched close to half the attackers already, he was pleased to see. The protoss made short work of the rest, energy blades carving through tough zerg hide and slicing off those nasty scythes. Within ten minutes the last of the attackers were dead or dying and Raynor was climbing into the shuttle to take stock. Cavez was waiting for him.

"Sorry, sir," his lieutenant started, and Raynor brushed away the apology. "We should have been ready to move when you gave the order."

"They would have caught you out in the open, then," Raynor consoled him, noticing the bloody bandage around Cavez's upper right arm. "Better off fighting from here. Why aren't you in armor?"

Cavez shrugged. "I figured the others needed it more," he admitted.

"Wrong," Raynor told him bluntly. "You're in charge of them. That means you need to be able to help them when they need it. You need the armor most. Without it you're a liability to them, not an asset. Don't do it again."

"Yes, sir!" The young trooper straightened and saluted, and Raynor fought back a smile. Damn, Cavez reminded him of Matt! The thought of the young pilot, and the *Hyperion,* sobered him a little.

"All right, all right," he said. "You're still alive so it wasn't too bad a screwup. Just make sure you've got armor next time." He glanced around. "Where's Abernathy?"

Cavez couldn't meet his eyes. "Dead, sir. She went to help Non get two of the wounded to the shuttle and a zerg stabbed her through the chest. I saw her drop."

Raynor nodded, then stopped. "Wait, stabbed her through the chest?" Cavez nodded. "Did it tear open her suit? Rip her apart?"

"Sir?"

He reminded himself that Cavez was young, and hadn't seen much combat before Char, particularly against zerg. Fortunately, he had. "Was her suit still in one piece when she fell?" he asked again.

Cavez stopped and thought about it. "Yes, sir," he said finally.

"Did the zerg keep on her after she dropped, or did it move on?"

"Neither." Cavez grinned proudly. "I took it down, sir—got it in the throat, ripped its head clean off."

"Good man." Raynor activated his suit's targeting systems and told it to search for damaged suits. It registered eight—two in the shuttle and five just outside. And one more a little ways beyond. "Come on." He was already hopping out and Cavez was right behind him, the lanky trooper doing his best to keep up as Raynor homed in on the signal. He was crouching beside the suit when Cavez ran up, gasping.

Cavez's memory had been right, he saw at once. Abernathy had taken a hit to the chest, damaging the suit's motors and probably shorting out some of its other systems. Without the servos working the entire suit had become dead weight and had toppled over, leaving her defenseless. Fortunately Cavez's shot had taken out the zerg before it could do more damage. And the rest of the brood had apparently been more interested in going after the still-active defenders. Raynor couldn't see any other damage to the suit beyond that one gaping hole. And though it had carved through the suit's armor easily, slicing open metal and plastics and wiring, he didn't see any blood.

"Give me a hand," he told Cavez, kneeling and fumbling for the suit's emergency catches. His own suit's fingers could handle a rifle but had trouble with clasps, and he'd only managed two by the time Cavez had an entire side open. Finally he got the rest and lifted the front of the suit off completely, tossing it to one side.

"Well, it's about bloody time," Abernathy said, sitting up and brushing bits of metal and wiring from her uniform. She grinned at them both, and Raynor could feel an answering grin on his face. "Did you leave any for me?"

"Don't worry," Raynor assured her, standing up and grabbing the rest of her armor to sling it over his shoulder; parts might still be usable. "Next time we'll leave 'em all to you."

Abernathy hadn't been the only lucky one, Raynor realized after the three of them had returned to the shuttle and done a quick head count. They'd lost ten soldiers in the attack, including three of the four who had already been wounded. Considering how many zerg had hit them, and how quickly the attack had occurred, they'd all been damn lucky.

"Gather your warriors," Tassadar told him a few minutes later. The protoss had placed themselves around the shuttle in a wide ring, Zealots on one side and Dark Templar on the other, facing outward to watch for additional attacks. "We must depart."

"I need to bury my dead," Raynor told him, and stood his ground when the Executor glanced down at him, eyes wide in apparent disbelief. "I'm not just leavin' them to rot," he insisted. "They deserve better than that."

He stared back at the protoss leader for a moment

and finally Tassadar nodded. "Very well. We will guard you until you are ready."

Zeratul hadn't interfered and didn't approach—Raynor saw the Praetor standing with his warriors, watching the horizon for any sign of zerg. Most likely the Dark Templar simply figured he'd leave when Tassadar did, which worked out fine.

The ground here wasn't that hard, the first few inches loose ash and dry, crumbling dirt below that, and the men took turns digging. They had the ten graves cut quickly, and then placed the bodies inside. McMurty was a chaplain and Raynor let him say a short prayer, then they filled the graves back in and grabbed their gear, redistributing the ten packs.

"All right, let's go," Raynor told Tassadar, who nodded. He heard a faint whisper again and the Zealots closed in, forming ranks around their leader. On the far side of the shuttle Zeratul must have heard or seen the command, because his Dark Templar grouped around him as well. Raynor nodded to Cavez and Abernathy, who shouted orders, and soon everyone was moving out, the humans forming a buffer between the two groups of protoss.

"I hate to leave it," Cavez admitted, pacing alongside Raynor and glancing back once toward the empty shuttle. "Seems like as long as we had that we had a chance of getting off this rock."

"Not much good to us now," Raynor pointed out, which was true. The zerg had done a number on the shuttle during the attack, carving several pieces from its wing and hull and using acid to eat large holes all across it. Even if they'd gotten engines from the protoss ships they'd have to rebuild the shuttle's hull before it could fly again. "And it's too easy a target."

"Where are we going?" Abernathy asked him from his other side. She'd claimed one of the other suits of powered armor, as had Cavez, and the three of them walked in front with Deslan. McMurty, and a few others. Ling and Non had charge of the rear, three other suited soldiers with them, and the remaining four covered the middle, two on either side, guarding the unarmored troopers.

"No idea," Raynor admitted, shaking his head. He jogged forward to where Tassadar and Zeratul led the way, still not speaking to each other. "Hey, where are we going?" he asked.

"To find a secure camp," Tassadar replied without turning.

"Yeah, great, thanks." Raynor glared at him but the Executor either didn't notice or didn't care. "And where's that?"

"You shall see it when we arrive" was the cryptic answer. Zeratul didn't add anything and Raynor dropped back to his lieutenants again, fuming.

"They're being coy," he told Cavez and Abernathy. "I guess we'll know when we get there."

"Why're we teaming up with them again?" Cavez asked, shuddering slightly as he glanced over at the protoss warriors stalking silently beside them. "Wouldn't we be better off going our own way and letting the zerg go after them?"

Raynor shook his head. "I thought so at first," he admitted, "because the zerg were leaving us alone. Now we're targets too, though. We're better off all together." He caught the look of revulsion on Cavez's face. "You don't have to like it," he told the young trooper. "I'm not askin' you to marry 'em. Just to treat 'em as allies." He grinned. "Hell, I'll take protoss over Duke any day."

They marched for four hours, reaching the mountains after two and climbing up among the sharp peaks. Tassadar stayed in front and never paused to look around or debate a path—Raynor couldn't tell if the Executor was going to a place he already knew or just sensing the route as he went. Either way he led them to a narrow gap between two peaks, which widened into a small valley almost totally concealed beneath a hanging cliff. A small stream ran down from the opposing peak and pooled at one end.

"Here" was all the High Templar said, his warriors already dropping into those cross-legged poses Raynor had seen them assume before. Zeratul's warriors did the same, none of the protoss making a move to eat or drink or even rid themselves of armor, and within minutes the valley was filled with what looked like protoss statues.

"Right," Raynor said, shutting down his armor and stepping out of it. "Let's set up camp over there," he said, gesturing to the wall under the cliff. "We'll set up a watch, just in case, though I'm sure the protoss will be keeping an eye out, too." He glanced over at his men, who were unshouldering packs and setting down weapons. "I don't know how long we'll be using this place," he told them, "so don't get too comfortable. But break out some food, let's refill our canteens, and I want to know what we've got left in terms of ammo and supplies."

His men got to work, setting up tents and checking equipment and making a quick meal, leaving Raynor and his two lieutenants to discuss their plans. Unfortunately there wasn't a lot to discuss.

"Nice to know what they're planning," Cavez muttered, jerking one thumb toward the motionless protoss. "Are we just tagging along like little brothers for now?"

"Yeah, something like that," Raynor replied, taking a swig from a full canteen Ling had just handed him. The water was cold and sharp, with just a hint of ash. "The good news is, we've got three times as many fighters now, and they're hell on wheels against the zerg. Bad news is, they're not exactly chummy with each other, let alone us. So don't go expecting cook-outs or singalongs."

"Well, are we hunting zerg or waiting for them to find us?" Abernathy asked. All Raynor could do was shake his head.

"No idea," he admitted. "I don't think either of these guys likes sitting around waiting," he added, nodding toward the statue that was Tassadar, perched cross-legged near the stream, and at the monument that was Zeratul, standing slightly hunched not far from the valley entrance. "So they'll probably take the fight to the Swarm if we go more'n a few days without getting jumped ourselves." He scratched his cheek, which still itched where the dream-Kerrigan had scratched him. "Could be a few days before it reaches that point, though." He slapped Cavez on the arm and Abernathy on the back, then stood up. "Best thing to do for now is get some rest."

Raynor's words proved prophetic. For two days they sat in that valley, doing nothing. The protoss behaved the same way they had when he had spied on the Zealots before, sitting immobile all day except for brief periods of stretching and exercise. Tassadar and Zeratul seemed to be on the same cycle and went from frozen to mobile at the same time but did not approach one another. Tassadar seemed to be deliberately ignoring Zeratul, though once Raynor caught the Executor staring at the Praetor, his eyes wide in confusion rather than narrowed in anger or hatred. The Praetor did nothing to disguise his own interest, watching Tassadar intently for several minutes each time they awoke, but did not speak to him or close the gap between them. Both groups of protoss ignored the humans in their midst, moving around them when necessary and not speaking to them at all.

For their part, Raynor's crew patched their wounds,

mended their gear, played cards, carved rocks, sparred, and otherwise did what soldiers did during downtime. Everyone kept glancing toward the aliens around them, and several soldiers jumped each time a protoss blurred from rest to activity. Raynor overheard several mutters of "Kill 'em all now, safer that way" and "Just a matter of time before they turn on us too" and "Just as creepy as the zerg" and other similar things. Finally he had to say something.

"I know they're weird," he told his assembled troopers on the second morning. "I know they're funny-looking with those heads and those eyes and no mouths and all that. And yeah, they ain't exactly friendly." He glanced from soldier to soldier as he spoke, making sure he had everyone's attention. "But they ain't the enemy. They ain't zerg. If they were, we'd all be dead already." He took a breath. "Listen, these guys are seriously bad-ass warriors. You've seen them fight. And they hate the zerg even more'n we do. And while they aren't lining up to dance with us, they do see us as allies. So let's just ignore their oddities and accept that, okay?" Several people nodded. "Okay?" Everyone nodded and he heard several yeses. "Good. You don't have to like them," he said, repeating what he'd told Cavez before. "You just have to be glad they're on our side, and stay out of their way."

"Easy enough when they're just sitting still," somebody called out, and everybody laughed, Raynor included.

"Yeah, they're really good at sitting," he agreed, but

just then a flurry of motion caught his eye and he stopped to glance over the troopers' heads. The protoss were all rising from their frozen positions, Zealots and Dark Templar alike, and moving toward the valley entrance.

"What's going on?" Raynor called out to Tassadar, who was striding toward him. They met midway between their two groups, Zeratul suddenly appearing next to them. Raynor started at the Praetor's presence, but Tassadar gave no sign of being surprised.

"We must find another haven," Tassadar explained. "The Swarm approaches."

"So we're just gonna run away?" Raynor asked. "We're not gonna fight?"

"They have far superior numbers" was Tassadar's reply. "We would not survive such a confrontation."

"We can't just let 'em scare us off," Raynor protested, stepping forward to block Tassadar's path as the Executor started to turn away. "We've got to take a few of them out, at least. If we do that each time we run into them, before long we'll whittle 'em down to nothing."

"The human is correct," Zeratul stated. "While we cannot win a direct battle this time, we can wage a small skirmish and inflict losses upon the zerg."

Tassadar frowned at the Dark Templar. "You would stay and fight?" he asked. Raynor could hear the surprise in his voice.

Zeratul nodded. "We can remove ourselves from the valley and position ourselves above it instead," he pointed out. "By gaining such elevation we will take the initiative and can strike quickly and then depart, leaving them wounded and confused."

The Executor studied his counterpart openly, blue eyes wide with curiosity. "I was taught that Dark Templar were cowards and weaklings," he admitted after a moment. "You are neither."

"Teachings come from the teacher," Zeratul pointed out, earning a small snort from Raynor, which he ignored. "Thus the lesson is influenced by the lecturer, rather than remaining unbiased truth."

Tassadar tilted his head to one side. "Perhaps," he said finally, "I will reevaluate my stance toward you and yours."

"The wise mind seeks its own answers," Zeratul agreed, "rather than relying upon the information of others."

"Yeah, I hate to interrupt," Raynor cut in, "but if the zerg are on their way we'd better get our asses in gear."

Both protoss swiveled to look at him.

"Indeed" was all Zeratul said, but Raynor could tell the Dark Templar was amused. Then both protoss leaders were turning back to their warriors and Raynor rushed to get his crew ready as well.

The ambush worked beautifully. They all moved up along the valley walls, protoss and human alike, and hid as best they could against the rocks and snow. Zeratul and his Dark Templar had the definite advantage there, fading completely from view. After perhaps ten minutes of waiting they heard the telltale clicks and hisses and scrapes of the zerg. Raynor and his people checked their weapons.

As with the shuttle assult, only a portion of Kerrigan's brood attacked, and again she was nowhere in sight herself. That was probably for the best. This batch of zerg was entirely land-bound, zerglings and hydralisks and ultralisks, and that made it easier as well—an ambush from above might not have worked against mutalisks and the other fliers. As it was, the zerg filed into the valley, intent upon slaughtering their prey, and halted in confusion when they found the place empty.

That was when the combined forces of Raynor, Tassadar, and Zeratul fell upon them.

It was a short, ugly fight. Protoss energy blades and human gauss rifles made short work of the zerg, who found their escape route cut off and their supposed prey armed and on every side. Within minutes, the zerg were dead on the valley floor.

"The rest of the brood will arrive soon," Tassadar warned, standing astride a hydralisk he had snapped in half as it reached for Non. "We must depart or face them all."

"Time to go," Raynor agreed, and gathered his men. They hadn't lost a single soldier in the fight. Neither had the protoss.

"That's more like it," Cavez said happily as they marched out of the valley and followed Tassadar to some new refuge.

"Not so bad working with protoss, eh?" Raynor teased him as they walked. His lieutenant managed to look a little embarrassed but keep grinning anyway.

"Not so bad," he agreed.

That first encounter set the tone for the next week. They would find a place to camp and settle in for anywhere from two hours to two days. The zerg would find them, or would wander close by looking for them. Tassadar, Zeratul, and Raynor would set up a trap for the zerg, attacking all of a small force or cutting off a portion of a larger force. They'd make short work of the zerg, protoss and human fighting together, and then abandon the area before Kerrigan could bring the rest of her brood after them. They were trimming her brood with each attack but avoiding her personally, and Raynor knew it had to be driving her nuts.

The protoss didn't exactly warm up to the humans. At least, the warriors still went into statue mode at each new campsite, and only moved to stretch or drink. But after that first battle, in which Raynor's men had held their own, the warriors did show more respect for his troopers. They also learned to work together a bit. The protoss were fearsome warriors, as strong and fast as a human in combat armor and deadly with those energy blades, but they were only effective right up close. Raynor's men, with their gauss rifles and targeting systems, could handle longer-range attacks, which meant they could thin the herd first and then provide support. The two races began figuring out how to take advantage of their repective strengths, and with each battle they improved their teamwork. Most of the protoss warriors still didn't talk to the humans, but they would point out a zerg target, or simply move aside to let a trooper take the shot.

For their part, Raynor's crew began to get a little more used to their alien allies. The protoss were still strange and still aloof but everyone agreed they were damn useful in a fight. And after several instances in which the protoss stepped in to save the humans from zerg attacks, the troopers began relaxing more around them. After all, why bother protecting someone if you wanted to kill him? Now they knew that the protoss really did see them as allies, and not only wouldn't kill them but would actively help them survive. It made a big difference. Troopers were able to sleep soundly without checking on the protoss's location every few minutes, and could walk calmly past a frozen protoss or even sit near one without worrying about being attacked. Everyone finally accepted that the protoss really weren't their enemies, which freed people up to worry about the zerg and only the zerg.

The Zealots and Dark Templar also formed an uneasy alliance. The two groups still didn't mingle, keeping to separate sides of whatever shelter they found and only following orders from their respective leaders. But they did fight alongside one another now. The Dark Templar seemed more relaxed about their strange partnership and regarded their Templar brethren with something like amusement and perhaps a little condescension. The Zealots still seemed wary of their dark kin but showed a grudging respect for their skills and gradually came to accept the fact that the Dark Templar were not going to attack them instead of the zerg.

The protoss leaders were less reticent than their warriors, and Raynor found himself spending more time with them both, and especially with the two of them together. Tassadar and Zeratul spent less time meditating now than their warriors did, and often sat near one another, communicating quietly—a concept Raynor had never realized could apply to telepathy before—or just sitting quietly. Raynor joined them whenever he could, fascinated by the interaction between the two and a bit surprised at the friendly feelings he found himself developing for each of them.

The two protoss were very different. Tassadar was a warrior through and through, direct and honest. He had no guile, though he was an excellent strategist and had no compunctions about employing feints and ambushes. But as an individual Tassadar seemed incapable of lying or deceit. He was fiercely loyal to his warriors and to his people in general, and Raynor saw in him the burning love of a true patriot, willing to die for his race's honor just as readily as for its survival.

But Tassadar cared about more than just his own people. As they sat one day at one end of their current camp, he turned to look at Raynor, and Raynor felt something like shame in that gaze. Zeratul also picked up on it.

"You feel guilt toward the humans," the Praetor commented softly, but after a moment's silence he corrected himself. "I mistake the source with the subject," he admitted. "You feel guilt because of the humans, but the guilt is toward our own people."

Tassadar started and stared at the older protoss, and for a second Raynor thought the Templar was going to attack again, though whether it was over Zeratul's reminder that they were the same race or his assessment of Tassadar's emotional state he wasn't sure. After a few seconds, however, the Executor simply shrugged and looked away.

"Is this about my ships?" Raynor asked. He had long since accepted what the protoss had done above Char and why. He still mourned the loss of his men, but he understood. In Tassadar's shoes—if the alien had worn any—he might have done the same thing. But Zeratul answered instead.

"The cause is much greater," the Praetor assured him, "and stems less from responding to events than from following directives."

If Zeratul knew any more about it he didn't say, but Tassadar finally turned back and looked at Raynor again. "My orders," the Templar explained heavily, "were to destroy those worlds already tainted by the zerg."

"Like you did to Mar Sara," Raynor said, and the Templar nodded.

"But far less taint is required to call down such a fate," he explained, and Raynor felt a chill wash over him.

"How much?" he demanded, leaping to his feet.

"How much contact with the zerg earns a world the death sentence? Do the zerg even have to land there?" He saw the reply in the protoss commander's eyes. "What, so you're just supposed to kill us all off now, just to be safe?"

"Yes," Zeratul replied, again speaking where the younger protoss seemed unable or unwilling. "Those were his orders."

"How do you know?" Raynor snapped. "It's not like you were involved!" He saw the two protoss glance at each other, then Tassadar looked quickly away, seeming embarassed. "What?"

"I know because the Executor has told me," Zeratul explained. "In these past few days we have discussed many things." He seemed pleased by this turn of events.

"Didn't feel like including me, eh?" Raynor asked Tassadar pointedly, glaring at him, then at Zeratul for good measure.

"He is still overcome with guilt," the Praetor replied. "But he wished to tell you. That is why I spoke for him."

"So you were supposed to kill us all?" Raynor asked quietly, numbed at the thought of those protoss warships hovering over each Terran world in turn.

"To eradicate your race's worlds, and prevent the Swarm from using them for fodder in the war between our species, yes," the Praetor answered. Then he eyed Tassadar carefully, and his tone turned warm. "But he did not obey."

"He didn't?" Raynor stared at the protoss, who refused to look up.

"No," Zeratul said. "He felt such actions were both dishonorable and unproductive. Instead he abandoned his post, his orders, and followed his instincts, to this world. Here he hoped to eliminate the zerg directly, thus ending the long conflict and sparing your people further harm."

Raynor didn't know what to say. He'd been so damn pissed at Tassadar when they'd first met, because the protoss had destroyed a few hundred men and their ships. Now he learned that the Executor had deliberately disobeyed orders to spare millions of other humans, and had come here looking for a way to end the problem before anyone else got hurt. It was one of the most selfless things he had ever heard of, and Raynor realized that Tassadar wasn't one of those fanatics who put their own race's desires above all else. The protoss commander was one of those far rarer beings who put their people's honor and dignity above even their own plans or orders, and who would do whatever was necessary to keep theie people's nobility intact, even if it meant sullying their own reputation.

"Yes," Zeratul agreed, and Raynor realized that the Praetor had read his thoughts. "He is rare indeed, and valuable beyond measure." There was no hint of condescension or sarcasm in the statement, only truth, pride, and perhaps a little envy.

If Tassadar was an open book, Zeratul was a tightly bound scroll, only hinting at his depths and content. Though a powerful fighter, the Praetor was first and foremost a scholar and teacher. He loved to explain things, though his preferred method was to present questions and make the student figure out the answers. He spoke in riddles without even realizing it and liked to consider everything two or three times before making a decision. Zeratul was a natural storyteller with a spellbinding mental "voice." He also had a wicked sense of humor, Raynor discovered, and his convoluted statements often contained barbs directed at Raynor, Tassadar, and even Zeratul himself. The first time Raynor made a joke at the Praetor's expense he wasn't sure how the Dark Templar would react and, in the silence that followed, was afraid he had gone too far. Then Zeratul started laughing, a dry cackle that washed over him and left him feeling as refreshed as from a mild summer rain. Even Tassadar had chuckled a bit, and after that Raynor and the Dark Templar traded quips and jabs daily. They both picked on Tassadar, who put up with their verbal assaults good-naturedly but did not volley back.

It was a strange trio they made, and their conversations often turned to subjects Raynor didn't really understand. After a few days Tassadar openly admitted that he was fascinated by Zeratul and his abilities. "You touch something I cannot," the High Templar said humbly, "but I feel the contact deep within, as if it echoed in my soul somehow."

"What you feel is the birthright of all protoss," Zeratul replied calmly, though the way he leaned forward and the way his eyes gleamed betrayed his excitement.

"I possess only those gifts native to us all. I have honed my connection with these forces, over these long years, but the power was there all along, as it resides within you."

"That's how you killed Zasz," Raynor commented, and was forced to explain that he had watched the combat between Praetor and cerebrate in that dark cavern, earning a nod of respect from the Dark Templar. "You used those powers to kill him for good," he continued.

"Yes," Zeratul agreed. "The forces we protoss possess are inimical to the zerg. By utilizing these gifts I severed the bond between Zasz and the Overmind, preventing his soul from being reborn."

"You are certain this Zasz was not restored after your attack?" Tassadar asked, and Raynor answered for the Praetor.

"He wasn't," he confirmed. "He's definitely dead." He thought back to the conversation he had witnessed between Kerrigan and Daggoth. "I saw Kerrigan talking about it," he explained, "before I ran into the two of you. Whatever you did"—he nodded at Zeratul—"it was the real deal." Then he remembered the other part of the conversation. "Damn."

"What is it?" Tassadar demanded. "If you know more of this, you must tell us!"

"Yeah, well, I—" Raynor couldn't bring himself to look at either of them, particularly Zeratul. "I guess when you did that, killed Zasz, you touched the Overmind itself."

"Yes, I felt it through its link to the cerebrate," the old protoss confirmed.

"Well, it apparently felt you too," Raynor explained. "And it tapped your mind while you were busy. That's how it found out about Aiur."

"No!" Zeratul shot to his feet but instantly tipped backward, flailing to catch himself. He looked for all the world like a drunken soldier, and his eyes alternated between blazing green fire and dull, colorless pools. "It *is* my fault!" His psychic cry was heart-wrenching. The Praetor turned to Tassadar and fell to his knees before the stunned Executor. "Truly I am to blame!" Zeratul wailed in their minds. "I have betrayed our people! Punish me! Take my life! End my suffering!" He bowed his head, clearly waiting for whatever punishment Tassadar chose to inflict.

For his part, the Executor sat unmoving for a moment. Then, surprisingly, he reached out and rested a hand upon Zeratul's shoulder. "You are the cause, yes," the Executor confirmed, "but your intent was pure. You sought to eliminate a foe, not expose our people. Your own grief and guilt are punishment enough."

Zeratul looked up at him, his eyes wide. "But through me the Swarm will strike at Aiur! Our people will suffer!"

"Yes," Tassadar agreed, "but the Overmind has sought our world obsessively. If not through your actions he would have found Aiur some other way. You have only hastened the inevitable." He turned, and his eyes blazed blue even in the daylight. "I must warn our people, however. They must be told of the attack—and that the cerebrates are the key." Then he bowed his head. "I have not the power to reach them alone."

"I will aid you," Zeratul offered, rising to sit next to Tassadar. The older protoss had apparently locked his grief away, for it no longer showed on his face or in his thoughts, though Raynor was sure the Praetor still felt it keenly. "Between us we may bridge the distance and let your warning be heard."

Tassadar nodded, and the two clasped hands, though not without a tiny shudder on the Executor's part. Raynor stayed where he was, too fascinated to leave and not wanting to disturb them with any sudden movements. He saw the air shimmer between the two protoss, taking on a rainbow sheen, and then two other protoss appeared, their images wavering as from a weak holograph. One was clad in the same uniform as Tassadar, and had sky-blue eyes. The other wore ornate robes of crimson and gold, and blue-gray eyes peered out from beneath his heavy hood.

"En Taro Adun, Executor," the hooded protoss was projecting, his thought-speech faint, and at first Raynor thought he was talking to Tassadar. But the image's eyes did not focus upon the High Templar, and after a second Raynor realized he was talking to the sky-eyed warrior instead. "Your defense of Antioch has restored my faith in the Templar caste. I admit that Tassadar's desertion had shaken—"

"*Indeed,* Aldaris?" Tassadar cut in, his thoughts

directed sharply at the hooded figure. "I would hope that the Judicator would put more faith in their Templar brethren. . . ."

Both of the protoss in the image whirled about, obviously looking for the thought's source.

"Tassadar?" the one named Aldaris queried, his eyes finally focusing upon the High Templar. "Where. . ."

"Be silent, Judicator," Tassadar warned. "There is no time to waste, and I have much to tell you." He nodded toward the second newly arrived protoss but did not pause to greet him otherwise. "As you know, the zerg vanished after the fall of the Terran world of Tarsonis. And though the Conclave bid me return home, I was compelled to remain. A powerful psionic call drew my attention to a remote, barren world named Char. Apparently, the call was answered by others as well. For upon Char, I encountered those who were once our brethren—the Dark Templar." Tassadar's eyes darted briefly toward Zeratul, hidden on the far side of the distortion, before returning to the image.

Aldaris's eyes had narrowed in rage. "Consorting with the Fallen Ones is heresy!" he proclaimed, his thoughts harsh and unforgiving.

"Enough!" Tassadar's own eyes flared into cobalt fire, and the Judicator fell silent. "Hear me, Executor," Tassadar continued, turning toward the sky-eyed protoss instead, "for I have learned much from the Dark Templar Prelate Zeratul. The Overmind controls its minions through agents called cerebrates. Strike down the cerebrates, and the Swarms will surely fall."

"My thanks, noble Tassadar," the other Executor replied, entering the conversation for the first time. "We will use this knowledge well."

"I pray we can trust you, Tassadar," Aldaris stated softly, still projecting anger but now mingling it with fatherly concern. "Already I can sense the taint of the Fallen Ones' influence on your mind. You must return to Aiur at once!"

"My concern is for the safety of Aiur, not the judgments of the Conclave," Tassadar replied calmly. "I will return when the time is right." *And when you have access to a ship,* Raynor thought, but he didn't say it. He understood that the High Templar didn't want to distract his people from the zerg invasion by asking for a ride home, and he admired the protoss warrior's dedication.

Tassadar lifted his hands from Zeratul's and swept them before his face, shattering the strange distorted circle and scattering the image's remains into the weak sunlight.

"My thanks," he told Zeratul quietly. "Perhaps now our people may have a chance."

"We may hope," the Dark Templar replied. "Though even targeting the cerebrates may not be enough."

"Why?" Tassadar asked. "Your attack was sufficient to destroy one."

Zeratul regarded him a second before answering.

"The powers you possess are formidable," he said finally, "but they are not your true gifts. They are merely versions of them approved by your leaders, diluted by their teachings and narrowed by their fears. You must grasp the full power within you to truly strike down the zerg."

Tassadar did not reply. Zeratul's suggestion hung above them, however, and several days later Tassadar responded.

"Tell me more about these gifts we possess" was all he asked, but it was a major step for him and Raynor knew it. From the first confrontation between the two protoss he'd seen how the Dark Templar were spoken of in normal protoss society, and how Tassadar had been raised to consider them evil. Fighting alongside Zeratul had convinced Tassadar otherwise, but he'd still considered the Dark Templar's abilities to be something foreign and perhaps tainted. To ask about them, and especially to speak of them as something native to all protoss, was a major step in breaking down his old prejudices and accepting a different, wider view. Even though Tassadar was far older than he was, Raynor felt proud of him, as if the protoss commander were a young man he'd just seen take his first step toward growing up.

CHAPTER 17

THE NEXT TWO WEEKS WERE A STRANGE MIX OF activity and leisure, study and idleness.

Zeratul had clearly been pleased when Tassadar finally expressed interest in learning about their protoss gifts, but the Praetor had hesitated before replying, glancing significantly at Raynor.

"These gifts lie at the very core of our being," he warned the younger protoss, "and may only be revealed to other members of our race, lest others gain unhealthy insight into our souls and abuse such knowledge to the detriment of our people." The language was convoluted, but Raynor got the gist.

"I'm outta here," he said, standing up and dusting off the seat of his pants. "You guys can do your little bonding thing." But Tassadar raised an arm and blocked him from leaving.

"James Raynor is our ally," the Executor told the wizened Dark Templar. "He is also a"—he paused for an instant; Raynor would have sworn he was taking a deep breath if the protoss had possessed mouths and nostrils and lungs—"friend," Tassadar said finally, and that one word carried a surprising amount of emotion. Not just for the protoss, either—Raynor rocked back on his heels at the statement and felt his eyes tear up. A part of him laughed at himself for being such a sap, but it was only a small part. The rest of him understood. The protoss didn't just read emotions and thoughts, they projected them, and so Tassadar's statement carried with it the full weight of his thoughts and feelings upon the matter. That was how Raynor knew it was such a significant acknowledgment. Tassadar wasn't just saying they were buddies—that had been encompassed in the word "ally." By referring to Raynor as a "friend," Tassadar was admitting to a strong bond between them, a bond that carried its own honor and required its own loyalty. The closest Raynor could come to a comparison was by thinking of blood brothers, men sworn to support one another as they would their own kin. It was a staggering honor, and one he never would have expected from the tall, taciturn alien warrior.

"Thanks," he told Tassadar, knowing the Executor would read into that one word all the gratitude he really felt. He could see from the protoss's eyes that he had. Then Raynor glanced over at Zeratul, who looked both amused and puzzled. "But I don't want to get in the way."

"You are not in the way," Tassadar informed him. "You are welcome." He dropped his arm, demonstrating that Raynor was still free to leave if he chose, and both of them turned to face the Dark Templar. Ball's in your court, Raynor couldn't help thinking.

Perhaps the Praetor heard him. Or perhaps he simply recognized that the two others were waiting for his response. The older protoss paused for a moment, perhaps for dramatic effect, before nodding slightly.

"You see beyond skin," he complimented Tassadar, "acknowledging the soul beneath and finding kinship regardless of form. Impressive." Something about his tone sounded almost jealous, and Raynor had a flash of insight. For all his learning and wisdom and counsel, all his talk about an open mind, Zeratul had very set notions about certain things. And Tassadar had just demonstrated that he could move beyond what he'd been taught, and think outside the box. It was a rare gift, and one the Praetor himself did not possess.

"Much of what I will teach you can only be learned by a joining of thoughts," Zeratul continued, "and thus our companion"—he nodded at Raynor—"will be unable to participate. However, I will share what I may, that he may learn more of us and our ways." He nodded again, but this was deeper, almost a bow. "Perhaps in this you will discover the true meaning of being protoss, and will understand us as no outsider has before."

"And perhaps," Tassadar added, "your perspective, unbounded by our heritage, will provide useful insight for us all."

Raynor thought about it for a second, but only a second. On the one hand, this might be pretty boring, especially when the two protoss were "joining thoughts," as

Zeratul had put it. On the other hand, the more he knew about the protoss the more fascinating they became, and this was a chance to learn things no other non-protoss knew. Things even most protoss didn't know, apparently. But the real deciding factor was Tassadar's calling him "friend." Raynor knew it was one of the most important moments of his life, right up there with the day he first left home and the day he met Mike Liberty and the day he walked out on Arcturus Mengsk. The Templar had invited him to participate in something incredibly important, and to refuse would be to insult their new bond. So he sank back down onto the rock he'd been using as a seat, and nodded. "Don't know I'll have much to offer," he admitted, "but thanks."

That apparently settled the matter. It was later that afternoon—because the old protoss refused to do anything without appropriate dramatic pauses—that Zeratul began their education.

As the Dark Templar had warned, Raynor wasn't able to follow all of it. Often the two protoss linked minds so the Praetor could demonstrate something directly. They had tried to include Raynor in the link but he'd wound up with no more than several strange images, a cascade of sounds, and a splitting headache. "Your mind is not meant for such uses," the Praetor pointed out afterward, sounding slightly apologetic, "and the link works best with only two minds, even among protoss." So for long stretches Raynor found himself just sitting between two statues, or getting up and wandering away while they were busy communing.

At other times, however, Zeratul lectured them on protoss history and theology, and Raynor listened along with Tassadar, though he could follow only some of the details. He learned about the Xel'Naga, the tribe that created the protoss millennia ago and been attacked for their troubles. He learned about the battles that tore the race apart, and about the Mystic known as Khas who reunited the people and created the Khala, the Path of Ascension. It was the Khala, with its rigid rules, that still defined protoss society today. And it was the protoss tribes who had refused to submit to its structure who were exiled from their homeworld and later became the Dark Templar.

"The powers you draw upon are those granted us by the Xel'Naga themselves," Zeratul explained, "and are entwined with the very fiber of our being. But they have been filtered through the Khala, restricted to a narrow channel defined by elder generations past. Our true powers are not limited in this fashion."

"Yet without these limits we would lose all control," Tassadar countered. "As happened long ago, when Adun failed in his duty and allowed the Tribes to unleash their power across Aiur, nearly destroying the world." Waves of shock and old pain rose from Zeratul, making Raynor flinch. "Yes, I know of these things," Tassadar admitted. "Rumors still exist, and when we rise high enough in our training Templar are instructed in the difference between lies and truth."

"Instructed, yes," Zeratul agreed, "but not fully. Nor are you given full truth, only the version the Conclave agreed upon centuries ago." He turned away, unable to speak further, and Raynor knew the lessons were over for the day.

It was actually three days before they discussed protoss history again. The zerg attacked on the second day, and after beating them back the protoss and human forces relocated to yet another hidden valley. They had honed the process to an art by now, the protoss actually helping to pack up the humans' tents and gear, and could be on the move in twenty minutes or less. With each battle and each new camp the rapport between the two races grew stronger, and between the two sides of the one race. Raynor knew the time he spent with Tassadar and Zeratul had something to do with that.

"They can't be all bad," Non said one morning over coffee, "or you wouldn't be sitting with them all day on these damn rocks." Everyone laughed.

"What're you talking about?" Cavez asked a little while later. "Or thinking about, or mind-talking, or whatever it is," he amended hastily. Most of the men still weren't comfortable with the notion of telepathy, and Raynor wondered if his history with Kerrigan had helped him accept the concept, and the practice, so easily. Not that it didn't still weird him out to have another's thoughts pop into his head, but he understood it and wasn't so much afraid anymore as just continually startled.

"History," Raynor answered honestly. "I'm learning their history." He took a sip of his coffee and thought about it a bit more. "It's an honor," he said then.

"They've never let another race know this much about them. And I can see why. The more they tell me about their past, the more I understand who they are now, and why."

"Is it . . . okay?" Cavez asked, a shadow of his former xenophobia showing on his face.

"It's fine," Raynor assured him. "Better than that, actually. We don't have to worry. The one thing they'd never do is betray us."

He knew it was true as he said it. The notion of honor and loyalty was at the very core of the protoss race, even before the Khala had made it such a large part of an individual's reputation. The Dark Templar, for all their rebellion and distrust, were still incredibly honorable. And still utterly loyal to their race. Tassadar saw that as well, and Raynor could see the Executor's respect for the Dark Templar, and particularly for their Praetor, increasing every day.

Especially after Zeratul's lessons began again. "We did nearly destroy Aiur," he admitted without preamble when he, Tassadar, and Raynor were seated on a small ledge by the valley's back wall that third day. "But it was not entirely our fault. Adun hoped to show us the error of our ways." His green eyes grew distant, and Raynor knew the Praetor was remembering ancient history—too ancient for him to have experienced it firsthand, but Tassadar had explained that protoss could share experience with one another so fully you felt you had been there.

"He came to us, with orders to destroy us," Zeratul

said softly, and turned at Tassadar's wordless cry. "This they did not tell you, of course. Why would they? Admit that they sent their Templar to slaughter their own kin, whose only crime was refusing to submit to their codes?" He nodded. "Now you see the depth to which you have been misled," he added, though he sounded sad rather than triumphant.

"But Adun refused," the Praetor continued. "He could not bring himself to kill his own kin. Instead he taught us that which Khas had taught, how to tap the power we all carried within us. He hoped our minds would link and we would then see our folly in resisting." Zeratul stopped, and for a moment it seemed as if he wouldn't continue.

"It didn't work," Raynor ventured finally, startling the older protoss and earning the mental equivalent of a bitter laugh for his efforts. But the reminder of an audience spurred Zeratul to resume his story.

"No," he admitted. "It did not. We learned our power, yes, but not the discipline to control it. That at least the Khala is good for: providing discipline from birth, teaching protoss to master their urges and thoughts. With such training our people can use our gifts without fear." He shook his head. "But the Tribes did not have this knowledge. Adun could teach us only so much—it would have required decades to train us in the necessary control, even if he could have. And many of us were too old, too set in our ways, to alter our patterns so fully." His eyes rested on Tassadar, and Raynor could tell what the Praetor was thinking. Here before him was a High Templar, a high-ranking member of the protoss society, but Tassadar was still young enough and idealistic enough—and honest enough—to change his patterns radically.

"Your power grew beyond your ability to contain it," Tassadar stated, and it was not a question.

"Yes," Zeratul agreed. "Storms rose from our minds, fueled by old enmities, and swept across Aiur. The Conclave scattered the storms, but not without grave cost."

"Yet you would have me follow this path," Tassadar said softly. The way he said it, Raynor felt the Executor knew better but still wanted to hear it.

He got his wish. "No!" Zeratul's reply contained the most emotion either of them had seen from the old protoss. "Not in that manner!" He calmed himself with a visible effort. "That was the beginning, and showed us the error of our ways," he explained. "After our exile, we continued to study the gifts Adun had shown us, and to unlock the powers within. But we also taught ourselves control, as strong as that granted by the Khala, but without its limitations. We learned to harness the powers of our race fully and control them completely, yet our minds remain unfettered by narrow codes and hierarchies designed only to protect those in power."

"The Khala is not a prison," Tassadar refuted, his thoughts quiet but the faith behind them hard and strong. "It is the foundation of our society, the bedrock of our people." He leaned back, his eyes half-closed. "It is impossible to describe fully," he warned, and Raynor could tell the thought was directed not only to him but to Zeratul as well. "We are as one within the Khala," Tassadar stated after a moment's silence. "Our minds are linked. But not as when we communicate—not as they are now. The Khala offers a deeper communion, a true bond between protoss. In some ways you lose yourself within that link, becoming one with all other protoss, a single glorious being."

Like the Swarm? Raynor couldn't help wondering. He didn't say it aloud, of course. But Zeratul was not so shy about airing his misgivings.

"This is why we refused it," the old protoss stated firmly. "We had no wish to lose ourselves. We are protoss, yes, but we are also individuals. That is important as well."

"Of course it is," Tassadar agreed, opening his eyes to meet the Praetor's gaze. "Never did I claim otherwise." He held up one hand to stop Raynor, who had just opened his mouth to protest. "We lose ourselves, yes, but not our identity, not who we are—just our loneliness, our isolation. I am still Tassadar within the Khala, but I am more than Tassadar, more than this body and this mind. I am one with all my brethren, part of the greater whole that is our race." He shook his head, releasing the mental equivalent of a sigh. "It cannot be explained properly, not without experiencing it." Now his look flashed over both of them, and Raynor saw something like pity in his eyes. "And neither of you will ever know it fully."

Raynor frowned. "I know I can't, because I'm not

protoss. But why can't he?" He jerked a thumb toward Zeratul, and saw Tassadar's eyes grow even sadder.

"The Dark Templar have removed themselves from our racial link," the tall protoss explained slowly. "They have forever severed their connection to our people, thrown away all that we are, turned their back on us."

"We never turned our back," Zeratul countered hotly, his eyes blazing. "We still keep watch over Aiur, over all of you! We have since our exile!" Then he let his eyelids drop, a deliberate setting aside of his anger. "But yes, we broke that link. We thought we would be lost within it, swallowed up by the Conclave, stripped of our identities. Perhaps if one such as you had explained it, we might have acted differently."

"You would consider rejoining us?" Tassadar seemed startled.

"Yes" was the Praetor's reply. "If we could, we might consider it. Not with the Conclave, for we do not trust their motives, but with those such as yourself, certainly."

"I am surprised to hear you discuss such a matter so calmly," Tassadar admitted, and Zeratul's mental snort made Raynor grin in reply.

"We consider all our actions, Executor. Every move is carefully inspected, debated, deliberated. We were not a hasty people to begin with, and we have learned patience from our time among the stars."

"Then you do not advocate giving in to every whim and emotion," Tassadar asked, and again it was clearly not a question, though Zeratul answered anyway.

"Of course not," the Praetor scoffed. "Those are tales

spread by the Conclave, painting us as rogues and fiends, little more than savages, unable to think clearly or act rationally, unable to control ourselves." He turned, raising his arms and sweeping them to include the valley behind them. "Are we irrational and uncontrolled?" Tassadar and Raynor both looked past him, where Dark Templar sat just as still as Templar and just as visibly at peace. No other answer was required.

"Poor, poor Jimmy. So sad, so lonely. So doomed."

Raynor jerked upright, sweat scattering from his sudden motion. He took a deep breath, forcing his racing heart to slow, and wiped his forearm across his brow, sweeping away the sweat that coated his skin. Damn. He couldn't remember all of the dream this time, but he knew it had been another one about Kerrigan. He had been having them more and more often ever since they'd abandoned the shuttle. But the tone of them had changed dramatically.

The ones that he did remember lately still involved him and Kerrigan. But they weren't happy. Or at least they weren't by the end. Each time the two of them were together, eating or running or making love or just sitting together, talking and laughing, full of life and love. But then something changed. Kerrigan pulled away from him, or simply turned cold in his arms. Her voice shifted, growing deeper, more raspy, chased by a strange echo that sent chills through him. Her complexion altered, fair skin mottling and darkening. And her look changed from love to anger, sorrow, even hatred.

"Too bad, Jimmy," she said each time. "You could have had it all."

Sometimes he woke up then. Other times he found himself running, fleeing this love gone wrong, only to be chased down. And tortured. He suspected this last dream had been one of the latter variety.

"I gotta stop doing this," he told himself as he stood up and made his way out of his tent, careful not to wake any of the troopers asleep in tents nearby. He was getting enough sleep, but it didn't feel that way. Often he was edgy, abrupt, antagonistic, particularly right after he'd woken up. His eyes burned, and sometimes the places where he'd taken wounds in the dream ached for hours afterward. Yet each night he hoped to dream about Kerrigan again, and each time he did he savored the start of the dream, before it all turned ugly.

"Why is she doing this to me?" he muttered as he knelt near the valley wall and splashed water on his face from the puddle that collected there.

"Perhaps her reasons are as muddled as your own thoughts." The reply came from behind Raynor, startling him enough that his handful of water splashed against his chest instead of his face. He turned around, already knowing whom he would find—the mental voice was distinctive.

"Zeratul."

The Praetor stood a few paces away, hands hidden within the folds of his robe, green eyes watching him carefully. "I did not mean to startle you," the protoss assured him.

"That's okay." Raynor scooped up more water, actually getting it to his face this time, then clambered back to his feet. "Just shaking off a bad dream."

The Dark Templar nodded. "Her touch still hangs heavy about you," he observed, confirming something Raynor had known but never stated out loud. The dreams really were from Kerrigan!

"She's torturing me," he admitted, walking a short ways to perch on a low rock. Zeratul sank down beside him with the easy grace of the protoss, curling in upon himself somehow so he resembled a ball of dark cloth with a head perched atop it.

"Not just you," the Praetor commented, but he didn't say more. His eyes bore a look Raynor remembered well from people like his mother, his teachers, and Mengsk. A look that said, *Figure it out for yourself.*

"I'm the only one getting these dreams, though, right?" That was his first worry, that she had infected all his men the same way. But he didn't really think she had, and indeed Zeratul shook his head no. "So who else could she be hurting with them? It's just me—and her." Raynor felt a chill run through him. He stared at the protoss, barely seeing him. "That's it, isn't it? She's hurting herself by sending me these dreams!"

"How could a dream hurt the sender?" Zeratul asked, though Raynor suspected the old protoss already knew the answer. He worked it out himself, talking it through, though he knew Zeratul could hear his thoughts as easily as his words.

"It'd hurt if she's giving up something she wants to

keep for herself," he decided. "Or if she's sharing something she doesn't really want to share. Or if she's reliving something she'd rather tuck away where she doesn't have to see it." He thought about the dreams, about their content, particularly how they started. "She's sending me images of how we could have been," he admitted, aching at the thought of it. "If we'd been together properly." In his mind's eye he saw them running together, dancing, laughing. "She's showing me that we could have been happy together."

He glared at Zeratul, squinting to blink away the sudden tears. "She's taunting me with what we could have had."

"Yes," the Praetor agreed. He waited, clearly expecting Raynor to continue.

"But she's also torturing herself with something she wants but can never have," Raynor realized. "Part of her still wants to be with me. That's where the dreams come from. She's twisting them because she knows she can't have that—can't have me. And using them against me because it's the only way to justify sending them at all."

Zeratul nodded. "You grasp truths quickly," he told Raynor, "once you free your mind from its constraints."

Raynor laughed. "If you mean I'm too pigheaded to see past my own nose half the time, you're right." He sobered again. "So I know she both does and doesn't want to send me these dreams. They're still torture. They still wake me in a cold sweat." He looked up at the old protoss. "Can't you stop them?"

"I?" Zeratul regarded him carefully. "They are not my dreams, either of my making or of my receipt."

"Yeah, but you can see them," Raynor insisted. "You can read them in my thoughts. Can't you block them somehow, so I don't have to get them? Turn them aside or something?" He knew he was grasping, but he was desperate. Knowing that part of Kerrigan still wanted him, still wished things had been different, only made the dreams that much worse.

But the Praetor shook his head. "These dreams are yours to bear," he cautioned. "It is not for me to turn them aside. You must confront them yourself, as best you can."

Raynor got up and was about to walk back to his tent when he stopped. Something in Zeratul's words, something in his look—he had a suspicion, and acted on it. "You could stop them, though," he said, turning back toward the Praetor. "If you wanted to. You could."

Zeratul met his gaze but did not reply.

"Why won't you?" Raynor asked. He stepped a little closer. "I'm not even asking you to, not now. But I want to know why. The truth."

For a moment he thought the Praetor would refuse to answer, or say something again about fighting one's own battles. Then a thin sigh escaped the old protoss, a hint of both amusement and chagrin.

"You are more like us than we know," Zeratul said, so quietly Raynor wasn't sure he'd heard him. Then, louder, he added, "You are correct. The dreams might be blocked, though only with difficulty. The bond between you is strong. Very strong." He paused, then went on. "It is clear to me, as a mottled band of light stretched between you."

"A band of light?" Raynor digested that. "Wait, you can see the link from Kerrigan?" At Zeratul's nod, he continued, filled with sudden understanding, "Then you know where she is!"

"I cannot see her precise location," the Praetor corrected. "But I can see from the intensity of the link whether she is near or far, yes."

"You've been using me!" Raynor snapped at him. "You let the dreams go on so you could keep track of her, keep us away from her!"

"Yes."

Raynor thought about that, thought about what he would have done in the same situation, and felt his anger wash away. "Good," he said finally. "It's a tool we can use."

As he walked back to his tent, he heard one last comment from Zeratul, little more than a whisper echoed on the wind. "More like us than we know."

CHAPTER 18

"YOU HAVE ALREADY BEGUN ALONG THE PATH, the truth path," Zeratul assured Tassadar a few days later during another of their strange trainings-lectures-discussions. Raynor sat off to the side, watching and listening as usual. "Nor did you require my instruction to take that first step," the Praetor continued, and Raynor thought he heard a hint of petulance, as if the old protoss was disappointed he hadn't been more necessary.

"I do not understand," Tassadar admitted. It was one of the things Raynor liked about the tall protoss warrior—he was willing to show his ignorance, and to own up to his mistakes.

"When we first met," Zeratul reminded him, and Tassadar hung his head in shame. After more than a month together, he clearly regretted attacking the Dark Templar during their first encounter. But the Praetor brushed any apologies aside with one hand

and continued speaking. "You manifested mental weapons, did you not?"

Tassadar nodded, and so did Raynor, remembering the glittering blue-white energy spikes protruding above the Executor's wrists.

"Yet you wore no bracers," Zeratul pointed out. Raynor was sure he saw Tassadar's eyes widen as he realized what the Praetor was saying.

"Okay," Raynor said, leaning forward slightly, "sorry to interrupt but I don't get it. So what?"

"The bracers amplify and focus our minds," Tassadar explained slowly. "They allow us to generate psi-blades. Yet I—" He paused, apparently unable to finish the thought openly.

"You created such weapons with no tools," Zeratul agreed. "Your mind alone focused your power and gave it form." He sounded proud, like a father watching a son fire a rifle for the first time. "Truly your mind has already made the leap away from the Khala and its restrictions." He rested his hands upon Tassadar's shoulders. "You are ready for the next step."

Raynor didn't follow much of what came after that. It was both too specific and too vague, instructions mixed with metaphors and sprinkled with poetry, as Zeratul showed Tassadar the true potential of the protoss mind. But he did witness the results as Tassadar mastered each new gift in turn, and he was present when, after the two protoss had sat silently communing for several hours, Zeratul finally rose and declared, "You are ready."

"Ready?" Raynor scrambled to his feet, cursing the pins and needles in his legs and massaging them absently back to life. "Ready for what?"

"The Shadow Walk," Zeratul explained as he led Tassadar down from the small nook they had found and across the valley they were currently using as their combined camp. "The test each Dark Templar must undergo to demonstrate his mastery of our skills."

Raynor, walking along behind the two protoss, suddenly understood what Zeratul was saying. All this time he had thought Tassadar was simply learning more about his heritage, and about the powers every protoss possessed. Apparently it had been more than that. Zeratul had been training the Executor, yes, but not just as a friendly gesture. He had been teaching Tassadar to become a Dark Templar!

"What happens if he passes?" Raynor asked as they neared the far end of the valley. The rest of the protoss moved aside, Tassadar's Zealots stepping back against the east wall and Zeratul's Dark Templar vanishing into the shadows along the west face, and Raynor gestured for his own people to stay where they were at the southeast corner.

"He becomes one of us," Zeratul replied.

"What about being a Templar, then?" Raynor demanded. "Does he lose that?" He wasn't sure why it was so important to him except that he had grown to like the Executor, and knew that his achievements as a High Templar were important to Tassadar.

Zeratul paused at the question and turned back to

study Raynor carefully. The old protoss's pale green eyes were as unreadable as ever, but Raynor thought he saw a flicker of amusement there—and perhaps of delight as well.

"Only one other has attempted to walk both paths," Zeratul admitted, but he did not explain beyond that. They had reached the end of the valley now, and the Praetor gently turned his pupil back the way they had come.

"What must I do?" Tassadar asked simply. He had followed Zeratul here as if in a daze, and only now seemed to waken from it, glancing around, his sharp blue eyes taking in every detail.

"You must traverse the valley to the far end," Zeratul replied. "Pass through the shadows only. Let none prevent your progress."

"That's it?" Raynor couldn't stop himself from asking. "That's all he has to do, walk across the valley?"

Both protoss glanced at him and nodded. Then Raynor's brain caught up with his hearing and he glanced down at the valley again, realizing what he'd seen as they'd passed. Tassadar's Zealots were all on the east side, in the fading sunlight. But Zeratul's followers had vanished into the shadows. The same shadows Tassadar was expected to stay within as he walked. Crossing a valley filled with invisible warriors who could attack at any time—yeah, that was a challenge.

"Good luck," he told Tassadar.

"Thank you, James Raynor," the Executor replied, his blue-white eyes wise and unblinking. Then the

High Templar turned and took three paces forward and to the left, the shadows rising about him like mist as he entered their domain.

"Will he make it?" Raynor asked Zeratul, who had also turned back toward the valley's far end but was staying outside the shadows.

"If such is his destiny," the Praetor replied. He did not offer any further comment, and after a few minutes Raynor found himself alone, the old protoss having vanished somewhere between one footstep and another. Raynor considered joining his own men but decided against it. They were at the front end of the valley, and Tassadar had already passed them. He wanted a better view, particularly for the end of the walk, which he suspected would be the hardest part. So he returned to the nook and settled himself there, back against the wall, to watch the show.

Tassadar was moving slowly but surely through the shadows. Somewhere before beginning the ordeal he had shed his uniform and now wore only the long loincloth, more ceremonial than necessary. His eyes glowed blue-white, pinpricks in the darkness. Shadows swirled about him, enveloping him as he walked.

Then the first Dark Templar struck.

It was difficult to follow, particularly from a distance. Raynor's first clue came when Tassadar twisted to one side, arm rising to block a blow. Then a protoss was standing beside him, angling for position, his hands wreathed in that strange beyond-dark glow Zeratul had manifested when saving Tassadar from the zerg. Those hands swung toward the Executor and Raynor thought he could feel the cold rising off them, though he knew it was just his mind playing tricks on him. Still, he breathed a sigh of relief when Tassadar blocked the first blow and tripped the warrior, sinking to his knees alongside, his own hand lashing out to land against his opponent's chest and pin him to the ground. That was a clear defeat, and the Dark Templar did not rise as Tassadar straightened and resumed his walk.

The second attack came from behind, a protoss appearing from shadows Tassadar had just passed. This one's hands also bore the darkness, stretched between them like a garrote torn from deep space, and with a quick flick the protoss tossed the band over Tassadar's head and around his neck. The Dark Templar tugged back sharply, planning to catch his quarry about the throat and yank him off balance. But Tassadar raised his right hand and his glittering psi-blade burst from it, the blade slicing cleanly through the dark band and scattering its shadowy substance. The warrior Tassadar dispatched with three quick moves, one to the chest and one to the throat and one to the space between the glowing eyes, and then he was moving again.

Everyone was watching now, human and protoss alike, knowing that this strange journey was somehow important. Raynor could see the look of awe on the faces of his men and knew he bore a similar expression. Tassadar's complete focus, his grace, and the powers he was demonstrating, seemingly without effort, put most legends and fairy tales to shame. Here was true power, true strength, manifested in a being who lived among them and fought beside them. Here was a true legend.

Tassadar's warriors seemed less impressed and more disquieted, though Raynor wasn't sure how he was getting that impression. They were all watching the shadows intently, barely moving, and though he could feel the occasional flutter he'd learned to recognize as mental communication it was too far away and too private for him to notice anything beyond its mere presence. He understood, though. The Zealots had watched their leader become friendly with Zeratul, someone they had been raised to believe was an enemy every bit as bad as the zerg. Even though they'd learned to respect the Dark Templar, it was still asking a lot for them to accept seeing their leader so chummy with one. And now they were watching what was clearly a test and an initiation. They probably worried that Tassadar would betray them, would become as dark and cryptic as the Praetor, and perhaps even as evil and ruthless and deranged as their legends of every Dark Templar. It was only their discipline and their tremendous respect for Tassadar himself that was keeping them from interfering.

Tassadar was halfway across the valley now. He had faced more than a dozen of the Dark Templar, defeating each one in turn. Some he had conquered with only his speed and strength. Others he had used his psi-blades to disarm. Still others he had bested with their own gifts, as when one had punched at him with a dark-shrouded fist and Tassadar had caught the blow, his own hand stealing the darkness and then releasing it harmlessly back into the shadows. Each Dark Templar, as he was defeated, moved aside to let him pass. But he still had half the valley to go, and many Dark Templar yet to defeat—including Zeratul himself.

As Raynor watched, however, he noticed something strange. Tassadar's eyes were still visible among the shadows, but now he saw a faint speck of light upon the protoss warrior's chest as well. A second appeared, then a third, forming an inverted triangle above the Executor's triple hearts. The tiny spots grew brighter, as did Tassadar's eyes, and slowly the glow crept across the rest of his body, until his entire frame was engulfed in a near-blinding light. It dispersed the shadows around him, scattering them into small pockets of stubborn darkness—pockets shaped much like protoss warriors preparing to strike.

Raynor blinked. For just an instant, as the glow had flared to full intensity, he thought he'd seen a flicker from it, like a candle bending in a strong wind. Or a faint shadow scurrying clear of the revealing light. But now it was gone and he wasn't sure if he'd imagined it.

He saw Tassadar, wreathed in light, continue his slow, steady march along the valley floor. Several of the Dark Templar straightened and let him pass without a fight, apparently accepting his tactic as a win since it had robbed them of their concealment and their tactical advantage. Others attacked but could not get close enough to strike, the light dazzling them and forcing them back before they could reach him. And still the Executor walked.

Finally he was just below the nook, and one last patch of shadow remained before him. As Tassadar approached the shadow spread out rather than shrinking back, extending tendrils to wrap around him and smother his light. The glow dimmed but did not die, and in return it lanced deep into the darkness, stripping away layers until the form of a tall, bent protoss was revealed. Zeratul.

"Excellent," the Praetor acknowledged, letting the shadows fall away from him now that they were no longer useful. "You have used both light and darkness to good advantage. Your skill with your Templar gifts is commendable, and you use our native gifts as one born to them. Truly you are worthy." Not for the first time Raynor could hear the grin in the old protoss's mental voice, the hints of laughter wrapped around every word. "Provided you can escape my grasp and reach the gathering place beyond."

Tassadar replied, the first time he had broadcast his thoughts since the challenge began. "Come then, old one, and let us see if my light or your darkness will prevail."

For an instant Zeratul's eyes flared as if in anger, and his response was sharp. "It is not about light or dark! I have told you this! It is about using what we are given!" Then, as if his anger spurred him on, the Praetor attacked. The shadows rose about him again, sheathing his limbs in their dark bands, and he drove them forward like twin blades, skewering the glowing form before him. Raynor almost called out in sympathy, until he saw that Tassadar was unfazed. His glittering aura had been pierced—in fact, the dark blades had driven deep into his shoulders as well—but he showed no signs of pain or even surprise.

Instead it was Zeratul who stepped back, confused. "Your mind is shuttered," the old protoss noted. "Good. But why conceal your thoughts when your body glows so brightly?"

Raynor got it just as Zeratul did, and watched the Praetor leap backward, pulling his blades free as he moved and twisted around. Both of them knew it was too late, however. One corner of the Dark Templar's shadow, an edge that had not wrapped back around him as he'd moved to battle, had swept past while Zeratul struck at Tassadar. Now that same wisp of shadow flowed up the rocks at the valley's edge, to settle squarely in the lesser shadows against the valley wall behind where Raynor sat. And then the darkness faded away, torn apart from within by a pair of small, diamond-bright blue lights, and Tassadar stood there, looking down upon Zeratul and the rest of the valley behind him.

"A ploy, then," the Praetor commented as he abandoned his own shadowy weaponry and climbed back up to the nook himself. "The light a mere decoy as you slipped past in shadow."

Tassadar nodded but did not otherwise reply.

For an instant Zeratul glared at him. Then he laughed, the mingled humor and pride washing over them all in a wave and briefly uniting human, Zealot, and Dark Templar alike.

"Wonderful!" Zeratul announced. "Inspired! Truly you took advantage of your abilities, old and new both, and our own prejudices as well. Without your Templar training that tactic might have failed, but without your newly awakened talents you could not have succeeded."

"Truly," Tassadar agreed, "I can feel the energies within me in ways as never before. The training I had as a Templar was a mere fragment of the whole, a carefully controlled sample of what lay beneath." He bowed his head. "Thank you."

"It is I who should thank you," Zeratul replied. He stepped forward and again placed both hands on Tassadar's shoulders. "And I greet you, brother, to the ranks of those who walk the true path of our race, through shadow and through light." He straightened to his full height and his next thought rippled across the valley, filled with power and grandeur that made the very rocks shake. "May you fulfill your destiny, child of Adun," Zeratul proclaimed, "and bring honor to us all."

From the rest of the Dark Templar, now assembled below them, came a mental shout, a wash of greetings and admiration. And from Tassadar's own warriors came an answering flow of cautious congratulation—respect for their leader and awe at his new skills, but concern over what he would now become.

"Nice going," Raynor said, offering his hand to Tassadar. The Executor stared down at it for an instant, then reached out and grasped it firmly in his own.

"Thank you, James Raynor." Tassadar's gaze swept across Zeratul and then the Dark Templar and his own Zealots, and even the rest of Raynor's people at the far end of the valley. "And thank you to all," he added, "for without the presence of so many, so different and yet so alike, I could not—"

But whatever he meant to say next was cut short, as a loud shriek split the air. An oily form followed it, wings beating hard as its awkward body dove down and acid flew from its mouth and splattered one of the protoss, who fell to the ground writhing in pain. The zerg had found them unawares. They were under attack!

CHAPTER 19

"DAMN IT!" RAYNOR LEAPED DOWN FROM THE nook and raced across the valley toward his men on the far side. He continued cursing as he moved. Why hadn't they thought to keep lookouts? Because they'd all been so entranced by the whole Shadow Walk thing. And he'd let his men get sloppy lately, allowing them to maintain only casual patrols, if that, because the protoss were always on alert and could detect incoming zerg better than they could, even in their suits.

And the suits! Their powered combat armor, so damn useful in a fight, sitting there useless against the valley wall. None of his men were suited up, though several were hurriedly climbing into the armor now. He just hoped they'd have time to get the suits up and running.

"Cavez! Abernathy!" he shouted as he hit the midpoint of the valley, hoping his voice would carry over the noise of the dive-bombing zerg. "Get rifles up and ready! Give us some cover fire!" Whether his two lieutenants heard him or simply anticipated his command, they turned and grabbed rifles, releasing a barrage of ammo toward the incoming creatures. Other troopers hoisted weapons as well, and soon the air above the valley was filled with glittering shards as the rifles fired wave after wave at the invaders.

By then Raynor was in the camp. He made a beeline for his suit, still sitting off to one side, and climbed into it as quickly as possible. He'd had years of experience with powered armor and had it sealed and in motion by the time he'd caught his breath from his run. Then he reached over his shoulder, unslung the canister rifle on his back, and began taking down zerg.

With the sky finally covered, the airborne zerg lost their advantage. They'd killed several protoss in the first wave but after that the Zealots and Dark Templar had moved to the safety of the walls and the fliers couldn't hit them as easily. Of course, the winged zerg weren't the only ones attacking—this time it was a larger group than usual, at least a hundred of them, and half were ground-based. They'd apparently found the valley and waited by the entrance until the fliers could distract everyone, then charged in. Raynor's camp was closest to the valley's front and so he and his men quickly found themselves swamped by hydralisks, zerglings, and ultralisks. The protoss moved to their aid and bolstered their ranks.

Raynor heard a strange noise over the sound of gunfire, a keening moan, and risked a glance toward the valley's other end. He saw Tassadar's Zealots using their psi-blades to take down any zerg that got close, and Zeratul's Dark Templar doing the same thing on the other side. He saw Zeratul himself, still perched in that small nook, casting strange bands of darkness like nets upon any flier that chanced nearby—even as he watched a devourer plummeted to the ground, its body wrapped in the inky strands.

And then he saw Tassadar.

The Executor had leaped down from the nook and was fighting his way across the valley floor, taking his Shadow Walk in reverse. Darkness rose behind him like a cloak, a curve of cold shadow that the zerg apparently could not pierce, but his glittering psi-blades flared from his wrists, now longer than a man's forearm and capable of reaching and searing through a soaring mutalisk with a mere flick upward. Raynor saw the High Templar turn and jerk his right arm in the direction of an approaching devourer. The psi-blade on that wrist lengthened somehow, going from a triangular blade to a long tendril like a glowing whip, and crackled as it lashed out. The gleaming tip struck the descending zerg just above its gaping snout and lanced clean through, causing a small spark of light to appear within the creature's mouth. Then the spark exploded and the creature fell, headless, to the ground as Tassadar retracted his weapon and used it, bladelike once again, on a hydralisk that had foolishly charged within range.

It was the most amazing display Raynor had ever seen. He had watched Tassadar fight before, and the protoss had always impressed him with his grace, speed, and accuracy. But now there was something new. Not only did the Executor possess these strange new gifts Zeratul had taught him, but he carried himself with more poise, more calm, more confidence. It wasn't posturing, either—if anything, the tall protoss warrior made less show of his authority now, but that somehow served only to deepen the aura of strength and power he projected. The zerg began backing away from him, sensing the same might Raynor saw, and Tassadar used that advantage, forcing them into his Zealots and the Dark Templar alike, clearing a path.

Within minutes the zerg had gone from conquering invaders to desperate defenders, the surviving brood members clustering together and striving to hold off their foes while they searched for a way out.

Then a small blip appeared on Raynor's screen and he turned, tracking the new arrival the suit had detected.

There, up along one of the ridges above the valley, hovered a large, familiar shape. One of the zerg overlords. But where had it come from? It hadn't been there before or his systems would have marked it. And the overlords were slow, clumsy, and vulnerable. They were also vital to maintaining the brood, providing a communications link between its controlling cerebrate—and Kerrigan above it—and the rest of the zerg. Kerrigan wouldn't send one into the mountains without adequate protection.

"Do not despair, my brethren," the overlord called down to the zerg still trapped in the valley. "More of our brood are close by, and will reach us soon. Pull back now, that your strength can add to the ferocity of our renewed attack."

Upon hearing this, the zerg below scattered. They gave up all attempts to hold off the protoss and human forces and scrambled for the walls, climbing and flying and crawling up to the ridge and then over it. In less than a minute they had vanished, leaving only their dead behind.

"Yeah!" Non shouted, raising his rifle high in both hands. "Run, you stinkers!"

"Shut it!" Raynor snapped at him. "Pack up! We're out of here!"

"What?" McMurty stopped slapping hands with one of the other troopers and turned, confusion written across his broad face. "But sir, we won! They've got their tails between their legs!"

"They're regrouping," Raynor corrected him. "They'll be back in minutes, and a lot more of them this time. We need to move on." He gestured. "McMurty, you and Ling take your rifles. I want you up on that ridge. The minute you see zerg, you start shooting. Got it?" He glanced at the rest of his crew. "Non, you and Deslan are on the valley entrance. Same deal—stand guard, keep frosty, and shoot anything that moves. The rest of you, get this gear packed!"

For a second his men stared at him. The victory had been so quick, so decisive, they clearly couldn't believe they were still in danger. But then their training kicked in and Cavez and Abernathy began bellowing orders, organizing the rest of the troopers while the four Raynor had singled out clambered up the slopes and stood guard high above.

It took them only ten minutes to pack and get moving, but Non began firing just as they had stowed the last tent. Deslan joined him an instant later, shouting, "Zerg! Heading toward us!" over his shoulder. It was the only good way out of the valley, but not the only way possible—Tassadar was too sharp a tactician to pick a site with no escape routes. Everyone else moved to the far end of the valley, filing up into the small nook where Raynor had so recently sat with his two protoss allies. Tassadar had already leaped onto a long, narrow ledge above the nook, which led them up and out of the valley and back onto a nearby peak. The troopers in armor helped those without to reach the ledge, then joined them. The Zealots and Dark Templar followed, Zeratul with them, and finally Raynor pulled his four guards back, covering them as they raced across the valley and then up and out. The zerg were still struggling to enter the valley, climbing over those already slain, when Raynor dropped down on the other side of the ridge and joined the rest of his forces in the quick march away from the recent battleground.

Several hours later, certain they had shaken their pursuit, Tassadar selected another valley and led them all beneath the shelter of its overhanging walls. They set up camp again with the ease of long practice, but this time Raynor set guards in armor to watch at every corner. He wasn't going to be surprised again.

"Nice call, chief," McMurty admitted as they crouched and ate some dried meat, washed down with superheated sludge-coffee. "How'd you know they were coming back?"

"I heard 'em talking," Raynor admitted, taking a cautious sip of his brew. "The overlord called them back to regroup."

He was still choking down the sludge when he realized the valley had gone very quiet. Looking up from his cup, he saw his men staring at him—and the protoss, sitting beyond them, as well. Even Tassadar and Zeratul were studying him closely, heads tilted to one side, eyes narrowed as if unsure they had heard correctly.

"They talk?" Cavez asked softly. "But, Commander, they don't talk. None of them do."

"What?" Raynor set his cup down and glared at his young lieutenant. "'Course they do. What, you think I'd make this up? I heard 'em!"

"The Swarm do not speak," Tassadar said, moving forward and crouching beside Raynor. Zeratul moved to his other side, he and Tassadar like a pair of statues at his arms. "Not as you do."

"They speak no more than we do," Zeratul confirmed, his green eyes watching Raynor intently. "What you call speech is not within their capabilities."

Raynor shook his head. "That's a crock!" he said, slamming one fist against his leg. "I've heard 'em!" He stared at Zeratul, daring him to deny his next statement. "So've you! What about when you talked to Zasz?"

The Praetor's eyes widened. "You heard this? How?"

"I was there," Raynor reminded him. "I watched the whole thing."

Zeratul tilted his head again, eyes narrowed now in contemplation rather than mere confusion. "The exchange was private," he explained after a moment, "a brief touch of minds that I might gauge the creature's attitude and study the effect my attack had upon it and its brood." His eyes turned back toward Raynor. "There were no words exchanged, not of the kind you would use."

"You're saying they talk in your head?" Raynor heard a hint of fear, actually more like terror, in Cavez's voice, and knew the younger man was imagining what that must be like.

"I guess," Raynor admitted slowly, thinking back. "I haven't actually seen their mouths move, now I think about it. But I've definitely heard them." He looked over at Zeratul again. "How else would I have known Zasz's name? Or that they were regrouping today?"

"You speak truth," Tassadar assured him from his other side. "This information was too accurate to be imagined. Somehow you have tapped into the Swarm's mind. You hear their thoughts to one another, just as we protoss hear each other in our own mental speech."

"Great." Raynor pressed his hands to his temples, hoping to squeeze the thoughts away. "I'm going bonkers. That's it, right? They say crazy people 'hear voices.' Now I'm hearing 'em too. Just my luck, the voices I get are zerg."

"Your mind is intact," Zeratul replied, "and your rationality undiminished." For an instant Raynor felt a soft, feathery touch inside his head, dry but gentle. Then it was gone and the Praetor nodded slowly. "Kerrigan," he announced.

"Kerrigan? What's she got to do with this?" But Raynor already had an idea what the Dark Templar meant.

"Your minds are linked," Zeratul confirmed. "She reaches out to you through this link, both to deliver you dreams and to monitor your welfare. But she is not careful." He chuckled, that raspy but soothing mental effect that always reminded Raynor of dry leaves in autumn. "She has not our experience at focus or control. Though her power is formidable, she cannot yet control it precisely."

"What's he talking about, sir?" Abernathy asked, staring at Raynor, her face gone pale. Raynor sighed, realizing he'd have to explain a few things he'd been hoping to avoid.

"Kerrigan's tapped into my head," he told his crew, ignoring the gasps that arose from his statement. "She's been messing with me for weeks, ever since we got here, in fact." Even before, actually, but he didn't want to go into that. "But it's a two-way street." He grinned at Abernathy, and was reassured to see her smile back. "She's sloppy, and Zeratul can detect the tag she put on me. He's been using it to keep tabs on her location, at least her general whereabouts. That's part of how we've been hitting them so well—we can tell if she's nearby and stay clear while taking out her troops." He shook his head, still absorbing the new information he'd just been given. "I guess there's another side effect. I can hear them talk, somehow. The zerg."

"You hear what she would hear, were she present," Tassadar explained. "She is linked to all her brood and thus all their communication reaches her. Most she ignores as beneath her notice, but she still receives it. When you are near zerg and those zerg communicate, her mind translates the thoughts into words you would understand."

"So she's keeping up a running translation because she hears it too, and automatically translates it into Terran if they're within my range?"

Tassadar and Zeratul both nodded in reply.

"Hunh." Raynor leaned back and thought about this, absently lifting his cup again and draining the thick liquid within. "So we can tell where she is," he said finally, putting the empty cup back down beside him, "and we can listen in on her troop reports." He looked at the two protoss leaders for confirmation, and when they nodded again he felt a small, hard smile crease his face. "That's one helluva advantage," he pointed out. He glanced around, at the assembled protoss and humans, not missing the fact that they were all there together, all listening side by side, not as three separate teams but as one larger unit. "I think," he said finally, "it's time we stopped running. Let's take the fight to her."

CHAPTER 20

IT TOOK THEM TWO FULL DAYS TO HAMMER OUT a plan. Surprisingly, Zeratul was the sticking point. Tassadar had agreed with Raynor that the time for hit-and-run tactics was past. But the Praetor was not as easily convinced.

"We must not leap carelessly into the dark places," he warned Raynor and Tassadar as the three of them sat together discussing their options. "Fight the zerg, yes, but maintain our focus and do not expose ourselves to unnecessary danger." He stared at Tassadar as if he expected the Executor to become reckless now that he was a Dark Templar.

"No one's saying we're gonna throw our lives away," Raynor reassured the old protoss. "But we can't hide forever, and I'm sure sick of it. We've got the tools to take her down—I say we use them and deal with her brood once and for all."

Tassadar, seated across from him, nodded. "I too feel

this conflict has continued past its proper time. We must resolve the issue, and soon."

Zeratul gave in then, though he continued to provide the voice of caution during their planning. But finally they had a course of action even he liked. And now they were putting it into effect.

The first step was Raynor's. He lay down, closing his eyes and taking slow, deep breaths until he felt himself slipping into slumber. And, as he'd expected, he found himself dreaming. He was standing on a small grassy hill, looking out over a green valley nestled between low, grain-covered mountains. The sun hung low in the sky, casting streamers of pink and orange along the horizon.

"Breathtaking," a husky voice said in his ear. At the same time he felt strong arms wrap around him from behind, and a warm, curvaceous body press up against him.

"Definitely," he replied, trying to keep his voice and his breathing steady even though his skin tingled where she touched him. He twisted to look behind him, and saw Kerrigan, the wholesome, happy Kerrigan of his fondest dreams.

"I wish we could stay like this forever," she said wistfully, tightening her hold on him and laying her head on his shoulder so her long red hair cascaded down over his shoulders and chest.

"Me too," Raynor agreed, reaching up to clasp both her hands in his own. "Sure beats the alternative." For an instant his mind flashed to the box canyon they were currently using as a hideout.

Behind him he felt Kerrigan stiffen, then relax, molding her body more tightly against him. "Oh, Jimmy," she said with a sigh, freeing one hand to stroke his cheek. He turned in her embrace until he was facing her, and was surprised to see tears glistening in her eyes. "I'll see you soon," she whispered, her voice thick, and she laid a soft kiss on his lips. Then she smiled, a smile that was both sad and triumphant—and vanished.

Raynor bolted upright, the dream driven from his head. He was lying out in the open rather than in his tent, and Zeratul was leaning over him, one gnarled hand resting on his shoulder. The old protoss was watching him closely, those pale green eyes narrowed.

"It went well?" the Praetor inquired.

"Perfect," Raynor replied, standing up and running a hand over his hair, shaking the last bits of sleep from his head. "She took the bait, hook, line, and sinker." He grinned at Zeratul. "Nice job. I said exactly what we'd discussed, and the image showed up right on schedule."

The Dark Templar's chuckle rippled over him again, and Zeratul's eyes widened slightly, a sign that he was definitely amused. "Potent indeed is your Queen of Blades," he explained, "yet for centuries I have experienced the communion of minds; I know many tricks she has not yet begun to suspect. And for one of such might she lacks all subtlety."

"Yeah," Raynor agreed, rubbing the back of his neck. "She always did."

A motion to his side caught Raynor's attention as Tassadar stirred and stepped closer to them. They had agreed that his linking to both protoss might have aroused even Kerrigan's suspicions.

"All set," Raynor assured the Executor, who nodded.

"You are certain?" Tassadar asked softly, and Raynor knew what he meant. Both protoss understood the deep feelings Raynor still had for Kerrigan.

"This attack does not require your participation," Zeratul agreed. "Your part is done. You may step aside and leave us to finish the matter, thus freeing you from confrontation."

"Thanks," Raynor said, and meant it. They all knew that, while the Zealots and Dark Templar might be able to do this alone, they'd stand a better chance with Raynor and his men alongside them. Though Cavez and Abernathy would do whatever he said, even lead the fight without him, they all knew he couldn't just sit by and watch his troopers go into battle without him. Nor could he let his friends take the risk alone.

"I can handle it," he said slowly, searching his head and heart as he spoke. "It'd hurt, taking her down, but I can do it. I have to do it. We all do." He thought again about Kerrigan as she'd become, as he'd seen her—taunting enemies, licking their blood from her claws, laughing at their misfortune—and shuddered. Yes, the woman he loved was still in there, but she was more than that now. She wasn't just Sarah Kerrigan anymore—she was the Queen of Blades. The enemy. And for all their sakes, she had to die.

"Very well." Tassadar rested one hand on Raynor's shoulder, and he could feel the sympathy and support pouring from the tall protoss. "We fight together, then, our fates still bound as one." The Executor nodded to Zeratul as well, and then he was moving, his long strides carrying him swiftly from the canyon and over the ridge beyond, toward the caves that lay just past them. They had deliberately chosen a location close to the hive entrance.

"Explain to me again why he's going and not you," Raynor asked as he and Zeratul watched their friend disappear. "You've done this before."

"Indeed," Zeratul replied, and his thoughts bore that heavy echo they sometimes carried when he spoke of important matters. "He requires the experience, however." That was what he'd told Tassadar as well, when suggesting the Templar handle this portion of the plan. "I have demonstrated the technique," the Praetor had explained, "yet to fully grasp it you must perform it yourself."

"All right," Raynor said finally, turning away from the place where he'd last seen Tassadar. "Let's get to work."

It felt like hours, but Raynor knew from his suit that it was only ten minutes before the first zerg appeared. He heard them before he saw them.

"Are you sure this is wise, mistress?" came a fluttering voice Raynor knew must be one of the overlords. "Taking our full strength when we do not know for certain—"

"Silence!" Kerrigan hissed, and the overlord wisely obeyed. "I tire of these games! We will find the little templars and their playmates and crush them all!"

Turning, Raynor signaled to his men, who were stationed beside him along the ridgetop. He didn't dare risk verbal communications with the zerg so close, but that was fine. They'd worked it all out beforehand.

"Go, and scout the area," Kerrigan ordered a moment later, and Raynor was sure he could feel the rush of air as the bulky overlord took flight.

It seemed like a mere heartbeart before his suit registered the approaching zerg, and he forced himself to stay still, gesturing for the others to do the same. They crouched there, hidden by the rocky overhang, their suits coated in ash to make them blend more closely, and waited.

At last he saw the shadow fall across the rocks to his left, and knew the overlord had arrived. An instant later he heard its update.

"I have found them, mistress!" Its mental call carried a note of triumph and pride. "They are in the canyon, just as you said!"

This was what Raynor had been waiting to hear. "Now!" he shouted, and Non and Ling opened fire. Their rifles had already been trained on the overlord and cut the bulky zerg to shreds, its lifeless body falling across the ridgetop not far from where Raynor waited.

As soon as the corpse dropped, he and his men were moving. So were the protoss below. They scrambled up and out of the canyon, using a narrow path Tassadar had found for that purpose. Raynor scuttled along the ridgetop, keeping low, until he and his troopers were safely beneath an overhang. It had taken a while to find a place that had everything they needed.

"They have destroyed your overlord, mistress!" he heard another zerg declare from somewhere nearby, but the creature was beyond his suit's range. Only Kerrigan's mental powers were letting him hear their communications at all. Which is what he had counted on.

"It matters not," she replied. "We know where they are. Swarm the canyon, my brood! Fill its walls with your flesh, smother the protoss and the humans with your bodies! Let none survive!"

"Here they come," Raynor muttered to himself. His hands tightened on the canister rifle and he reflexively checked the readouts on his suit. Green across the board. He was ready, at least physically. Mentally, he wasn't so sure. Could he kill Kerrigan if it came down to that? He was about to find out.

The zerg came boiling over the ridge and through the mouth of the valley, just as Kerrigan had commanded. There were more of them than Raynor had seen at any time since that first excursion into the caverns, several hundred at least, and he was a little shaken despite their careful planning. All those raids, all those zerg they had killed, and still her brood outnumbered them at least three to one! If things didn't go exactly as planned this could easily become a slaughter—with him and his men and their allies as the victims.

He had to trust that Tassadar would handle his end. Fortunately, he couldn't see the Templar as someone who considered failure an option.

Staying still was difficult. Every muscle in Raynor's body, every impulse, screamed at him to stand up and start firing. There were so many zerg it would be impossible to miss. But that wasn't the plan. He had to stick to the plan, he reminded himself again and again. It was their only chance to survive this thing, much less win it.

As the brood topped the rise and started down into the canyon, he heard their mental cries change from glee to confusion, from hatred to rage. Several faltered, only to be dragged along by their kin in the mad rush to the bottom. Soon all the zerg were there, milling about, searching desperately for something to attack.

The only problem was, there wasn't anything there.

"What?" Kerrigan was the last one down, her wing-spikes flared as if to slow her descent, long claws digging into the rock as she skidded toward the bottom. It was the first time Raynor had seen her in the flesh since teaming with the protoss, and his breath caught in his throat. Despite the dreams, despite what she had become, he had forgotten how beautiful she was, and her presence sent him reeling. If she had confronted him now he wouldn't have been able to pull the trigger, or do much of anything. Fortunately she was focused on something else entirely. Specifically, on the canyon floor—and its complete and utter lack of targets.

"Where are they?" she screamed, her wings flexing in rage, hands closing spasmodically as if they would tear the very air apart in search of her prey. "They were here!"

Her brood looked around as well, but no one answered. They didn't know either. Instead they all stood there, uncertain what to do next.

And that was the perfect moment. "Now!" Raynor whispered, though he knew no one would hear him. That was fine. He wasn't the one sending the signal this time.

From his vantage point, he could just see the shadowy ledge near the far end of the canyon. And, magnified by his suit's targeting system, he thought he saw a faint green gleam at one end. But even without a visual he knew that Zeratul stood there, and that right now the Praetor was reaching out telepathically, through the link he had forged with Tassadar.

And the Executor, hearing the mental signal he had waited for, turned toward the creature he had snuck up on so stealthily. And struck.

"Arghhh!" Kerrigan reeled backward, hands clasped to her head, wings scraping the wall as she staggered into it. And all around her, her brood erupted into chaos and violence and frenzy.

"No! Stop!" she shouted, one hand still pressed to her temple, but it was to no avail. The brood had lost control.

And that was the signal for Raynor and his men to stand up and start shooting. The zerg weren't able to control themselves, and they died beneath the barrage, unable to focus long enough to realize their enemies stood upon the ridge rather than down with them in the canyon.

"Like fish in a barrel!" Non shouted as he cut a hydralisk in half with one burst. "Damn!"

It had gone perfectly.

They had known they couldn't take Kerrigan and her brood in a fair fight. So they'd made sure it wasn't fair. First Raynor had let her see their location. Then they'd let the overlord confirm it. But they'd left only a handful of protoss in the canyon, just enough to convince the zerg it had seen the entire force. Once it was dead they'd pulled everyone out along the walls. The canyon had high, steep walls and a nice wide space at the bottom—a perfect killing ground. The zerg thought they'd sweep in and take their opponents by surprise, overwhelming them before they could respond or flee. But they hadn't realized Raynor, Tassadar, and Zeratul had orchestrated all this.

Nor had they known that, while Kerrigan was leading her entire brood out of the caves, Tassadar was slipping past them, cloaked in shadows. Or that he would wait patiently beside the nameless cerebrate, who alone among the brood was too large to leave the caverns. And, when Zeratul gave the word, Tassadar struck just as Zeratul had with Zasz, killing the cerebrate and severing its link to its brood.

Driving them insane.

Kerrigan was strong enough to control her own brood, of course. But she wasn't trained for it, or bred for it. She had been created for a different purpose. So when her cerebrate died she was unable to take command and reestablish the links. She was powerless to stop her brood from collapsing into a mad frenzy, slaughtering each other by sheer reflex.

And the rifle fire from on high cut them down that much more quickly.

"Come out, little templar!" Kerrigan howled, scraping the claws of one hand along the valley wall for emphasis. Several of Raynor's troops targeted her with their rifles but the high-velocity metal spikes stopped just shy of hitting her, rebounding from a glittering, almost oily disturbance in the air around her. She ignored them, weapons and shooters alike. "I know you are here!" she shouted instead, eyes narrowed as she searched every nook and cranny. "I can feel you! Face me!"

A moment passed, and no reply. Kerrigan reached out then and snagged a devourer from the air, her wings pinning it against the wall beside her. "Obey!" she commanded, and Raynor was sure he saw a burst of yellowish-green light leap from her eyes and into those of the captive zerg. Its struggling ceased immediately, and when she released it it hovered above her, awaiting orders. She did this with several more, taking them one at a time, until she had five devourers once more linked to her. Then she grinned and looked straight at Raynor.

"Kill the humans," she instructed, and the airborne zerg hastened to obey.

Next she reclaimed a trio of hydralisks and set them to scouring the edges of the canyon, avoiding their still-crazed brethren and searching for the elusive protoss. Raynor caught only glimpses of her actions then, because he and his men were busy fending off the devourers, which swooped in quickly and moved too fast for them to shoot down at such close range. By the time they'd taken down the last one Raynor had lost several of his troopers and needed a minute to locate Kerrigan again.

A large portion of her brood was dead now, the bodies strewn about the canyon floor. And the protoss had apparently decided they were tired of waiting to be found. Or perhaps they felt she needed an additional distraction to keep her from restoring order to the rest of her zerg minions. Whatever the reason, Raynor stepped away from the last devourer and glanced down just in time to see a pair of Zealots leap at Kerrigan, psi-blades glittering in an arc.

Kerrigan's wings blocked the first warrior's attack, shearing partway through his arm in the process, and her claws tore the second one's arm from his shoulder, tossing it aside in a shower of blood. Then her wingtips pierced the first one's chest, neck, and head, even as a vicious backhand ripped the second's head off. She let the bodies fall behind her, but she had noticed their origin point and turned her attention toward the ledge.

Next to attack her were two Dark Templar, materializing from the shadows on either side and stabbing quickly toward her with their psi-blades. But she had apparently sensed their presence, and her wings drove them back before they could reach her. One fell against an ultralisk, which bellowed and used its massive tusks to carve him open. The other righted himself and attacked again but Kerrigan's hands drove forward, into and then through his chest, and the poor protoss was dead before his body hit the ground.

Kerrigan straightened and made a show of wiping the blood from her hands. "Once again," she called, "I grow tired of slaughtering your servants. Have the mighty Templars lost their infallible courage?"

"Well spoken, concubine of the zerg," came the reply. It was Zeratul, still ensconced in shadows, and his statement reverberated through the valley, the power in it causing several zerglings to collapse in helpless spasms. "But though we strike at you from the shadows," the Praetor continued, "do not think that we lack the courage to stand in the light. You would do well to abandon this attack."

"You seem overconfident of your abilities, *dark one,*" Kerrigan answered, snarling, her eyes attempting to burn holes in the shadows of the ledge. "I am no helpless cerebrate to be assailed under cover of darkness. I am the Queen of Blades, and my stare alone would reduce you to ashes." She stalked toward the end of the valley, those zerg still alive smart enough to move out of her way. "You and your ilk cease to amuse me," she called out as she neared the ledge. With a single leap, wing-spikes beating behind her, she reached the ledge. "Prepare yourself for oblivion's embrace," she announced, and a sickly yellow light rose from her flesh, driving back the shadows. Zeratul and his Dark Templar stood revealed before her, and Kerrigan smiled, a nasty, hungry smile, when she saw him.

"Now, *protoss,*" she all but purred, flexing her wing-spikes and her clawed fingers, "you shall know my wrath. Now you will know the fury of the Queen of Blades!"

She lashed out, her wings piercing the nearest Dark Templar and then sweeping outward to fling his body from the ledge and into the zerg still rioting below. Zeratul gestured and the rest of his warriors leaped down, skirting the crazed zerg and climbing up toward the ridge where Raynor and his men stood and picked off those zerg who showed signs of leaving the general chaos. The Praetor himself waited calmly for Kerrigan to reach him, his eyes blazing and an answering gleam emerging above his wrists as his psi-blades ignited.

"Come then, Queen," he challenged her, "and let us see if either of us fares better than the last time we crossed paths." The darkness rose up around him again, though it did not conceal him. Instead it hung about him like a mantle, in much the way Tassadar had used it recently, for protection.

Tassadar! Whether it was Zeratul's thinking of the Executor that triggered it or a mere coincidence, Raynor suddenly caught a glimpse of motion at the top of the canyon's back wall, above that same ledge. It was a mere flicker, nothing more, a brief hint of color against the ash-coated rocks, but somehow he knew what it meant. Tassadar had returned! And with that knowledge Raynor realized something else—Zeratul was stalling, biding his time until he and the Executor could attack Kerrigan together.

"Aw, hell," Raynor muttered. "Cavez, Abernathy, keep everybody sharp. I've got something I need to do." And he started making his way around the side of the canyon, eyes still focused upon that ledge, rifle idly picking off random zerg as he went.

During the planning stage he and the two protoss commanders had agreed that none of them could take Kerrigan alone. Two together stood a slim chance, but all three would fare better. And that's what they'd decided to do—attack her together, all at once. And now here were Zeratul and Tassadar getting into position without him. Damn it! On the one hand he was furious that they would try to cut him out of the attack. On the other, he was relieved at the thought that he wouldn't have to face Kerrigan in battle, that he wouldn't have to make that hard decision. And on yet another hand he realized that was why his friends were about to act without him, to spare him that problem. Which was entirely too many hands.

"I said I'd do it," he whispered to himself as he half-ran along the ridgeline, "and I will."

Zeratul was still taunting Kerrigan, still staying outside her reach. Tassadar was almost to the ledge now, moving carefully and quietly, the noise from below providing plenty of cover. And Raynor was a hard jump away. Another second and they'd have her.

They didn't get it.

"Enough!" Kerrigan shouted, her temper finally flaring out of control. She lunged at Zeratul, both wings lancing forward over her shoulders, determined to spear him and tear him open. His darkness blunted the blow but could not stop it entirely, the glow around her body piercing it as her claws hoped to pierce his flesh, and he was shoved back against the wall. As he parried a blow from her right hand, the left clipped him on the shoulder, leaving deep scratches there, and his brow furrowed in pain. But he did not fall or falter.

"No pretty words now, little protoss?" Kerrigan asked mockingly, waving her claws before him. "No challenges or cryptic replies? Nothing left to say?" Zeratul did not reply. "Then die!"

She speared again, claws and wings both, all aimed for his chest. Raynor, seeing her dart forward, gave up on subtlety and hurled himself at her, pivoting midair to plant his heavy boots on her back and smash her to the ground.

He wasn't fast enough.

Fortunately, Tassadar was.

The High Templar had been right above the ledge and swung himself down as she moved, flipping forward with both hands gripping the rock just above Zeratul's head. As Tassadar uncurled, his legs swept down, knocking Kerrigan to one side and causing her hands and wing-spikes to grate harmlessly against the valley wall, inches from where Zeratul stood. Then Tassadar released his grip and dropped the rest of the way, to stand beside his friend and mentor.

"Now, o Queen of Blades," he announced, "you shall face us both."

Kerrigan straightened and began to reply. But before she could speak Raynor's feet struck her full force, sending her sprawling. He stumbled himself, but caught himself with one arm and stayed upright.

Now they were all there, he and Tassadar and Zeratul, in a rough triangle. And Kerrigan stretched out between them.

It was Tassadar who reacted first. His psi-blades flared into existence even as he dropped to one knee, fists plunging toward her head and neck. Her wing-spikes arced up, however, catching his wrists and turning his attack.

Zeratul was right beside Tassadar, his own psi-blades aimed not at Kerrigan's head but at her wings. These blows connected, and Kerrigan screamed as the glittering green beams cut into her appendages, ichor seeping from the wounds.

Raynor leaned in as well, canister rifle at the ready. He rested the barrel against her head and—overruling the cries from deep within his heart—pulled the trigger.

And just as he did, Kerrigan raised herself to a crouch and pivoted, one leg sliding out to trip him. Despite the suit's servos he toppled, the gun firing spikes in an arc along the valley wall. She was on him before his back hit the ledge, clinging to his chest like an oversized spider, her face inches from his helmet.

"We'll play later, Jimmy," Kerrigan assured him softly, her eyes glittering. She planted a kiss on his faceplate even as her fingers twitched along his side, then she was spinning away from him. He tried to rise but discovered he couldn't move. His suit was frozen.

"Damn it!" Raynor let loose a whole volley of curses, thrashing as best he could within the suit's confines. She'd triggered the emergency lockdown! It was meant to help immobilize wounded troopers, or to shut down a shorted-out suit before it could misfire. Kerrigan knew these suits at least as well as he did, maybe better, and she'd activated his lockdown, trapping him inside until someone could set him free. All he could do was lie there, stretched out on the ledge, and watch the battle that would occur just above him. Now that he had no chance to participate in it, he wanted to do that more than anything.

He watched as Zeratul and Tassadar faced off against Kerrigan, their psi-blades versus her wings and claws. The two protoss moved together perfectly, each motion complementing the other, their attacks in perfect harmony, a mix of shadows and light, strength and wisdom, knowledge and power. It was a devastating charge, and Raynor knew that few creatures could survive it.

Kerrigan was one of them.

Her wings acted of their own accord, it seemed, parrying and attacking without her conscious control, so that she always fought with an ally at her back. Their spikes blocked strikes and stabbed back in return, scoring both protoss several times, and her claws were just as fast, leaving furrows in their skin. The yellow glow around her intensified, weakening their shadows and blocking their light, and she moved with the grace and danger of a panther, lithe and lovely and deadly.

Tassadar drove his blade toward Kerrigan's heart and she caught his wrist between her wings, stopping the attack inches from her chest and trapping his hand. She spun then, hands rising to ensnare his wrist, wings flaring to hurl Zeratul back against the wall with such force he dropped to his knees. Tassadar raised a shadow around himself but Kerrigan tore it away with one glowing wing, and then she slowly, deliberately pierced his side with the other, until the pain made him wince and the shadows fled.

"Trapped again, little protoss?" she whispered to Tassadar, tugging him to her until her lips brushed his leathery cheek. "How familiar this all seems, yes?" She smiled and twisted the wing within him, the pain so intense he would have fallen if she had not held him up. "The end to our little drama. I swore to kill you slowly, but I think not. You are too dangerous to risk. So, this is farewell, little protoss. You led me on a merry chase." She kissed him on the brow, right between the eyes, and her other wing reared up behind her, spikes angled to strike all three of his hearts at once.

"No!" Zeratul's cry roared through their minds,

shaking the rocks all around, sending loose stone down into the valley and overwhelming many of the surviving zerg in an instant. Kerrigan merely grinned at him.

"Do not worry, Dark Templar," she assured him. "You will be next." Then she turned and slowly, provocatively, winked at Raynor. "You I'm saving for last, dear Jimmy." Her wing-spikes flared outward again, then leaped forward—

—as the ledge just beyond her disappeared in a shower of fine dust, obliterated by a beam of light so intense it was colorless.

A beam that had come from the graceful ship descending upon them now.

A protoss ship.

A second beam lanced out, carving away more of the ledge. A dozen zerg disappeared as well, caught in the beam near the cavern floor. And Kerrigan reeled backward, one arm raised to shield her eyes from the light. Tassadar dropped to the ground as she stepped away.

"This is not over," she assured the three sprawled before her. "There will be a reckoning." Then she leaped forward, her claws stabbing deep into the rock overhead and pulling her up above the ledge and onto the ridgeline. She quickly vaulted that crest and disappeared from view.

"Indeed there shall." Zeratul's thought was so soft Raynor wondered if it had been meant as a reply or if it was merely the Praetor's own musings. "But a reckoning for whom?" Then the Praetor reached forward and helped Tassadar stand.

"Can you stand, James Raynor?" Tassadar asked after a second, ignoring his own wounds to stagger over to where Raynor lay.

"Not without unlocking this thing," Raynor replied. "Give me a hand, willya?" He thought about the sequence to remove the lockdown, and the tall protoss nodded and duplicated the process. Raynor sighed with relief as the suit's warning lights blinked out and he felt control return. Then he took his friend's hand and stood up.

"Well," he said after he was on his feet again. He glanced up at the protoss ship, still on the descent, and then down at the carnage below. Most of Kerrigan's brood was dead, and though here and there a protoss or human body lay among them, by far the largest body count belonged to the zerg. Raynor grinned at his two allies.

"That went better than I expected."

EPILOGUE

THEY STOOD THERE, WATCHING THE SHIP DESCEND. But Raynor noticed that Zeratul had stepped back into the shadows, and was fading from view even as he turned to comment.

"Hey!" Raynor said. "What gives?"

Tassadar turned as well, and the Praetor reappeared from the darkness, though it seemed he did so grudgingly. "The time has not yet come for us to return to our brethren," he told them gravely. "It would be best if we were not present when the ship alighted."

Raynor started to protest, but Tassadar merely nodded and stepped forward. "I will honor your decision," the Executor stated, his thoughts strong and soothing as always. He rested his hands on the older protoss's shoulders. "But know that your counsel shall be missed . . . my brother."

Zeratul placed his hands on Tassadar's shoulders as well. "Thank you, my brother. Know that you will always be in my thoughts, and thus close to my spirit.

If you have need of me I shall find you." Then he turned to Raynor and nodded so deeply his chin scraped his chest. "Fare well, James Raynor," the Dark Templar intoned, his words ringing through Raynor's head. "Truly you are protoss in spirit if not in flesh, and I acknowledge you as a brother in kind if not in race. If ever you require aid I will be there as well."

"Yeah, thanks." Raynor reached out to clasp Zeratul's hand. "But hey, where're you gonna go?" He jerked his free hand back toward the descending ship. "That's the only ride in town."

Zeratul's eyes crinkled in what Raynor recognized as the protoss equivalent of a smile. "Not quite," he admitted.

"What? That cerebrate Daggoth said he destroyed both your ships!"

"So he thought," the Praetor said. "But for centuries I have honed my arts, and long ago I mastered illusions such as no zerg could penetrate." Raynor could hear the old protoss's mental laughter. "Though he thought his mission successful, yet the *Void Seeker* waits for my return."

"Wait a second." Raynor shook his head to make sure he'd heard right. "You're saying your ship is intact?" Zeratul nodded. "But what the hell? We were stranded here for weeks—months! And you could have left at any time? Why the hell did you stick around? Why didn't you get off this rock?"

The Praetor looked at him, pale green eyes guileless for once. "Such was not my destiny," he replied. He turned to look at Tassadar. "I was meant to be here, as were we all. Thus has our race's future been assured." Then, without a sound, he bowed and backed away, disappearing into the shadows.

"Hunh." Raynor stared after him for a moment, then turned back to Tassadar. "Well, guess that leaves just us, eh?" The tall protoss nodded—he had not watched Zeratul go, and was now looking at the arriving protoss ship again.

Together they watched the protoss ship finally touch down. It looked almost exactly like the ship Tassadar himself had arrived in, and Raynor thought about the changes that had occurred since he had watched that first ship land and the Executor emerge. Back then the protoss had been a strange, alien race, possibly allies but possibly enemies and certainly dangerous and unreadable. Now he stood here with one of their high commanders, side by side, and knew he could trust the protoss with his life and those of his men. It seemed like so little time had passed, but at the same time it felt like an eternity.

The ramp unfurled from the ship's side and the door irised open. Several protoss warriors stepped out and arrayed themselves at the ramp's base, standing at attention as two tall figures followed them down. Raynor recognized them immediately as the two he had seen when Tassadar, with Zeratul's help, had contacted his people to warn them of the Swarm invasion. The first one, Aldaris, wore the same long heavy robes of crimson and gold, the long hood still covering his face completely so that only his blue-gray eyes were visible beneath the shadowy cowl. The second figure was the one Aldaris had called Executor and Tassadar had named Artanis, and his garb was the same as Tassadar's, though the newcomer's clothing and armor were undamaged and glittered in the weak sunlight. His sky-blue eyes locked on Tassadar immediately and he looked only at the High Templar as he approached, projecting a mixture of friendship, respect, and embarrassment.

Tassadar saw them both and strode forward eagerly, his eyes ablaze. Raynor followed behind him.

"Aldaris?" Tassadar called as he approached. "Artanis? How is it that you've come here? I was about to abandon all hope of rescue!"

He and the newcomers were now face-to-face, with Raynor right beside Tassadar. The High Templar bowed slightly, a mark of respect among equals, and Artanis matched his movements. Aldaris did not, however, and his eyes narrowed instead.

"I have come to arrest you," the Judicator stated, his mental words as cool and distant as his eyes, "and bring you home to Aiur to stand trial."

Tassadar straightened and stepped back slightly, eyes widening in obvious surprise. "*Arrest me*? Aiur burns at the touch of the zerg, and you travel all this way to arrest *me*?"

"Don't let it get to you, man," Raynor said, knowing what his friend was going through. "This happened to me once. . . ." He flashed back to his own arrest and incarceration, back on Mar Sara, and how Mike Liberty had rescued him and then introduced him to Arcturus Mengsk. It had been the first step on the long road that had led him here.

Aldaris turned and stared at him, his eyes cold. "Who is this human, Tassadar?" Raynor could feel the disdain in his question, and bristled at it.

"The name's Jim Raynor, pal," he replied, stepping forward to glare at the protoss commander. "And I won't be talked down to by anybody. Not even a protoss."

"Amusing . . . ," Aldaris said, though his eyes and his tone showed no humor. "Tassadar, your taste in companions grows ever more inexplicable." He turned back toward Artanis. "Executor, prepare to take Tassadar into custody."

Tassadar turned to study the second protoss, and his eyes narrowed for an instant. Then he nodded. "I did not fully appreciate the change in title before," he admitted. "You have been promoted to my former position, Artanis. I take it, then, that I no longer hold that title?"

Artanis fidgeted slightly, which made Raynor think he must be young. In some ways this sky-eyed protoss warrior reminded him of Cavez. "The Conclave felt it best," the new Executor replied. "I am sorry, Tassadar." Raynor could feel the warrior's sincerity, and he was sure Tassadar could as well.

"You are a wise choice," Tassadar assured the younger protoss. "I know you will protect our people well." Artanis dipped his head, and Raynor was sure he would have been blushing if the protoss had been capable of such a feat.

"Enough of this," Aldaris commanded, and with a gesture he summoned the guards waiting nearby. "You will be held, Tassadar—you and your companion—until such time as we may return to Aiur for your sentencing and punishment." The scorn radiating from the Judicator left no doubt about the verdict he expected.

"Executor, wait," Tassadar asked, raising both hands. "I do not know what they have told you about me, but what I've done, I've done for Aiur. Help me find Zeratul and his Dark Templar." If he noticed how Aldaris and many of the warriors recoiled at the name, he ignored it. "They alone can defeat the Overmind's cerebrates. Once we've won I'll gladly submit myself to the judgment of the Conclave."

Aldaris's eyes blazed with anger. "Unthinkable!" he announced, the word ringing like steel. "You presume that we would side with the *Dark Ones* as you have? You have gone quite mad, Tassadar."

This time it was Tassadar's eyes that flared, and even Aldaris backed away, clearly awed by the power the Executor wielded. "You shall speak of them with respect, Aldaris." Then he calmed himself and turned back toward Artanis. "Executor, there is much that I can explain to you, if only you'll help me find Zeratul."

"I thought he said he wasn't ready to rejoin your society," Raynor pointed out quietly.

"He said the time had not yet come," Tassadar corrected him. "I have reconsidered, however. I believe we must stand together once again if we are to protect our homeworld."

"You think he's reached his ship yet?" Raynor asked. Tassadar shook his head.

"Our minds are still linked," the High Templar explained. "I would know if he had departed this world." He turned back toward the newly arrived protoss and addressed not Aldaris, who stood seething in front of him, but Artanis and the warriors behind him. "Hear me, my brethren," he called, his words a soothing blanket that drifted across their minds. "You know me, for I am Tassadar, High Templar and once Executor of our forces. However, I speak to you now not as your leader but as your brother. Our world, our people are in danger. Only by reclaiming our ancient birthright may we save them. And only the Dark Templar, whom we have wronged these long centuries, can aid us in this process." The warriors stood unmoving, neither accepting nor rejecting, and Tassadar nodded. "If you cannot accept them yet, so be it. But I ask that you trust me in this matter, for truly it is the only path for our survival."

"You have become corrupted!" Aldaris claimed, but Artanis stepped forward and held up one hand, palm out. Tassadar mirrored him, and the two protoss touched palms, a faint glow forming between and around them. They stood thus for a moment before the young Executor lowered his hand and stepped away.

"The tenor of your thought is different," Artanis

admitted, "but I sense no evil about you. And your devotion to our world and our people is as strong as ever." He bowed. "I will trust in your wisdom, noble Tassadar. It shall be as you wish."

"You defy my orders?" Aldaris's mental query was as sharp as a well-honed knife, and Raynor could feel the anger that accompanied it. This one was a dangerous foe. But Artanis, for all his youth, faced the Judicator with composure.

"You wish Tassadar returned to Aiur," he stated. "And so he shall be. His impressive achievements for our race have earned him respect, however, and we shall not treat him as a criminal. Let him go before the Conclave with his head held high, that all might hear him and judge for themselves whether he has done right. We shall retrieve these Dark Templar, too, as Tassadar suggests, and bring them before the Conclave as well. For surely our people would know the truth of this matter, and within the Khala none may dissemble." For an instant the young Executor's eyes blazed a vivid cobalt blue, a glimpse of strength waiting to be tapped and daring to be challenged, and Raynor got the message. As did Aldaris, apparently, for the Judicator backed away and did not again object. The protoss warriors moved forward then, flanking the four of them. But Raynor could see from their posture, and the way they bowed to Tassadar, that they were treating him as their commander again, or at least as an honored guest, rather than a prisoner.

"You have my thanks, Executor," Tassadar told

Artanis, nodding in return. "Now let's find Zeratul and speed our way home."

He turned back toward Raynor. "And what of you, James Raynor?"

Raynor started to reply, but just then a small light began blinking in his helmet. It took him a minute to realize what it meant. It was an incoming call.

He stared at it for a second. A call? He and his men had routed their communications through the shuttle—when the zerg destroyed it they'd lost the ability to do more than line-of-sight communication. And this was way too strong a signal for that. Cautiously, he opened the link. "Raynor," he said.

"Captain?" The voice was young, male, and utterly familiar. He'd hoped to hear it for weeks now, but Raynor still felt tears in his eyes as he responded.

"Matt? Matt! Damn, am I glad to hear you, son!" He scanned the skies overhead, and sure enough now that he looked he saw a familiar outline off in the distance. The *Hyperion*!

"Thank you, sir," Matt Horner replied. "Same here. Sorry it took us so long"—he sounded embarrassed, and Raynor could practically see the young lieutenant sitting in the captain's chair, his face wearing that abashed look that always made Raynor think of a puppy that had just peed on the rug—"but the emergency jump took us a ways out and crashed some of our systems. We had to make several repairs before we could get back."

"Don't worry about it," Raynor said. "I'm just glad

you made it back. Any chance you can send someone down to get us?"

"Already done, sir," Horner answered. "Belloc is on his way down in a shuttle, locked in on your signal." Raynor vaguely remembered Belloc as a short, round man who laughed a lot, often at the worst possible moment. But right now he was ready to kiss him upon sight.

"Great, we'll be here," he said, and closed the link.

"I am glad your ship has returned." He turned to find Tassadar watching him, the protoss's blue eyes sympathetic. "Now you too can depart this world."

"Yeah." Raynor thought about that. He'd come here to save Kerrigan, and he'd failed. A lot of people had died as a result. But he'd met Tassadar, and Zeratul, and forged a friendship with them, a friendship between two different races. Perhaps that was worth all the lives. He thought maybe it was.

"What will you do now?" Tassadar asked again, ignoring the obviously impatient Aldaris and even the puzzled Artanis beside him.

Raynor thought about it. He had his ship back, if understaffed. Cavez and Abernathy had both survived somehow, as had McMurty, but he'd lost Non, Ling, Deslan, and several others. The crew totaled forty now, himself included. Not enough to take the war to Mengsk, really. But perhaps enough to tip the scales on Aiur. Besides, he wanted to be there when that slimy Overmind got what he deserved. And Kerrigan was probably heading toward the protoss homeworld as well. Besides, he, Zeratul, and Tassadar made a good team. It would be a shame to break that up.

"I think I'll tag along, if you don't mind," he said finally. Aldaris flinched, clearly offended, but Raynor ignored him and concentrated on Tassadar. "I'd like to see this to the end."

Artanis turned toward Tassadar, clearly not sure how to respond.

"James Raynor is a valued friend and ally," the High Templar assured his counterpart. "I for one hold him most welcome, and I am honored that he would accompany us."

Taking his cue from Tassadar, Artanis turned then and bowed to Raynor. "You are welcome among us, James Raynor," his thoughts proclaimed, quiet and uncertain and slightly formal, but honest nonetheless. "You and your people both."

"Let us locate the Praetor and his Dark Templar, then," Tassadar said, and Raynor could feel the warmth of his friend's affection and thanks. "And then, indeed, we shall end this together."

Raynor grinned. "Well, all right, then. What are we waiting for?"

ABOUT THE AUTHOR

AARON ROSENBERG is originally from New Jersey and New York. He returned to New York City seven years ago, after stints in New Orleans and Kansas. He has taught college-level English and worked in corporate graphics and book publishing. Aaron has written novels for Pocket's *Star Trek: Starfleet Corps of Engineers*, White Wolf's *Exalted*, and Games Workshop's *Warhammer* lines. He also writes educational books and roleplaying games and has his own game company, Clockworks (www.clockworksgames.com). Aaron lives in New York with his wife, their two-year-old daughter, their infant son, and their cat, unless they've moved out while he was chained to his desk again.

COMING SOON

STARCRAFT®
GHOST
NOVA

A novel by

KEITH R.A. DeCANDIDO

THE PREQUEL STORY TO
BLIZZARD ENTERTAINMENT'S
HIGHLY ANTICIPATEL
STARCRAFT: GHOST

TURN THE PAGE FOR A PREVIEW. . . .

As soon as she felt Cliff Nadaner's mind, Nova knew that she could destroy her family's murderer with but a thought.

She'd spent days working her way through the humid jungles of the smallest of the ten continents of Tyrador VIII. *Funny how I tried so hard to avoid this planet's twin, and now I wind up here,* she had thought when the drop-pod left her smack in the middle of the densest part of the jungle—before the rebels had a chance to lock onto the tiny pod, or so her superiors on the ship in high orbit insisted. The eighth planet in orbit of Tyrador was locked in a gravitational dance with the ninth planet, similar to that of a regular planet and a moon, but both worlds were of sufficient size to sustain life. They also both had absurd extremes of climate, thanks to their proximity to each other—if Nova were to travel only a few kilometers south, farther from Tyrador VIII's equator, the temperature would lower thirty degrees, the humidity would disappear, and she'd need to adjust her suit's temperature control in the other direction.

For now, though, the form-fitting white-with-navy-blue-trim suit—issued by her teachers at the Ghost Academy when her training was complete—was set to keep her cool, which it did, up to a point. The suit covered every inch of her flesh save her head. The circuitry woven throughout the suit's fabric might interfere with Nova's telepathy, and since her telepathy was pretty much the entire reason *why* she was training to become a Ghost, it wouldn't do to interfere with *that.* This suit wasn't quite the complete model she would be using when she became a Ghost—for one thing, the circuitry that allowed the suit to go into stealth mode had yet to be installed. Once that happened, Nova would be able to move about virtually undetected—certainly invisible to plain sight and most passive scans.

But she wasn't ready for that yet. First she had to accomplish this mission.

The suit's design meant that sweat dripped into her eyes and plastered the bangs of her blond hair to her scalp. The ponytail she kept the rest of her hair in was like a heavy damp rope hanging off the back of her head. *At least the rest of my body is comfortable.*

The suit's stealth mode would probably have been redundant in this jungle in any case. The flora of Tyrador VIII was so thick, and the humid air so hazy, she only knew what was a meter in front of her from the sensor display on the suit's wrist unit.

Intelligence Section told her that Cliff Nadaner was headquartered somewhere in the jungle on this planet. They weren't completely sure where—though still only a trainee, albeit not for much longer, Nova had already learned that the first half of IS's designation was a misnomer—but they had intercepted several communiqués that their cryptographers insisted used the code tagged for Nadaner.

In the waning days of the Confederacy, Nadaner was one of many agitators who spoke out against the Old Families and the Council and the Confederacy in general. He was far from the only one who did so. The most successful, of course, was the leader of the Sons of Korhal, Arcturus Mengsk—in fact, he was so successful that he actually did overthrow the Confederacy of Man and replaced it with the Terran Dominion, of which he was now the emperor and supreme leader. Nadaner did somewhat more poorly in the field of achieving political change, though he was very skilled at causing trouble and killing people.

Days of plowing through the jungle had revealed

nothing. All Nova was picking up was random background radiation, plus signals from the various satellites in orbit of the planet, holographic signals from various wild animals that scientists had tagged for study in their natural habitat, and faint electromagnetic signatures from the outer reaches of this continent or one of the other nine more densely populated ones. All of it matched existing Tyrador VIII records and therefore could be discarded as not belonging to the rebels. And now she was reading a completely dead zone about half a kilometer ahead, at the extreme range of the sensors in her suit. *This is starting to get frustrating.*

She had completely lost track of time. Had it been four days? Five? Impossible to tell, since this planet's fast orbit gave it a shorter day than what she was accustomed to on Tarsonis, with its twenty-seven-hour day. She supposed she could have checked the computer built into her suit, but for some reason she thought that would be cheating.

Let's see, I've got enough rations for a month, which means ninety packs. I've been eating pretty steadily, more or less on track for three squares a day, and I've gone through fourteen packs, so that makes—

Then, suddenly, it hit her. *A dead zone.*

She adjusted the sensors from passive scan to active scan. Sure enough, they didn't pick up a thing—nothing from the satellites, nothing from the animal tags, nothing from the cities farther south.

Nothing at all.

Nova smiled. She cast her mind outward gently and surgically—not forcefully and sloppily, the way she always had back in the Gutter—sought out the mind of the man who killed her family.

In truth, Nadaner had not personally killed her family. That was done by a man named Gustavo McBain, a former welder who was working a construction contract on Mar

Sara when the Confederates ordered the destruction of Korhal IV—an action that killed McBain's entire family, including his pregnant wife Daniella, their daughter Natasha, and their unborn son. McBain had sworn that the Confederacy of Man would pay for that action. However, instead of joining Mengsk—himself the child of a victim of Korhal IV's bombardment with nuclear weapons—he hooked up with Cliff Nadaner's merry band of agitators.

Nova learned all that when she killed McBain. Telepathy made it impossible for a killer not to know her victim intimately. McBain's last thoughts were of Daniella, Natasha, and his never-named son.

Now, three years later, having come to the end of her Ghost training, her "graduation" assignment, which came from Emperor Mengsk himself, was to be dropped in the middle of Tyrador VIII's jungle and to seek, locate, and destroy the rest of Nadaner's group. Mengsk had even less patience for rebel groups than the government his own rebel group had overthrown.

Within five minutes, she found the mind she was looking for. It wasn't hard, once she had a general location to focus on, especially since they were the first higher-order thoughts she'd come across since the drop-pod opened up and disintegrated. (Couldn't risk Dominion tech getting into the wrong hands, after all. If she completed her mission, they'd send a ship to extract her, since then they could land a ship without risk, as Nadaner's people would be dead. If she didn't complete it, she'd be dead, and her suit was designed to do to her what was done to the drop-pod if her life signs ceased. Couldn't risk Dominion telepaths getting into the wrong hands, either, dead or alive.)

It was Nadaner. Also about a dozen of Nadaner's associates, but their thoughts were focused on Nadaner—those that were focused at all. The man himself was chanting something. No, singing. He was singing a song, and half his people were drunk, no doubt secure in the knowledge that no one would find them in their jungle location, with its dampening field blocking any signals. It probably never occurred to them that an absence of signals would be just as big a signpost.

Complacent people are easier to kill, she thought, parroting back one of Sergeant Hartley's innumerable one-sentence life lessons.

She was to kill them from a distance, using her telepathy. Yes, her training was complete, and she should have been able to take down Nadaner and his people physically with little difficulty—especially since half of them were three sheets to the wind—but that wasn't the mission.

The mission was to get close enough to feel their minds clearly and then kill them psionically.

That was the mission.

For the next two hours, Nova ran through the jungle, getting closer to her goal. After her "graduation," the suit would be able to increase her speed, allowing her to run this same distance in a quarter of the time, but that circuitry hadn't been installed, either.

The hell with the mission. That bastard ordered McBain and the rest of his little gang of killers to murder my family. I want to see his face when I kill him right back.

Soon, she reached the dead zone. She could hear Nadaner's thoughts as clearly as if he'd been whispering in her ear. He'd finished singing and was now telling a story of one of his exploits in the Confederate Marines before he got fed up, quit, and started his revolution, a story that Nova knew was about ninety percent fabrication. He had been in the Marines, and he had been on Antiga Prime once, but that was where his story's intersection with reality ended.

With just one thought, she could kill him. End him

right there. *That is the mission. You don't need to see his face, you can feel his* mind! *You'll know he's dead with far more surety than if you just saw him, his eyes rolling up in his head, blood leaking out of his eyes and ears and nose from the brain hemorrhaging. Kill him now.*

Suddenly, she realized what day it was. *Fourteen packs, which means the better part of three days.*

Which means today's my eighteenth birthday.

It's been three years to the day since Daddy told me I was coming to this very star system.

She shook her head, even as Nadaner finished this story, and started another one, which had even less truth than the first. A tear ran slowly down Nova's cheek.

It was such a good party, too . . .

Constantino Terra had long since given up throwing surprise parties for his daughter. She always knew they were coming and ruined the surprise. *In retrospect,* he thought, *that should've been the first clue.* But other evidence had also presented itself, and soon Constantino realized that his darling Nova was a telepath.

Were he someone else, Constantino would have been forced to give in to the inevitable and turn his daughter over to the military for proper training. But the Terra family were not "someone else," they were one of the Old Families, descended from the commanders of the original colony ships that had brought humanity to this part of space from Earth generations ago. The Old Families did not turn their daughters over to anyone they didn't want to. And Constantino refused to put his little girl through that.

Her mother agreed. There was little that Constantino and Annabella Terra agreed upon, but that Nova should stay out of government hands was assuredly one of them. Not that they needed to agree on anything save that they remain married. Like most Old Family marriages, theirs was based on financial expediency, a union of two fortunes that would work better together than apart, and would also produce worthy heirs. Those heirs were created by an injection of Constantino's seed into Bella's body, thus saving him the distasteful task of sleeping with the wretched woman. He had his mistress for that, just as she had her jig, as was proper. Constantino had heard whispers among the servants that Bella was growing tired of her jig and seeking out other household employees for her sexual sport. But then, he'd also gotten word of similar rumors regarding him and his beloved Eleftheria, and he would never betray her trust. The mistress-husband bond, and the jig-wife bond, for that matter, was far too strong and important to the household for him to consider sundering it.

Instead of his daughter spending her fifteenth birthday in some government facility being trained to use her psionic talents as a tool against the alien threats the Confederacy now faced, she was instead being thrown the finest party since—well, since the last time one of the Old Families' children had a birthday. It was a competition, in many ways, with each family throwing a more and more outlandish shindig to prove that they loved their children the most.

As a result, the domed roof of the penthouse atop the Terra Skyscraper was decked out as it had never been decked out before. The dome had been polarized to provide an optimum view of the city of Tarsonis without interference from the sun. (The Terra family's building was one of the few buildings that had a virtually unobstructed view, matched only by that of Kusinis Tower and, of course, the Universal News Network Building.) A massive chandelier, six meters wide, hung in midair atop the dome, supported by state-of-the-art antigrav units guaranteed not to fail. (The guarantee was that Constantino would drive the manufacturer to complete ruin if it did fail.) Food from all across the Confederacy was laid out, as expected, but he actually managed to get his hands on Antigan buffalo meat and a limited supply of Saran pepper slices. The price for the latter two items was higher than the aggregate salaries of any ten of Constantino's employees, but it was worth it for his little girl.

All the important people were there—at least three representatives from each Old Family on Tarsonis, and a few from offworld—and UNN had dutifully sent all its gossip reporters, and even one of its news reporters, a woman named Mara Greskin. Constantino smiled at her presence. *She must have cracked off somebody to get assigned to cover a birthday party.* Usually such occasions were fodder only for gossip columns; news reporters considered such assignments beneath them, which was why Greskin simply had to have annoyed somebody important—or gotten in UNN editor-in-chief Handy Anderson's doghouse.

Then again, if they're covering this, it means one less paranoid story about how aliens are going to wipe us out. It seemed all UNN was talking about these days were the horrors in the Sara system and the emergence of a strange alien threat. Constantino knew more than UNN did, of course—for example, that there were, in fact, *two* alien species fighting a war that the human race somehow got caught in the middle of—which only made him worry more, especially since Arcturus Mengsk and his band of butchers in the Sons of Korhal were using the invasion as a propaganda tool to stir uprisings on planets from here to Antiga Prime.

In the face of all this, Constantino threw a party. It was, after all, his daughter's birthday, and he was damned if he'd let Mengsk or alien scum distract him from *that.*

Nova was becoming a woman. According to the girl's nurse, she had started what the nurse insisted on calling "her monthly time"—as if Constantino wasn't familiar with the female anatomy and its functions—and she had started to develop a woman's chest. Soon, the prepubescent disdain for the opposite sex would give way to hormonal imperatives. *Which means an endless array of unsuitable suitors for my little girl.*

In truth, Constantino was looking forward to it. There was nothing quite so satisfying as watching a young man trying desperately to impress one of the most powerful men in the Confederacy and failing miserably, that failure compounded by Constantino holding him to an impossible standard. He'd already gone through it with Nova's older sister, Clara—now engaged to young Milo Kusinis—and was looking forward to it again with Nova.

Now, Nova stood in the center of the domed space, wearing a beautiful pink dress that had a ruffled neck, the white ruffles opening like a flower beneath her chin, a formfitting top, and a huge hoopskirt that extended outward half a meter in all directions and came to the floor. She walked with such grace and ease that the skirt's hiding of her feet made it seem as if she were floating when she walked. (Other girls achieved the same effect by attaching gliders to their shoes, unseen under the skirt's voluminous mass, but Nova, the darling girl, had always felt that to be cheating.) She wore very little makeup, simply enough to highlight her green eyes; her smooth skin needed no cosmetic enhancements, and so far the ravages of adolescence had not blemished her visage.

Her normally straight blond hair had been curled for the occasion and piled atop her head elegantly. Constantino made a mental note to apologize to Rebeka. He had doubted the hairdresser's word when she said Nova would look marvelous with curls; he should have known better after all these years. After all, Rebeka had made even Bella look presentable on more than one occasion.

All around them, the partygoers were partaking of the food on the tables, the servants ably refilling any plates that were in danger of emptying. The punch bowl remained three-quarters full no matter how much of it was imbibed—and, it seemed, old Garth Duke was determined to imbibe most of it himself; Constantino made a mental note to have Boris keep an eye on him in case he started undressing again—and the empty glasses and plates were whisked away. As ever, Constantino had the most efficient servants. If he ever had an inefficient one, he didn't have that one for long.

There were those who expressed confusion at his employing of human servants—most of whom were among the younger, newer rich, the so-called "bootstrappers" who had made their fortune during the boom a decade earlier. Robots, they pointed out, were more efficient, and you only had to pay for them once. Constantino generally just smiled and said he was old-fashioned, but the truth was, he owned Servo Servants, the largest robotics company in Confederate space, and he knew that you paid for them a lot more than once. Planned obsolescence and sufficiently inefficient mechanisms that required regular repairs were what kept SS in business.

Besides, he preferred to keep people employed. The more he employed, the fewer were infesting the bowels of the Gutter.

Nova glided over to him. "Daddy, you're always going on about how wonderful the servants are—but you never let them partake."

"I beg your pardon?" Naturally, if he was thinking about the servants, Nova would know that, even if only subconsciously, and talk about them with him.

"They're people too, Daddy—and they work *so* hard. Don't you think they deserve some of this fantastic Antigan buffalo a lot more than, say, *him*?"

She pointed over at Garth Duke, who had apparently decided that the punch bowl was a wading pool, and was taking off his boots. Constantino looked around, but Boris was already making a beeline before Garth could make a scene. *Or, rather, more of one.*

"Well?"

Turning back to look at his daughter, he found himself unable to resist her pleading green eyes. It wasn't the first time she had begged an indulgence for the servants, and she usually got what she asked for—a weakness of her father's that she hadn't taken nearly as much advantage of as she might have. Eleftheria said once that her telepathy probably allowed her to think of the servants as *people* rather than servants, since they had thoughts just like everyone else.

Nova herself didn't know this, of course. She simply imagined herself to be a very perceptive young woman.

He reached across to cup her cheek in his hand. "My darling girl—you know I can deny you nothing." He turned around and activated the microfone built into the button of his suit jacket.

Amplifiers placed discreetly throughout the room carried his voice over the partygoing din. "May I have everyone's attention, please?" As the room started to slowly quiet down, he grabbed two glasses of wine off the tray of a passing server and handed one to his daughter. "Today is the fifteenth birthday of my beautiful daughter, November Annabella Terra. She is the last of our children to reach that age, and indeed the last of our children." He tipped his glass toward where Bella stood, her arm in that of her jig, and she was kind enough to return the gesture and provide an almost-genuine smile. "But being younger than her sister Clara or her brother Zebediah does not make her inferior or any less loved. Indeed, the day she was born was one of the four happiest days of my life, the other three being when her siblings were born—and, of course, when Continental went out of business, granting me a monopoly on holocams."

Ripples of laughter at the admittedly mediocre joke spread throughout the room. Nova just glared at her father, apparently not appreciating the humor. Or maybe she just didn't like it when Constantino used her full name.

"In any case, because that day made me so happy, it pleases me more than I can say that all you good people are here today to celebrate that day's anniversary. So I ask you all to raise your glasses and wish my darling Nova a happy birthday."

Everyone in the room did so, and the words were spoken raggedly throughout. Nova smiled and her cheeks flushed.

After everyone had drunk, Nova looked at Constantino and said, "*Dad*dy!"

"Of course, my dear. And now, I'd like to ask everyone to please step back from the food and drink tables for a time. My household servants have worked hard for weeks to get this party ready, and have worked even harder to keep things running smoothly now that it's begun. So as a reward and to show my great appreciation, I invite all the servants to come forward and partake of this magnificent spread."

Several chuckles spread throughout, and a smattering of applause. Constantino noticed that most of the patrons were less amused. In particular, Bella looked like someone had poisoned her drink. And many of the patrons looked unhappy at having to move aside for servants.

Nova, however, beamed at him with a radiant smile. Turning around, he saw that Eleftheria was favoring him with a similar smile. Those were the only two reactions Constantino cared about.

A moment later, Zeb came sidling up to his father. "Dad, did you *have* to use my full name?"

Nova rolled her eyes. "Don't be such a baby, Zeb."

"Oh, that's funny. I suppose you liked him calling you 'November,' huh, *little* sister?"

"I'm fifteen years old, and I'm taller than you."

Constantino chuckled again. "She's got you there, son." Nova was already taller than both her siblings, and almost as tall as her father, and he doubted she was done growing yet.

Zeb shrugged it off. "That's just the clothes."

"You just keep telling yourself that, 'big' brother."

"Mr. Terra!"

Constantino whirled around to see Lia Emmanuel. Constantino himself was the president of every one of Terra's business ventures, with the individual day-to-day left to assorted vice presidents. Lia was the vice president in charge of the vice presidents, as it were, and Constantino counted on her as his right hand in all matters relating to his many and varied businesses.

She was dressed in the same suit she always wore. Lia had twelve identical suits, and wore a different one each day, laundering them when time permitted or when twelve days passed, whichever came first. Constantino doubted she owned any other clothes—which was a pity, as she was the only one in the room in business attire. Everyone else was wearing a much more celebratory brand of formalwear.

Moving away from the sibling argument—which would probably keep going for at least another five to ten minutes—Constantino approached his vice president. "Lia—haven't seen you all night. Where've you—?"

"Sir, I'm sorry, we need to talk." Lia stared at him intently with her piercing brown eyes. Her curly brown hair was tied sloppily atop her head, as if she just wanted to get it out of her way as quickly as possible. "In private."

Constantino sighed. "Why didn't you simply buzz me?"

Lia's stare intensified into a glare. "Because you turned your fone off and left it in your bedroom, sir."

"Imagine that," Constantino said dryly. "You'd think I was throwing a party that I didn't want interrupted by business."

Now Lia winced. "I'm sorry, sir, truly, and I wouldn't have interrupted Nova's party normally, but—"

Again, Constantino sighed. It was true, Lia would never have been so gauche as to have business intrude upon family like this unless it was urgent. "All right, all right, what is it?"

"Rebels, sir. They've attacked and destroyed the plant in Palombo Valley."

Constantino blinked. "Destroyed? The *entire* plant?"

"Effectively, sir. I believe some of the structure is still intact, but the plant is functionally useless at present, sir. This will set back production of the 878 and 901 hovercars and especially the 428 hoverbikes by—"

Waving it off, Constantino said, "I don't care about that right now, Lia—how many people—"

"The entire night shift, sir. The ID tag scans of the wreckage matches all but three of the night-shift employees, and of those three, one was on vacation and the other two called in sick. Everyone else is dead. DNA verification will take another hour, but we're pretty sure—"

"I want all three of them investigated—find out if they're collaborators." Constantino let out a breath through his teeth, trying to rein in his temper. It wouldn't do to cause a scene here, especially with so much of his competition present.

"That's already under way, sir. The attack was such that it *had* to be an inside job. The bombs used were very specifically targeted to the areas of the plant that either would be most densely populated during the night shift or would have the equipment that would be most expensive to replace."

Knowing this was a stupid question—who else would do this sort of thing, after all?—Constantino nonetheless had to ask, "We're sure it's rebels?"

Lia nodded. "Completely sure, sir. Mengsk did one of his pirate broadcasts at the same time as the attack, condemning the Old Families in general and you in particular as symptomatic of the decay that has gripped—"

Again, he interrupted, not caring about Mengsk's propaganda. "All right, fine. Keep on it, and prepare a full report. I'll read it when the party's over." He sighed. "Dammit. This was a good evening, too."

"Sir, the news gets worse. I've run the financials and—well, you can either rebuild the plant or you can give bereavement pay to the families of the victims. You can't do both."

"Then we'll put off rebuilding the plant," Constantino said without hesitation, "we—"

"Sir, we were counting on that plant to produce enough vehicles, especially the 428s, to counteract last year's falloff."

Sales of most Terra products had flattened out of late, due in part to an economic downturn, in part to fear of rebel attacks driving down consumer spending. The one exception to this was the 428 model of hoverbike, which was incredibly popular among both children and younger adults.

Lia continued: "We can stave off maybe a few months, but we *have* to get that plant back up and running right away. Mengsk didn't choose it randomly—he knew that without that plant, our ability to get back into the black will be next to impossible without—"

"Without screwing over the families of the victims of his attack." Constantino shook his head. "Bastard. If we don't rebuild, we start falling apart. If we do rebuild, we give him more fodder for his crap about how we exploit the workers." He had to resist the urge to spit. "Dammit. All right, Lia, thanks."

"Sir, I'm afraid—"

"I'm not going to make a decision about that now."

"Sir, that's not what I need to tell you about. There's more bad news—the Protoss have wiped out Mar Sara. The Confederacy managed to pull back, but I'm not sure how many got out alive."

Constantino shook his head. He knew the experiments being done on the zerg they'd captured in the Sara system would come back to haunt them all. They'd already wiped out Chau Sara, and now Mar Sara had gone the same way. And who knew where these Protoss bastards would stop?

"Thank you, Lia. We'll talk after the party, all right?"

"Yes, sir." She turned on her heel and headed for the lift.

Looking down at his left hand, Constantino saw that he still had the glass of wine in it. Aside from the sip he took for Nova's toast, he hadn't touched it.

Now he swallowed it all in one gulp. The fruity taste almost made up for the sting of the alcohol as it plunged down his throat faster than wine was intended to be drunk, but right at the moment, Constantino didn't care all that much.

Eleftheria intercepted him on his way back to Nova and Zeb. As was often the case with mistresses, Eleftheria was the opposite of Constantino's wife. Where Bella was a short, stout brunette with olive skin and an hourglass figure, Eleftheria was a tall, willowy redhead with pale skin and a slim figure.

"That was Lia. She came late, talked to you for two seconds, then immediately left. That usually adds up to bad news."

"No flies on you, m'dear." He chuckled without mirth. Eleftheria had always been observant. He told her about what happened to the Palombo plant—he couldn't tell her about the Protoss. That was something she wasn't cleared to be aware of, much as it pained him to keep anything from her.

Eleftheria's already-pale face grew paler. "My God, that's awful. How could they *do* that?"

"Apparently, we *all* have to pay for the sins of the Council's idiotic decisions." Constantino had been the loudest among those arguing furiously against the bombing of Korhal IV as too extreme a solution, but many of the Old Families took the Council's side—as well as that of the military—in believing that extreme problems *demanded* extreme solutions.

Except that Constantino and his allies had been correct. Korhal IV had backfired rather spectacularly, turning public opinion further away from the Confederacy. And the bombing gave rise to Mengsk and his band of butchers, not to mention dozens of other smaller rebellious groups who didn't have Mengsk's profile, but were irritants just the same.

He looked over at Nova and Zeb, now talking more civilly to each other. *Lia said it was an inside job. Maybe one of the three who were out. Maybe one of the corpses in the plant, willing to be a martyr for Mengsk's cause.*

"What are you thinking?" Eleftheria asked.

"That we're going ahead with the plan." He put down the wineglass and grabbed another glass from a passing server.

His mistress's eyes went wide. "I thought you said—"

"I said I was considering abandoning it, but this attack

makes it imperative." *Not to mention what just happened in the Sara system.* "If they can get someone inside the plant, they can get someone inside this household." He smiled grimly. "Security's a lot more stringent for my businesses than it is for my home, I'm afraid." He took a sip of the wine. This was an inferior vintage to the previous one. *We must have run out of the '09. This tastes like the '07.* As he recalled, the grape crop on Halcyon was awful that year. He made a mental note to ask the wine steward why they had any of that vintage in the wine rack at all.

Eleftheria asked, "But if one of the household staff was untrustworthy, Nova would know, wouldn't she?"

"Not necessarily. She's not trained, she doesn't know what to look for." *And whose fault is that?* a little voice in his head asked, but Constantino tamped it down. The only way to get that training was to lose his daughter altogether, and that he *would* not do—not to the very same imbeciles who nuked Korhal IV and started this entire nonsense.

"When are you going to tell her?" Eleftheria asked.

"After the party. Let her have a good time tonight—then I'll tell her that she's going to have to go offworld for a while."